"All you have to do is look at a man and he can't help falling in love with you." Drew bent his head and kissed her softly.

"Oh Drew..." She lay back on the sand and pulled him down to her.

"Marcy," he whispered. He kissed her again, his soft tongue caressing the edge of her lips so she trembled at the sensation. She closed her eyes, enjoying the feel of his mouth, then gasped aloud as a shiver ran through her body. She could feel her heart beating wildly.

"Oh, please..." she breathed, and pushed him away. It was almost too agonizing to endure.

She looked at him through half-closed eyes. His face in the firelight was strong and angular, elegant with its patrician nose and wide mouth. She had never wanted anyone or anything as much as she wanted him. She sat up and smiled, slowly unbuttoning her shirt...

Forever
Wild

Forever Wild

Louisa Rawlings

POPULAR LIBRARY

An Imprint of Warner Books, Inc.

A Warner Communications Company

POPULAR LIBRARY EDITION

Cover art by John Ennis

Popular Library books are published by
Warner Books, Inc.
666 Fifth Avenue
New York, N.Y. 10103

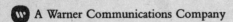 A Warner Communications Company

Printed in the United States of America

First Printing: October, 1986

10 9 8 7 6 5 4 3 2 1

_____ *Acknowledgments* _____

Many thanks to the following:

The good people of Long Lake, especially dear friends Ellen and Don Gordinier, who were so kind and hospitable, and Mrs. Frances Seaman, the town historian, who gave me insights into Long Lake's history; with the hope that they'll overlook the few liberties I took! (Reuben Cary and Mitchell Sabattis each acquired a fictitious son, and Clear Pond— now called Lake Eaton—grew an island for the purposes of my story.)

The staff of the wonderful Adirondack Museum at Blue Mountain Lake, who were so helpful to the lady who haunted the premises for a whole week.

The staff of the Brooklyn Public Library who answered— thoroughly and well—many an odd question posed to them over their hotline.

Rudolph Herz, and Ann and Martin Fishman, for research material.

My editor, Fredda Isaacson, who's a solid anchor in the lonely sea of writing.

My agent, Al Zuckerman, for his encouragement and advice.

And last, but scarcely least, my husband, Sid, who introduced me to the glorious Adirondacks years ago.

"In the woods we return to reason and faith. There I feel that nothing can befall me in life . . . which nature cannot repair."

—RALPH WALDO EMERSON

Chapter One

The streak of lightning knifed out of the sky and slashed at a solitary hemlock on the far shore. Marcy sucked in her breath sharply, watching in horrified fascination as the tree splintered and crumbled, a puff of blue smoke rising from the charred spot where the lightning had hit. She lifted a hand to cover the involuntary cry that had sprung to her lips, and saw that her fingers were shaking.

"Tarnation, Marcy Tompkins," she whispered. "What ails you?" She'd seen a hundred storms, and laughed in the face of thunder and lightning. She took a deep breath, stilling her thudding heart, then giggled aloud.

Look at you, miss, she thought. Scared and shaking like an old woman, because of a bit of lightning. She looked up at the mountains that ringed the lake; the pines of Owl's Head were beginning to sigh in the wind.

Why should I be afraid? she thought. This is mine. The mountains. The wilderness. It's always been mine.

And the lake. Especially the lake. There were a thousand of them in the Adirondack Wilderness, but only one Long Lake. Her lake. Part of the chain that stretched for more than

a hundred miles to the border of Canada. She'd paddled its
length countless times, her boat gliding smoothly on the current. She knew it as a lover would—its every mood, each
bend and curve, its rages when the wind whipped across it,
as now it did, its friendly silences. It was in her blood, this
aching love of the lake, of the wilderness.

She smiled, remembering. Her father had felt it, too, that
long-ago day, standing on the veranda of their small cabin
that looked out upon the ten-mile length of Long Lake. Just
come home from the war, he was. And still wearing the sash
of his New York regiment, with a bit of black crape pinned
on out of respect for poor Mr. Lincoln.

He'd kissed her mother, then walked silently out to the
veranda, while Marcy tagged behind, wishing he'd notice
what a big girl she'd become since he'd marched off to fight
for the Union. He'd gazed out on the lake, the western shore
already in shadow, the tops of the bordering pines still on
fire with the last rays of the sun. A golden eagle had swooped
low, then wheeled and turned, heading toward Round Island.
Her father had stood there, the tears washing his weather-
beaten cheeks. Then he'd gulped, cleared his throat, and
harrumphed loudly.

"Marcy," he'd said, "you reckon Pickwacket Pond is fished
out yet?"

"I love you, Daddy," she'd whispered, and clasped the
hand he'd held out to her.

So long ago. Marcy sighed, then ducked under a tree as
the first raindrops began to fall. She'd never make the cabin
now. Might as well watch the storm a little longer, then head
for Uncle Jack's barn during a lull.

Yes. It's in my blood, she thought. This region. Just as it
had been in her father's. Then how explain her sudden panic?
The heart-tearing urge to run as far from the mountains as
she could get? She'd come down to this sheltered cove, as
she so often did, to watch the storm, to hear the thunder
building far away across the lake, rolling through the valleys
and echoing against the side of Owl's Head. It never failed
to thrill her. The air so still, oppressive almost. The black

clouds gathering silently. The lake like glass. Then the first messenger of the storm: a gust of wind, bending the tops of the trees, working its way down the lake in serrated ranks like a ghostly army, ravaging the smooth surface.

Then the lightning had struck the hemlock tree, splintering it, and Marcy had shuddered.

"Nature is good," her father always said. "Mother Nature. She looks after her children."

"What else do we need?" her mother would ask, mending her worn dress one more time. "We have each other. We have this beautiful country. Nature is good to us."

"No," said Marcy softly, her heart twisting with pain. "No!" she cried. She raised tear-filled eyes to the shattered hemlock across the lake. The tree is dead, she thought. Why? How can Nature be good? What did the tree ever do, except to give comfort and shelter? And now it's dead.

Almost against her will, she turned to look at the ruins on the edge of the shore. And her parents were dead, buried in the wreckage of their cabin.

Explain that, Mother Nature, she thought in bewilderment. Why did the earth shake so hard that the chimney toppled? They didn't deserve that. They trusted in you.

She shivered involuntarily. The earthquake had happened seven months ago. And since then, sleeping in her bed in Uncle Jack's cabin, she'd never felt completely safe. Not ever again.

She sighed and wiped at her cheeks. Maybe she should get away. Leave the North Woods. It wasn't that she was actually *afraid*, of course. She still loved her mountains and her lake. But maybe it was time to see a little more of the world. She'd been to Albany only once, and Saratoga three times. And though she hadn't much patience for the city slickers who'd crowded into North Creek since Dr. Durant had extended the railroad up from Saratoga Springs in '71, she had to admit that the women's gowns and parasols were the prettiest things she'd ever seen. She'd look nice in pretty dresses like that. She was a woman now. Eighteen last month. And even if her mirror hadn't told her so, she knew she was good-looking.

Every time she went over to Mr. Sabattis's Boardinghouse to help out in the kitchen or clean the rooms for a few extra dollars, the fancy Dans, up for a few weeks of fishing and hunting and "roughing it," would eye her like hungry kids at a strawberry festival.

Yes. She was good-looking. Not as tall as she would have liked, and a little rounder, and stronger, and healthier-looking than those frail, pale creatures who came up from New York City for rustic pleasures and pure air and didn't even have the sense to leave their corsets behind. But her hair was a rich mahogany with reddish glints, and her eyes were the blue-green of the rocks that shimmered in the bed of the Opalescent River. She'd look pretty in a fancy dress.

But first she had to get away from the North Woods.

And do what? she thought. She could take care of herself in the woods, but in the city . . . what was she fit for? She couldn't hunt and fish in the city. She could clean other people's houses, of course. But for that, she might as well stay in Long Lake and work in the boardinghouse.

Or she could get married.

She laughed aloud at the sudden thought. Tarnation! Why not? The summer was just beginning. The tourists and sportsmen would be invading the mountains, as they had every year since Mr. Murray had published his book on his adventures in the Wilderness. "Murray's Fools," they'd called them in the summer of 1870, three years ago. That flock of greenhorns who'd come swarming into the mountains for a summer of disaster and cold and crowding. But the men were young and knew the ways of the world. And if she were ever to leave, they would be her ticket. Her friend Zeb Cary, the blacksmith's son, had somehow stopped being a marriageable prospect ages ago, though she still let him kiss her and take some liberties.

It might be fun—to live in a city, to marry one of those nice young men, to wear pretty dresses.

To feel safe again.

Not that she was afraid of the mountains that had taken her parents from her. No. She shook the unwelcome thoughts from her brain. It was only natural to want to see something of the world. To have all the things she'd only dreamed of. She'd find a man to marry her and take her away.

It was raining harder now. She giggled at her own impulsive scheme, and raced for Uncle Jack's barn, holding the back of her skirt over her head and shoulders to protect her from the driving rain. The barn was dark. Marcy shook the rain from her skirt and leaned against the closed door, catching her breath.

"You're a sight for sore eyes, Marcy Tompkins."

"Zeb!" Marcy turned, peering through the gloom at the raw-boned young man lolling against a buckboard wagon. "What are you doing here?"

"Old Jack asked me to look at this wheel rim. The storm caught me. I thought I'd wait it out. Still mad at me?"

Marcy shrugged. "You can't help it if your maw never taught you to dance. But you could have tried when the reverend brought in the fiddler especially for the church supper."

"Then you're still mad."

"No."

"Then come kiss me."

Marcy made a face. "Tarnation, Zeb..."

He moved toward her, scowling. "You used to like my kisses. Used to like a lot of things!"

"We were both kids, Zeb." She was glad for the dim light. Her face felt as if it were burning with shame. Remembering. They had grown up together. Shared their first tentative kiss at sixteen. By the time they were seventeen she had allowed him to fondle her breasts. She enjoyed it. Her body had felt pleasure at his touch, in the same way that her body responded to the warm sun, the icy winds, the soft breezes. What were bodies for, if not to *feel*? Only once had she felt a pang of guilt. Just after her parents had died, she and Zeb had been kissing at night, lying on the sandy shore of the lake. She had allowed his hand to stray up under her petticoat, to invade her drawers, to explore territory that had been inviolate until then. It had been a delicious sensation, thrilling and comforting all at the same time. She'd only felt wicked afterward, when she had returned to her room at Uncle Jack's and found blood on her flannel drawers.

And someone had seen them in the moonlight and told Uncle Jack. Despite Zeb's protests that they were both old enough to do what they wanted, Uncle Jack (with Zeb's father's blessing) had marched the young man to the woodshed for a session with his razor strop. The knowledge that her mother would have done the same to her with a hairbrush had she been alive filled Marcy with added remorse. Since then, Zeb's caresses had been confined to the region above her waist.

"We're not kids anymore, Marcy," Zeb growled, strong hands gripping her by the shoulders.

"Don't you dare, Zeb Cary!"

He dropped his hands. "I don't know what's got into you, Marce. The last few months . . . No. Even before then. After your parents died. When you came to live with your uncle. A body can't tell what you're thinking anymore, you're that changed."

He looked so forlorn it nearly broke her heart. But he was right. She *had* changed. Had it been there all this time—and she unaware of it—the fear, the confused longing to leave the mountains? From the day her parents died. Maybe it had been in her brain all that time, and she hadn't even known it herself.

Not until the lightning hit the tree.

"Oh, Zeb . . ." She put her arms around his neck—a gesture of friendship. Of sympathy.

His arms tightened around her and he kissed her full on the mouth. Hard. She resisted for a moment, angry that he should have misread her kindness, then relaxed against him. She really did enjoy being kissed. She closed her eyes and allowed his mouth to take hers again, savoring the pleasant sensation of his lips, the way his hands had begun to move lightly over her back. It was even more pleasant when his hands moved around to the front, cradling the roundness of her breasts. She groaned in contentment and nestled more firmly in his arms, feeling his hardness even through her skirts. It was only when he began to unbutton the top of her dress that she came to her senses. "Stop it, Zeb," she murmured, pushing against him.

His voice was strained and hoarse. "Please, Marcy. Please . . . just this one time before I go plumb crazy wanting you!" He tried to pull her down to the straw-covered floor.

She felt an edge of panic. She couldn't let Zeb make love to her. She couldn't afford to be sidetracked. She'd be trapped forever in these mountains. "No!" she said firmly, pushing him away from her.

He shook his head, bewildered. "I thought maybe you'd marry me . . ."

"Marry you?" She threw back her head and laughed. "*Marry* you? If you're not every way a jackass, Zeb Cary . . ."

"Why?"

She realized her cruelty and softened at once. "You know there was never any chance of that, Zeb," she said gently.

"Why?"

"Let it go."

"Drat it, Marcy. Why?"

"Don't make me say it."

He grabbed her roughly by the shoulders. "*Why?*"

His fingers were painful through the thin calico of her dress. "Because you're green as a sapling," she snapped. "Because I want a better life than you can give me!" She saw the pain in his eyes. "Because I'm not sweet on you, Zeb," she said softly. "Never have been. You know it."

"You let me kiss you often enough!"

"Kisses aren't everything." She swept past him and threw open the barn door. The rain had almost stopped.

He gave a low growl behind her. "You let me take a walloping for you, Marcy. You owe me something for that, at least!"

She whirled in anger, hands on hips. "I don't owe you one blamed thing, Zeb Cary! I'm remembering that you didn't mind kissing *me*!"

"But I was waiting for more, and you know it!" he said,

and lunged toward her. She sidestepped nimbly. He clutched at her, managing to catch her wrist; but she swung around and smacked him, open-handed, in the groin. Not very hard; he was still her childhood friend. He yelped in surprise and released her wrist, his hands going to his injured parts. "Darn you, Marcy!" he bellowed, standing forlornly in the doorway, as she raced out of the barn and up the small rise to the cabin.

Uncle Jack turned from the window when she slammed the door behind her and leaned against it, breathing hard. He jerked his thumb in the direction of the barn. "What in tarnation was that all about?"

Crossing to a rough-hewn sideboard, Marcy tied on her apron, then pulled down a sack of beans from a shelf and measured a handful into a saucepan. She added some water from a covered pitcher, set the pot on the small cast-iron stove. "Zeb wants me to marry him."

"And . . . ?"

She took a slab of salt pork from a stone crock and began to dice it into little bits. "I turned him down. With no chance for a change of mind."

"I'll be jiggered! Are you daft, girl?"

"No. Just coming to my senses. I reckon I can do better than Zeb. A city slicker with an eye out for a wife . . ."

He gaped in surprise. "Why would a fancy feller want to stay in Long Lake?"

"What makes you think *I* want to stay?"

"You *are* daft! If ever a body was married, it's you . . . to these mountains."

Her chin jutted in defiance. "Well maybe I want to be unmarried! Maybe I want more than just Zeb and Long Lake and the rest of it! Maybe I want to live in a city!"

He shook his head. "I don't know where you get these notions. You're the contrariest girl, when you want to be. Miss Flibbertigibbet, like your paw used to call you!"

"What's wrong about wanting to live in a city?"

"And married to a city feller? That you don't love? That you don't even know yet?"

"You wouldn't have cared if I married Zeb, and I don't love *him*!"

"But you were suited! Tarnation, girl, do you know how hard it is to live in a city?"

She frowned in bewilderment. "What do you mean?"

"You need money, girl! Life in a city is hard without money."

"I never thought of that. Do you really think so?" She bit her lip, feeling terribly young and untried.

"I *know* so! Bill Peterson and his wife were never the same again after they came back from New York City. It right near broke their hearts to live so mean. Give up this silly idea!"

She stirred the beans thoughtfully, then turned to him, her blue-green eyes lighting up with the innocent joy of a child. "Why then, I'll marry a *rich* man!" She smiled in delight. It seemed such an easy solution.

"Dag nab it, girl, if you don't beat all! Haven't you heard what I've been saying?"

"Bosh! Why should I? I'll marry a rich man, that's all." She resumed her task with the salt pork, her knife clicking determinedly on the cutting block.

"You're as stubborn as your father was, once you set your mind to it. And how do you mean to bag your game, miss? Those rich fellers only stay a couple of nights at the boardinghouse before lighting out for the woods."

"Don't you have a group of sportsmen coming up in a couple of weeks?"

Old Jack scratched the graying stubble on his chin. "A biggish party, like as I can make out. One of the Sabittis boys is spoken for, and Amos Robinson, and Alonzo. One or two more, maybe. We'll need four or five guideboats, I reckon."

"Hunters?"

"Science folk, too, seems like, from their letters. A Dr. Marshall and his wife. Coming over from North Creek. They mean to set up at Clear Pond for a couple months. Use it as their base camp."

"Hmmm. There'll be at least one eligible bachelor in the lot, I'm sure."

"Now, Marcy . . ."

She set down her chopping knife and wiped her hands on her apron. "Let me come along, Uncle Jack. I haven't in ages. If your feller is soft and weak, you might need an extra paddle!"

"But it's not like the old days. You're not exactly a little girl anymore. He might not like it. And he's paying."

"Then I could go in Amos's boat. Or one of the others. And it's not as if I'd be the only woman there. Mrs. Marshall would probably take kindly to company. And if the men don't seem like good prospects, I could always make some excuse and come back to Palmer's or Sabattis's, and wait for the next batch."

He scowled in disgust. "You surely shame me, Marcy, with such talk. You make it sound like a quail shoot!"

She turned toward the window, watching the last rivulets of rain course down the old panes. "Please don't scold, Uncle Jack," she said softly. "I don't know what it is, but . . ." She turned back to him, her aquamarine eyes shimmering behind crystal tears. "I was down to North Creek last week. There was a railroad car. One of those fancy things the swells use to ride up here. All cut-glass windows, with swans and flowers scratched into them. Just for *decoration*! And polished brass and shiny wood— It even smelled special." She sighed. "I wanted to peek inside, but old Tom at the depot shooed me away." She looked up and blinked, and the brimming tears mimicked the rain on the windowpanes. "It wasn't just the fanciness. It was like that car was all the things I want, that I never had. That I never did. I kept thinking . . . that car has traveled out of the mountains. It's seen the world. And I'll live and die here." She brushed the tears from her cheeks. "Help me, Uncle Jack. I'm aching. I don't even know what it is, but I want . . ." Her voice trailed away on a sob.

"What? What do you want, girl?"

"I don't know. Everything. To leave here. I don't know . . . I think I'll never be safe until I'm away from here."

"Safe from what? This has always been your home! Safe from what?"

She buried her face in her hands. "I don't know. I'm so mixed up inside, Uncle Jack..."

Awkwardly, he draped his arm around her shoulders. "You're my own brother's child. You know I'll do whatever I can to make you happy, Marcy," he said gruffly. "You can ride in the boat with me. And if my feller makes a fuss, I'll hit the rapscallion with my oar!" He smiled in relief as she sniffled and giggled. Then he shook his head, his face suddenly serious. "But I think you're going against what you are, girl. This crazy notion—to leave the mountains—I only hope it *does* make you happy!"

She smiled in gratitude. "I'll never know if I don't find out," she said softly. "Now!" She squared her shoulders. "I reckon I'll go down to the barn and ask Zeb to stay for supper. I ought to feed him, at least!"

"Ali ben Tibor smiled and took my hand in his. 'Pray give me your trust, Lady,' he murmured. I leave you, gentle Reader, to divine the joy with which my heart was filled at his words. The touch of his fingers was..."

"Did you want that book as well, Miss Bradford?"

Startled, Willough closed the slim volume with a snap, set it down, and brushed the dust from her fawn gloves. "Certainly not!" She managed to smile uneasily at the clerk, though she could still feel her heart pounding beneath the amber silk bodice of her gown. She prayed that she wouldn't blush and make a complete fool of herself. "How can people write such foolishness?" she asked primly to hide her embarrassment.

"Mrs. Buchanan has a large following, ma'am," said the clerk gently.

"I suppose there are those who find it worthwhile to read romances. As for myself... if you will arrange to have delivered to me the volumes on iron and steel production that I ordered... and Mr. Ruskin's latest lectures, if they have arrived."

"Certainly, ma'am. I'll see if they've come in."

Willough nodded and turned away, glad for the opportunity to compose herself. She felt like a child who's been caught stealing cookies in the pantry. Thank heaven it had only been the clerk, and not one of her father's friends who had found her reading that frivolous book! What would Daddy have thought of her then?

She sighed. It was always the same. She never meant to look at the foolish things, so silly and romantic, with their sighing heroines forever needing to be rescued from some scrape or other. Falling helplessly into the arms of passionate and totally unreal men. As though a woman had nothing better to do with her life! That's what Daddy would say.

And yet—and this was what was so strange—she was always drawn to the books, almost in spite of herself, the words leaping out of the pages, setting her heart to thumping and her pulse to racing madly beneath the fine kid of her wrist-length gloves. The handsome men in the romances, who loved their women with passion, still treated them with honor, and respected their virtue. She smiled ruefully to herself. In all her twenty-one years, there had never been a real man who had been worth a second glance; they were all so *earthy*, the lustful animal within kept barely in check. They seemed so *possessive*, wanting . . . she hardly knew what. Her independence. Her freedom. And something more. Something dark and nameless that she scarcely understood—yet somehow feared. Perhaps that's why she'd always concentrated on the future she'd mapped out for herself, one that virtually excluded men. If, by some chance, the right man should come into her life, she'd surely know it. He'd be far grander, more worthy of her pure love and respect than the callow young men who had come courting in the last few years. She knew it with a certainty! Maybe that was why the heroes of the books held such a fascination for her, despite her attempts at indifference.

The clerk had returned, bearing her order pad. "The Ruskin book has not arrived as yet, ma'am. We expect it within a day or so. Shall I have the ironworks volumes sent out to your coachman?"

"No. I shall be in the north of the state for a good part of the summer. You may send the set to me there. Miss Willough Bradford, Saratoga Springs."

The clerk frowned, writing. "W-I-L-L-A?" she asked. "Is that how it's spelled, Miss Bradford?"

"No. W-I-L-L-O-U-G-H."

"What an unusual—and lovely—name!"

"Thank you." Willough smiled. "You will notify me at my Gramercy Park address when the Ruskin arrives?" Without waiting for a reply, she swept up the pleated train of her skirt and made for the door of the bookshop. She nodded at the young man who held open the door, then waited on the stoop, surveying the noise and hustle of Fourteenth Street, while her coachman brought up her open carriage. He jumped from his seat and held out his hand to assist her. She stepped into the open carriage and sat down, smoothing her taffeta skirts.

The coachman scrambled onto his seat and turned to her. "Will you go to Lord and Taylor now, Miss Bradford?"

Willough pulled at the elastic watch fob on her bodice and snapped open the little case. Three-thirty. "No," she said, closing the watch and settling back against the leather cushions. "It's nearly time for tea. I'll go straight home." She opened her parasol to shade her complexion from the strong May sun. It was surprisingly warm in New York City for this time of year. Far warmer than it had been in Chicago with cousin Hattie. Well, she'd be off to Saratoga in another two or three weeks, before the weather got too hot. And before she had become so thoroughly sick of her mother's company that she hardly could be civil. To avoid being with her mother, she had spent very little time at home in the last six years. The years at Vassar, the tour of the Continent with the Reverend Gordon and his wife, the visits with cousin Hattie. And of course the months at a stretch when she lived with her father in his house at Saratoga.

She was startled out of her reverie. The carriage had stopped between Third and Fourth avenues, where a group of squalid urchins was fighting in the road. Willough frowned in dismay at their obvious poverty, feeling helpless, wishing she'd brought a few coins in her purse. The coachman cursed and waved the boys out of the way. Willough looked up as the carriage began to move again. Just to her right was the large red brick building of the Tammany Society, the most powerful political club in all of New York City. Even in Chicago over the winter, the papers had been filled with the accounts of Mr. Tweed's trial for bribery, forgery, larceny, and all manner of political chicanery. The trial had ended with the jury being unable to render a verdict. A month later, fifteen new indictments had been handed down against Tweed, with the new trial scheduled to begin some time in June.

And there was talk there would be more indictments to follow. The Tammany Hall cronies of "Boss" Tweed were quaking in their boots, according to the *New York Times*, and corruption would be rooted out from high places and low. Willough leaned forward and tapped the coachman on the shoulder with her parasol.

"Is Mr. Gray expected for tea this afternoon?" she asked.

"I don't know, Miss Bradford," he said, turning his head to speak to her. "We've not seen much of him this month. He's been out of town. Albany, I think."

It was hardly surprising news. Willough nodded at the coachman and settled back again in her seat. Arthur Bartlett Gray. Man-about-town. Charming. Quite obviously wealthy, though he never seemed to do much except travel back and forth to Albany when the Legislature was in session at the state capital. He carried himself like a man of breeding and birth, but he was always close-mouthed in the matter of his antecedents. He was a lawyer who had never bothered to hang out his shingle. And a member of the Tammany Society and a friend of that selfsame William M. Tweed who was daily being pilloried in the newspapers. No wonder Arthur had arranged to be out of town for the last month or so!

The carriage turned up the avenue toward Gramercy Park. Willough closed her parasol, and tucked in a stray curl at her temple. It must be five or six years now since she'd seen Arthur. She had been home so seldom, and he had spent a great deal of time in Albany. They had always missed each other.

Besides, she'd been unwilling to truly accept him or his visits to the house since the day she'd seen him kissing her mother.

"I don't know why you can't call me Uncle Arthur as your brother does, Willough," he'd said. All warm and friendly. Uncle Arthur. And then he'd gone off like a thief in another man's house and kissed her mother. Was that why her father had bought the house in Saratoga?

Still, it might be interesting to see Arthur again. There was a certain rakish charm to the man. He didn't try to charm her often, but when he did he could always make her laugh. Joking about her name, her awkwardness as she shot up in her teens, all gawky arms and legs.

"Willough," he'd say, laughing. "Willough. Are you sure they didn't mean Will*ow*? If you grow any taller, you must never wear a bonnet with leaves on it, or the birds will be tempted to nest."

"Oh, Mr. Gray," she'd say, blushing.

"And when you cry — which I fervently hope you do not — will they call you Weeping Willough?"

She'd giggled. "Don't be silly. They called me Willough for Daddy's Grandfather Willoughby. I was supposed to be a son, not a daughter."

Willough sighed as the carriage pulled up to the curb in front of the elegant town house that faced Gramercy Park. She hadn't thought about it much in those days, her name. But this last year, watching her father grow older, seeing the loneliness of his life, she felt a pang that was equal parts pity and guilt. Poor Daddy. A wife who cared for another. A daughter who should have been a son.

Give me a chance, Daddy, she thought. I'll make you proud of me.

After alighting from the carriage she mounted the stairs and passed through the hastily opened door to the cool vestibule. "Thank you, Brigid," she said to the parlor maid who had opened the door for her. "I'll go to my room until tea is served. I've some letters to write."

"Oh, Miss Willough..." Brigid said in her soft Irish brogue, "'tis Mrs. Bradford. She's feelin' very peevish today. Said she wanted to have tea straightaway as soon as someone came in. She can't wait. She's that impatient for her cup o' tea."

"Why can't she drink her tea alone?" muttered Willough.

"Ma'am?"

"Never mind. Is Mr. Drewry expected for tea?"

"Your brother went out after lunch to the Academy of Design. He *said* he'll be back. But you know what will happen if he gets to paintin'..."

Willough sighed in resignation. "Very well. Tell cook to put up the kettle." She pulled off her gloves and laid them on a marble console along with her parasol and purse. She pulled out the hatpins that anchored the small forward-pitched arrangement of horsehair and feathers and ruched ribbons that her father had bought for her in Paris last year. It was a very fetching hat, and still the height of fashion here in New York.

She studied her reflection in the mirror. She was not displeased with what she saw: a serious face, strong and angular, with a straight nose and wide-set eyes. Her lips were thin— or perhaps it was just the way she held her mouth, firm and prim. Her skin was very pale and creamy, a striking contrast to the ebony curls swept back from her temples. She turned her profile to the mirror and patted the neat roll at the nape of her neck. The back hair had been twisted in a thick coil, then doubled back on itself in a vertical figure-eight, and pinned snugly to her head. She rather liked the new style— it made her look purposeful. More so than a cascade of ringlets.

I look like a woman capable of running a business, she thought with satisfaction. *And I know I can. I'm not like other women. Not dependent and dishonest, like my mother, who has to wheedle every penny out of Daddy and pretend to the world that they're not estranged.*

She frowned, searching her face in the glass. She was a

little less pleased with her eyes. Blue-violet. Soft. Velvety. They made her seem weak and helpless. She would have much preferred to have eyes like her brother Drewry—ice-blue, and as cold as he wanted them to be when he was angry.

Her figure was another matter; she viewed it with a certain ambivalence. She was tall, and still as willowy as she had been when Arthur had made fun of her, but her bosom had developed at an alarming rate since those days. From the point of view of fashion, she knew her figure was perfect, with the voluptuous curves necessary to wear the severe-cut bodice they called *en princesse*, after Princess Alexandra of England.

On the other hand, it was the kind of figure that made her look almost too feminine, attracting unwelcome stares from men. And hardly designed to persuade her father that she could be as useful to him as a son, the proper heir to his vast enterprises.

Steeling herself, Willough crossed the vestibule toward the parlor, where her mother waited. Isobel Bradford was re-clining on an overstuffed chaise; she looked up as her daughter entered. Willough had to admit she was beautiful, in a frail way, though she was beginning to show her years in her thickening waist, slight puffiness around the chin, gray streaks in her glossy black hair. She was wearing a tea gown, a frilly garment of ruffles, tiers, and swags, extravagantly trimmed with lace. And loose enough, Willough knew, so she could discard her corsets.

Isobel smiled sourly at her daughter and sighed. A martyr's sigh. "You might have given a thought to me, Willough, while you were gadding about on your errands. But never mind."

"I've sent for tea already, Mother. Have you had your tonic?" It was a foolish question. Willough could see from the brightness of her mother's eyes, the way her hands flut-tered and fussed at the small lace cap perched on her hair, that the daily dose had not been forgotten.

"It did nothing but give me a headache! I know I shall never sleep without a bit of laudanum tonight. Not that your father would care," she said bitterly. "When you're in Saratoga with him you might mention that I could use a larger bank draft next month. Mrs. Astor has recommended a wonderful doctor, but his fees are extremely high."

"What's the matter with Dr. Page?"

Isobel Bradford sniffed in disdain. "They say when Mrs. Lenox suffered her sick headaches last month Dr. Page could do nothing for her."

"Mrs. Lenox drinks too much," said Willough dryly. "But of course Mrs. *Astor's* recommendation goes without question!" Or Mrs. Belmont, or Mrs. Goelet, thought Willough with disgust. Anyone whose name was better than theirs.

Her mother looked shocked. "The Astors are among the finest families in the city!"

"I daresay."

"Don't you take that tone with me, Willough! I shan't forget I'm a Carruth, though you might!"

Willough felt her insides churning, as they always did when her mother began her genealogy lecture. "Let's have it again, Mother," Willough said tightly. "The Carruth name goes back over two centuries, while the Bradford name . . ."

"The Bradford name didn't exist thirty years ago."

Willough crossed to the window and pulled back the lace curtains. She felt suffocated, wishing herself out-of-doors with the children who played in the street, laughing and romping in the park across the way. "Whatever possessed Daddy to change his name for you?"

Whatever possessed him to marry you? she thought in anguish. An insufferable snob.

Her mother laughed. "I was a Carruth! I could never have married a man whose name was MacCurdy! Mrs. Brian *MacCurdy*! It's absurd.

"But you didn't mind the MacCurdy money."

"If I had thought for a minute it was to be doled out in niggardly fashion, the way it is to me—and to you and Drewry too!—I should certainly have thought twice about marrying him!" It seemed to Willough that her mother's very tone revealed the endless hours she had spent collecting and nursing her grievances. "Ah, at last. Tea!" Isobel said, as the door opened and Brigid struggled in, carrying a large tray. "Not near me, Brigid," she snapped. "Can't you see I'm not well today? Over on that table, where Miss Willough can pour."

"Yes, ma'am." The maid turned clumsily with her burden and just managed to set it down in front of Willough's chair. The sudden jolt of the tray on the table set the teacups rattling, earning for Brigid a scowl from Isobel. She curtsied hastily and fled the room.

Isobel struggled to pull herself upright on the chaise as Willough poured the tea and handed her a cup. "These girls will be the death of me," she said, casting her eyes to heaven. "They come off the boat with no manners, not a lick of training..."

"Really, Mother. She's very pleasant. And she knows her place."

"Yes, that's true." Isobel sipped daintily at her tea. "Heaven knows, it could have been worse. She could have been a Hebrew."

Willough's stomach was now actively protesting. She took a small swallow of tea, wondering how she could even manage to keep it down.

"Have a teacake, Willough."

"No, thank you."

"A small sandwich, then."

"I'm not hungry, Mother."

"If you didn't lace your corsets so tightly, perhaps you could manage to eat a bit more."

"They're not too tight, Mother. My waist has always been small."

"But eighteen inches, dear..." Isobel's voice was heavy with criticism. "Vanity, Willough. Vanity. Your grandmother Carruth used to say: *The upright life is free from Vanity*."

"Grandmother Carruth must have done nothing but spout aphorisms from morning until night," muttered Willough.

"Don't be impertinent! God knows, you're your father's child. Your manners have always been a trial to me. You're entirely too independent and brazen in your ways. And do sit up straight!"

Willough flinched inwardly as the waves of her mother's disapproval and dislike washed over her in a bilious tide. She put down her cup and pressed her lips tightly together.

She thought: What's the matter with me? I'm a grown woman. Why should my mother still have the power to hurt me with her cruel attacks?

"Are my two favorite girls at it again?"

"Drewry! Dearest boy!" Isobel held out her arms to her son, watching from the doorway. "You're in time for tea. I feel better already."

Drewry Bradford laughed, an easy, comfortable laugh, and sauntered into the room. Look at him, thought Willough. She felt a surge of love for her brother, then a twinge of envy. He moved with the assurance of a man who was used to being pampered, admired, loved.

He tossed his hat onto a sofa, bent over to kiss his mother, then plopped his lean form into a deep chair, draping one long leg over the arm. Isobel beamed.

Why don't you tell *him* to sit up? thought Willough, then frowned at her own mean thoughts.

Drewry smiled at his sister. "Pour me a cup, Willough, honey. Mum, you'd feel a lot better if you could manage to toss out that tonic!" He nodded his thanks as Willough handed him his tea. "We see you so seldom anymore, little sister, that it would be nice to find a smile on your face. Life can't be *that* difficult." He winked good-naturedly at her.

Willough managed a small smile, then bent her head, concentrating on the patterned carpet, reluctant to look Drewry full in the eyes. She had never managed to return the open affection that he gave to her. It was not that she didn't love him; it was just that he had always been neutral when war had raged between her mother and her. She felt so alone, so abandoned in this house since her father had moved out, and she needed total loyalty from Drewry. His careful neutrality had created a gulf she could not cross. "Brigid said you were at the Academy of Design this afternoon," she said. Small talk. Safe and impersonal.

Drewry laughed. "Yes. That homage to Venice on Twenty-third Street! What a monstrous building."

"I like it," said Isobel. "It reminds me of the trip the two of us took to Italy. Do you remember, Drew?"

He wolfed down a teacake in two bites and smiled at her, his blue eyes twinkling. "Indeed I do, Mum. I remember how you flirted with Signore Fornaio, that day on the *piazza*."

"Oh, Drewry!" Isobel giggled like a schoolgirl and hid her face with her hands.

"Oh, Mum, you're not really blushing," he teased.

Watching them laughing together, Willough felt a pang. Why do they all love you, Drew? she thought, parlor maids and debutantes, governesses and shopgirls. There had never been a time when women had not smiled at him, held out their hands to him. And men too. In a different way, of course.

And Isobel. Today, as always, she looked past her daughter and saw only her son.

Willough sighed and poured herself another cup of tea. Maybe it was his looks. It was really quite odd, when you stopped to think of it. She and Drewry looked so much alike, even though he was four years older than she was. But the sharply defined features that made her look purposeful and a trifle severe for a woman were somehow subtly transformed on his face into a handsomeness, a beauty that was almost soft for a man.

And there was more than that. There was a sweetness in Drewry's nature, a sunniness that touched everyone. Oh, Drew, she thought miserably, how did you learn to laugh when I never have?

She stirred uncomfortably in her chair. She was an intruder. "Did you paint today, Drew?" she asked at last.

"No. I was going to sit in on a class. They had a good model. But I changed my mind." His face had suddenly gone serious. "They had some new paintings in the gallery. From Paris. Those Frenchmen are doing the most remarkable things with light and color. Not at all what I've been doing." He looked at Willough for a moment, then turned away. She was surprised to see the pain in his eyes.

"But you paint beautifully, Drewry dear," said Isobel.

He glared at her impatiently. "I paint like a damned amateur!" When his mother looked dismayed, he smiled quickly and shrugged away his anger. "But those French paintings look as though they'd been done by madmen."

"They accepted two of your paintings for exhibit at the Academy last winter, didn't they?" asked Willough. "You can't really think you're an amateur. Didn't they pay you?"

"The still life sold for fifty dollars." Drewry grinned crookedly. "I treated a bit of fluff to a steak dinner at Delmonico's with the money, and then had to borrow against my next month's allowance to make it through the week."

"Since when do steak dinners cost fifty dollars?" said Willough.

The grin deepened. "If you were a bit less straitlaced, little sister, I'd tell you what else I paid for that night!" He laughed aloud as Willough colored.

Isobel was already launched on a different tack. "Well, I think it's outrageous that you should have to depend on your father to dole out money as he sees fit!"

Drewry shrugged. "Not at all. I know the conditions, and so do you. I have only to give up this foolishness with the painting, and take up the family enterprises. And if I work diligently, and please my father—and learn that money is king—I will be rewarded with a partnership. 'Bradford and Son.'" He rose and moved easily to the mantel mirror, picking up his hat along the way. "No, thanks. I'll let Willough do it."

Willough frowned, hearing disapproval in his voice. "Someone has to!" she said defensively.

"Ah, yes. Mum told me. Did you enjoy springtime at the MacCurdy sawmill, learning the ropes?"

"I'm *proud* to be a part of it! If I can be of service to Daddy . . ."

"Has he promised you a partnership?"

Willough hesitated. "Yes. In time."

Drewry shook his head. "Don't get sucked in, Willough."

"I consider it a privilege . . . an honor . . ."

"You're a fool, little sister. He'll break your heart, and you can't even see it."

Stung, Willough glared from Drewry to Isobel and back again. "Well, we both have our blind spots," she said sourly.

Drewry smiled broadly. "So we have. Did you see my new hat?" He turned to the mirror and set the hat at a tilt on his head. Round, low-crowned, and wide-brimmed, of dark brown felt, it was the type of hat a country farmer might wear on Sunday to go to church. It looked incongruous with his well-cut black frock coat and gray trousers, the formal cravat and fawn-colored waistcoat. An outfit that cried out for a silk top hat.

Willough made a face. "A 'wide-awake' hat! I didn't notice it when you came in. I trust you didn't wear it out-of-doors with your frock coat. It looks ridiculous."

"Indeed, I did wear it. And I intend to wear it all summer long, until it's well broken-in."

Isobel looked uneasy. "A country hat in the city?"

"I don't plan to be in the city this summer."

"You're not going to Saratoga." Isobel's voice was heavy with accusation.

"Well, in a way I am. When are you going up, Willough?"

"The tenth of June. Though it's not definite."

"Make it the seventh, and we'll go together." Willough nodded in agreement.

Isobel had begun to flutter nervously. "You're *not* going to see your father?"

Drewry's blue eyes twinkled mischievously. "Don't worry, Mum. You haven't lost me. I'll stop off for a day or two, that's all. And when Father and Willough are set to leave from MacCurdyville, I'll head for the North Woods."

"What in Heaven's name will you do *there* all summer?"

"Paint. I ran into an old friend from Harvard the other day. Ed Collins. He's been living in Philadelphia. It seems there's a botanist professor and his wife from the university who are getting up a group to spend the summer in the Adirondack

Wilderness. Very high-toned. Sort of like Emerson and Low-ell did in 'fifty-eight. There's a geologist, I think. And an amateur surveyor. There'll be hunting and fishing, of course, and plenty of roughing it, but it won't be all frivolity. So you needn't look so scandalized, Willough!"

"I . . . I never . . ." she stammered.

His blue eyes softened. "Poor dutiful Willough. It would probably do us both more good if *I* spent the summer at the mines and the ironworks, and you took off your corsets and had a real holiday. At any rate, Ed asked if I'd like to come along, and I agreed. I haven't been camping in years. And I've been meaning to try more outdoor paintings. They say the scenery is spectacular in the High Peaks. I'll come home with a lot of field sketches, and maybe a painting or two if I can set up my easel at the base camp." He smiled in pleasure. "I intend to pack my traps with nothing but comfortable old clothes. All the rest can go into camphor for the whole sum-mer."

Isobel had been listening intently, leaning more and more heavily into the cushions of her chaise. Now she sighed and looked at Drewry with woeful eyes.

It was a look all too familiar to Willough, one she had learned to ignore; but it was devastatingly effective on her brother. How can he be so blind? she thought.

Isobel sighed again. "You're leaving for the entire summer . . . and you didn't even tell me."

"Now, Mum . . ."

"The entire summer! And stopping off to see your father too."

"He's still my father. Besides . . . once I've bought my hunt-ing and fishing gear, I won't have enough money left to buy a penny's worth of coffee unless I make the pilgrimage to Saratoga."

Isobel dabbed at her brow with a lace handkerchief. "I hope you prick his conscience for his tight-fistedness. Tell him he should be ashamed to treat us all so meanly. Oh, I feel so poorly today. Will you stay for supper, Drew dear?"

Here comes the kill, thought Willough.

Drewry looked uncomfortable. "I . . . I have an engagement. Isn't Uncle Arthur coming?"

"I don't know. He's been in Albany. Please stay. How important could your engagement be? Postpone it. For my sake."

He grinned wickedly. "My stomach might not mind a postponement. Other parts of me might not be so agreeable."

"Drewry! Merciful heaven, what a thing to say!" cried Isobel.

Willough felt her face turn red with embarrassment. "Why do you always have to talk about your *amours*?" she asked primly. Somehow they seemed less vulgar to her if she used a foreign word.

Drew clucked his tongue, looking from one shocked face to the other. "What a pair of prim Nellies. This is the first time I've seen you agree on anything!"

Isobel sighed again. "I suppose I must seem old-fashioned to you. I'm sure your . . . female companions are far better company at supper than an old woman who can't forget she's a lady."

"Now, Mum . . ."

Isobel's face had fallen, as though she had suffered a mortal blow. "I can hardly blame you for wanting to rush away. She must be charming. And it's not as though I won't see you once or twice for supper before you go off to spend the *entire* summer away from me."

Willough could see that Drew was weakening.

"Well . . ." he said.

"No. No. Pay no attention to me, silly boy. Go and have a lovely evening. If my sick headache has not prostrated me before you return, perhaps you'll knock at my door and read me a chapter or two of Mr. Lever's novel before you retire."

Drewry threw up his hands helplessly. "Oh, Mum. How can I go out when you're feeling so poorly? The young lady can wait. But I ought to send flowers round with my excuses, unless I want to get crowned with a parasol the next time I see her!"

Isobel looked suddenly panic-stricken. "She's not . . . *special* to you, this young lady . . . ? That is . . . more than usual . . ."

"No. She's just a charming lady. Like all the rest."

"Well, then." Isobel exhaled. "I think flowers would be appropriate. If you wish, you may order them from Sylvestre's, and have them put on my bill."

"Indeed I shall. I'll see you at supper." He hugged his mother, blew a kiss to Willough, and made for the door. Murmuring about the need to write a few letters, Willough followed him.

"Now who's the fool," she said, once they were in the vestibule. "You think she hasn't got her hooks in you?"

"It's not quite the same, little sister. You're giving up your whole life for Father. All it's cost me is a night's frolic."

"So far, big brother. So far."

Drew shrugged, set his hat more firmly on his head, tapped the crown, and went out.

"Willough!" Isobel whined from the parlor. "Come back and pour me another cup of tea."

Willough sighed and returned to the room, ignoring the gleam of triumph in her mother's eyes: for the daughter's obedience, for the capture of the son. She measured out the sugar, added the milk, poured the tea with deliberate slowness—a trifling rebellion. Resentment twisted at her insides.

She thought: Why don't you love me, Mother?

"Forgive me for not knocking. Brigid said you were still at tea." Willough looked up. Arthur Bartlett Gray stood in the doorway, every inch the gentleman, from his tall silk hat to the short gray suede gaiters over his patent leather shoes. His frock coat was impeccably tailored, with padded "American" shoulders that seemed to add to his stature; his trousers were crisply pressed, his collar starched, his cravat fastened with a discreet diamond. He smoothed his well-manicured brown mustache and crossed to Isobel, taking her hand in his and bringing it to his lips. "As always, my dearest, you look enchanting." He glanced at Willough and smiled, then looked again. "My word! Is that our little Willough, all grown up?" He put down his hat and walking stick, and turned to her in pleasure. "It must be years! Five or six at the very least! Stand up and show Uncle Arthur how you've grown."

Reluctantly, Willough rose from her chair, then covered her embarrassment at his searching gaze by holding out her hand in a businesslike way. "How are you, Mr. Gray?" she said coolly.

He shook her hand solemnly, his brown eyes appraising her; but when she would have pulled away, he held fast to her fingers. "No," he said. "After all this time, I'm entitled to more than a handshake." He moved closer and bent his head to kiss her.

She watched in horrified fascination as his lips came close to hers. In the years of growing up, she had always thought of him as an older man; he was seventeen years her senior. Now the realization struck her that she was a woman, not a child anymore—and he was younger than her mother.

Dare I let him kiss me? she thought. Then scolded herself, remembering what Grandma Carruth had always said, according to Isobel. *Proper ladies of a marriageable age never allow a bachelor to kiss them on the mouth.* She turned her head aside, so that his kiss grazed her cheek. He searched her face for a moment as though he were reading her thoughts, smiled gently in understanding, and released her fingers. He had a nice smile. Willough had never realized it until now.

"I can't expect you to call me Uncle Arthur anymore," he said. "Not when you've become such a grown-up—and beautiful—young woman. But 'Mr. Gray' sounds so cold and unfeeling. After all these years, don't you trust me enough to call me Arthur?"

Absurdly, Willough found herself remembering the novel she'd glanced at this afternoon. *Pray give me your trust, Lady,* Ali ben Tibor had said. Now, with Arthur's warm gaze enveloping her, she felt her heart fluttering. She turned quickly to the tea tray and fussed with the cups. "Do sit down... Arthur. I'll pour for you."

He laughed, and pulled up a chair next to Isobel's chaise. "I do believe you're blushing, Willough. I should think you'd be used to compliments by now. From dozens of beaux. Unless they're blind fools."

"Oh, do have your tea, Arthur, so Brigid can clear the tray!" Isobel's voice had a sharp edge.

"Isobel!" He took her hand between his own two. "How pale you are, *cara mia*. I should have seen it at once. Do you want me to go?"

Isobel softened at his tone. "No. I feel better. And I shan't burden you with my sufferings."

"But that's what friends are for, my dear."

"No. I shall be cheerful for you. Drink your tea. How was Albany?"

"In a panic. Or exulting, depending on which side of the aisle a man sits. I'm afraid our Mr. Tweed will pull down the whole house of cards. It isn't even so much his political enemies—though half of Albany knows that Judge Davis was bought off to steer the jury to a conviction."

"Which he couldn't do, anyway!"

"Not for the lack of trying. You mark my words. They'll try Tweed again, and this time they'll convict. But the newspapers are having a field day. *The New York Times*, and that abominable Mr. Nast and his cartoons in *Harper's Weekly*. It's the newspapers that everyone is afraid of. Once they get their hooks in a man, his career is ruined."

"But surely you have nothing to fear, Arthur. Just because of a friendship with Mr. Tweed..."

"No. No, of course not." Arthur stroked his mustache thoughtfully. "Isn't George Lenox connected with the Broadway Bank?" Isobel nodded. "I should very much like to meet him. It might be wise to switch my accounts at this time."

Isobel thought a moment. "I'll have the Lenoxes for tea on Thursday. You can drop in. Then you can send your card around to him the very next day. Now, no more business! How is the house on Fifth Avenue progressing?"

"The plasterer assures me that the walls will be ready for murals in another week. And the drawing-room paneling is in. I'm really quite pleased. I expect it will be only a few more months before I can move in. And then I shall give a great party, and you"—he paused to kiss her hand—"and Brian, of course, will come."

Isobel smiled, her eyes shining with delight. "You must let me help you with your guest list!"

"I had every intention. I couldn't do it without you. And you must let it be known in your circle that I'd look upon a refusal with disfavor."

"Rest assured," she said with determination, "they'll have to deal with me if they slight you."

Willough stood up from her chair, smoothing her skirts. "If you'll excuse me..."

Arthur turned to her. "No. Stay," he said. His eyes were like a caress, soft and gentle on her face. "Will *you* come to my party, Willough? And bring your latest beau."

"I...that is..." What was the matter with her, stammering like a schoolgirl? She had always been so cool, so controlled.

He chuckled. "If you blush like that, you'll stampede every man there in his haste to dance with you!"

"Willough doesn't have a beau," purred Isobel. "I don't understand it. At her age, I was already married. Why, I had ten beaux alone the winter I 'came out.' I think she wants to be an old maid."

Willough felt a pang, the sting of her mother's words. I *don't* want to be an old maid, do I? she thought. She had her soft dreams, like any other woman. Misty dreams of a husband and children and a blissful future. But the noble men in those dreams bore scant resemblance to the brash young suitors who had come calling. They had asked nothing more from her than to look pretty and flutter helplessly. When she'd tried to talk about serious topics, they'd laughed and assured her that a woman needed only to be decorative. She'd even allowed herself to be kissed a couple of times, by the only serious suitor she'd ever had, just after she'd turned nineteen. It was quite a pleasant sensation, but scarcely worth giving up her independence, or her wish to become Daddy's partner some day.

And once—it made her sick to remember it—she had been grabbed by one of Drew's friends at a party. Grabbed, held,

kissed, his tongue forcing its way between her lips, one sweaty
hand on her bare shoulders, the other kneading at her rump
as though it would work its way through skirts and petticoats
and bustle. She had found it frightening and disgusting. She
had only a vague idea of the relations between men and
women—what her mother called "that fate worse than death."
The servants gossiped about it, of course, but she'd only
caught brief snatches of mysterious talk that left her still in
the dark.

Oh God, she thought miserably. Surely there was a man
somewhere who didn't expect her to be merely a silly or-
nament; who wouldn't frighten her with violent, lustful kisses,
nor leave her indifferent with soft ones.

"Yes," repeated Isobel, with a certain satisfaction, "I think
Willough wants to be an old maid."

"Nonsense," said Arthur. "She's just waiting for the right
man. A man who knows how to treat a woman with tender
affection and respect."

Willough trembled. It was almost as though he could read
her heart, her most intimate longings.

His voice was very deep and resonant. Now it dropped to
a soft murmur. "*Will* you come to my party, Willough? And
drink champagne with me?"

"I'll be in Saratoga and MacCurdyville!" she blurted out,
an edge of panic in her voice.

He smiled. "Then perhaps I'll bring the champagne to
you."

"I really must write those letters," she said, and fled the
room.

Arthur watched her go, then turned to Isobel. "I had no
idea she'd changed so. I still remember her as little Willough."

Isobel's eyes narrowed. "Damn you," she said softly.

"Isobel! You can't really be jealous."

"Do you still love me, Arthur?"

"Always, *cara mia*." The words came automatically.

"And you're not sorry you never married?"

"I'm not the marrying kind. You know that."

She closed her eyes, fighting back the tears. "How I must vex you. Growing old and tiresome . . ."

He examined her dispassionately, noticing the tight lines around her mouth, the cheeks that now needed a spot of rouge to maintain the illusion of youth. Ten years ago she had been a beauty. Ten years ago he had been a man of twenty-eight, wildly infatuated with a woman of thirty-four. Now he was in his prime—and she was growing old.

Do I still love her? he thought. He had ached with passion in those days, seeing past her pretense of a happy marriage, sensing her loneliness, her estrangement from her husband. He had wooed her, pursued her, waited impatiently for the moment when she would surrender to him, body and soul.

Body and soul, he thought bitterly.

When had he first realized that she never would? She loved him, that was certain. Loved to be petted, kissed, flattered, courted. But not to be loved as a woman should. Fool that he was, he had kept his hopes alive for years, relieving his frustration with a succession of mistresses who bored him and aroused her jealousy. But never enough to goad her into his bed. He began to remember gossip he had heard about Brian Bradford and other women. For the first time, he understood why. Isobel was like far too many women of this age, repressed and inhibited by all the nonsense they were taught, kept ignorant of the joys of sensual pleasure. An ice princess. He had thought her reticence charming in the days when he had burned with love. Now he saw it as prudery that had long since chilled his passion, leaving only comfortable friendship and habit. She was still good company—a woman of breeding and elegance. And with an impeccable lineage and useful connections.

But an ice princess.

And raising her daughter in the same mold. It would have been funny, if it hadn't been so pitiful, the way Willough had flinched at his kiss. Still . . .

He paraded Willough before his mind's eye. She had become more beautiful even than her mother, though she seemed unaware of the fact. And despite her cool exterior, there was

a vulnerable softness in her. She had blushed and trembled
at his affectionate words and tone, though she had tried to
hide it; then she had fled in fear. He suspected that it wasn't
because she feared *him*, but because she was afraid to acknowledge her own feelings. He felt an unexpected stirring
within him. How sweet it would be to woo Youth, to fan the
innocent spark to a mature flame, before the rigid conventions
had frozen her. He sighed, regretting the wasted years.

"What are you thinking of, Arthur?" Isobel smiled uneasily,
her mouth puckered in a prissy imitation of pleasure that made
her seem older than her forty-four years.

He shook off the disquieting thoughts. "Nothing, *cara mia*.
Nothing."

She searched his face, her eyes dark and filled with pain.
"Am I losing you, Arthur?"

"Of course not."

"If I lose you, Arthur, it will break my heart." Her expression was suddenly hard. "But if I lose you to Willough, I'll
never forgive you!"

He smiled thinly. How tiresome she had become. There
had been a time when he'd wanted to tear off her laces and
silks, hold her naked in his arms, force her to take all of his
love. But that was long ago and before he'd seen Willough.
Willough, who blushed and sighed. Willough, with her red
lips and sensual body. He smiled again at Isobel, and said
nothing. What could he say, without his voice betraying him?

Isobel stared at him for a long minute; the clock on the
mantel ticked in the silence. "I'm tired," she said at last.
"The tonic has made me sleepy. Please go."

"Do you want me to return for supper?"

"Do you want to?"

"Will Drew and Willough be there?"

"I suppose so."

He hesitated, seeing the look of apprehension in her eyes.
He felt a moment's pity. For what had been, and was no
more.

"Then I shan't come," he said. "Make it tomorrow night,
when I can have you all to myself."

* * *

"I spoke to Dr. Marshall yesterday at the boardinghouse, Marcy. He didn't think my feller'd mind your riding in the boat. And he didn't fuss at the rise in price. Figured you'd be useful."

Marcy squinted and shielded her eyes from the glare in the east, gazing out over the mists that shrouded Long Lake. Soon enough, she knew, the morning fog would burn away with the rising sun, and it would be hot. She rolled up the sleeves of her flannel shirt. "Thank you, Uncle Jack. He didn't happen to say . . . um . . . if any of the men are single . . . did he?"

"You're still set on that, my girl? Well, I couldn't very well ask the man right out! I only know *he's* spoken for. Mrs. Marshall seems an odd one for a trip like this. I didn't meet the rest of 'em. They just come over by stage from North Creek last night. Why don't you just give it up?"

Marcy stuck out her chin. "No. I mean to get me a husband."

He shook his head. "I don't know why my brother didn't paddle that stubborn streak out of you years ago! And even if any of them is single, you're not forgetting what I told you about needing money, are you? How will you know which of 'em is rich? Tell me that!"

She bit her lip in consternation. "I don't suppose I could *ask* them . . . could I?"

He snorted and turned sharply. "Mind you watch that boat, Tom!" he called to one of the other guides. "See that the gear is stowed proper."

Tom Sabattis ambled over to where Marcy and Old Jack stood on the small dock. He grinned at Marcy, and hitched at his wide leather belt. "Will you ride the Oxbow Rapids, Marce?"

She put her hands on her hips, answering the challenge. "They never scared me yet, Tom! You were the one that took the spill the last time we went together!"

"Aw-w-w. That's because I was with a greenhorn. I thought he'd darn near puke, he was that scared. Anyways, I sure am glad I'm not Amos. Taking the Marshalls. Mister Marshall looks a decent sort, but *she* showed up for supper last night dressed like it was Saratoga. All fancylike. And when she sat down to table, a body could hear her stays squeak! I thought my maw would drop the whole danged platter of flapjacks, she was trying that hard to hold in her laughter." He eyed Marcy from head to foot, scanning the flannel shirt that failed to hide the curve of her bosom, the men's trousers that accented her hips, the knee-high boots and snug leather belt that held a sheathed hunting knife. "It wouldn't surprise me none if she takes a fit at the way you're dressed!"

"Bosh! I reckon I'm not about to take the rapids in a dress, no matter what the city slickers do! But I packed a skirt for Sundays, in case they're the type who needs a little praying once in awhile."

Old Jack scratched his head and grumbled, his eyes inspecting the five oddly shaped boats drawn up onto the spit of sand. "We're going to waste the whole danged morning if those folks don't get amoving. If the lean-to up at Clear Pond blew down in the last storm, we could be at it all day, just setting up camp. And no chance for a spot of fishing."

"Don't fret, Uncle Jack. It's still early. Just past five, I reckon. And Amos and Alonzo aren't back from Palmer's yet with the last of the provisions." Marcy smiled in understanding. "But if it'll make you any happier, I'll go on up to the boardinghouse to see if any of 'em are stirring yet."

"If my maw don't look too frazzled in the kitchen," said Tom, "whistle down to me. I sure could use a second breakfast right about now."

Marcy nodded and left the beach, climbing the heavily wooded hill to Sabattis's Boardinghouse. The path was dim and well worn, the exposed cedar roots rubbed smooth by constant footsteps. On either side of the path, the forest floor was cluttered between the soaring trees, damp and matted dead leaves of yesteryear pierced here and there by white-blossomed hobblebush and feathery clumps of new ferns.

Marcy noticed with pleasure that the wintergreen had begun to flower, and made a mental note to see if the wild roses had opened yet on the sheltered shore of Clear Pond. She moved slowly on her way, her eyes on the brush, seeking some new growth that had not been there yesterday, a patch of glossy clubmoss that announced that June had come at last. Her footsteps were soft, trained by years of tracking at the side of Uncle Jack and old Mr. Sabattis, an Abenaki Indian—though, of course, that fact wasn't generally known to the tourists and city folk, who were more prejudiced about such things.

"Don't move!" An urgent whisper broke the morning stillness.

She looked up. There on the path was a man, half dressed. His feet were bare, and his gallused corduroy trousers were pulled on over a woolen undervest. That was all he wore. In his hands he held a large pad and pencil. He hadn't even looked at her, not even when she stopped; now she followed his gaze to see that he was concentrating on a white-tailed doe some ten yards off the path and to her left. The man seemed to be drawing, his head bent over his sketchpad, a shock of black hair falling across his forehead. At his hissed command, the deer had stopped feeding on the leaves of a small bush and looked up, startled; then, sensing no menace, it had resumed its breakfast.

Marcy felt a slight breeze ruffle her loose curls; the deer was upwind, and far too busy to be spooked by her if she were quiet. Moving carefully, she continued on up the path.

"I said, don't move!" he whispered, still without looking at her. His pencil moved furiously on the paper.

She ignored him. City slicker, she thought. The deer would need more than her quiet progress to frighten it off. Besides, she was curious to see his drawing. She covered the last of the distance between them, and stood near his left shoulder. He was very tall; she had to raise herself on tiptoe, and still she couldn't see his sketch.

He continued to be absorbed in his drawing. "You're a stubborn hayseed, aren't you?" he said softly.

It had been said good-naturedly, but the word stung. "And you're a dad-blamed fool for coming out here without your boots," she hissed. "If the red ants are biting, you'll be scratching for a week. *Greenhorn!*" she added with malice.

He chuckled under his breath, his eyes still on the doe. "And a bit of a shrew, too, are you?"

She gasped in outrage, and turned to march up the hill.

His voice cut like a knife, sharp and unexpectedly menacing. "If you move again before I'm through, I'll knock you down!"

She froze in her tracks, seeing the sudden tenseness in the square shoulders, the set of his jaw in profile.

As quickly as the anger had come over him it passed. He relaxed and resumed his drawing. "I saw her from my window," he whispered, jerking his chin in the direction of the doe. "I didn't want to stop to dress."

She was still smarting from his high-handedness. "I'm surprised you bothered to put on your britches!" she said with sarcasm.

For the first time, he lifted his head and looked at her. His eyes were icy blue and clear, with a piercing intensity that took her breath away. They traveled over her in an unhurried appraisal, peeling away her clothing in a manner that left no doubt as to his thoughts. Then he grinned, and the eyes twinkled. "You're lucky I *did* put on my britches!" He waited to see the blush color her cheeks, then returned to his work.

She didn't know whether to be flattered or angry. No one had ever looked at her like that before, not even Zeb with his hungry yearning. "You're a fancy artist?" she asked in an off-handed way, then cursed silently to herself, dismayed to hear the quaver in her voice. She thought: Danged if I want him to know how his eyes turned me to jelly!

"A fancy artist?" He laughed softly. "Well, I try to be."

"Does it pay well?" She was surprised at her own boldness.

"Not very," he answered dryly, "but I . . . damn!" He swore as the doe, disturbed at last by their voices, lifted its head, sniffed once, and bounded away. "Oh, well . . ." He closed his pad, and put the pencil in his pocket. "I guess I got enough." He grinned at her again, the self-assurance of his smile pricking her like a cocklebur under her collar.

"Can I move now?" she asked coldly, remembering his threat.

He laughed. "Did I ruffle your feathers?"

She pursed her lips primly. "You had no call to talk to me like that."

His face was suddenly serious, though she wasn't at all sure he wasn't laughing at her. "You're right. No call at all. I'm sorry." His eyes twinkled with a devilish gleam. "Of course, if I hadn't been busy sketching, I might've found a better way to keep you from moving. And it surely would have pleased you more."

"What do you mean?" she asked, then gasped and blushed as the realization hit her. He would have held her in his arms—that's what he meant! Pleased her, indeed! She began to sputter in anger. "Why you . . . snaggle-toothed wolf! You swell-headed, puff-britched, conceited son of a . . ." She was too angry to continue.

He leered wickedly. "Damned if I can't think of a way to still your shrewish tongue! And close that pretty little mouth of yours!"

She blushed even more furiously. She was half tempted to rear back and slap him as hard as she could, but he towered over her, and she wasn't at all sure how he'd retaliate. Besides, his eyes were on her lips now, and he'd stepped closer. She gulped. His face was beautiful under its shock of black hair. Strong and beautiful. And his eyes were pale blue and mesmerizing, seeming to bore into her, to the very depths of her, until she felt wondrously, frighteningly naked before him.

Her heart began to pound beneath the coarse flannel of her shirt. It made her shiver, to have him so near.

Retreat seemed the wisest course. "Oh-h-h!" she cried, and turned on her heel and stormed back down the path to the lake.

Behind her he roared with laughter. "You'd better run, girl. Next time I see you, I intend to take my kiss!"

Chapter
Two

"Tom Sabattis, don't you dare laugh!" Marcy stifled her own urge to giggle, and shot a warning look at the young guide.

"If she don't beat all, Marce," said Tom under his breath. "She looks like she's come straight out of one of them fancy catalogs, without even stopping to get dust on her boots!"

Marcy nodded in agreement as a tall and buxom woman emerged from the wooded path and advanced across the small spit of sand to where the guides waited beside the mound of supplies and stacked rifles. To Marcy's way of thinking, she looked sturdy enough to stare down a bear. She was encased in the very latest mountain gear, or at least what the city folks took to be the right way of dressing for "roughing it." A knee-high walking dress over Turkish drawers fastened tightly at the ankles; thick balmoral boots, with rubbers for added protection; a pair of buckskin gloves with chamois armlets sewn on at the wrists and buttoned snugly at the elbows (to keep out the black flies, thought Marcy); and a large felt hat with a net of fine Swiss mull poised on the edge of its broad brim, in case the mosquitoes should start to bite. A pair of funny little glasses was pinched onto the tip of her nose, forcing her to peer out of them with her head tilted far back, like a turtle sniffing the air.

"She'll see fine going *up* mountains," whispered Tom. "I just don't want to be in front of her when she's coming down! And I sure wouldn't want to be Amos!" He looked with sympathy at Amos Robinson, one of the guides, struggling along behind the woman, and sweating under the load of a bulging carpetbag, several blankets, a waterproof coat, and two fur hats.

Marcy nearly choked, swallowing her laughter.

She thought: That must be Mrs. Marshall. The lady with the squeaking corsets. I hope she's not still wearing them. With all that gear, and corsets besides, she'd most likely swamp the boat!

"Lewis. *Lewis!*" said Mrs. Marshall in a shrill voice that reminded Marcy of the quavering of a loon. "Did you remember to pack the special envelopes for the leaf specimens?"

"Yes, my love." Dr. Marshall was a gentle-looking man half a head shorter than his wife. His forehead was lined with years, but his cheeks and nose were pink and round and cherubic. On his head he wore a floppy straw skimmer studded with fishing flies.

"And a spare flannel undersuit for yourself? You know how important a 'change' is in the wild."

Dr. Marshall blushed and tugged at the collar of his shirt. "Yes, my love."

Marcy ignored Tom's snicker beside her, and concentrated on the men who had followed the Marshalls down to the beach. Uncle Jack had said there were five men in the party— and Mrs. Marshall, of course; not counting Dr. Marshall, that left four prospects for marriage. It seemed a bit cold-blooded, to take stock of them like boots in a dry goods store, but she was nothing if not stubborn, once she'd made up her mind to something. And she'd made up her mind to find a husband this summer. Before she became an old maid. Before it was too late to leave the mountains.

She discounted the first man almost at once. He seemed

dry and old—forty at the least. And there was an uppishness
in the way he carried his head, looking toward the assembled
guides and boats, that she didn't much take to. As a last
resort, she thought.

The next man was decidedly good-looking. His straight
brown hair had been allowed to grow into long side whiskers
in front of his ears, which gave a dashing appearance to his
square-jawed face. Like the pictures of buccaneers that Marcy
had seen in one of her father's books. His eyes, casually but
thoroughly assessing her where she stood with the rest of the
guides, were certainly a buccaneer's eyes, on the lookout for
plunder. Dangerous, she thought, but a distinct possibility.
Over one shoulder he carried a tripod and several odd-looking
instruments. Marcy remembered that Uncle Jack had said one
of the men was planning to measure and survey some of the
territory.

She was disappointed in the next man who appeared. He
was younger than the first two—much closer to her own
age—and he was handsome, with pale yellow hair and fine
features. But he seemed to be everything she most disliked
about the city folk who came to her mountains. He picked
his way carefully down the path, frowning as he kicked aside
a small rock that stood in his way; and when a stray branch
caught at his well-tailored frock coat, he brushed away the
offending twig as though it had clutched at him intentionally.
His jaunty top hat, sprigged with a turkey feather in a deliberate attempt to appear "country," didn't look substantial
enough to withstand the first rainfall. Marcy knew tourists
like that. They pretended to love the wilderness, and treated
their stay in the mountains as an adventure, but they did
nothing except complain, and wish that the country could be
more like the city.

She sighed. He *might* be rich; he was certainly soft and
spoiled.

The last man, his soft felt hat tilted rakishly over one eye,
bounded onto the beach laughing, and knocked his comrade's
top hat onto the sand. He laughed again, stooped to retrieve
the hat, brushed the sand from the fine plush, and returned

it to its owner. Then he looked around the clearing, his blue eyes widening at sight of Marcy.

"Well, well," he said softly.

She felt her knees go weak. Her fancy artist. She smiled tentatively, not sure whether she was glad or not to see him again. Then he grinned—a crooked, funny smile—and her heart began to thump madly at the thought of spending two whole months in the wilderness with him.

She thought: he'll see me blush. And turned away in embarrassment, moving to where Old Jack was checking the straps on a valise.

"That tall one looks a good prospect," she said quietly, trying to sound off-hand and indifferent.

Old Jack straightened, quickly appraised the man, then turned back to her in disgust. "That one? Huh! You might's well stay in Long Lake and marry Zeb Cary. You wind up in the big city with *that* one, and you'll be boiling rats from the cellar for his dinner!"

"Oh, bosh, Uncle Jack, what do you know?" But it was so, of course. After the first shock of seeing him again, she had begun to notice his clothes. His hat was battered and old-looking, and his heavy boots were dappled with paint. His shoulders were broad and manly under the billowing shirt he wore, which only added to her dismay. For the shirt itself had begun to fray at the cuffs, and the scarf tied so casually under the soft, turned-down collar was no more than a simple cotton neckerchief. She wondered if he even owned a second shirt. He was carrying his coat slung over one shoulder, and both the coat and his snug-fitting waistcoat had obviously seen better days.

I don't care! she thought defiantly, then remembered what Uncle Jack had said about the Petersons, beaten down by the poverty of the city.

She thought: I can't afford even to consider him. And if I stay in the mountains, I'll die. She sighed unhappily and forced herself to look again at the other three men. Dressed in new, fancy clothes. And not a one of them with a wedding band. That was a good beginning, at least.

The blond man replaced his top hat and grimaced at the artist. "Do you intend to ruin my hat before our jaunt begins, Drew, old fellow?"

Marcy thought: Drew. What a nice name.

"Begging your pardon, Mr. . . . " Old Jack stepped forward to the top-hatted man, and tugged politely at the brim of his own flat-crowned felt.

"Collins, my good fellow. Edward Collins."

"Well then, Mr. Collins. If you reckon on keeping that hat in a stiff breeze, you'd best tie a string to it and hook it on your lapel. A tall hat don't usually last long in the wilderness. You oughtn't to have brung it."

Collins looked faintly annoyed. "Do you hear that, Drew? My first morning in this backward territory, and already I'm being lectured by a yokel."

Drew's blue eyes were like ice. "Don't be a prig, Ed," he said quietly. "I told you not to wear your good clothes."

"If the rest of this summer is like the past two days, my clothes will be old in no time!" Collins rubbed his rump in dismay. "Ten hours in that coach from North Creek! And those roads . . . ye gods!"

"Now, now, Edward!" said Mrs. Marshall in a hearty voice. "Have you forgotten so soon that this is to be our great adventure? All the hours that you and Lewis and I spent in planning? Think of it! The forest primeval. The sacred wilderness!" Her eyes began to glow with religious fervor. "Treading paths hitherto trodden only by our noble red brethren. To return to Nature is to return to God!"

Tarnation! thought Marcy. She *will* want praying on Sundays.

Collins smiled ruefully and rubbed his chin. "Our 'adventure' seemed more exciting in a gaslit drawing room than after two days in a dingy railroad car and a bumpy stagecoach! But . . ."

"Come, come, my lad," said Dr. Marshall. "Haven't you been longing to see the ring lichen in its native habitat? Even an amateur botanist must venture into the field once in awhile.

Why I remember once in 'sixty-eight, with some of my students..."

Mrs. Marshall cut in sharply. "There'll be time for that later, Lewis!" She turned to Marcy's uncle. "Old Jack. I understand that you and my husband have made all the arrangements. Will you please assign us to our guides and boats?"

"My pleasure, ma'am. There are five boats. You and Dr. Marshall are with Amos in the first one. Most often we ride two to a boat, one guide for one sportsman. But the doctor wished for you to be together."

Dr. Marshall looked concerned. "I knew the task of paddling a boat would be too strenuous for your delicate constitution, my love."

"Quite so."

Marcy nearly laughed aloud as Mrs. Marshall attempted a delicate expression. She looked away, flustered, when she saw that the man Drew was grinning, too, sharing the silent joke with her.

"Young Tom, here"—Old Jack indicated the Sabattis boy—"is to go with that gentleman there."

"That's Mr. William Stafford," said Mrs. Marshall.

The dashing buccaneer has an ordinary name, thought Marcy, as Stafford handed his surveying instruments to Tom, and pointed to a valise and knapsack on the small beach, which Tom immediately began to stow in one of the boats.

Old Jack beckoned to another guide. "Alonzo will take that tall feller there."

"Drew's my name."

"*Mr.* Bradford," corrected Mrs. Marshall primly. "We don't want too much familiarity, Drewry. Do we?"

Drew's eyes twinkled wickedly, but his smile was as innocent as the day. "Why not, Mrs. Marshall? You and I met only three days ago, and I asked you to call me Drew soon as we shook hands. Now Alonzo here will practically be... so to speak... my bed partner for the next two months. Why can't he call me Drew?"

Mrs. Marshall looked scandalized. "Mr. Bradford!"

He hastened to appear contrite. "My dear Mrs. Marshall. It was only a figure of speech, I assure you. But you do see my point..."

She adjusted the pince-nez on her nose, tugged at the buff ribbon that held the glasses around her neck. Then she tilted back her head and peered coldly at Drew. "You may be as democratic as you wish, of course, Mr. Bradford. But you'll reap the consequences."

"I quite understand, Mrs. Marshall," he said solemnly. "I shall endeavor to avoid being overfriendly with the guides." His expression still serious, he deliberately winked at Marcy.

Tarnation! thought Marcy, feeling her face burning again. If that long-eared devil doesn't stop making me blush...

"Humph!" said Mrs. Marshall, indignantly turning her back on Drew.

"Old Jack," said Dr. Marshall quickly, "you haven't finished assigning the guides."

"Yes, sir." Old Jack indicated the first man who had come down the path. "That's Mr. Heyson, isn't it?"

Stuck-up Mr. Heyson, thought Marcy.

"You said he collects rocks," continued Old Jack. "I thought Jerry there would be just about right for Mr. Heyson. He's a strong 'un."

Jerry stepped forward, a strapping lad of eighteen, and grinned at George Heyson. There was a gap where his front teeth should have been. "I can carry any pack you can load up, Mr. Heyson, sir!" He flexed his arms to show the bulging muscles of his biceps.

Heyson eyed him critically. "Just don't chatter away," he said in a voice as colorless as his face. "I don't enjoy unnecessary talk. And I expect a day's work from you." He frowned at a large pebble on the beach, then scooped it up to examine it more closely.

"It sure is getting warm." Ed Collins pulled a handkerchief out of his pocket and dabbed at his forehead. "I guess that leaves me with you, Old Jack."

"And Marcy."

George Heyson turned indignantly to Dr. Marshall. "Lewis. Is that girl coming with us?"

Dr. Marshall cleared his throat. "I'm sorry. I haven't had the opportunity to speak to all of you. The girl is Marcy Tompkins, Old Jack's niece. He asked me about her yesterday. I didn't think any of you would mind." He turned to his wife. "She'll be good company for you, my love."

"Yes . . . perhaps." Mrs. Marshall's disapproving eyes traveled over Marcy's shirt and trousers. "Is that what you intend to wear, girl?"

"It's what I'm comfortable in, ma'am," Marcy answered. "But I did pack a skirt for Sundays," she added quickly.

"Well . . ."

Drew Bradford pulled off his hat and ran his fingers through his black hair. "I hate to be crass, Dr. Marshall, but is the girl hiring on? And if so . . . who's to pay for it?" He looked at Marcy and shrugged apologetically. "Sorry, honey. But by my reckoning, I'll be lucky to have a ten-dollar greenback in my vest pocket at the end of the summer. And glad I already have my ticket home."

Marcy's heart felt as if it had dropped into the pit of her stomach. He was obviously poorer than she had imagined. A man like that wouldn't want the burden of a wife.

"Don't fret, Drewry," said Dr. Marshall kindly. "Old Jack said she's skilled at roughing it, but we both agreed that the going rate of two fifty a day was a little steep for a female. We settled on a dollar fifty a day, plus her weekly board of two dollars for supplies. And her meal vouchers if we stop at any hotels or boardinghouses along the chain. And I don't see why we can't divide the cost among ourselves—it doesn't amount to that much per man. What do you say?"

Drew shook his head. "I don't know. I make that out to be fifteen, twenty dollars—at the very least—for every man. I just don't have that kind of money with me."

"See here, Bradford. I'll pay your share." William Stafford fished a cigar out of his breast pocket and bit off the tip. He struck a match against the sole of one fine leather boot and took several deep puffs of his cigar. The smoke that drifted in Marcy's direction was rich and aromatic.

She thought: Whatever the buccaneer does for a living, he must do it well.

"Well, Bradford? You can pay me back whenever you're able. I'd quite understand." For a moment Stafford's eyes focused on Drew's paint-spattered boots, then he smiled at the other man and exhaled a stream of blue smoke.

"I can forward you the money as soon as I return to New York City," said Drew softly. "I'm obliged to you, sir."

Stafford allowed his gaze to travel the length of Marcy's lush form. "I'm not sure I'm doing it for you, sir."

Drew smiled disarmingly. "I'm not sure that's a gentlemanly thing to say, sir."

Marcy bit her lip. In a strange way, they seemed to be engaged in some sort of battle, though neither man had stopped smiling. And she seemed to be a part of it. It was frightening and exciting all at the same time. And brand-new. Zeb was a boy. These were men—strange and unfamiliar to her. She felt a moment's panic.

She thought: Am I getting in over my head?

"Well, I don't like it." George Heyson's fingers played with the rock he still held. "A female doesn't belong on a jaunt like this!"

"I beg your pardon, George!" Mrs. Marshall's face began to turn red.

"Cynthia . . . I . . . I didn't mean . . . you're not . . ."

"Not what, George? Not female?" Mrs. Marshall's voice was growing shrill. "In all the years you've known Lewis and me, I've never heard you say a crueller thing."

The fingers had now become quite agitated. Marcy thought the rock would fly out of Heyson's hand.

"That's not what I meant at all. Not at all," he stammered. "I just don't see what a young chit like that can contribute to the seriousness of our expedition."

Old Jack stepped forward. "She's a good hunter, Mr. Heyson. She'll more than earn her keep in game. You won't regret it."

"I don't like it, Lewis. We don't need her."

"I don't see why Miss Tompkins can't come along," said Drew.

Old Jack turned to Mrs. Marshall. "I appeal to you, ma'am," he said mournfully. "The girl had her heart set on going. My poor dead brother's only child . . . orphaned and alone in the world, with no one but me. To be at the mercy of strangers while I'm away . . ."

Tarnation! thought Marcy. What's Uncle Jack trying to do? She'd begged him to do what he could to arrange things, but she didn't expect he'd start pouring out all that hogwash! He sounded like the actors in the melodrama she'd seen last year down at North Creek.

And all because that high-nosed Mr. Heyson didn't think that females could do anything.

"Oh, balderdash!" she cried. Marching to the rifles lined up on the beach, she snatched up her own weapon and slammed a cartridge into the breech. She whirled angrily to the men.

"Toss up that rock, Mr. Heyson!"

George Heyson looked shocked, his eyes widening at the sight of the rifle barrel pointing in his direction. "Now just a minute, young woman . . ."

"Go it, Marcy!" Laughing, Drew strode to Heyson, pulled the stone from his limp fingers, and flung it high in the air. Marcy swung the rifle to her shoulder, sighting and squeezing the trigger simultaneously. There was a loud crack, and the rock shattered into a thousand pieces.

"Well done!" said Stafford. "I for one think we can use you on this jaunt." By the look in his eye, Marcy wasn't quite sure *what* he meant.

"I agree," said Mrs. Marshall, taking charge once more. "But I trust you will all remember you are gentlemen. And while Marcy scarcely has the refinements of young ladies of our class, she is, nevertheless, a member of the fairer sex, and as such merits the proper behavior you would all show toward your own mothers and sweethearts." She turned to Collins. "Now, Edward. Are you agreeable that the girl and her uncle should ride with you?"

Collins looked petulant. "I don't fancy having a girl show me up every time we go out for deer. And if there's some hard paddling to be done, I'd just as soon not have the extra weight in the boat."

"I'll switch places with you. You can have Alonzo." Drew's voice was a humorous drawl. "I'd be delighted to have Marcy do my shooting for me. And if she can spell me at the oars now and again, so much the better!"

Mrs. Marshall sniffed her disapproval. "That's not a very manly view."

Drew scratched his ear. "No, ma'am, it's not."

Impatiently, Old Jack picked up a large knapsack from the beach and tossed it over one shoulder. "If we don't pack up right soon, we'll lose the daylight long before we reach Clear Pond!" While the sportsmen watched and supervised, the guides began to load their boats. Each man had a carpetbag or a soft leather valise, loaded with his clothing and blankets. The hunting and fishing gear—fly-rods and creels and ammunition—packed into knapsacks, was stowed in the flat-bottomed boats. Their provisions and cooking utensils were carried in ash-splint baskets, some two by three feet, which could easily be strapped to a man's back for the carries between lakes. The Abenaki Indians were skilled in the weaving of these baskets; often Marcy had sat with Tom Sabattis's kin, while they twined the supple splints and told stories of the old times and the old ways.

His mouth pinched tight in disapproval, George Heyson insisted that Jerry repack his gear, while Mrs. Marshall flapped about like a large hen in the barnyard, her net veil fluttering, worried that she had not brought enough warm clothing. Ed Collins had already removed his top hat and frock coat, and was now pacing the dock and complaining about the heat, while he mopped the inside of his hatband with a handkerchief.

Only Drewry, his hat and coat thrown aside, worked alongside Marcy and Old Jack, carrying his own rifle and carpetbag down to the boat, and returning for his painting supplies—a worn satchel filled with rolled-up canvas, sketchpads, a paintbox, and a handful of brushes and pencils tied up with string.

Marcy stooped and reached for the straps of the provision basket, grunting as she lifted it, and swung it onto her back. Fresh-stocked for the journey, with coffee, tea, flour, and other staples, as well as pots and plates, the basket weighed almost seventy pounds. But she was strong, and had carried heavier loads.

"Here. I'll take that. You take my painting gear." Drew bent down, his blue eyes warm with concern.

Marcy felt her body go hot, just from the look in his eyes. Dang him! she thought. She was angry—angry at him for looking the way he did, angry at herself for allowing him to have such an effect on her.

"Bosh!" she snapped, adjusting the basket and standing up. "I can carry this old thing!"

He shook his head. "I said it before, and I reckon it's so. You *are* a stubborn filly!"

Stung, she turned away and made for Uncle Jack's boat, trying to move as though the basket were as light as a feather. It was heavier than she had imagined: She nearly tripped as she reached the boat. Drew had followed her; without a word he pulled the basket from her back and dropped it onto the beach. She felt angrier than ever, thinking he might be laughing at her.

Then he put his hand on her arm. She looked up and saw that he was smiling. A friendly smile.

"I'm glad you're coming along," he said quietly.

Her mouth went dry. "Mr. . . . Bradford . . ." she stammered.

He grinned. "Drewry. Even better, call me Drew. It's only fair. Now that you and Old Jack will be . . ." he chuckled, " . . . you know. Instead of Alonzo . . ."

Bed partners. He'd said it to Mrs. Marshall. She felt the blush creeping up to her hairline once again.

"Damn," he said softly, his eyes examining her closely. "I wish I had my paintbox at the ready. I wonder if I could ever mix that lovely shade of pink. I think that's why I like to see you blush so often!"

"You're making fun of me!" she said in indignation.

"No, I'm not. Truly." He reached out and brushed a curl from her forehead. His fingers across her skin sent a flutter racing through her insides. "I don't have the pigments to capture all those glorious colors. That hair . . . those extraordinary eyes . . . and your skin, when you blush . . ."

"You *are* making fun of me!"

He laughed. "Not at all. I'm probably thinking of you as an unpaid model for the next couple of months! It's my good fortune that Stafford agreed to lend me the money. I don't think I could have come up with that much this month. And I didn't want the Marshalls to shoulder the expense—they're already paying for two."

"But he's a doctor. He can afford it."

"No. Not that kind of doctor. He's just a professor at the university. He teaches botany—that's to do with plants, though I'll bet you could teach him a thing or two about plants."

She shrugged. "It's easy when you've grown up with them. But he oughtn't to call himself a doctor if he isn't one!"

"He *is* a doctor—just the wrong kind. So you better not take sick."

"Don't fret none about me! I could show you plants and mushrooms in these mountains that'd cure half a hundred ills. And more that could cause 'em!" She giggled. "I could feed you something that would turn your skin green. And then you could match *that* with your paints!"

He laughed, his teeth white in his tanned face. "Damned if you're not one first-rate girl, Marcy Tompkins!"

She smiled back, feeling wonderfully comfortable with him, as though she'd known him all her life. Why, she thought, he doesn't even make me blush anymore! And then he leaned in close, and murmured a few words, and she felt her face flaming.

He said: "I haven't forgotten about that kiss you owe me."

He was so matter-of-fact, so confident. It scared her. It wasn't like being with Zeb. It was easy to keep the upper hand with Zeb, to call the tune. She should be able to do it now. After all, she'd already made up her mind that she couldn't have anything to do with Drewry Bradford.

Then why did she feel so helpless when he looked at her?

"You're mighty cocksure," she snapped. "What makes you think I'll give you a kiss?"

One black eyebrow arched up in cool amusement. "What makes you think I'll *ask*?"

She gasped and backed away from him, glancing nervously around at the others on the beach. "If you want to be helpful," she said quickly, "you'll find a place to stow that basket in the boat while I go and see if Uncle Jack has more supplies for us."

She managed to keep her distance from him until the boats were loaded and the party was ready to leave. Old Jack made a last-minute inspection of the provisions, and then frowned.

"Marcy," he said, "what happened to the linen bandages and salves, and the rest of that stuff? Did you pack 'em?"

She shook her head. "No, Uncle Jack." She pointed in the direction of a small shack at the other end of the spit of sand. "Maybe you left them in the boathouse. I'll go look."

"Bring 'em along if they're in there," he said, bending down to stow the paddles under the wicker seats of the boat. "And the jug. I forgot that too. I must be getting old."

Mrs. Marshall was at once aroused. "Jug? Did you say jug, Old Jack? Are you speaking of hard spirits?"

"Well, yes, ma'am . . ."

"I'm 'Temperance'," she said indignantly. "I cannot tolerate license on a jaunt such as this. We are here to experience the cleansing and healing powers of Mother Nature. Our souls may be refreshed by our surroundings; our bodies can scarcely be so, if you intend to bring along such poisons!"

"Now, now, Cynthia," said Dr. Marshall soothingly. "I'm sure that Old Jack intends such spirits for medicinal purposes only. Isn't that so, Old Jack?"

Uncle Jack scratched at his stubbly chin. "Sure enough. There's nothing can ease the peskiness of the black flies when they get to biting, except the insides of a good jug!"

Mrs. Marshall looked bewildered, as though she were trying to figure out how the whiskey might be administered; before she could ask another question Old Jack quickly jerked his head in the direction of the shed. "Tarnation, Marcy, what are you waiting for? Go fetch that stuff!"

"I'll help you." Drew Bradford swung into step beside Marcy as she moved toward the boathouse.

"It isn't necessary, Mr. Bradford, I . . ." She stopped, seeing the look in his eyes as he towered over her. She thought: He means to kiss me, whether I want to or not! And the boathouse was dim, and far away from the others. She lengthened her stride. "I don't need your help, Mr. Bradford," she said sharply.

He chuckled. "You're just a little bit of a girl. Do you really think you can walk faster than I can? And my name is Drew."

She found herself almost skipping to get away from him. "I don't want your help." Her voice shook. She didn't know whether she was nervous because of his intentions, or angry because he was so cocky about it. "I don't *want* your help!" she said again, more firmly this time.

"Hasn't anybody ever tried to do something about that stubborn streak? A good dose of castor oil every spring, or something?" He took her by the elbow and propelled her forward to the shack, pushing her inside and closing the door softly behind him. Even in the dim light, she could see the devilish twinkle in his eyes. "Now . . ." he said.

She backed up against the far wall. "Don't you come near me!"

He grinned. "I promised you I'd take that kiss."

"I'll scream!"

He clucked his tongue. "Tsk, tsk! What would Mrs. Marshall say? She'd take a conniption fit, and we'd both have to stay behind. You don't want to scream." He advanced toward her and put his hands on the wall on either side of her shoulders.

She looked up and gulped. She hadn't realized how tall he was. At least eight inches taller than she. Panicky, flustered, she thought about ducking under his arms; but he had already moved nearer and was now so close that she had no space to maneuver.

"Didn't they teach you any manners?" she asked in a quavery voice.

He shook his head. "Not a lick." His arms came down from the wall and circled her waist, pulling her close to him. "At least not where pretty girls are concerned."

She was trembling. His eyes were the clearest blue she'd ever seen, pale and limpid, seeming to look right through her skin. And ringed with black fringes of lash that matched the rakish curl that had fallen over his forehead. She felt an odd tickling at the back of her throat. She thought: What's he waiting for? Not that she *wanted* him to kiss her, of course; she'd already decided that she wasn't interested in him. But if he intended to do it, why didn't he just get it over with? Then he grinned, that funny, crooked smile of his, and she felt herself getting hot under the collar. Danged if she was about to let him have the upper hand!

She tried to look as indifferent as she could manage, with those eyes boring into her. "Don't take all day, Mr. Bradford. I have better things to do than waste the time with you. Take your kiss, if you must."

His blue eyes widened in surprise. "You're a cool one. I take it this won't be your first kiss."

Somehow that angered her more than anything else he had said. "Certainly not!" she snapped. "Now take your kiss, or let me go!"

He gathered her more firmly in his arms and bent his head to her mouth. She closed her eyes, feeling the softness of his lips on hers as they moved gently back and forth and pressed against her closed lips. She felt weak and breathless, as though a tight band was wound around her chest. Zeb had never managed to make her feel like this.

Abruptly, Drew raised his head and frowned. "Haven't you ever been kissed by a *man*?"

"Wh-What?" She was still trying to catch her breath.

"Honey," he said gently, "a man expects you to act as if you're enjoying it." He smiled, the corner of his mouth twitching. "Otherwise, I might as well go and kiss one of Mrs. Sabattis's flapjacks!"

"Oh!" Her voice was an outraged squeak. "If you're not every way the most conceited..."

He laughed and pulled her hard against him, almost lifting her from the ground. His mouth closed over hers, stilling her words, stilling everything but the roaring in her ears, the wild pounding of her heart. She slid her arms around his neck and clung to him, and this time when his mouth moved on hers she responded, straining against him with her lips, her arms, her breasts. He kissed her very hard for a moment, then lifted his head. She was glad he hadn't released her from his embrace; her knees were so weak that she would have fallen.

"That's the sweetest kiss I've ever had," he said.

Eyes still closed, she sighed and leaned up against the wall, letting her hands fall away from his neck. But when she heard him laugh softly she opened her eyes with a start, suddenly afraid he was mocking her. "Tarnation," she said. "I don't know why I just don't kick in your shins for being so uppity!"

He shook his head. "Only if you didn't like my kiss."

Drat! She was blushing again!

He frowned, studying her face. "Vermilion, I think."

"What?"

"Vermilion. With a touch of madder lake. The color of your blush."

"Dang you, Mr. Bradford...!"

"Drew."

She knew she was blushing again, and she didn't even care. "Dang you... Drew! You better watch out, or I just might push you overboard!"

He laughed and reached for the stone jug on the boathouse floor. "Come on, before they come looking for us." He opened the door and laughed again, his eyes twinkling mischievously.

He said, "*You'd* better watch out. I'll take another kiss when I can!"

* * *

Willough Bradford peered out the window of the railroad car as the trees sped past. There was a small crack in the pane, a thin line that jagged across one corner of the window. It annoyed her. She knew that it would be repaired as soon as Daddy sent the car back to Saratoga, but it annoyed her all the same. This was Daddy's private railroad car. His world. It should be perfect.

She turned from the window and smiled across the dining table at her father. "Shall I have Keller bring you another cup of coffee, Daddy?"

Brian Bradford leaned back in his red plush chair, unbuttoned his frock coat, and patted the buttons of his waistcoat. "No. I've had more than enough. That was quite a dinner. Now, if it'll sit comfortably, for a change..."

Willough smiled uneasily. Daddy had been complaining a great deal lately. Perhaps he was eating too much.

"Would you like some mineral water?" she asked. "Keller brought a bottle or two from Saratoga."

He made a face and reached for a cigar from the silver humidor. "Never mind. If Mrs. Walker's cooking is as bad as ever, I won't want much supper when we reach Mac-Curdyville." He bit off the end of his cigar and spit it toward the cuspidor on the floor, eyeing it with indifference when he missed. "Give us a light, lass."

She struck a match and held it to the end of his cigar. He was feeling good. She could always tell. He called her "lass," he let his voice slide into the soft lilt of his native Scotland, he ignored the graying hair that drooped carelessly over his forehead. How handsome he must have looked when his hair was still all black, she thought. Like a wild gypsy coming over the moors. There was an air of danger to him that she had never quite got used to. As much as she loved him, wanted to please him, she'd always been a little bit afraid of him. But he was feeling mellow right now. It was a good time to speak up.

She hesitated, choosing her words with care. "I hope you haven't forgotten your promise to name me the chief clerk at the ironworks. It's all I've thought about for months, since we were at the sawmill. I've been reading the financial notes in *Harper's Weekly* and the *Times*. I can quote you the figures for pig iron for the last six months, and I know what the stock was going for last week. I even wrote to your manager, Mr. Clegg, with dozens of questions. He very kindly answered them as best he could, and assured me that"—she laughed nervously—"whenever you're ready to give me the job, of course, he would be happy to help me through the difficulties of the first few weeks. So you see, I haven't been idle."

"Good. Good. It's not an easy job . . . to run the ironworks." Brian Bradford stood up and impatiently brushed back the wayward lock of hair. He paced the length of the railroad car, dropping cigar ash on the flowered carpet. "God!" he burst out, "I wish your brother Drew . . . it needs a man . . . !"

She felt the old familiar pang. Why hadn't she been born a son? His son Willoughby. Drew was Mother's child. Even his middle name—Carruth—had been given out of pride. Her name had been given out of disappointment.

"I can do it, Daddy," she said softly. "You'll see. I've always been good with figures. You know that. I'll be able to fill the clerk's spot."

He looked doubtful. It made her uneasy.

She smiled with a brightness she didn't feel, and tried to sound off-hand. "If the sign is to read Bradford and Bradford someday, I should get to know the ropes. And soon."

He sat down, grimacing, and rubbed his hand against his stomach. "Someday," he said sourly. "But you'll have to earn it first. If you can."

She felt her control slipping. "I'm your daughter!" she said rising to her feet and glaring at him. "If you can do it, why can't I?"

His dark eyes flashed; he pounded the table with his fist so the dishes rattled. "Don't you raise your voice to me, miss! I'm still your father, no matter how grown-up you get!"

She subsided into her chair, trembling. The last thing she'd wanted to do was make him angry. I'm sorry, I'm sorry, Daddy, she thought.

She was saved by the appearance of Keller with a decanter of port. Brian downed one glass quickly, rubbing again at his stomach, then poured another glass. He sipped slowly at it while the tension drained out of his face. He leaned forward to extinguish his cigar and his front curl drooped again on his forehead. He let it stay. He stretched, took another sip of port, and smiled at Willough. "It's a hard job, lass. I was fourteen when I started. Fourteen. Puking my way across the Atlantic on that foul boat to come to this land. But I was determined to make it. I wasn't about to spend my life like my father in Scotland, grubbing a living out of a rocky soil that didn't give a damn for a man."

Willough gazed at him in adoration. She could almost see him as he must have been. Young and reckless. Bold and daring and handsome. "You started with the bloomery forge, didn't you?"

He nodded. "Hot as hell it was, working day and night to pound that red-hot mass into good cash. But the ore was there, lying on the ground, for the taking." He made a fist, peering intently at the knotted muscles of his hand. "Seventeen years. *Seventeen years!* To bend that land to my will. To show them that MacCurdy was a man to be reckoned with!" He laughed bitterly. "And then I built my house at MacCurdyville and went looking for a wife."

"Oh, Daddy," she said, near tears.

He waggled his finger at her. "No, lass. The Carruths were a classy lot, and don't you forget it. I guess it's what I wanted at the time. I was thirty-one, rich as the devil, and rough as they come. And your mother at eighteen was a beauty. I kept thinking of the old laird back home. Five daughters, he had. And they'd throw mud at me for sport. But they couldn't hold a candle to your mother for class."

"And you didn't mind changing your name for her?"

He laughed. "It didn't change *me*! Which fact your mother sometimes regretted, I think."

Willough looked down at her hands. "I hate her," she whispered.

"No, lass, you mustn't. Pity her instead. With nothing but her tonic and her laudanum to keep her going."

"And Arthur," she said bitterly.

He stared at her for a minute, and then began to laugh. "Arthur? You don't really think . . . a tumble in the hay with her skirts up . . . ? My God, you do!"

"Daddy, please." She put her hands to her burning cheeks.

"There's nothing between them, Willough. There never has been. Not with a woman like your mother." He laughed again. "My God, not with *any* man!"

"But . . ."

He shrugged his shoulders and reached for another cigar. "Oh, he was infatuated with her for years. I knew that. But it was harmless. I knew that too. And she seemed to enjoy his attentions. All his pretty ideas of romance." He shook his head. "I never remembered to bring her flowers. Your mother always set great store by little things like that. But I think Arthur's lost interest in the last few years."

"Then why did you leave? I always thought it was because of Arthur."

"I left because it just seemed better to move out. I couldn't make her happy. And Arthur always kept her amused." He exhaled a puff of blue smoke. "I like Arthur, by the way."

Unexpectedly, she felt herself blushing, remembering how Arthur had looked at her, kissed her on the cheek. She plucked at a piece of lint on her skirt. "I do too," she said softly. How noble of Arthur, she thought. Worshiping her mother from afar. It seemed so courtly and chivalrous—to burn with an unrequited love, and ask for nothing more.

She felt a surge of tenderness for Arthur. For his strength and purity. Perhaps she had misjudged him all these years.

"Arthur's been very helpful this last year," her father said. "Business has been booming. When I needed more woodland for charcoal—that big tract over near New Russia—I showed you on the map—Arthur was able to get a change in legislation up in Albany."

"Through Mr. Tweed?"

Brian laughed. "No, thank God. When Tweed's indictment came down there were a lot of men who were sorry for the deals they'd made! Arthur was a little more discreet on my behalf. He covered his tracks." He stood up and looked out the window. "We should be reaching Crown Point soon. You'd better get set."

"You ... you haven't forgotten about the clerk position ... ?"

Brian buttoned his frock coat. "We'll see. Don't you worry. I'll have something for you to do."

"I'd best get my hat and gloves." Willough stood up and smoothed down the pearl-gray cashmere overskirt of her gown, fluffing out the large pouf in back, which had become creased from the hours of sitting on the train. There was nothing to be done about the pleats of her brown silk underskirt; they were quite crushed beyond repair. Perhaps Mrs. Walker would have someone at the rooming house who could press the skirt for her before she wore it again.

Brian scowled. "Is that all you have to wear?"

Willough looked down at her costume. She thought it a rather handsome dress herself. The snug gray bodice was trimmed with lapels and cuffs of the brown silk, and the fullness of the skirts, with their rather high bustle and pouf, accented the slimness of her waist. "It's the very latest walking suit," she said. "Don't you like it?"

"Too plain. I want the world to know Brian Bradford's women can dress well!"

She thought: I've disappointed him again. "It's the best gown I've brought."

He waved an impatient hand. "Well, fancy it up with something," he muttered. "I ought to shop with you. I don't like what you pick out. Not enough ... frills, frou-frou ... you know."

"I'll see what I can do," she said quietly. She traversed the length of the parlor, nodding to Keller as she passed him working in the galley, pulled open the heavy door, and went into the narrow corridor that led to the bedrooms. The train

rattled around a sharp curve; she steadied herself against a
wall before opening the door to her bedroom.

Quickly she stripped off her basque jacket and threw it
across the olive green velvet of her coverlet, then turned about
and ran a bit of water into the marble basin tucked into a
corner of the room and connected to the water closet by shiny
brass pipes. She splashed at her face and bosom, taking care
to pull her corset cover low enough so it wouldn't get wet.
After she dried herself, she dabbed on a bit of cologne. She
put on her jacket again, eyeing herself critically in the large
mirror on the wall. Too plain, Daddy had said. She thought
for a moment. She had a lavender silk sash that she'd packed
to wear with the only evening gown she'd brought. Rum-
maging through her valise, she brought out the sash and tied
it into a large bow; another quick search produced a cameo
pin with which she attached the bow to the collar of her suit.
Very fetching, she thought. It was a pity she wasn't in Saratoga—she had several lavender silk flowers there with which
she might have trimmed her hat. Well, the gray hat with its
brown silk leaves would have to do. She anchored it firmly
on her black hair and picked up her gloves. At the last moment
she remembered a white batiste handkerchief with a delicate
edging of lavender lace; she fetched it out and tucked it into
the cuff of her jacket so the bright lace peeped out and echoed
the color of her bow. She nodded in satisfaction at her reflection and went out to join her father.

The small public coach they boarded at Crown Point was
a far cry from Daddy's private car. Rickety and old, its green
plush seats worn thin, it reeked of train smoke, stale food,
and perspiration. But the track was narrow on this line, which
serviced the mines and the ironworks in the region, hauling
loads of pig iron and ore as often as miners and foundrymen.
Too narrow for Daddy's car, which had been sent back to
Saratoga to be restocked and cleaned, awaiting its next summons to Crown Point.

Well, it would be only an hour's ride to MacCurdyville.
While her father dozed in the seat beside her, Willough stared
curiously out of the window. It had been years since she'd

been to the ironworks. Her only memory was a vague recollection of the glow of the furnaces at night—the sense of
awe and mystery and romance, knowing that somewhere beneath those flames which mounted to the heavens was the
raw ore that was magically being converted into iron.

It was a beautiful day. As the small train chugged out of
Crown Point, Willough admired the view from the window,
the way the evergreens stood out darkly against the clear blue
of the sky. The trees here—farther north—were taller than
in Saratoga; taller, darker, more mysterious. She felt a sense
of serenity that was surprising. Drew had often spoken of the
awesome beauty of the North Woods, had tried to persuade
her to venture beyond the manicured prettiness of Saratoga;
for the first time she began to understand what he had been
talking about.

It might be nice, she thought, to run among those trees,
to tear off her clothes and her constraints, to lie down in
those tantalizing green meadows she glimpsed so briefly as
the train hurtled along.

Then she frowned. Here and there she began to see bare
patches, large tracts where the forests had been cut, acres of
nothing but jagged stumps. The grassy meadows, unsheltered
from the sun, had already begun to turn brown, though it
was only the beginning of June. After awhile there were no
trees at all, only the ravaged landscape, naked and ugly.

She'd never thought of it before: The lumber had to come
from some place. She'd spent the spring at the sawmill with
Daddy. But that was at the town of Glens Falls. The logs had
simply been there. Hundreds of thousands of them, floating
on the Hudson River. Branded with the markings of a hundred
different mill owners. She'd never stopped to think of the
living forests that supplied those mills. It really was quite
awful, what was happening to the forests.

No. She shook off the unwelcome thoughts. The land had
to be bent to a man's will. That's what Daddy said.

Brian Bradford stirred and sat up, leaning forward to peer
out the window. He pulled his gold watch from his waistcoat

and snapped open the case. "We should get there right on time."

"Will Mr. Murphy, your clerk, meet us at the station?"

Brian snorted. "Not likely! He'll be packing right about now. I told Mr. Clegg to sack him today. I'm fed up with his spendthrift ways. I didn't break my back building up this business for some Paddy to throw my money away with both hands!"

Willough held her breath, scarcely daring to hope. "Today? Did you mean it for me? As a surprise?"

"A surprise?" Brian frowned.

"Was it in your mind to let me take over as clerk . . . with Mr. Clegg's help? Was that why you let Mr. Murphy go today?"

He grimaced in disgust. "You as clerk? Are you daft? You're just a girl!"

"But . . . but you promised . . ."

"Don't tell me what I did," he snapped. "It's *my* business, and don't you forget it! You're my daughter. You'll be my partner some day. But I'll not put you in as clerk until you're ready."

She stared at her gloved hands, fighting back the angry tears. "And who's to be clerk?" she asked.

"One of my founders. Nat Stanton. Been with me four years now. He's a hard worker . . . with a head on his shoulders. He can do a man's job."

A *man's* job. Willough stared sightlessly out the window while the words tore at her insides.

Brian patted her knee. "Come now, lass," he said gruffly. "Don't look so down at the mouth. You can work under Stanton and learn the ropes from him."

She felt betrayed. How could Daddy do this to her? "And I'm to take orders from a founder?" she asked bitterly.

The train screeched to a stop. Brian lumbered to his feet, his face purpling in indignation. "Take orders? No, by God! You're a Bradford! And my daughter. I don't expect him to forget that. And you damn well better not either! You can learn from the man, but I expect you to put him in his place if he gets out of line!"

She stepped off the train, feeling numb. She scarcely noticed the conductor handing down their baggage; or Mr. Murphy on the platform nodding icily to her father as he boarded the train; or the whistle and chug of the engine as it continued its journey. She didn't recognize the old man who met them with the small carriage; at her father's introduction she greeted him mechanically and clambered aboard.

Nothing mattered. *A man's job.* Daddy still wanted a son. She felt herself burning with anger. Whoever this Stanton was, she hated him already. She'd have to work twice as hard to earn the right to wrest the job from him. It would be a fight to the death—with no quarter given—but she'd win. She'd show them all, including that upstart Stanton!

"I thought we'd go to Number Three before we settle in at the rooming house," said Brian. "I want you to meet Nat. He was supposed to blow in Number Three today . . . it's been closed for repairs. It'll be his last job as founder—showing the new man how to start up a cold furnace."

"Whatever you say, Daddy."

"We'll have him for supper tonight. He stays at Mrs. Walker's anyway, but now he'll be entitled to eat with us and Mr. Clegg."

The carriage was now ascending a steep hill. Far below, on the left, were the ore banks, deep gouged-out pits, looking as though a giant hand had torn at the earth and left it raw and bleeding. But the blood that poured out was long lines of men and carts transporting the crushed rock to the furnaces. What a mournful image, thought Willough. I wonder why I thought of it.

She hadn't remembered the pits, nor the black soot that seemed to cover everything the nearer they came to the furnaces. Sooty children played in sooty roads around ramshackle sooty houses, and the few trees that were still standing were gray-green.

The carriage drew up at last to a large building crowned with a smokestack belching flame, bright red and smoky. The

deep roar of the flame was a sonorous contrast to another
sound that seemed to come from within the building, a steady
creaking and whooshing, like a giant bellows. On the side
of the building was painted a yellow number three.

Two men were standing on the gravel path, staring up at
the chimney, as Brian and Willough alit from the carriage.

"I don't like the look of that flame, Nat," said Brian.

One of the men turned. "Nor do I, Mr. Bradford. There's
too much flux." He turned back to the other man. "Put in
another charge of ore, Bill, and let's see what she does." As
Bill nodded and vanished into the building, the other man
held out his hand to Brian. "Nice to see you again, sir."

"Nat." Brian shook the proffered hand, then jerked his chin
in the direction of Willough. "Nat Stanton. My daughter
Willough."

Nat stepped closer to Willough and held out his hand. "Miss
Bradford."

Willough sucked in her breath, feeling as though she'd
been hit in the pit of her stomach. She'd been prepared to
hate the man—simply for what he represented. She wasn't
prepared for this feeling of panic that swept over her at sight
of him. He wasn't excessively tall . . . perhaps a few inches
taller than she. And his looks were not remarkable: sandy
blond hair, tightly curled, shaggy eyebrows that veiled light
brown eyes, a wide nose, a straight mouth. His jaw was
square, and looked stubborn, but otherwise he had the face
of a pleasant enough man. About thirty, she guessed.

But his body . . . oh God, his body . . . she felt her mouth
go dry. His body was the most beautiful—and frightening—
thing she had ever seen. And the way he was dressed left
nothing to the imagination. His work pants were tight; his
hard-muscled thighs and calves bulged beneath the sturdy
fabric. And above the waist he was almost naked, with only
a skimpy leather vest that barely covered his powerful shoulders and fell open in the front, revealing a thick patch of
yellow curls. His sinewy arms were darkly tanned beneath a
light dusting of golden hairs. She was mesmerized, seeing a
sudden vision of herself being crushed lifeless by those over-

powering arms. All the terrible things her mother had ever told her came crowding back into her brain—rapacious men, savage animals filled with lust. She found herself trembling violently.

He was still holding out his hand to her. She couldn't bring herself to shake his hand. The thought of his touch, the raw sexuality of the man, was too frightening to endure. She took a step backward, nodding her head. "Mr. Stanton."

Without a word he withdrew his hand. "Did you want to see anything here, Mr. Bradford?"

Brian shook his head. "No. Let me talk to Clegg for a few minutes, if he's here. Then when I come back, you and I can take Willough over to Number Four. I want her to see a furnace in full operation this afternoon. And as long as you're still firing up here..." He looked up at the flame of the chimney. "Tell Bill to make that two charges of ore before we go." Brian turned about and strode off into the furnace building.

Willough stood where her father had left her, trying desperately to keep her composure. She didn't dare look at Nat Stanton, though she could tell, just by the way her skin tingled, that he was gazing intently at her.

"My hand is clean, Miss Bradford." His voice was low and edged with mockery.

In spite of herself she found her eyes drawn to his face, then his broad chest, damp and glistening from his labors.

Frowning, he followed her glance, looking down at his chest and arms. "And it's honest sweat," he growled.

Was I staring at his body? she thought in horror. "Really, Mr. Stanton..." she said primly.

"Does even the word upset you? Don't fine ladies 'sweat'?"

She felt like a caged animal. "I find you very rude, Mr. Stanton."

He smiled thinly. "And I find you very attractive, Miss Bradford. Though not at all what I expected."

"What do you mean?" Could this be her own voice? So prissy? So cold and unnatural? Oh God! she thought, anguished. *Why doesn't he cover himself?* "What do you mean,

I'm not what you expected?" she asked again, using the harshness of her voice as a shield.

"I mean," he said, "that I hardly expected the daughter of Brian Bradford to be a snob."

The injustice of his words tore an outraged "Oh!" from her throat. She glared at him in fury, clenching her hands at her sides.

He smiled crookedly, bringing an unexpected dimple to his bronzed cheek. "You don't really intend to slap my face, Miss Bradford," he said. "You wouldn't want to soil your glove."

She wanted to cry, she wanted to scream, she wanted to flee the frightening masculinity of him. But well-bred young ladies did none of those things. She thought: He thinks I'm a snob. If he's too coarse to see the difference between snobbery and proper behavior, he must have had a frightful upbringing. And Daddy had said she was not to allow him to get out of line.

She pulled the lace-trimmed hanky from her cuff and dabbed at her upper lip. "If we're to work together, Mr. Stanton," she said coldly, "I can only hope that this afternoon was merely a lapse on your part. I trust you shan't forget your place again."

He scowled in anger; for a terrible moment she almost thought he'd strike her. The golden eyes had become hard amber, glittering and cold. "A snob, Miss Bradford," he said quietly. "A damnable snob." Turning on his heel, he stalked away.

Willough watched his retreating back, feeling the blood pounding at her temples. She dabbed again at her face; then, fingers shaking, she replaced the handkerchief in her cuff.

Chapter Three

M arcy closed her eyes and leaned back in the square stern of the boat, feeling the lovely warmth of the sun on her face.

"I'm sorry you tied up your hair, Marcy. It's too pretty to tie up."

She opened her eyes, sat up, and glared at Drew Bradford, who sprawled in the middle of the boat, facing her. The summer's jaunt had barely begun. Did the lop-eared rascal intend to torment her every mile of the journey? Even the way he was sitting in the boat had been planned to get her goat. She was sure of it. Uncle Jack was on the oars in the pointed bow of the boat, facing to the back. When the boat was rowed it needed weight toward the front of the craft, which was why Drew had had to sit in the middle. Only when the boat was handled like a canoe, being paddled at both ends, was it supposed to be evenly balanced; at those times, Uncle Jack would steer from the stern, and Marcy would take the middle.

But, dang him! thought Marcy, frowning at Drew. Why did he have to face in her direction?

He smiled wickedly. "Don't make faces. Old Jack will wonder what's the matter." He spoke in a low voice. Old Jack, plying his oars behind Drew's back, heard nothing.

"You're supposed to sit facing the other way, Mr. Bradford," she hissed. "Why don't you?"

"Drew. Because I prefer to look at you. Your hair. Why did you tie it up?"

"It'd only get tangled!"

He shrugged good-naturedly. "I suppose it's sensible. And you *do* have nice ears."

"My ears are my business, Mr. Bradford." In spite of herself, she found herself nervously touching her lobes.

"Drew," he corrected again.

She ignored that. "I think you *enjoy* making me blush!"

He grinned. "I think I do. It's nice to know, when I'm giving a compliment, that it's being appreciated."

She felt a queer feeling in the pit of her stomach. "A . . . a compliment?"

"Yes. I thought you understood that. It seems I must be more explicit. Well . . ." He put his hands behind his neck and leaned back comfortably, allowing his pale blue eyes to assess her thoroughly where she sat. "To begin . . . your hair is glorious, especially with the sun on it. It's quite red in the sun. A wonderful color. Burnt sienna with highlights of crimson, perhaps. Your skin is healthy looking . . . I find pale city girls tiresome after awhile. I haven't yet been able to figure out what color your eyes are; sometimes I think they're blue, sometimes green. Your ears, as I mentioned before, are quite nice. No. More than that. They're like delicate shells . . . so beautifully curved . . . I haven't decided yet whether I'd prefer to sketch them, or kiss them . . ."

"Please, Mr. Bradford," she whispered. She'd never felt so flustered in her whole life.

"Drew. Shall I go on to your mouth?"

"No!" At the sharpness of her tone, Uncle Jack stopped rowing and looked up at her from the bow. She smiled in reassurance. "It's all right, Uncle Jack. I was only telling Mr. Bradford that it'll be just another moment until we clear the

creek and break out into Clear Pond. He . . . he can't believe it's taken such a short time."

Old Jack grunted and bent again to his oars. A few more strokes and their boat, leading the other four loaded with sportsmen and guides, reached a sharp bend in the creek. Another turn, and they found themselves on the edge of Clear Pond, a glassy body of water some two miles around. In its center was a small, tree-covered island.

Mrs. Marshall clapped her hands in wonder, and stood up in her boat, nearly capsizing it. "Oh! Isn't it magnificent! Mother Nature in all her glory!"

"Sit down, ma'am," muttered Alonzo, fighting with his oars to keep the boat upright.

Drew put his hand over his mouth to keep from laughing, and turned about to survey Clear Pond. He studied it for a long time, then turned back to Marcy. "It *is* beautiful, though," he said seriously. "I've never been camping this far north. I've just been a little above Saratoga. This is far more breathtaking and wild. What's that peak?"

"Owl's Head. You can see it from Long Lake, but not so well."

"I'd like to sketch it. Where do we set up our base camp?"

Marcy pointed to the distant shore just opposite. "There. Can you see the lean-to? It's a nice sheltered spot, with plenty of room to leave our extra supplies. And only a three-mile carry to the next lake."

"Carry?"

"Honestly, Mr. Bradford. Don't you know anything about this region?"

He grinned. "Don't you dare call me greenhorn again. But, no. I guess I don't know much."

"This whole Adirondack Wilderness . . . the waters only flow in two directions. South to the Hudson River . . . most of the streams in the High Peaks run that way. Just last fall they found out where the Hudson begins. Right on the top of Mount Marcy."

"That's where you got your name? From Mount Marcy?"

"Uh-huh. Anyway, they said it's the source, a little pond

on top of Marcy. And they called it Lake Tear-of-the-Clouds."
She shook her head in wonder. "Isn't that pretty?" she whispered. "As if the clouds had wept." She gulped, fighting back
the sudden urge to cry. Beautiful things always did that to
her. Feeling foolish, she stole a sidelong look at Drew.

His eyes were warm and serious. "You're enchanting, Marcy
Tompkins," he said softly.

"Tarnation! Don't start that again! Anyway, the rest of the
waters flow north to Canada. And the thing is, you can put
a boat into the water at Blue Mountain Lake and travel clear
up to the Saint Lawrence River and the open sea."

"I'll be damned! And never touch land?"

"Well, sometimes you have to take your boat overland a
few miles to the next lake."

"Which is why it's called a carry?"

"Yes. Most of the carries are three, four miles or so. That's
all."

He laughed ruefully. "That's *all*? With a boat on your
back?"

She patted the painted siding of their craft, a sleek boat
some fourteen feet in length. "Didn't you notice the boats?"

"Well, they looked a bit queer to me. Like wide, square-
sterned canoes."

"They're made especially for the Wilderness. My . . . my
father helped design them. He'd build a boat, and then every
time a guide would come back from using one, they'd talk
over the changes. First off, they have to be big enough to
carry supplies, like a regular rowboat. But they have to be
flatter. Because some of the lakes are shallow."

"Why can't they use a regular flatboat?"

"Too heavy. You're forgetting the carries. And a *canoe*
isn't big enough. Not sturdy enough. These boats are built
as light as canoes. Pine planking as thin as pasteboard."

"But shallow, like flatboats. About ten inches deep, I'd
guess."

"And with a pointed bow," she said. "And rowed like
rowboats, most of the time." She pointed to two grooves on
either side of the boat, just in front of Drew. "You see those

cleats? There's a shoulder yoke stashed up front under Uncle Jack's boots. For a carry, he'll put the yoke in there, up-end the whole boat, and lift it on his shoulders."

"Good God! I'm glad I don't have to do it!"

She laughed. "It weighs only about seventy pounds. You and I will have to carry the *rest* of the supplies, including the oars, unless Uncle Jack makes two trips!" She laughed again as he groaned. "Now aren't you sorry you didn't stay in the city?"

"Not a bit of it." He shook his head. "Damned if you're not beautiful when you laugh."

She felt her face flaming again. "Oh, *please* turn around, Mr. Bradford!" she begged.

He smiled wickedly. "Only if you promise to call me Drew all summer long." He held up an admonishing finger. "And if you forget—even once!—I'll make you blush right in front of Mrs. Marshall, and then you'll be sorry!"

She giggled. He *was* a charmer.

"Well?" he said, frowning. "Is it a deal?"

"Yes."

He cocked one black eyebrow at her.

"Yes . . . Drew," she said, blushing once more.

He grinned again and turned about to face Uncle Jack.

In another quarter of an hour the boats pulled up to a wide expanse of sandy beach on the shore of Clear Pond. Set back from the beach, and nestled up against a line of deep green spruce trees, was a lean-to. About the size of a small cabin, its three sides were made up of stacked logs; its fourth, open side faced out toward the pond.

As soon as the party had clambered ashore, Mrs. Marshall began to examine their surroundings, exclaiming in delight at the rustic charm, the joy of dining in the open air, of sleeping with the stars as a coverlet.

She frowned suddenly, nervously adjusting her pince-nez. "Where . . . where *do* we sleep, Old Jack?"

Marcy's uncle pointed to the floor of the lean-to. "Right there, ma'am. You'll find it cozy enough with some fir boughs as a mattress."

She looked doubtful. "And the women? Marcy and I?"

"That's the only lean-to there is, ma'am."

"I'm not sure I approve of that! I'm not concerned for myself, of course. I'm a respectable married woman. But Marcy..."

"I can look after myself, ma'am..." began Marcy, only to be cut short by Mrs. Marshall's snort.

"And the men?" she asked with suspicion.

Drew Bradford stepped forward. "I can assure you, Mrs. Marshall," he said solemnly, "that I, for one, have no intention of storming Marcy's person in the dead of night."

She peered at him through her glasses, her mouth pinched tight in disapproval. "I don't like your levity, young man. I warn you that I shall be eternally vigilant in the matter of Marcy's virtue. Eternally vigilant, gentlemen!" she added, glaring at the assembled party.

In the end, with much fuss on Mrs. Marshall's part, it was decided that Marcy should sleep at the farthest corner of the lean-to, shielded from the rest of the men by Mrs. Marshall and then Dr. Marshall.

There were still some hours left of daylight. The supplies were unloaded from the boats and stowed in a large covered storage box. Since the company would be returning regularly to Clear Pond during the summer, it wasn't necessary to travel with all they had brought.

Stafford, Collins, and Heyson shouldered their rods and reels and set out upon the lake once again with boats and guides, to see if they might catch some fish for supper. Mrs. Marshall, delivering shrill orders to Dr. Marshall and a patient Alonzo, proceeded to reorganize the camp to her liking. Drew Bradford rummaged in his satchel and pulled out a pencil and a small sketchpad. Seating himself on a tree stump, he opened the pad and gazed out across the lake.

Old Jack stuffed a handful of cartridges into his pocket and picked up his rifle. "If we could bag us a deer before sundown, we'd have fresh venison for the carry. Come on, Marcy. Let's see how good your aim is today." He turned to Drew. "You're staying here, Mr. Bradford?"

Drew looked up, grimacing at the sight of Mrs. Marshall. "All she needs is a broomstick," he said quietly. "I'm not sure I want to be abandoned." He closed the pad and stood up. "I'll come with you." He waited until Old Jack had started down the narrow trail, then fell in beside Marcy, putting his hand lightly on her shoulder. "Besides," he whispered, "you're much better company than Mrs. Marshall."

She looked up at him and brandished her rifle. "I just might shoot *you!*" she hissed, but she let his hand remain.

Moving quietly along the path, they came at last to a small rise that looked out over a broad meadow made up of marshy patches and tall grass. The grass seemed to be bent and beaten down in spots.

Old Jack pointed. "The deer bed down there," he whispered to Drew. He indicated the rise. "This is as good a place as any to wait. You stay here with Marcy. I'll go down aways." Skirting the meadow, he moved off, finally settling down some twenty feet to their right.

Marcy sat on a fallen log, loaded both barrels of her rifle, and placed the weapon across her knees. Against her better judgment, she left room on the log so Drew could sit beside her. She knew he was looking at her, and leaning in close, but she kept her eyes determinedly on the far side of the meadow, where a break in the line of grasses marked the deer run.

"They're even prettier up close," whispered Drew. "Your ears."

"*Sh-h-h!*" Marcy strained her eyes, peering at the line of trees beyond the meadow. Was that a movement, there beside the silver birches?

She gasped. She felt a tickle in her ear, a slight current of air that caressed the inner edges and sent a shiver down her spine. He was blowing in her ear! Hanging on to her control, she turned carefully and scowled at him. Drew Bradford was smiling like a saint in a Sunday school book.

She thought: Deer or no deer, I'll give him a piece of my mind! And then she saw something out of the corner of her eye. A small doe, just in among the trees. She held her breath, waiting for it to emerge into the meadow. Uncle Jack was already slowly raising his rifle to his shoulder in anticipation of a clear shot. The doe stopped, sniffed the air, hesitated.

And then Drew Bradford blew in her ear again.

"Dang you!" she whooped, leaping to her feet. The doe vanished.

"Tarnation, Marcy!" Uncle Jack shouted. "If you're too fidgety to hunt today, go on back!"

"That's a good idea, Old Jack," said Drew. "Even better, maybe Marcy can show me a place near the edge of the pond where I can get a good view of Owl's Head."

"Right enough. Take him on down to Miller's Cove, Marcy. I'll bag us a deer."

Angrily, Marcy rose from her seat and stormed back down the path, taking a fork that was narrower than the first one. She parted the overgrown branches with impatient hands, deliberately allowing them to snap back at Drew. After about five minutes, during which the path grew more dense with growth, Drew reached out and grabbed her by the shoulder.

"Whoa!" he said, turning her around. "Are you trying to kill me?"

"It wouldn't be a bad idea! Why'd you say you'd come hunting if you didn't want to?"

"What was my alternative?" he said mournfully. "Mrs. Marshall?"

He looked like such a woebegone little boy that Marcy had to laugh in spite of herself. "Drew Bradford, you're a devil!"

He grinned and rubbed at his cheek, where a branch had left a small scratch. "And you're an imp! Now lead me to Miller's Cove, while I try to dream up a story to explain *this* to Mrs. Marshall."

While he knelt on the small beach of the cove and drew the outlines of Owl's Head Mountain, Marcy wandered down to the water's edge. From its still surface she plucked a water lily, soft golden velvet with a ruby center, and held it to her nose, inhaling deeply of its rich scent. Drew was absorbed in his drawing; it gave her a chance to examine him at her leisure. He was beautiful, there was no denying that, with that reckless black curl falling over his forehead. And those liquid blue eyes. Beautiful and charming.

And impossible.

She felt herself torn with longing, remembering the sweetness of his kiss. Maybe . . .

No! The mountains had killed her parents. How could she stay? But the city had broken Bill Peterson and his wife. How could she live there with a poor artist? Just for a moment she yearned to be a child again, when life had been so simple.

He had finished his drawing and was frowning down at the page. She walked to him and knelt beside him on the sand, peering over his shoulder at the sketch. "It's beautiful," she breathed.

"It's dreadful," he growled. He sighed heavily and snapped shut the pad. "Well, maybe when I work it up in color . . ." He turned to her, then burst into laughter. "You have pollen on your nose! It's all orange." He held her chin in one hand while he wiped the tip of her nose with his handkerchief, but when he was finished he still held her chin. Leaning down, he kissed her softly on the mouth.

No! she thought, feeling her heart melt. I can't let him. I can't! She pushed violently against him. "Now you just quit that!" she cried. "I can't marry you!"

He rocked back on his heels as though she'd struck him. *"What?* Who's talked of marriage?"

"Well . . . no one . . . but . . . but . . ." She felt like a fool, stammering idiotically. "But a girl has to think about those things!" she finished with defiance.

The corners of his mouth had begun to twitch. "And you're on the lookout?"

She tried to sound as grown-up as she could. "As a matter of fact, I am."

His eyes narrowed thoughtfully. "Wait a minute. This little excursion. All that humbug Old Jack was spouting—poor helpless orphan, can't leave her behind, and all that rot. Were you figuring on hunting deer this summer? Or husbands? From among our jolly band?"

She turned red with embarrassment. She hadn't meant for anyone to know.

He shook his head. "I don't suppose it's because you *have* to get married. No. I thought not," he said dryly, as her eyes widened in horror. "Not when you kiss the way you do."

She felt young, stupid. He was so worldly and experienced. It made her angry to have him treat her like a child. "I just decided one day it was time to get married," she said grandly.

He smirked. "Just like that."

"Just like that!"

"Yes. I can see you—with your stubborn little chin stuck out—making up your mind to it."

"Don't laugh at me!" She swung her fist at him, but he grabbed it and wrestled her to the sand, holding her immobile beneath him. He kissed her hard, then released her.

"But you can't marry me," he said.

She sat up and inhaled shakily. "N-no."

"Why not?"

"Because I have to marry a rich man."

"Well I'll be damned!" Laughing, he rose to his feet. He plunged his hands into his pockets and turned them inside-out. A solitary silver dollar fell to the sand. "Then I'm not the one, that's for sure."

That settled it. Even if she'd wanted to marry him, it was clear *he* didn't want the expense of a wife. "That's for *blamed* sure!" she said sulkily.

He dropped to his knees beside her, pocketing the coin. "You're joking, of course."

"Don't laugh at me!"

He frowned. "You're *not* joking."

"Of course not!"

"You innocent child! And you think that's how it's done? You just 'decide' on it?"

"Isn't it? Don't the ladies in the city marry well?"

"Yes. Usually."

"And don't they set out to catch a rich man?"

He laughed ruefully. "With a little more subtlety, perhaps. But why on earth are *you* doing it?"

"I *told* you," she said, as patiently as she could. "Because I want to live in the city and be very rich."

"In God's name, why?"

How can I tell him? she thought. What can I say? That I'm afraid? It hardly made sense to her—how could she explain it to him? And he already thought her a silly child. How could she tell him of her childish fears? "Because I want nice things," she said. It seemed the easiest lie.

"A house with lace curtains, I suppose."

"And a carriage with four horses!" she said defiantly.

He was grinning again. "A dozen silk dresses in your wardrobe."

"Two dozen! To change into, five times a day, if I want! And show the likes of you! Dang you, stop laughing at me!"

"We haven't even talked of jewels. I suppose you fancy diamonds. . . . "

She'd never even seen a diamond, and cared even less. "A whole handful! But it's clear I'd never get 'em from you," she added spitefully. He didn't even flinch. The thick-skinned timber wolf!

"No," he said, trying to look serious. "A starving artist isn't for you. Well then, which one of our fine gentlemen is worth snagging for matrimonial purposes?"

She eyed him suspiciously. "What are you saying now?"

He tapped at his teeth with his pencil. "I don't see why we can't do this in a scientific manner."

"What do you mean 'we'? This is my business!"

"But I'm happy to be of service. Besides, I know more about the gentlemen than you do."

"Like what?"

"Like money, for instance. Except for Ed Collins, I don't know the others very well. But I know how rich they are."

"Really?" She still wasn't sure if he was making fun of her. "I ought to start with the richest, I suppose."

"That'd be George Heyson. He's a banker from Philadelphia."

She made a face. "The one who's collecting rocks? The stuck-up one?"

"I'm afraid so."

"Ugh! I don't like him much."

He was grinning again. "If you're going to marry money, you can't be fussy."

"Who's the next one?"

"Mr. William Stafford. Boot manufacturer."

"Is he as rich as Mr. Heyson?"

"Nearly."

"Um. He's a good prospect. And he's interested. I can tell by the way he looks at me."

He looked surprised. "If you've noticed that, maybe you're not quite as green as I thought."

She ignored the jibe. "Then you think I ought to try for him?"

"Just watch out," he warned, suddenly serious. "I'm not sure about him."

"Bosh! I can handle him!"

He smiled and stood up. "Come on. Let's get back to camp. I want to see if Mr. William Stafford can resist those beautiful eyes." He held out his hands and pulled her to her feet. Before she realized what was happening, he was kissing her again.

"Tarnation!" she said, when she was finally able to catch her breath. "I thought you were going to help me!"

He looked innocent. "I am! That doesn't mean I can't kiss you once in awhile, does it?" He grinned. "Consider it my fee for being a matchmaker." She glared at him, feeling bested once again. "And stop looking so fierce," he said. "Most men like their women soft."

"I *will* push you overboard," she said through clenched teeth. Stooping, she picked up her rifle and slung it over one shoulder, then stalked off toward the trail.

Behind her he chuckled. "And try to look helpless, if you can manage to fake it."

Willough loosened the lacings on her corset, and stretched out on the wide bed, staring at the carved wooden headboard.

Ornately festooned with roses and swags, it had been Daddy's idea of the height of gentility when he'd built this house for a wife. A wife who'd found it beneath her. Now Mrs. Walker rented it from him and took in boarders.

She sighed and rubbed the back of her neck. It had been a tiring afternoon, touring the furnace with Daddy and Nat Stanton. She'd found herself vacillating between dislike of the man and the need to be friendly, to prove to him that she wasn't a snob. And all the while to be so close to his person...

But it had been fascinating, to see what she had only read about. The great blast furnace—one of four that Daddy owned—like a giant chimney, really, encased in a three-storied shed. At the top was the charging room, where the charcoal and ore and limestone were carted in, weighed, then dumped into the tunnel head, a round hole in the floor that adjoined the top of the furnace. The men who worked there were protected from the heat by broad leather aprons, but Willough had noticed that several of the men had singed their eyebrows in a sudden spurt of flame as they charged the stack. A dangerous job. She hoped Daddy paid them well.

The next level down was where the blast was created to fan the furnace. A waterwheel, twenty-five feet across, filled the space and was reached by several rickety staircases and walkways. Originally its power had pumped a giant bellows; the bellows had now been replaced by a blowing engine, which consisted of two wooden tubs some six feet high and six feet in diameter. Flat disks within the tubs served as giant pistons, moving rhythmically up and down with each turn of the waterwheel, and maintaining a steady blast of cold air that was fed to the furnace near its base, just above the molten ore.

The waterwheel itself was no longer turned by water; a steam engine, its boiler heated by the gases near the top of the stack, was connected to the large waterwheel by a small flywheel and several gears. Nat had pointed out to Willough the deep pit under the slowly turning waterwheel, where a creek had once flowed. The water had been diverted, he explained, the flow closed off by a sluice gate outside the furnace house. Now, when they were "blowing in" a furnace, they waited until it was in blast, in order to create the steam which ran the wheel.

At the lowest level of the furnace was the cast house. This was where the molten ore was tapped, and run off into channels dug in the sand floor. While the guttermen had smoothed the molds—dozens of small depressions on either side of the narrow channel—Nat had poked at the red-hot ore with a long rod. As founder, it was his job to assess the readiness of the ore for tapping. He had barked an order to one of the men, who had skimmed off the slag from the top of the molten iron; then Nat had probed the ore again and declared it ready to be run off. Someone had rung the cast house bell, which hung just outside the door; it had seemed to be a signal that everyone was awaiting. Half a dozen molders and their assistants had come running. Afterward, Daddy had explained to her that the casting was usually done twice a day, once at six in the morning, and again at six at night. Willough had wondered what kind of a life it could be for a man, who had to be on call like that.

Yes, it had been a fascinating day, with much to see. Willough frowned and sat up. Then why did she keep remembering the sight of Nat's knotted muscles as he hoisted the iron rod?

You're a fool, Willough Bradford, she thought. The best thing to do was to freshen up for supper and put Nat Stanton out of her mind for as long as she could. He'd be coming to supper, of course. But Daddy and Mr. Clegg had gone down to the depot to wait for another furnace owner. There'd be three other men at supper besides Nat Stanton. She could ignore him. In the meantime, Mrs. Walker had said there was lemonade in the parlor; it suddenly sounded quite inviting. She washed up at the washstand, pouring out a bit of cool water from the pitcher, then slipped into her gown. It was simply cut, of prune-colored faille, with a prim white muslin ruff at the high neck, and the smallest of bustles. She had always liked its severity, but now, remembering Daddy, she looped a gold chain and locket around her neck to dress it up a bit. Smoothing her coiled chignon, she went down to the parlor.

She had just poured herself a glass of lemonade when she heard a step behind her.

"Miss Bradford."

She turned. Nat Stanton was standing there, dressed for supper in a neat frock coat and starched collar. With his arms and shoulders covered, he seemed less forbidding. She began to feel a little foolish for her earlier reaction. She smiled timidly. "Mr. Stanton." What could she say now? "Would you . . . care for some lemonade?"

"Please." He seemed as uneasy as she. He sipped at the drink for a moment, his amber eyes guarded and distant. "I hope you'll forgive me, Miss Bradford," he said at last. "I *was* rude this afternoon. It couldn't have been easy for you, in unfamiliar surroundings . . ."

"No. No. I'm sure I must have appeared . . . a dreadful snob. I didn't intend it."

He smiled. He was almost boyish suddenly, with an unexpected dimple in his cheek. "Did you enjoy the tour of the furnace?"

"Very much. But I'm surprised we're still using cold-blast. All my reading indicates that a hot-blast furnace makes more efficient use of fuel."

He shrugged. "Some men—and your father is one of them—seem to think that the supply of charcoal in the Adirondacks is limitless. Less costly than putting in hot-blast machinery."

She didn't like his tone of voice, the implied insult to Daddy. "I trust his judgment," she snapped. "He's been at it longer than you have!"

His eyes glowed in sudden anger. "Some of us had to stop and fight a war," he growled. "It tended to destroy the continuity of our lives."

She felt a pang of remorse. Her family had been fortunate. Daddy had been too old, and Drew too young to serve. "I'm sorry," she said softly. She sipped at her lemonande. "Did you work in the iron industry before the war?"

"No. My father had settled down near Troy. I'd planned to be a teacher." He laughed in bitterness. "The war ended that."

"Couldn't you go back?"

He eyed the glass of lemonade with distaste. Putting it down, he crossed to a sideboard and poured himself a glass of whiskey. "It suddenly seemed more rewarding to beat iron than to cane schoolboys," he said savagely. "I worked in a forge, pounding red-hot iron all day. Very satisfying." He lifted the glass of whiskey and tossed it down in one gulp.

Willough shivered. Even fully clothed he had an aura of naked power that was frightening. "I'm surprised you'd be happy with the clerk's job," she said at last.

He poured himself another whiskey. "I didn't really want it. It doesn't require an intimate knowledge of the iron workings. Just a head for numbers and organizing, and an ability to learn the market. I've known many a son or nephew who was appointed and didn't know a damn thing about it. But he learned quick enough how to keep the company books, and handle the payroll and the credits at the company store. And buy and sell at the best prices." He shook his head in disgust. "I don't even know what pig iron is selling for."

"Ninety dollars a ton this week," she said sharply. She ignored his surprised expression and turned away, feeling the anger building in her. He didn't even want the job! "Why did you take it, then? The clerk's position?"

"I'll be frank with you, Miss Bradford. I want to be manager when Clegg retires. It didn't make sense to refuse your father's offer. But as far as I'm concerned he could have given the clerk job to anyone."

She whirled to face him. "He promised it to me!"

He studied her face for a moment, then finished the last of his drink. "Perhaps he should have given it to you," he said quietly. "If you'd like, I'll speak to him on your behalf. I don't see why . . ."

"No!" She drew herself up, fighting to regain her composure. "No, Mr. Stanton," she continued, her voice controlled and icy, "I'll earn it. I want no favors from you for being a woman. If you want to feel manly, find a helpless shopgirl to patronize!"

His face was as hard as steel. "You'll *get* no favors from me, Miss Bradford. Now...I see your father and Clegg coming up the walk with Mr. Doyle. Perhaps we can both keep our tempers during supper."

Supper was a disaster. Sam Doyle, like Willough's father, had started with nothing and built an iron empire. But there had been no Isobel Carruth in *his* life, Willough thought. She tried not to show her displeasure as he dribbled soup on his beard, scratched his belly, belched loudly. She dabbed daintily at her lips with her napkin, managing to smile even when he spilled a glass of water across the table. Finally he put down his fork, pushed away his plate with a careless sweep of his hand, and planted his elbows firmly on the table.

"All right, Brian," he said. "Let's talk business."

Brian Bradford leaned back in his chair, rubbing his stomach in distress. "Damn Mrs. Walker's cooking," he muttered. "There's nothing to talk about, Sam. As soon as the lease comes through for the new tract, I'll have more lumber than I know what to do with, even with the sawmill. I figure I can send a crew in this winter to clear. You need charcoal for your furnaces. All you have to decide is whether you want the raw lumber or the finished charcoal. I'm prepared to supply either. There are enough colliers around to do the job for me."

"But your charcoal price, Brian..."

"Then buy the raw wood."

Sam Doyle scratched his beard. "That's a long haul from New Russia to my forge at Hague. And then I'd have to whistle up the men and the space to make my own charcoal. Easier to cart your charcoal from MacCurdyville..."

"Well, think about it, Sam. You know my prices. Let me know in a week or so."

Mrs. Walker appeared with the coffee. Willough poured, and handed around the cups, but it seemed a bit foolish to

be concerned with the niceties in a place like this, and surrounded by crude men like Sam Doyle. And Nat Stanton,
too, she thought, watching in distaste as he poured half the
sugar bowl into his cup.

Nat stirred his coffee slowly, a frown creasing his forehead,
then leaned forward to Brian. "The tract in New Russia, sir.
Where is it exactly?"

"Just north of Goodman's farm."

The frown deepened. "But that's not supposed to be cut.
It's state land!"

Brian smiled in satisfaction. "Not anymore."

A taut muscle worked in Nat's jaw. "And the men who
make a living on that land? Hunting and fishing?"

"Let 'em come work for me. I'll be hiring lumbermen all
this fall. Twenty-five dollars a month and room and board."

Sam Doyle snorted. "Ordway's paying two, three dollars
a day to lumbermen over at Eagle Lake."

"Ordway's a fool. He doesn't know how to get value from
a dollar."

Doyle chuckled in delight. "I'll say this about you, Brian.
You're a Scotsman through and through. You know how to
hold on to a greenback until it squeals! Like a good woman."

Brian roared with laughter. "Like a *bad* woman!"

Willough felt an uncomfortable flush warm her face; she
was embarrassed that Daddy would talk that way in her presence. She looked up. Nat Stanton was watching her. Somehow, that made it worse.

He turned to a still laughing Brian. "Miss Bradford was
telling me how much she enjoyed the tour of the furnace
today," he said quietly.

"That so?" Brian looked at his daughter. "Glad to hear it,
lass. Of course, I'm sure there was a lot you didn't understand. It's to be expected in a *woman.* . . ."

"It was quite clear," she said crisply. "I understood the
workings perfectly."

"All of it?"

What's the good of getting upset over a few careless words?
she thought. Daddy didn't mean it. She forced herself to

smile. "Well, truthfully," she said, "there's one thing I don't understand."

"What's that, lass?"

"Why do you call it 'pig' iron?"

"I'll tell you, Miss Bradford," said Doyle, grinning. "It goes back years. Did you see the shape of the molds in the cast house floor? The long feeder channel with the little molds on both sides? The men say it looks like a big sow with all her little piggies sucking at her tits." He threw back his head and roared with laughter as Brian smiled broadly.

Oh, God! Willough could feel herself beginning to tremble inside. She folded her napkin neatly and placed it on the table before her. "I think I'll take the air on the veranda. I'll leave you gentlemen to your port and cigars."

"*Port*?" exclaimed Brian. "Port be damned! You're not in that fancy city house now, Willough! Clegg, fetch that decanter of whiskey from the parlor. We've got some serious drinking to do!"

"If you'll excuse me," whispered Willough, and fled into the night.

The air was cool on the veranda, fanning the hot shame that still burned her cheeks. How was she ever going to manage to get along here? How could she ever get used to the way the men talked? She took a shaky breath and gazed out into the night, letting its tranquillity soothe her.

The rooming house was on a hill. From here she could see the flames of the furnaces, lighting up the sky, glowing like four shining beacons in the dark. She felt again that sense of wonder; despite her tour of the workings, it still seemed awesome and mysterious and magical.

The veranda door slammed. She turned. Nat was standing there. "I just couldn't listen to them anymore," he said. His voice sounded hard and angry. He crossed to the porch railing and looked out over the landscape. "You're admiring the view?" He laughed shortly. "It's the only time it's beautiful. At night."

"Oh, but it has a grandeur, a majesty..."

"How do you live?" he snarled. "With your eyes closed?

It's ugly. Ugly! We've torn this land apart. We've ripped up the earth, and stripped it of its trees . . . Have you ever seen it when it rains? The place drips ink. Black blood. It pours off the eaves and down the gutters. And when the furnace is burning badly, it belches more soot into the air. Wait until you try to wash your pretty finery and find it gray with soot."

"There's a price for progress. It always must be so."

"And the price here? We're doing more than destroying the land. Half the water in the east comes from here. And every time we destroy another forest, another river dries up. And no one gives a damn."

She felt she had to defend Daddy. "Are you suggesting that my father . . ."

"Your father is no better nor worse than any of the rest of them," he said tiredly. "Just smarter. If he hadn't managed to get his hands on that state land near New Russia, someone else would have. But they'll ruin the land. All of them. The greedy bastards."

"Mr. Stanton, I do protest your language!"

"Christ!" he muttered under his breath. "Look, Miss Bradford, if you want a place in a man's world, you'd better get used to it. Including people like Sam Doyle and his crude remarks about sows and pigs. There's no room here for prudery."

That stung. "There's no reason why a man can't behave like a gentleman."

"If he doesn't, that doesn't mean he's less a man."

"I disagree. I've never known a real man who wasn't a gentleman first." Arthur was a perfect example, she thought. There was nothing frightening about Arthur.

He laughed. "A real man. Gentlemanly and polite. Kiss a woman's hand. Safe. No need to fear in the presence of a man like that."

"Yes!"

He shook his head. "Men like that only exist in those books the ladies read."

She felt naked, her secrets betrayed. She wanted to hurt

him. "What can you understand? *You're* no gentleman! But I know men like that."

"You don't know them very well, then. You'll find that every man's the same in bed, gentleman or not."

She gasped, and whirled away from him. With her hand shaking, she reached for the door latch.

"Wait," he said. She turned. "Look," he said, "I'm sorry. We seem to have started out badly today. I'd like to declare a truce, if we can."

She wasn't ready to forgive him his bad manners. "We'll work together, Mr. Stanton," she said frostily. "I'm sure I can learn a great deal from you. But I don't have to like you."

"You don't have to be afraid of me either," he said quietly.

"I'm *certainly* not afraid of you!"

He held out his hand. "Then I'll take that handshake now."

She hesitated. Her slim fingers would be lost in his powerful grasp. No! I'm not afraid, she thought. Resolutely, she clasped his hand. He took a step nearer. For a terrifying moment she thought he would wrap his arms around her. She shook her hand free and backed away.

He sighed in weariness. "It makes no difference to me, Miss Bradford, but why in the name of Christ didn't someone ever teach you to enjoy being a woman? Look at you. In a gown my grandmother wouldn't wear. Do you ever let your hair down?"

She felt her heart beginning to pound. She was speechless with outrage.

He shrugged and answered his own question. "No. You probably sleep with it tight and knotted. In your tight little virginal bed."

"Oh!" She cast her eyes about the veranda, looking for something to throw at him. She'd never felt so reckless in all her life. A small iron doorstop in the shape of a cat was sitting on a windowsill. She lunged for it, but he reached her side first and closed his hand around her wrist. She looked up. The menace in his eyes made her tremble.

"I'm not a gentleman, Miss Bradford," he said quietly.

"You said so yourself. If you raise your hand to me, you'll regret it." He released her hand and she straightened, although her entire body shook. "I'll see you in the clerk's office in the morning," he said. "Perhaps we can both forget that this night ever happened."

Chapter
Four

"**I** won't have it, Marcy! He'll kill you *and* himself!"
"Oh bosh, Uncle Jack!" Marcy turned, grinning.
"You won't kill me, will you, Drew?"

Drew Bradford laughed, his eyes twinkling. "Maybe your uncle is right. I've never handled a boat in the rapids before."

She smiled back. It made her feel good, just to hear him laugh. "I've watched you these last couple of weeks," she said. "You're good with oars *and* paddle."

"I warn you, I may not be that good. Sculling on the Charles River in Cambridge isn't exactly the same as shooting the rapids."

Old Jack frowned. "I'll go down with him, Marcy. You get in the boat with Dr. Marshall."

"No!" she said stubbornly. "Honestly, Uncle Jack, how many times do we have to go through this? Mrs. Marshall is scared to run the rapids, but she wants Amos to tramp through the brush with her to the next campsite. She won't have anyone else."

"Exactly! So you go with Dr. Marshall in his boat, and take the oars. I'll go with Drew."

Marcy shook her head. "Drew wants to be on the oars himself. Besides, I don't think Dr. Marshall would feel safe with me. He's a regular fraidy-cat. And I can give directions to Drew as we go."

"Ah-h-h!" With a look of disgust, Old Jack marched off to Dr. Marshall.

Drew chuckled. "Sometimes I like that stubborn streak of yours! Now, what do we do first?"

Marcy knelt to their boat. "First off, we have to lash down everything to the sides of the boat. Your fishing rod, and both our rifles. And the paddles. We only need the oars to run the rapids."

"And our gear?"

"Tie it to the bottom. And unless you want to lose your hat, you'll stow that too."

Drew took off his battered hat and stuffed it into his carpetbag. "I can't afford another one this summer. As it is, the rain nearly destroyed it last week!" He smiled, his blue eyes warm on her face. "By the way, you looked mighty pretty in the rain. I meant to tell you so, but I was busy sketching you."

She blushed. "Why do you always say things like that?" she whispered.

He put on an expression of innocence. "Like what?"

"Like you were . . . courting me, or something!"

He grinned. "Don't be silly. I'm the poor artist you can't marry. Why should I court you?"

Dang him, she thought. She *knew* it was impossible, of course. But every time he reminded her of how poor he was, it was like a knife to her heart. "Put on your moccasins and stow your boots," she said. "If we're dumped, we want to take to the water light. Even if the boat wrecks, it'll drift to shore with our gear."

He unlaced his boots and slipped into his soft camp shoes. "Your 'beau' comes back tomorrow, doesn't he?"

She glared at him. "I'm sorry I ever told you about my plans! You've just had great sport these last weeks, making fun, twitting me every chance you can!"

He laughed. "And not kissing you nearly often enough!"

"Not for the lack of trying, dang you!"

He took off his coat and packed it away. Then he rolled up the sleeves of his shirt. Marcy noticed how tanned his arms had become in the month or so they'd been camping. "So your beau's coming back tomorrow," he said.

How maddening he could be! "Uncle Jack said Mr. Stafford and Tom should meet us at McBride's on Tupper Lake tomorrow night. But he's not my beau yet!"

"I don't know why not. You had more than a week before he went off with Heyson to do some surveying. I was expecting you to make your move right away."

"Well..." She fussed with the ribbon around her hair, feeling uncomfortable. "The truth is, there was never a chance to be alone with him, except the one time he forgot his rifle on the carry at Rock Pond and I had to go back with him."

"The perfect opportunity! A lonely setting, a beautiful girl with blue-green eyes..."

"It was a little *too* lonely. I'm not so sure I trust him. I want to have some promises...."

He snorted. "I'd hold out for a ring."

"Well ... *something*! At least before I get too far away from help."

"I'm not worried for you. I haven't forgotten how loud you hollered when you landed that trout. Mr. William Stafford better not try to take liberties!"

"I swear I'm going to let the rapids take you if you don't stop funning me!"

He laughed and stood up. "I don't believe that for a minute. I think you like to be teased."

She felt her cheeks coloring. It was bad enough that he could see right through her; it was even worse when he *told* her! "I think you're just a conceited..."

"You're blushing again."

"Bosh!" She stood up and put her hands on her hips. "Do you want to ride the rapids or don't you?"

He tried to look serious. "All right. What next?"

"You'll sit in the middle of the boat, facing downstream. I'll be behind you. I'll be on the bottom of the boat, so I won't be able to see the river as well as you. I can tell you what lies ahead—I've done this stretch often enough—but you've got to look out for hidden rocks as we go. Keep her straight in the currents, and use your oars to hold her steady. Uncle Jack always says, 'Smash your oars before you smash your boat.' The only time you'll let 'em trail is when we go over the falls."

He frowned. "How will I know when we reach the falls?"

She smiled in malice. "Don't worry, you'll hear them. And by that time, it'll be too late to back out, Mr. Smart-Aleck!"

They settled into their boat, Drew perched lightly on the caned seat, Marcy cross-legged on the boat bottom in back of him. Old Jack strapped Dr. Marshall into his boat, while Ed Collins, with Alonzo as his guide, jammed his top hat firmly on his head, smiled nervously toward them, and clutched the sides of his boat until his knuckles were white. Old Jack gave the signal and the three light boats moved into the center of the river.

The current was swift, the river flowing downhill, pulled by a force that could not be seen, only vaguely heard in the distant roar of the falls. Marcy watched Drew's back as he plied the oars, following in Uncle Jack's wake; his strokes were sure and strong, guiding the boat over the relative smoothness of this stretch.

He needs a haircut, she thought, longing to reach out and touch the black curls at the nape of his neck.

"Bear to the left," she said. "There's a large rock to our right. You see where Uncle Jack is going? There's a strong eddy there. It'll pull us too far over unless you lean into your right oar."

He nodded, negotiating the swift current with ease. In a moment the smooth surface of the river was broken up as more and more rocks came into view. The boat picked up speed. Drew worked furiously, steering this way and that, taking advantage of the whirls and eddies to propel their craft forward. They topped a sudden rise and darted down a steep incline. The wild spray shot across the bow.

The roar of the falls was now quite loud. Drew grinned over his shoulder at Marcy. She laughed aloud. "That's only the *first* one!" she cried.

They glided on, swerving past giant boulders, bouncing and tossing on the foam, as the roar grew louder. Marcy looked up. She could see the rim of the falls. "Now!" she shouted. "Throw yourself against the oars! When we crest the falls let go and lean forward! And hang on!"

Drew nodded without turning. He bent to the oars. The boat leaped forward, shivered slightly, and plunged over the falls. They drifted for a moment in the shallows beneath the falls, then Drew steered them to the side of the river just behind Old Jack's craft.

Ed Collins wiped the foam from his face. "I've lost my hat," he said in a hurt tone. "And there's more to come?"

He looks like he wishes he were still in the city, thought Marcy.

"I, for one, wouldn't mind a rest," said Dr. Marshall shakily. "That's the most harrowing fifteen minutes I've ever spent!"

"*I'm* ready to go on," said Drew. "How about you, Marcy?"

She smiled and nodded. He was so wonderfully devil-may-care. She'd never met anyone like him. "We'll wait for you down below, Uncle Jack," she said.

"Now, Marcy . . ."

She laughed. Drew had already maneuvered the boat toward the center of the current. "Wait," she said. "There's a shallow patch ahead. Watch out for it. If you have to, back up and take us another way. Then we'll hit the short drop. We'll come around a sharp bend. Then the current's very swift, and there's only one channel deep enough. I'll point it out to you. As we come out of it, we hit the second falls. You won't have time to catch your breath. Stay on the oars till the last minute, and after we go over, row like crazy or the falls will swamp us."

"I understand."

They hit the current. The boat was alive, dancing in and out of small whirlpools, flying past jagged rocks that cut the river to shreds and sent the spume whipping into their faces. Marcy laughed in delight; it had never ceased to thrill her, the heart-stopping excitement of it. But now her life, her safety, were in his hands; it made it all the sweeter.

They passed through the shallows and dashed toward the first drop. She could feel the wind on her wet cheeks. The falls loomed ahead, then the boat was on the crest. They dropped in a great splash of foam, spun dizzily for a minute, then hurtled around the sharp curve of the river.

Marcy leaned forward and pounded Drew on the back. She pointed. "There!" she screamed, over the noise of the water. The wind whipped the words from her mouth. He shook the spray from his eyes and nodded, fighting with the oars to guide the boat to the space between the rocks. They hit the channel. They seemed to be sucked by some great force toward the roaring unknown. They shot out of the channel, oars trailing, and raced to the rim of the raging falls. The boat shuddered, paused, then plunged. For a moment they seemed to hang suspended. Drew let out a whoop of joy. They hit the seething water with a great splash; then Drew clutched at the oars and rowed them into the calm shallows.

Breathing hard, he turned around in his seat and smiled at Marcy. His eyes were shining with excitement. "My God!" he exclaimed. He wiped his wet shirt across his wet face and laughed. He grinned and reached out his hand, dabbing at the spray on her cheek. The grin faded. Leaning forward, he kissed her tenderly on the mouth. "I wouldn't have shared it with anyone but you, Marce."

Oh, drat! she thought, feeling her heart leap at the sweetness of his kiss, the gentleness of his words. No! I can't let him get to me! He's only playing a game to amuse himself. He has no intention of marrying. He said so himself. She cocked a skeptical eyebrow at him. "I'll bet you say that to all the girls!"

His mouth twitched in amusement. "We're usually sharing some other experience when I do." He pointed to the falls behind her. "Look. Here come the others."

She turned just in time to see the two boats come flying over the falls and land in a whoosh of water at the bottom. Dr. Marshall was shaking like a paper birch in a storm; he tried weakly to rise, but was restrained by Old Jack.

"I say, Drew, that was capital!" shouted Ed Collins. He smiled brightly, turned green, and vomited over the side of the boat.

By the time they reached their campsite farther down the Raquette River, it was late afternoon. There was no lean-to here, only a small stretch of beach. The guides propped the boats upside-down with a strong sapling at one end; they would sleep under their craft tonight.

Mrs. Marshall was in rare spirits. She and Amos had spent the afternoon fishing, and had caught enough trout to furnish them all with supper, and breakfast besides.

Marcy had to laugh. She'd watched these past weeks as Mrs. Marshall had slowly discarded bits and pieces of her costume. The gloves had gone first, then the hat with its netting, and the funny little glasses on her nose. She could only guess when the corsets had been put aside; but it was now quite plain from the bulges around Mrs. Marshall's waist that her underpinnings had been stowed with the rest of her "city" clothes.

And yet, thought Marcy with amazement, she's as stiff and proper as the first day she arrived. Still giving orders, still treating the men with suspicion when it came to Marcy. She saved her sternest lectures for Drew, who was entirely too "frivolous" for her taste, cautioning him to let the "pure and rarified air" that filtered through the trees cleanse his wicked nature.

While Amos cleaned the fish and Alonzo mixed some pancake batter, Old Jack examined the up-ended boats. "Marcy," he said, "I think we're about to spring a leak."

She peered over his shoulder at the hull of their boat. There was a deep gash in the wood. "I was afraid of that. We scraped a bit going over that last slide."

"Aren't we near that spruce bog?"

She pointed away from the river. "Half a mile in. I blazed a fresh trail in the spring. Do you want me to go?"

He nodded. "I should help Amos with the fish. You get us some spruce gum for the boat."

"I'll come with you, if you don't mind," said Drew.

Mrs. Marshall had been taking a proprietary interest in the preparation of her fish, but at Drew's words she turned to him, frowning.

"Did you intend to go into the woods with Marcy, Mr. Bradford? Alone?"

"Yes, ma'am, I did," he said solemnly. He bent to the pile of supplies on the sand and grasped his rifle. "If our boat isn't repaired, it could mean our lives. But if it grows dark before Marcy returns from her noble mission, who's to protect her from the savage beasts that may lurk in the wilds?"

Mrs. Marshall smiled uneasily, unsure of his sincerity.

Marcy thought: If she starts in lecturing him, we'll never get out of here. "Mr. Bradford's right," she said. "I'll feel much safer with his protection." She grabbed for a tin cup, motioned to Drew, and made for the narrow path beyond the beach.

Behind her, Drew laughed under his breath. "Safer?" he whispered. "Really?"

As soon as they were out of sight of the others, she slowed to let him walk beside her. "Honestly, Drew Bradford," she said. "You'll burn in Hell for all those lies!"

"I wasn't lying. I didn't say *I'd* protect you!"

She giggled. "And I didn't say who I thought the savage beast might be!"

"Anyway, what are we doing?"

"There's a big swamp ahead, ringed with spruce trees. The sap is hard and sticky. I'll scrape off a few chunks into this cup, and Uncle Jack will cook it up with some bits of shredded rope. When it cools a little he can caulk the seams of the boat."

He looked around. "How do you know where we're going?"

She pointed. "See that tree? That thin gash in the bark? That's how you blaze a trail. I was out here last spring. That's my mark."

"You're a regular Hiawatha."

She ignored that, content to walk beside him in silence, taking in the sights and smells of the wilderness she loved so well.

He seemed to feel it too. "It's so silent," he said at last. "I guess I've noticed that from the first day, but it didn't register in my brain. Dark and silent and mysterious. Why's it always so quiet? I can't remember the Catskills being like this."

She shivered unexpectedly. "It's scary, sometimes," she said softly. "Like it's haunted. The Indians felt it too. They didn't live here, you know. They just hunted and fished. Then went home again. Some north, some south."

"But why is it this way? So eerie?"

"Haven't you noticed? The trees. Dr. Marshall was talking about it yesterday. He made it sound so ... scientific. It's colder here than the Catskills. And rockier. So there're more evergreens. Pine and spruce and tamarac. And lots more. Look at all the patches of needles on the ground. That's not good ground cover for the little animals. It doesn't give them much to eat."

"Nor the birds. I've mostly heard chickadees."

"Well, anyway, that's why it's so quiet."

He laughed. "I'd like to hear *Mrs*. Marshall's explanation sometime. The majesty of God. The silence of the spheres..."

"It's nice enough without her trying to find highfalutin reasons. Come on. There's the spruce swamp." They circled the marshy patch until Marcy had found a tree to her liking. Pulling out her knife, she hacked off several large wads of the thick resin that oozed from its bark, and filled her cup.

"My God," said Drew. "Look at that sky."

Marcy turned. Large fleecy clouds, touched with gold and

red, were cradling the setting sun. Above it, the sky glowed in bands of bright color, deep ruby and pale green and, finally, clear blue. And the evening star.

She'd never been able to make a wish on the first star. What could she wish for beyond the beauty of the star, the glory of the sky? She gulped, feeling the tears well in her eyes.

"Good Lord, you're crying!" Drew turned her to face him.

She stuck out her chin. "So what if I am? Can't a body cry when . . . when something's so beautiful?"

He stroked the side of her cheek. "Then I should cry every time I look at your face."

She sniffled and pushed him away. "Bosh! You're just buttering me up to steal another kiss."

He grinned. "Oh. Then you're *not* beautiful?"

She looked disgusted. "Well, I'm not a fool either. I know I've got looks. But I'm not about to let a devil like you turn my head!"

His blue eyes narrowed. "Now I really *am* going to kiss you."

"You'll have to catch me first!"

"Easy enough." Before she could flee, he had swept her into his arms. "Now, my beautiful Marcy . . ." he said, holding her close. "Damn!" He released her and slapped his neck. "I thought we'd seen the last of the black flies!" He rolled down his sleeves, buttoning them tightly, and brushed at the air in front of his face.

She swatted at a swarm of insects. "It's gnats. The black flies are done for the season. Maybe it's just the swamp," she said hopefully.

He scooped up his rifle and grabbed her arm. "Then let's get out of here!"

Laughing, they raced back toward the campsite. At last Drew stopped, breathing hard. He smacked at his cheek. "No. They're still with us."

"If we're lucky," panted Marcy, "the wind will blow them away from camp."

He chuckled. "I'm hoping not. I'll personally take great

delight in smearing Mrs. Marshall's face with that foul slime
your uncle mixes up."

"It's just tar and castor oil. It keeps the bugs off. Why are
you so mean about Mrs. Marshall?"

He laughed. "It's only that I can't do this when she's
around." He bent and kissed her. "Two in one day. Fancy
that! Well, I've got to get them while I can. Tomorrow I lose
you to Mister Moneybags William Stafford!"

The following afternoon Drew watched as Marcy began
her campaign when the group sat together at McBride's boardinghouse.

"You're looking mighty pleased with yourself, Mr. Stafford. Did you have a good success?" Marcy smiled warmly
with what she hoped was a seductive expression. On the other
end of Mr. McBride's veranda, Drew cleared his throat and
turned away. Dang him! she thought, and smiled again at Mr.
Stafford.

Stafford stroked his side whiskers. "Very good. Very good.
I took some barometrical observations of Wall Face Mountain,
and explored a bit of the Ausable River. Should be good for
an article or two in *Harper's Weekly*."

"Oh, how wonderful!" she breathed. As though half the
city slickers didn't write stories for the newspapers the minute
they left the Wilderness! But she couldn't think like that.
She'd already made up her mind to marry; she'd better start
finding good things to think about William Stafford. He certainly was handsome enough, very distinguished—even if
that gleam in his eye made her nervous.

She was glad she'd put on a skirt and lady's waist; it was
plain, but far more attractive than a man's woolen shirt. She
was sorry that she'd left her mother's earrings back at the
cabin in Long Lake. But she'd brushed her hair until it shone,
and left it loose.

Mrs. McBride came out onto the veranda and struck the
dinner gong. William Stafford smiled at Marcy like the buccaneer she had come to consider him; his eyes swept her ripe
curves. "Miss Tompkins," he said, presenting his arm, "may
I escort you to supper?"

"I'll be eating with the guides," she said. "I always do."

"No. I've paid for your meal voucher. You'll sit with me."

"I'd be right pleased." She slipped her arm through his, feeling very grand and ladylike.

McBride's was elegant compared to most of the boarding houses on the more remote lakes. Indeed, a sign over the doorway proclaimed it a "Hotel," and Mrs. McBride had brought in a Persian rug and a shiny new piano for the parlor. In the dining room, the guides' table was plain, and tucked into a corner, but the guests were treated to white linen and fancy dishes. For the proper "rustic" touches (earning squeals of delight from Mrs. Marshall), the cloth had been strewn with fresh leaves, and the glass salt cellars were set into hollowed-out pinecones. The men were instructed to hang their hats on the antlers and hooves of a mounted deer, and the chairs around the table, cushioned with bright calico, were made entirely of branches of silver birch.

Marcy smiled in pleasure as the hired girl brought around the platters of food and Mr. Stafford insisted on serving her himself. She didn't know if that was the way it was always done in the big city, but it certainly made a girl feel special to be fussed over by a man. She laughed gaily all through supper, ignoring everyone else at the table except Stafford. Especially Drew Bradford, who watched her all during the meal, one devil's eyebrow cocked in mocking amusement.

When supper was finished the guides went outside to sit on the veranda and swap stories. As soon as Mrs. Marshall retired to the parlor, Mr. McBride brought out a bottle of whiskey and a deck of cards, and Collins, Heyson, and Stafford settled down for some poker. In the parlor, Mrs. McBride began to play a slow waltz on the piano.

"Come on," said Drew, pulling Marcy by the hand. "I'll dance with you." He swung her into his arms, holding her tightly, and swirled her around the floor, carefully avoiding the Marshalls, who were also waltzing—with more grace than Marcy would have imagined.

I could dance like this forever, thought Marcy, feeling herself swept up in the sensuous rhythm of the waltz. She was conscious of Drew's size and strength, the warmth of his arms, the clasp of his hand. *His silence*. She frowned and looked up at his face. Like a closed book.

"Are you angry about something?"

"Why should I be angry?" he said. There was an edge to his voice she'd never heard before. "I watched you at supper. You made a good beginning. You took to it like you were born to the purple."

"What does that mean?"

He laughed shortly. "It means when you marry your rich man, you'll fit right in. And Stafford certainly took a shine to you."

He seemed so strange. "Drew..." she said hesitantly.

"You dance very well. By the by, I thought you were a bit coy with Stafford. Not even the empty-headed city girls giggle all the time."

"You *are* angry."

He grinned. "Not at all. And to show you my heart's in the right place, I'll play Cupid. In a little while, when we've finished dancing, go down to the edge of the lake. I'll send your 'beau' to you."

"Bosh! How are you going to do that? He'll be at the cards all night."

"Not if I tell him that you've gone to look at the lake by moonlight. He'll come running like a hound to the scent."

"I'm not sure..."

"You've talked about it often enough. Are you afraid to put your plan into action?"

Dang him and his teasing! "No!" she said. "I'll catch me a husband tonight. Just you wait and see, Mr. Drewry Bradford!"

The moon shone on the still water of the lake, making a silver path to the opposite shore. A loon cried mournfully. Marcy shivered. You're daft, Marcy Tompkins, she thought. Maybe it wasn't too late to run.

"You shouldn't have come out without a wrap, Marcy." The voice was smooth, confident.

She turned. "Oh, Mr. Stafford! You gave me a start."

"You must be chilly. Take my coat."

"Oh, no. Really, I..." It was too late. He had already taken off his frock coat and wrapped it around her shoulders, holding it close so her arms were imprisoned.

"I feel cheated, Marcy," he said. "I had nothing but George Heyson's company for nearly three weeks. The others had you."

"Oh, but... the time just flew... we fished and hunted ... I'm sure you and Mr. Heyson..." Tarnation! She was babbling like an idiot.

He slid one arm under the coat and around her waist. "You looked charming this evening. I'd surely like to see you in a fancy gown. Perhaps you could come to Philadelphia. I could show you a good time."

She wriggled uncomfortably, wishing he would let her go. But she knew so little of the ways of men and she wasn't sure if he truly had wicked intentions; it wouldn't do to make him angry. He might take it out on Uncle Jack and the others. "Would you invite me to your home in Philadelphia?" she asked coyly.

He laughed, a low ugly sound in his throat. "I don't think Letty would approve."

His face in the moonlight seemed suddenly frightening. He *is* a buccaneer, she thought, picturing the evil flash of a gold earring. "Who's Letty?"

"My wife. Now, we were talking about you. In a gown that shows off your figure. Would you like that?"

"I don't think..."

"Green. Green velvet. The color of envy. Because every man will be jealous of me. A gown that fits just so. Here"— his hand on her waist had dropped lower, caressing her hip— "and here." Deliberately, he cupped her breast with his other hand.

"Tarnation!" she cried, almost leaping away from him. "Isn't that Uncle Jack calling me? You must tell me about Philadelphia some other time. Good night, Mr. Stafford. Thank you for the use of your coat." She almost threw it at him. While he bent to retrieve it, she fled toward the hotel. She was glad there was a back door. She was too ashamed to meet up with Drew or the others in the parlor. She crept up the back stairs and into the small room under the eaves that she was sharing with the hired girl. She stripped down to her chemise and crawled between the sheets, hating Mr. William Stafford and Drew. And herself. She slept, and dreamed of a pirate with one gold earring and a green velvet hat.

She awoke at the first chirping of the birds, and sat up in bed. She felt dirty, thinking of the way Stafford had touched her. It was still early; she could take a swim in the lake and be back before anyone else was up. She pulled on her drawers and her man's shirt and trousers, slipped her bare feet into her moccasins, and tiptoed out of the room.

The morning fog was still on the lake, vertical ribbons of mist rising to the fast-brightening sky. So clean. So pure. Men like Stafford shouldn't even be allowed in her Wilderness, she thought. She undressed quickly, keeping on her chemise for a bathing dress. The water was cold and crystalline; she swam slowly, reluctant to make ripples on its glassy surface. She looked up. Drew was standing near the edge of the lake, grinning at her.

"I thought I was the only one who couldn't sleep," he said. "How goes your affair of the heart?"

She stood up in the shallows and glared at him. "I don't know why I let you talk me into last night," she said, wading furiously toward shore. "That varmint, that . . ." She stopped, seeing the look in Drew's eyes.

"If we're to talk," he growled, "you'd better get some clothes on."

She looked down at herself. The chemise clung wetly to her curves, revealing the outlines of her firm breasts, her nipples grown hard from the cold water. "Well, you don't have to look!"

He laughed and turned his back. "You're right. Get dressed. But hurry up. I want the whole story of Stafford."

She stripped off the wet chemise and dressed without it, donning her clothes as quickly as she could. She didn't like being naked and vulnerable. Drew Bradford might not want a wife, but the look in his eyes made her wonder if she was, perhaps, a little less safe with him than she had thought.

"Well?" he said impatiently. "What about Stafford?"

"You can turn around now," she said, tucking her shirt into her trousers. "I'll *tell* you about Stafford! He's got a wife!"

"Why that old goat!" Drew was trying hard not to laugh. "I *am* sorry. But from the way he talked about the ladies, I naturally assumed he was single."

"What do you mean, *talked about the ladies*?" She was beginning to sputter. "Tarnation! Do you think I'd want to be married to a man like that?"

"Well, he *is* rich."

"With a wife in Philadelphia." She frowned. "What's Philadelphia like?"

He shrugged. "It's just a city."

"No. Tell me. Is it wonderful and beautiful? With tall buildings? And women in pretty gowns? And fine houses? Oh, tell!"

"My God. Look at you. Your eyes are shining!" He shook his head. "How can you get excited about just a city when you have all this?" He waved an impatient arm in the direction of the lake.

"What do you know?" she grumbled.

He sighed. "Not very much. I certainly don't know you. You're so serious about this. So solemn. Good God! I've watched the way you look at a flower or a bird on the wing. And then you talk about a city as though it were the end of the rainbow!"

"Leave me alone. It's none of your business."

He stared at her, frowning, while she wrung out her chemise. Then he laughed. A forced laugh. "You're right." He picked up a pebble and threw it into the lake. "Who's next? George Heyson? He's mighty rich."

"I don't like him. I don't care how rich he is. He's old. And he said mean things about Tom."

"Tom Sabattis? Stafford's guide? He's a nice fellow."

"But he's an Indian. At least his father is."

"So what?"

"Mr. Heyson called him ... a red savage ..."

He scowled. "Mr. Heyson's a pompous ass."

She nodded, then began to giggle. "And I don't think he likes girls much."

"I don't think he likes *anybody* much! Well, what about Ed Collins? Of course, he's not nearly as rich ..."

"Huh! City slicker!"

"He's just out of his element. He's not a bad chap. And a lot younger. What about him?"

It no longer seemed to be a game. Why was he forcing her to play it? "Stop it, Drew," she said softly. "Really, I ..."

He smiled, the corners of his mouth twitching in a devilish smirk. "Maybe you could plan to have him come upon you swimming. The way I did. Only it might be a good idea to leave your shift with the rest of your clothes."

"Oh!" She smacked him in the face with her wet chemise, and stormed off toward the hotel, hearing his mocking laughter until she reached the veranda.

Willough lifted her head from the opened ledger and put down her pen. She rubbed at her stiff shoulders and looked across at the other desk. "I don't like it, Nat. We haven't had near enough rain this summer. Every one of our farmers says there won't be enough hay and oats to see the horses through the winter. Even if the skies open up next month, there are too many dry fields. Three months is such a short growing season. We'll be lucky to have enough potatoes for the company store."

Nat stood up and stretched, tugging impatiently at his stiff collar. He looks like a caged lion, thought Willough. There was something frightening about all that pent-up power. "God, I hate sitting for hours," he muttered. "What's the problem, Miss Bradford? We're buying extra to make up the shortfall."

"Not enough."

"We can always buy more if we get into September or

October and find our supplies running short. Mr. Murphy did it last year."

She tapped the ledger. "At twice the cost. I'd rather put in an order now than be forced to do it with our backs to the wall. I've had some correspondence with a farmer down near Ticonderoga; if his grain is as good as his price, it might be worth our while."

He nodded. "When I go down to Ingles on Sunday, I can stay over and take a look around. If you'll give me the farmer's name, I'll scout around on the sly, and then you can follow up with a letter."

She smiled in satisfaction. They worked well together. He seemed to understand the way her mind operated, her approach to the business. She had learned a great deal from him in the past few weeks, but surely he had learned from her as well. You're your father's daughter, he'd often say, though sometimes she wasn't sure he meant it as a compliment.

Restlessly he moved around the small office, riffling books, opening and closing his desk drawers, toying with the sturdy briar pipe on his desk. That was something she still found terrifying about him: the way he filled a room with his masculine presence. But she'd done her best to ignore it, avoiding anything but talk about the business, the running of the MacCurdy Ironworks. Thank God there had never been a repetition of that first disastrous day! "Ingles," she said. "Is that where you go every Sunday, when Daddy and I are at Saratoga?"

"Yes."

"And what's there? A wife? A sweetheart?"

His mouth twitched sardonically. "Why is it you can make even a simple question sound like a challenge? My grandfather lives in Ingles."

"Oh." She looked at her hands, feeling uncomfortable under his searching gaze. It *had* sounded like a challenge, cool and superior. Designed to make him squirm. She thought: He certainly brings out the worst in me. "And you visit him every week?" she asked more kindly.

"*Every* week, even in winter. And even if I have to travel half the night."

She looked at him in surprise. "That's very dutiful of you."

"He can't walk. He's dependent upon me for his food. And his firewood in the winter."

"What a heavy burden for you. Can't you find someone to care for him, when you're not there? That is . . ." She felt herself blushing. Perhaps he couldn't afford it.

"It isn't a question of money, Miss Bradford, if that's what you're thinking. Gramps is a queer duck. He doesn't much like people. I'm his only contact with the outside world, and that's just about the way he likes it."

"Still, it's a burden."

He turned to the window and stared out at the gray sky. One powerful hand still clutched his pipe. "You said it yourself. I'm dutiful. Filled with a sense of duty." There was an edge of bitterness to his voice.

He seemed more human than she'd imagined him to be. Human and vulnerable. "Why do you permit him to tyrannize you?"

"It isn't tyranny. I do it to myself. Because he's the only family I've got." He turned to look at her.

Oh, God, she thought. His eyes. Like glowing amber, stripping her naked where she sat, burning into her flesh. She couldn't allow it! "That's perfectly foolish!" she snapped, drawing herself up. "To turn your life upside-down . . . !"

His eyes narrowed in sudden anger. "How well you play the grand lady, Miss Bradford! Do you do it because you're bored? Or fearful? Or because you truly *enjoy* being a snob? I care about my grandfather because while men like your father were making money casting cannon, men like *my* father were dying in front of those cannon! I had two brothers as well. They died together at Gettysburg. Gramps may chain me to him—but four years of war, four years of hell forged those chains!" His hand had become a fist. Willough gasped in horror as the pipe shattered in his grip.

He could crush me as easily as that, she thought, shivering.

Nat exhaled slowly and uncurled his hand. "I'm sorry. I didn't mean to frighten you."

I'm sorry, she thought. I didn't mean to sound snobbish. It always seemed to be the only way to keep him at a distance. To pretend a superiority she didn't feel, in order to hide the strange uneasiness she *did* feel in his presence.

The door opened. Brian Bradford strode into the office. "Afternoon, Nat. Willough." He frowned at his daughter. "Haven't you sent for more gowns yet? Never mind. There'll be time to shop in Saratoga in August. Nat, Clegg tells me he's closing down Number Two for repairs next month."

"Yes, sir."

"Good. It will ease your work. I want you to come to Saratoga for a couple of weeks. Stay at the house. I have some bankers coming in. I want to discuss an expansion. . . . I'd like you to be in on it."

"What about the clerk's duties? Will Miss Bradford stay here?"

"Willough? Good God, no. Bill can fill in as clerk. I need Willough in Saratoga."

He needs me, thought Willough. She'd never felt more pleased at something her father had said. "Daddy . . ."

Brian smiled at her. "Will all those men around, lass, *someone's* got to be my hostess."

Her heart sank.

"You might find Miss Bradford more useful if you had her sit in on the meetings," Nat said quietly.

Brian looked doubtful. "Yes. Well . . . we'll talk about it in Saratoga. One other thing, Nat. This note about paying the fillers more. Do you think I'm made of money?"

"The note came from me, Daddy."

Brian turned. "You? Are you daft, Willough?"

"There's been a lot of talk. The fillers aren't getting much more than the woodcutters. And the work is twice as dangerous. Two men quit last week. They went over to Eagle Lake to work for Ordway. You can't run your furnaces if no one will charge them."

"Let them all be damned. Bleeding me dry," growled Brian.

She sighed in exasperation. "Jim Hopewell nearly died last week when the furnace flared up and set him on fire! The fillers are angry. Clegg's heard dangerous talk ... an extra dollar a week won't break you."

Brian banged on the desk with his fist. "Dammit, Willough, I won't have you telling me how to run my business!"

Nat cleared his throat. "If the fillers refuse to work, it'll cost you more than a dollar a week to bring in new men. You won't be able to get anyone local. The word will get around."

Brian looked thoughtful. "You think so?"

"Sometimes it's just plain short-sighted to cut corners. You don't want to get the men grumbling. You won't get any work out of any of them."

"Maybe you're right, Nat." Brian pulled a cigar out of his waistcoat pocket and headed for the door. "Give the fillers a raise." He lit his cigar and opened the door. "Not a dollar, damn 'em! Seventy-five cents a week." He scowled. "But fire the first bastard who complains!" He went out of the office, slamming the door loudly.

Willough stared at the bottle of ink on her desk, feeling an irrational urge to hurl it across the room. Daddy had changed his mind because of Nat. *Her* advice had meant nothing.

"Your father's a damn fool, Miss Bradford."

She frowned. He'd just bested her with Daddy. The last thing she wanted now was his sympathy. "I dislike swearing, Nat," she said coldly.

"I'll say it anyway. He's a damn fool. For not knowing what he's got in you."

"It's not for us to question him," she snapped.

He ran his fingers impatiently through his blond curls. "Christ! Can't you even take a compliment? I'm trying to tell you I think you're one hell of a woman!"

She felt trapped by his presence. "I told you, I don't like swearing!"

He shook his head. "We always seem to end up fighting," he said tiredly.

She was still thinking of Daddy. "Perhaps we're rivals," she said with bitterness.

"Not in my mind. I can work my way up to manager— even buy into a share some day. But the business will be yours. You're a Bradford. You could fire me tomorrow, and there wouldn't be a damn thing I could do about it. I don't see any rivalry there."

She was beginning to feel a bit foolish. He *had* been her ally with Daddy. "Maybe I meant we seem to be . . . at cross purposes."

"I don't know why. We certainly think alike when it comes to the business. The only difference between us seems to be that I'm a man and you're a woman." He smiled, bringing the boyish dimple to his cheek. "And that's a difference I've always found interesting."

She made a face. "You have a fondness for vulgarity. Perhaps that's why we don't get along."

"And you, Miss Bradford, seem to think that cloaking the truth in a kind of prissy gentility makes it more palatable. Frankly, I prefer to say what's on my mind."

"Then do so," she said coolly, surprised at her own boldness.

"All right. I don't know whether you dislike me or not. Sometimes I think you're afraid of me. It doesn't really matter. We make a fine team in this office. I consider us equals, not rivals or adversaries. I would hope you do the same."

She smiled shyly, feeling chastened. "Your point is well taken. Perhaps we can begin by being equal in the matter of names. There's no reason why you shouldn't call me by my Christian name, since I've been calling you Nat."

"I've been hoping you'd say that . . . Willough. I was mighty tired of calling you Miss Bradford."

She giggled as a sudden thought hit her. "You made it clear from the first that you didn't consider yourself a gentleman. I'm surprised you waited for my permission to do what you wanted!" She was delighted to see him blush. It made him human. She wondered why she *did* fear him.

And then his eyes swept her body and came to rest on her

face. He smiled. "Perhaps there'll come a time when I won't ask your permission."

She shivered at the naked desire in his eyes. She was right to fear him. How did a woman handle a man like him? She'd been taught how to behave among men with manners—like Arthur.

At the moment Willough's thoughts had turned to him Arthur Bartlett Gray stepped out of the railroad car and brushed a bit of soot from his patent leather shoe. My God, he thought, but MacCurdyville is ugly. No wonder Isobel had refused to live here! He'd thought Brian's house in Saratoga was primitive enough, but at least the town of Saratoga had a certain charm, and the hotels were always filled with pretty—and accommodating—young women. He looked around with distaste at the shabby buildings and barren hills, then sighed. Well, it couldn't be helped. He needed Brian's signature on that lease today. Needed it enough to go out of his way to get here to MacCurdyville. But if all went well, he'd be able to get the signed papers back to Albany tonight. And the ten thousand. Brian had raised the roof over that, but in the end he'd given in. He'd make ten times that much on the New Russia land.

He looked about. A grimy little urchin was standing on the station platform, staring at him. He frowned and fished a penny out of his pocket. "You. Boy. Go over to the livery stable and have them send round a carriage for me." He flipped the coin in the direction of the boy, who grinned toothlessly and scampered down the street.

Arthur thought: ugly little child. They ought to be kept out of sight until they're old enough to put in a decent day's work. God knows they're good for nothing else.

The carriage was old and creaked, but at least it would get him to the ironworks. He leaned back on the hard seat and looked at his surroundings.

Brian Bradford's domain. A mill town, like a thousand others. The rows of workers' shanties, the stables, the ice house with its pond, the schoolhouse, the rickety little church. Behind him the ore pits; beyond, the four furnaces belching flame into the sky. The workers, like ants, crawling over the whole scene, carting ore and iron and charcoal day and night.

The carriage labored up a steep hill toward the MacCurdy Ironworks. Brian Bradford's domain, Arthur thought again, glancing up at the distant building marked "Office." He squinted at the figure that had just emerged from the office, and smiled to himself.

And Brian Bradford's daughter. He hadn't realized until now how eager he was to see Willough again. She seemed to be preoccupied with one of the furnaces, peering intently in that direction. It gave him the perfect opportunity to examine her at his leisure as his carriage approached. My God, she was magnificent! Tall and stately, with a lushness of form that made his hands itch to touch those breasts, that young body. And the face of an angel.

He laughed softly. And the virginal innocence to match. It had been a long time since he'd seduced a virgin—it might be a delicious challenge. She was easily disarmed by flattery and charm; he'd already discovered that in her mother's house. He could begin his campaign today—soften her up with sweet talk. And Brian had said they were going to be in Saratoga for a week or so next month. He could plan to be there himself. Stay in a hotel, so it wouldn't seem a contrived plan. A stroll in the garden, boating on the lake. He could charm her into his bed in no time. He cursed under his breath, remembering the fear in her eyes. God knows what Isobel had told her about men and sex! He would have to assume she feared everything but knew almost nothing. In some ways, it was to his advantage. She might not realize she was being compromised until it was too late. And then, of course, if she resisted he could always force her. But he would have to be very careful not to frighten her off until the moment when...

She turned and saw him in the approaching carriage. Smiling, she lifted her hand and waved. He smiled back, and tipped his hat to her.

I'll have you, Willough Bradford, he thought. One way or another, I'll have you!

Willough held out her hand shyly. "How nice to see you again, Mr. Gray." She thought: I really am glad to see him. Such a gentleman. He was her mother's admirer; that didn't prevent him from being *her* friend. Somehow the seventeen-year difference in their ages seemed less and less important.

He took her hand in his. "You've forgotten so soon that you were to call me Arthur," he chided. He lifted her hand to his lips and kissed it. She could feel the soft tickle of his mustache on her flesh.

She was aware she was blushing. His kiss on her hand, his courtly charm made her as helpless as a schoolgirl. "Arthur. It will take time to get used to."

"Not too long, I hope. I feel as though I missed so many years while you were away. Years when I might have watched you growing more beautiful. When you stopped being the child who called me Uncle Arthur. Do you remember when I called you Weeping Willough?"

"I thought it was amusing, but I was afraid to tell you so."

"Weeping Willough," he repeated. "I should never wish to see tears in those lovely eyes."

What was the matter with her, trembling like a fool. "Please..." she whispered, pulling her hand away.

He seemed to sense her discomfort. "Forgive me. I'd forgotten how it distresses you to be complimented. I'd promised myself after our last meeting that I'd never again tell you how beautiful you are." He smiled warmly. "At least not more than once a day!"

She giggled. "What am I to do with you?"

"You might say you're pleased to see me. You might say you're extravagantly *delighted* to see me. You might ask if I've come to see *you*."

"Have you?" she asked, then blushed again. She sounded like a tart, all coquettish charm.

He laughed. "As a matter of fact, no. I've come to see Brian on business. It couldn't wait. But you're the truffle on the pâté."

"That's not a very flattering thing to say! Truffles must be rooted out by swine."

"But they're precious and difficult to find."

"Anyone can hunt for truffles," she countered.

His voice dropped to a murmur. "Only a man who knows their worth can find the rare jewel hidden in the forest. Other men might pass it by."

She felt quite giddy. No one had ever talked to her like that before—the easy banter that hinted at deeper meanings, the romantic games between a man and a woman. And yet, so *safe*. For she could take his words at face value and nothing more, if she chose. Whereas, when a man like Nat looked at her . . .

"Daddy's up at the rooming house," she said. "Let me take you to him."

"Willough, did you see if that charcoal arrived at Number Three?"

Willough turned. Nat had emerged from the office and was hurrying along the path to them. "Yes, Nat," she said. "They were just unloading when I came out." She indicated Arthur. "I'd like you to meet Arthur Gray. Arthur, this is Nathaniel Stanton, the company clerk."

The two men shook hands. Nat frowned. "Gray. The lawyer?"

"As a matter of fact, yes."

Nat's eyes were cold. "You're the one who arranged that lease over at New Russia?"

"I had a hand in it."

"And a purse as well?" Nat's voice cut like a knife.

Willough was horrified. The man had no manners! "You have no right to question Arthur!" she snapped.

"Of course not." Nat bowed mockingly. "I only wondered how a man arranged to have state boundaries redrawn at will. Or whether Mr. Gray will stop to mourn when the next rainfall brings a flash flood to the local farmers because there are no more trees to hold back the deluge."

Willough stamped her foot angrily. "Nat. Stop!"

"Willough, my dear. Please." Arthur smiled benevolently. "I don't like to see a frown on that pretty face. I'm sure Mr. Stanton was only expressing his concern for the Adirondacks.

Quite admirable of him. We all take an interest in this region.
I meet with legislators every day in Albany who are deeply
involved in the fate of the Wilderness. Ah. I see your father
on the veranda. Let me take care of my business." He turned
to Willough and smiled. "Will I see you before I go?"

"I don't know . . . I . . ."

He took her hand. "If I stay long enough for tea, will you
pour for me as you did in the city?"

"Mrs. Walker is not very good at tea," she stammered,
feeling flustered again. "There'll be no cakes or sweets."

"I won't even need sugar in my tea if you're there," he
said, kissing her hand. "I'll see you later."

Willough turned away as he mounted the path to the rooming house. Her face was flaming. And yet there had been
something thrilling in the way he spoke to her. As if he could
hardly wait to see her again.

It would have been perfect except for Nat. And now he
was staring at her, his amber eyes boring into her. She stuck
out her chin. "Well? What have you to say for yourself? You
insulted the man unforgivably! And now you're standing there
thinking . . . what? I can read your disapproval! You believe
in speaking your mind. Well, perhaps you'll do so now!"

"Do you really want me to?" he asked quietly.

"Yes!"

"Quite aside from his obvious shrewdness as a lawyer, I
think he's out for no good."

"In what way?"

"In the matter of . . . you."

"What do you mean?"

"Must I be more blunt?" he said with a sigh. "In plain
English, he'll seduce you if he can, or I miss my guess."

"Oh! If it weren't so amusing, I'd find your crudeness
despicable! I've known Arthur for years. He's an old friend
of the family. I'm sure he's . . . fond of me"—she felt herself
blushing again—"but he's a man of honor." Hadn't he respected her mother's married state all these years? How could
Nat think for a minute that he had unholy designs? The very
idea of it! "Perhaps that's *your* style with the ladies, Mr.

Stanton! You can hardly be expected to appreciate a gentle-man's behavior!"

He swore under his breath. "You're the most exasperating woman! I'm trying to tell you for your own good. Watch out for the man. He'll get you into bed if he can. And you're such a blind little fool, he won't even have to work hard to do it!"

"I'm sure he has no such thoughts," she said coldly.

His lip curled in scorn. "If a man's nails are manicured, you wouldn't begin to know his intentions."

"I'd know *your* intentions, Mr. Stanton."

"Would you?" He eyed her contemptuously, his insolent glance raking her body. "I'd have to be interested first."

She took a deep breath, stilling her thudding heart. "We have a business to run, Nat," she said. "You keep out of my private life, and I'll keep out of yours!" Whirling on her heel, she marched back to the office, and the safety of her imper-sonal ledgers.

Marcy pushed through the last of the brush and emerged onto the shore of Clear Pond. It was a cool afternoon, rare for July. She threw down her rifle and rubbed her fingers together.

Drew glanced up from the easel that had been set up in front of the lean-to, then resumed his painting. "Where are the others?"

"Mr. Stafford bagged a deer. I never saw him so happy in all my life! Tom and Uncle Jack are dressing it in the field before they bring it in. They sent me on ahead to get the fire roaring and boil up some coffee. Did you remember to stop for lunch?"

He dabbed at his palette and applied the color to his canvas. "I wasn't hungry enough to cook a can of beans. I worked on those apples your uncle brought back from Long Lake the other day."

"What'd you do with the cores?"

"I didn't toss them into the woods, if that's what you mean. Though I wonder why you make such a fuss over a few apple cores."

"You wouldn't want to be visited by a panther or a bear in the middle of the night. That's why Uncle Jack covers the food or keeps it near the fire."

"Panthers and bears. You make it sound so melodramatic! I can't imagine . . ." His voice trailed away. He frowned at the picture, stroked on another bit of paint, then threw down his brush in disgust. "Oh, hell! I can't get that sky to look like anything but a flat blue smear."

"Why don't you quit? You've been at it all day. You should have gone fishing with the others at least."

He laughed. "You're a regular mother hen today. The marriage bug bit you again? Is that why you're being so domestic?"

She blushed. "I told you to quit that teasing! It was a foolish plan and I've changed my mind and I don't want to talk about it anymore!"

He chuckled. "I'll take some of that coffee when it's ready." He cleaned his brushes and tied them up with string, then wrung out a rag in a bit of water and placed it carefully over the blobs of paint on his palette, so they wouldn't dry out.

Marcy knelt to the fire, watching the pot of coffee. "Oh!" she squealed. Drew had crept up behind her and wrapped his arms tightly about her. "You lop-eared devil! Stop that!"

He kissed her on the neck. "Why? Have you decided to set your cap for Ed after all?"

"I've decided that I don't want you to kiss me again," she said firmly.

"Really? Why?"

She thought: He's so off-hand. He doesn't care a fig for me, dang him! "Why do you kiss me?" she asked, stubborn chin jutting forward.

"Because you're nice to kiss. Why do I need any other reason?"

Her heart fell. "Well, I don't want you to anymore."

He laughed and stood up. "If that coffee's not ready yet,

let me do a sketch or two of you." He reached for his pad and a small piece of charcoal. "Sit on that rock." He knelt in front of her, propping the sketchpad on one knee.

She shivered. It always felt so strange when he drew her picture. The blue eyes searched her face with an intimacy that was almost embarrassing. And yet a part of him didn't really see her—it was like being examined by a stranger. She never knew if she liked it or hated it.

He sketched in silence for about five minutes, then the stranger's eyes were replaced by an unmistakable twinkle.

"What are you up to now?" she asked suspiciously.

"Sh-h-h! I'm sketching your mouth. That soft, lovely mouth. That sweet taste of honey ... that I'm not supposed to kiss anymore." His voice was gentle, like a caress. "What a pity. I had so many more kisses to give that sweet mouth. I've wondered what it would be like to run my tongue along the edge of your soft lips ... to invade your mouth with my kisses. Would you have minded, I wonder?"

She felt faint, her heart pounding furiously. Her throat was dry. "Drew ..."

"Hush! You can't talk while I'm drawing your mouth."

She gulped. "But don't you want ..."

He looked innocent. "To kiss you? I can't! You've forbidden me!"

She gasped in sudden understanding. "Tarnation! You rapscallion! You've been funning me!" She reached for a handful of grass and threw it at him. But when he began to roar with laughter she forgot her anger and joined in his mirth. At last she stopped laughing and took a deep breath, shaking her head in mock disapproval. "You're always making fun. Everything's a joke with you."

He shrugged. "Why not? Life's a lark. I'm having too much fun to take anything seriously."

"Except your painting," she said softly.

He laughed sharply. "Don't be silly."

"You can laugh all you want, Drew. But I've seen your eyes. When you draw. When you paint. Even when you make jokes about it."

He put down his pad and pencil and stood up, turning his back to her. "You're a Paul Pry, do you know that? You're not supposed to look so carefully." His voice sounded choked.

"It matters to you, doesn't it?"

Silence. Then, "I want it so badly, sometimes it hurts." The words dragged out of him.

"Money?"

He laughed and turned back to her. "Good God, no. That's the least of it. Acclaim, maybe. I don't know. I need to paint. God, I *need* it! I want to be the best there is. That's all there is to life, as far as I'm concerned. The rest is just"—he waved a hand in the air—"a puff of smoke."

She stood up and moved to him, seeing the pain in his eyes. "But you're good! I'm sure of it. I've seen other painters. Mr. Tait comes to Long Lake every summer. He's a success. But you're as good as he is."

"No. No. There's something wrong. Something missing. I've been thinking about it all summer long. I saw some work before I left New York . . . things they're doing in France . . . with color and light. If I could get to Paris, study with someone . . ."

She fought back her tears, feeling helpless to ease his anguish. Reaching up, she pushed back the lock of black hair that had fallen over his forehead. "Why does your hair always fall in your eyes?" she whispered.

He stared at her for a moment, then pulled her into his arms, clutching her fiercely to his chest. He kissed her hard, his mouth pressing on hers, taking, demanding all the comfort she could give. When she felt the tip of his tongue probing gently she parted her lips, welcoming the thrilling sensation of his possession.

Her mouth was his. Her heart was his.

He grunted in anger and thrust her away. "I must be losing my mind!"

"What . . . what do you mean?" she gasped, swaying unsteadily.

He smiled in mockery. "I nearly forgot. At my peril." He turned about and snatched up the drawing of her. "Look," he said, sketching rapidly. "I've given you a tiara. And diamond earrings. It's a pity I didn't draw you full-figure. I would have dressed you in a ball gown." His blue eyes were cold and hard. "That *is* what you want, isn't it?"

She'd never cursed in her life before. "Damn you," she said softly, "I *will* go after Heyson!" She stared down at the pot of coffee that was boiling furiously over the fire. Drawing back her boot, she kicked it viciously and sent it flying, then raced into the woods so he wouldn't see her weep.

She had to stay away from him, she decided. Yet the following week, during an outing, she was at the river's edge with him, sharing a sight she knew would delight him.

"You see, Drew? What did I tell you?" Marcy leaned over the grassy bank and pointed to the rocks in the shallow riverbed.

"I'll be damned." Drew knelt beside her, frowning into the water. "Look at the way they catch the sunlight! Like blue-green fire. I never saw anything sparkle so." He scooped up a pebble from the riverbed, turning it back and forth in his hand. "You have to hold it just right to make it shine."

"I told you. It goes on that way for miles. That's why they call it the Opalescent River."

"But what is it?"

"I always called it the shiny rocks. But Mr. Heyson gave it a funny name when he took some samples yesterday. Lab . . . lab . . . labradorite, I think he said."

Drew chuckled. "Leave it to George Heyson to take the romance out of everything! Is that *all* you were doing? Looking at rocks?"

She sat up and wrapped her arms around her bent knees. "I told you last week I don't want to talk about it."

"You also told me you didn't want me to kiss you anymore. But I don't believe it. I think you've been avoiding me."

"Why should I do that?"

He laughed. "Because you're stubborn. And you can't let on that you want to change your mind."

She leaned forward and stared into the river, unwilling to look at him. She'd never felt so miserable in all her life. He'd made it clear, often enough. He was too poor to marry. And even if—by some wonderful miracle—he *did* marry her, he'd hate her soon enough, because it wasn't what he wanted. He wanted to paint. He wanted to go to Paris. He didn't want a wife.

She thought: You're daft, Marcy Tompkins, for even hoping. Marriage. Marriage, indeed! When any fool could see it was all a game to him—the kisses, and the teasing, and the jokes about helping her to find a husband. And she'd made it worse by telling him her idiotic plan.

He was still playing with the labradorite crystal. "It really does look like an opal. It reminds me of your eyes. Blue, then green. And flashing with every change of color."

"That's what my father always said."

He looked at her quizzically. "Do you live in Long Lake with your father?"

"No."

"Mother?"

She gulped. Grief had a way of catching a body unawares. "I live with Uncle Jack," she said softly.

"Your parents?"

"Both . . . dead. An accident."

"Marcy. I'm so sorry."

She felt herself beginning to quiver. She shook her head, fighting off the tears. "It was more than eight months ago. You'd think by now . . ."

"Marcy." He reached out and touched her cheek.

She bit her lip. "Sometimes, I feel so frightened," she whispered. "So alone." She felt a surge of anger. "Sometimes I *hate* these mountains!"

He smiled tenderly. "I'd like to kiss your tears away."

She struggled back from the edge of the black abyss of her fears. She sniffled and wiped her sleeve against her cheeks. "Tarnation! I should have known that's all you think about!"

He grinned. "What else?"

She flopped onto her stomach, her face close to a patch of shining clubmoss. "Look. I always thought they looked like little trees, close up."

He lay down beside her, peering intently at the bright green plants. "So they do."

"I used to play with them when I was younger. The little pods. Here. If you lift the top of one ever so carefully, you can shake out the seeds."

"And the little men, who live among the little trees, will think it's snowing," he said solemnly.

She giggled and rolled over onto her back. "I never thought of that."

He leaned over her, his blue eyes warm on her face. On her lips. "Marcy . . ." He kissed her softly, then deepened his kiss, his chest pressing against her heaving bosom.

No. No. How could she let him kiss her—and the memory of her parents still fresh in her mind? *I have to leave the mountains!* she thought. *I can't think of him. It's hopeless.* She felt as though her brain would explode with the tangled thoughts and longings that crowded in. A great sob rumbled up from her chest. She pushed him roughly from her, feeling overwhelmed by her grief. "Don't *do* that!" she cried, bursting into tears. "I don't want you to do that anymore!"

He sat up, bewildered, and searched her face. "No you don't, do you," he said at last, frowning. The eyes had become blue ice, cold and distant. He rose to his feet. "My mistake. I seem to have . . . misread . . . It won't happen again. I'll see you back at camp." He turned about and moved purposefully toward the path that ran along the river.

Marcy curled herself into a tight ball, sobbing out her unhappy confusion until there were no more tears left.

Chapter
Five

"*A*re you sure you have enough wood for the week, Gramps?" Nat Stanton pushed the wicker wheelchair toward the small cot, and bent to pick up the frail old man.

"Consarn you, boy, get your hands off me! I'm not completely helpless!"

Nat stepped back, watching in concern as the old man struggled out of the wheelchair, leaning heavily on his right arm and leg. His lined face reddened with the effort. He managed at last to fall across the bed, face-downward; after a moment's rest he rolled over and dragged himself to a sitting position, readjusting his useless left arm and leg with his right hand. Nat shook his head. Stubborn old codger, he thought. "The wood, Gramps. Will it last you?"

The clear gray eyes that stared at Nat were astonishingly young under their shaggy white brows. "Why in thunderation not? It's August, not December!"

"I just don't want to find you eating cold mush by the time I come back next Sunday."

"I'll manage. I've eaten cold mush many a time when my

body was still whole, and it didn't kill me! Many's the time I'd be out trapping and didn't have food at all! I don't know why you make such a fuss, boy. I've got my books and my pipe. It's enough."

"I wish I could get you to move closer to town. I'm sure there's someone in Ingles who could..."

"Hell, boy! There's no one in Ingles—or any other fool town—who's worth a tinker's damn!" He peered through the small window at the horse that waited outside. "'Course if it's a question of the time it takes you to get here..."

"Don't be daft."

"The cost of the train ride and renting a horse...?"

"Dammit, Gramps, you know that's not it at all! I worry about you! I don't like to be up there at MacCurdyville all week wondering how you're getting on."

"You worry too much. You'd probably be better off if I was dead."

"Christ, Gramps! What a thing to say."

"You'd be out west now, if it weren't for me and my stroke." The old man pounded the bed. "Damn this useless body of mine!"

Nat walked to the window, stared out at the small clearing among the trees. He thought: Would I feel more free, out west somewhere riding the plains? Or had the dream of going west after the war been only an escape? Eight years since the war. *Eight years*. And still he had nightmares. Of the black-edged letter from the War Department telling him about Dad. Of stumbling across the bloody field of Gettysburg and finding Jed and Pete side by side—brothers together in death as they had been in life. He'd barely made it to the end of the war after that without losing his mind. Those last two years had been a blur of hatred—of senseless battles that took his comrades, of killing.

Yes. The west had seemed an escape. He had wanted to run away, to live out his days on some isolated mountaintop. And then Gramps had had his stroke, and duty—and something else (the need to cling to the last remnants of family?)—had kept him here.

He'd no longer had the heart to be the teacher he'd planned to be. There was still too much anger and bitterness in him. He'd sought work that taxed his body, exhausted his strength, so that at night, falling into bed, he'd sleep without dreams.

"Are you sorry you didn't go west, boy?"

Nat turned, and shook his head. "No. Someone has to stay. I hate what's happening, how the Wilderness is being torn up. But without industry, the towns would die." He clenched his fist. "And, by God, if I can make enough money, maybe I'll have the power to change things!"

"You're getting on as clerk for old man Bradford?"

Nat paced the room. "It's not the job for me. I'm used to working up a sweat, dealing with the men. Not counting sacks of flour or flattering a banker. But I have the feeling Bradford will put me in Clegg's position when he retires. He's taking me down to Saratoga with him on Sunday night. For a few weeks of business. Some deal with a banker. He wants me to be there."

"Does that mean I won't see you next Sunday?"

"Of course not. Bradford's railroad car will pick me up at Ingles on Sunday night, after our visit. And while I'm at Saratoga, I'll still arrange to come up to see you."

"That's a long haul. I don't like to see you taxing yourself for me."

Nat smiled mockingly. "In a pig's eye, you don't! I wouldn't dare suggest that I could have someone else look in on you, bring you supplies, while I'm in Saratoga!"

The old man chuckled, clearly pleased with himself. "Hand me my pipe, boy. By the way, what about Bradford's filly? You don't talk much about her."

"She's fine to work with. Quick, smart as a whip, able as a man. More suited to the job than I am. But sometimes I can't figure her out."

The old man cackled. "What's to figure out with a woman? You kiss 'em often enough, and give 'em a smack on the tail if they don't behave!"

Nat laughed. "I think she'd have a fit if I so much as touched her hand."

"She sounds like a cold bitch."

"No. Sometimes I think it's because she's a rich girl, looking down her nose at me. And then I see a look on her face, and damned if I don't think she's afraid of me. That's the thing of it. There's something inside her that so's gentle. And fragile." He sighed. "She has the most beautiful eyes I've ever seen," he said softly.

"You're not sweet on her, are you, boy?"

"Good God! I'm not even sure I *like* her! She always manages to rile me up, and then I lose my temper and pretty soon we're quarrelling." He frowned. "I get so damned tired of the battles. One way or another, I always seem to be fighting a war."

"Will you ever find peace, Nat?" The old man's voice was gentle.

Nat rubbed his hand across his eyes. "I hope to God I do," he said hoarsely. "I'm getting older, Gramps. I'll be thirty-one in November. I feel as if I've lost my youth in the war, and there's no time to get it back."

"Hell, boy. What you need is a wife. You ought to marry and settle down. A good woman under the covers keeps a man young!"

"I haven't found the right girl yet." He picked up his hat. "I'll see you next Sunday." He kissed his grandfather on the forehead and went out to his waiting horse. He found himself suddenly whistling.

It was odd, but the only thing he could think about at that very moment was the blue-violet of Willough's eyes.

"Mr. Collins, do you want a sample of this fern?" Holding her knife poised above the luxuriant growth, Marcy looked up at Ed Collins.

He grunted his assent and continued to peer thoughtfully at the young maple tree before him. He ran his fingers along the bark and rubbed his chin. He looks like a schoolmaster, thought Marcy, resisting the urge to giggle. They had spent

half the day tramping through the brush, while Mr. Collins
had made a great show of his knowledge of "woodland lore,"
as he called it. What a silly ass, she thought. She cut off a
frond of the fern and popped it into the special envelope he
had given her, then stuffed the envelope into his knapsack,
which lay on the ground. He cleared his throat. She knew
what was coming. Another lecture on some plant that she
had grown up with, while she forced herself to smile and
pretend it was all new to her, so he wouldn't take offense.
He *was* a paying customer, after all. Still, she was glad she'd
never made a try for him when she'd first dreamed up her
harebrained scheme. She didn't know how he was in the city,
but in the woods he was less than useless.

She sighed. She regretted the whole stupid affair. Not that
she didn't still feel the aching need to leave the mountains.
But the silly business about catching a rich husband, and then
telling Drew about it . . . She sighed again, gulping back her
tears. Drew. Cold and indifferent. He had drawn away from
her since that day at the Opalescent River, when she'd cried.
She longed for the devil-may-care Drew she had grown used
to. The Drew she had laughed with.

Don't be a fool, Marcy, she thought. It was just as well
that they'd reached this pass. There was only a little more
than a week remaining of the Marshalls' expedition. It would
be easier to forget Drew if they spent these last few days as
strangers. She had even managed to talk Alonzo into taking
Drew out fishing while she tramped the woods with Collins.

"Look at this, Marcy," said Collins pompously. He tapped
at the bark of the maple tree. "Look at these peculiar marks.
Like torn spots, but quite regular in size and shape. A disease,
no doubt, that has attacked the maple. I've seen carbuncles
like these on a crabapple tree. Perhaps we ought to take a
sample of the bark."

Oh, bosh! she thought. Paying customer or not, she couldn't
listen to any more twaddle! "It's squirrels," she said dryly.

"Squirrels?"

"In the spring they like the maple sap. They chew through
a bit of the bark, then scoot down aways and lick up the sap

as it flows. They use their front teeth to gnaw—that's why all the cuts look the same."

"Oh." He laughed sheepishly. "I guess you figure us all for fools. Though I suppose Lewis is familiar with this."

"How did you come to know the Marshalls? Did you study with Dr. Marshall at his college?"

"No. They're friends of my father's. After I left Harvard I began to take an interest in botany. Dr. Marshall very kindly guided my studies." He mopped at his forehead. "God, it's hot! I'm mighty sorry I lost my top hat in the rapids." He examined a tear in his trousers. "I should have listened to Drew, and worn old clothes." He shook his head. "I think Drew has owned that coat and waistcoat since our days at school together!"

"*Drew* went to Harvard College?"

"Yes. We took rooms in the same house."

"Uncle Jack says it takes a heap of money to go to that school. Drew must have had a fine benefactor."

Collins chuckled. "He did. Ever hear of the MacCurdy Ironworks?"

"Of course. After they closed the furnace at Tahawas a lot of the men started going over to MacCurdyville to work. He owns a lumbermill down at Glens Falls, too, I think."

"Who does?" Collins was smiling broadly.

"The ... the owner." She frowned. "I think his name is ..." What was it? Bingham? No. Bradley? "Brad ... Bradford!" she gasped aloud.

"The very same. Drew's daddy."

She rocked on her heels and sat down hard in the clump of ferns. A Bradford! And all that talk about the "poor artist" who couldn't support a wife—it must have been part of the game for him! Tarnation! There was no reason why they couldn't get married. She could change his mind. They'd be good for each other. She could make him see that. She nearly laughed aloud, her heart singing with joy. And all this time she'd been afraid to let herself love him, thinking that marriage was impossible for him.

She got to her feet and grinned, brushing the leaves from

the seat of her britches. "Are you just about set to go back to camp, Mr. Collins?" She wanted to see Drew. To tell him what was in her heart. She almost ran back to their campsite; Collins, gasping for breath, begged her to go more slowly.

Drew was sitting on a rock, drawing pictures in the sand with a long stick, when they emerged into the clearing.

Marcy knelt beside him, smiled brightly up at him. "How was your fishing?"

He shrugged. "We came up empty-handed. Unless the others were luckier, we'll have to settle for flapjacks and salt pork for supper."

"Alonzo doesn't know the good fishing holes. Remember how many trout you caught the day you and I went out?"

His blue eyes were cold. "Just luck."

"No. You said I was a siren, tempting all the fish."

He stood up and erased his sand drawing with the tip of his boot. "Did I? I don't remember."

She looked longingly up at him. "Do you want me to pose for you right now?" She smiled with what she hoped was a seductive expression. "I promise I won't talk, so you can draw my mouth."

His lip curled in disgust. "What's the matter? Didn't Collins take the bait?"

"What are you talking about?"

He flung the stick into the lake. "I didn't really think I was the only one who went fishing this afternoon. You managed that very well—being alone with Ed."

She felt her heart sink at the anger in his voice. "No. Drew ... please..." she said softly. "You don't understand...."

"I'm going for a walk," he said. "Alone, if you don't mind. Tell Old Jack I'll be back in time for supper." He turned on his heel and strode off down the trail.

She felt like crying. If she could only take back that day at the river. She thought: We're right for each other. I know it!

But it would never happen if she couldn't break through that wall he'd put up. Maybe tomorrow she'd think of something.

One morning several days later Drew was alone, sketching as usual, but the work was not going well. He threw down his charcoal and cursed. He couldn't concentrate today. Most of the others were gone for the whole morning: Heyson and Stafford and their guides hunting for grouse, the Marshalls and Collins on a trek up the side of Hay Stack Mountain, Old Jack off to Clintonville for fresh supplies. He didn't know where Marcy was, and he wasn't sure he cared. He stood up and stretched.

The view was beautiful from here. The sandy beach where they'd camped was on the edge of a calm, shallow bend of the Ausable River, which formed a glassy pool. He could hear the faint roar of a waterfall in the distance (Old Jack had said they'd have to carry the boats around the falls), but this spot was serene. Then why couldn't he concentrate?

Well, perhaps he'd follow the river for awhile, see what the falls looked like; the exercise might clear the cobwebs from his brain.

The "carry" was some yards back from the riverbank; following the well-beaten path, he could only catch glimpses of the river as it flowed along, picking up speed. He saw a patch of white water, then the trees obscured his view again. The roaring increased in intensity. He knew he must be very near the falls now. The path dipped sharply down, and suddenly he was in the open again, below the waterfall.

"My God," he whispered, and stepped back into the shadow of the trees.

Below the falls was a foam-filled pool. Marcy was there, washing her hair. Naked. The morning sun glinted on her firm young body, and when she stepped under the falls to rinse her soapy hair, the water cascaded off her breasts, setting rainbows to arching in the sun-touched spray. Her skin was radiant and tanned; her wet hair flowed down her back and glowed like burnished mahogany. He caught his breath, enchanted—and disturbed more than he wanted to admit. He couldn't stand here all day watching her. Quietly he turned about and retraced his steps.

Damn her! he thought, as a sudden idea crossed his mind.

Had it been *deliberate*? Had she wanted him to see her? He
remembered he'd told her, half joking, that that was the way
to catch a man. Was that exhibition meant for him?

But why? He'd made it clear enough he had no money.
She didn't know about his father's "conditions," and he wasn't
about to tell her. Maybe she *didn't* care about a rich husband.
He shook his head, as if to rid it of all the confusion. None
of it made sense. She seemed to be a naive innocent—a child
of nature. Was that false? She had responded to his kisses;
he was sure of it. Dammit, he was sure of it! But . . . maybe
that was false. And the last time he'd kissed her. Her tears.
The pain and grief in her eyes. Surely *that* hadn't been false.

He sighed and leaned up against a tree. And this nonsense
about catching a rich husband. He'd treated it as a joke at
first. She was so young. So stubborn, with a crazy idea fixed
in her head. But maybe her desire ran more deeply than he
thought.

He plucked morosely at a leaf. If he could only pick and
choose those traits that drew him to her—to say to himself
these qualities make the real Marcy—and reject the others,
separate the ambitious Marcy from the girl he'd grown to
love.

Love. How easily the word had come into his thoughts.
Love. It had never crossed his mind before. All the pretty
New York belles he'd courted and kissed. And bedded. But
they never laughed, any of them, the way Marcy laughed.
They never wept at a sunset, or whistled back to a loon. They
pouted over a torn hem, and squealed at the gift of a lace
handkerchief, though their sachet-scented bureaus might be
stuffed with a hundred lace handkerchiefs. And Marcy wanted
to be like that? It didn't seem to fit, somehow.

Yet when she spoke about leaving the mountains to go to
the city, there was a dark intensity in her that was almost
frightening. It wasn't just a passing fancy. It was a hunger.
He frowned and stared at his hands, smudged from his charcoal. A hunger he couldn't begin to satisfy.

She had the right idea. Ed Collins or even Heyson could
give her what she wanted, though all her joy and laughter

might be stifled in their staid, conventional world. Yes. That was the best course for her. God knows a struggling painter couldn't offer her anything.

But why had she begun to tantalize him? He was almost sure he wasn't imagining it—the coy smiles, the girlish giggles, the sidelong glances and sighs these last few days. It was so artificial it made him sick. He wanted to grab her, and shake her and shake her until the mask fell away and tears sprang to her eyes. And then he'd kiss the tears away and hold her in his arms and—

Oh God! he thought. Let me just get out of here. Get to Paris. Before I go mad with wanting her!

He groaned, remembering. That body. That beautiful body, caressed by the river, kissed by the sunlight.

"Get out of my life, Marcy Tompkins," he whispered. "Get out of my life!"

And keep her out of his life he did, until two days before the end of the trip. Marcy was in total despair.

"Oh, Uncle Jack, I've lost him!" She sat down on a moss-covered log and buried her face in her hands.

"What's that, girl?" Old Jack squinted at the twilight sky, adjusted the brace of rabbits on his shoulder and leaned on his upright rifle. "Lost who?"

She looked up at him, her eyes brimming with tears. "I don't know what to do. And it's too late! I only have tomorrow and the next day. And then he'll be gone forever!"

"Tarnation, girl! Who?"

"Drew."

"I thought you two got along just fine."

"Not anymore. I . . . said something. A couple of weeks ago. And now I'm sorry. But it's too late! I've tried every way I could think of, but he's just . . ."

"Is that why you said you'd come out with me?"

"I had to talk to someone. I don't know what else to do."

"Well, if we're going to talk for a bit, you'd better fetch out your pocket lantern. It looks like it'll be dark before we get back to camp."

She pulled from her pocket a small copper lantern and a

candle. Unfolding the lantern, she inserted the candle, then brought out a box of matches. "I don't think we need it yet."

"All right. Now tell me about Drew."

"It's just that . . ." She felt herself blushing. "He's the one I want to marry."

"Did you tell him?"

"No. I was going to, and now . . . now he's angry with me and I can't talk to him and now I'll lose him!" She had begun to cry again.

"Dag nab it girl, tell him!"

"I've tried every which way I can, and now we're going home the day after tomorrow! What'll I do, Uncle Jack?"

He shook his head. "The only way *I* know to catch a man and keep him hooked is at the end of a shotgun!"

Her eyes widened in astonishment. "I'll be jiggered! Why not?"

"Have you taken leave of your senses?"

"No. Listen, Uncle Jack. You know how Mrs. Marshall has behaved toward Drew all summer long. Like he was some sort of scoundrel. Well, since tomorrow's our last full day, Drew wants to spend it on the island in the middle of Clear Pond. He thinks he can get a good view of Owl's Head from there. I said I'd go with him." She gulped. "Though I don't think he wanted me," she added unhappily. "Anyway, why can't I . . . cast our boat adrift when he's not looking? You can keep the rest of 'em from looking for us until it's too dark. Then, in the morning, when you find us on the island, you can make a big fuss about our being together all night. Alone." She looked down at her hands, ashamed of her own wickedness. "You know what I mean," she said softly. "And Mrs. Marshall will raise the cry and then . . . then he'll *have* to marry me!"

"Good God, Marcy! *No!*"

She sniffled. "I know it's awful of me. But I want him so much, Uncle Jack. I'm just plumb aching for him. This is my last chance. And it'll be good. You'll see. I'll be the best wife for him he could ever have!"

"I won't do it, Marcy!"

"I'll probably burn in Hell, but . . . Oh, please, Uncle Jack. Please! I don't know how else to get him."

He grumbled and looked up at the darkening sky. "I must be the jackass of all time. Light that fool lantern and come on."

"But . . . Drew?"

"Hell! You know I can't refuse you. And I can't talk you out of it once you've set your mind to a thing." He sighed. "If he's what you want, girl, he'll find himself at the end of my rifle and in front of a preacher before he has time to pull his wits together! Now come on, before it gets too late to cook these rabbits for supper."

As she had planned, Marcy took over as Drew's guide the next day.

"The boat'll be fine here, Drew," she told him as she splashed ashore on Clear Pond Island, surveying the narrow spit of sand. Good. She couldn't see the camp from here. That meant that they couldn't be seen by the others either, so there was no way that a signal fire would do them any good tonight. Tonight. She took a deep breath. She thought: I don't want to think about *that*! But if she played her part right, Drew would never suspect it had been planned. He'd just think they'd been stranded by accident. She doubted he'd try to take advantage of her just because they were alone; he'd always been a gentleman. Not like that skunk Stafford, who'd pawed her the first minute he could.

Drew pulled in the oars, slung his painting satchel over his shoulder, and followed her out of the boat. He tugged at the rope and pulled the craft well up onto the shore. "Why don't we get it out of the water altogether? Maybe turn it over, in case it rains?"

"No!" She bit her lip nervously when Drew frowned at the sharpness of her reply. "That is . . . I figure on going out to catch us some fish for lunch."

"Oh. Of course." He glanced around at the thick vegetation and leafy trees that crowded the small beach. "Is this the only clear patch on the whole island?"

"No. The center of the island is a big flat rock covered

with moss. It's a lot higher than this spot. You'll be able to see Owl's Head much better from there."

"Is there a path?"

"Not so you could pick it out. The whole place is covered with witch-hopple, and it grows so fast. Follow me, but watch where you're going. It'll trip you, if you're not careful." She led the way through the tangled undergrowth of shiny leaves and bright berries, walking cautiously to avoid the ground-level runners and roots that lay hidden beneath the greenery.

When at last they emerged onto the moss-covered clearing, Drew put down his satchel and glanced back at the witch-hopple. "That was rough going," he said. "I nearly tripped half a dozen times! What did you call it?"

"Witch-hopple. Dr. Marshall calls it hobblebush." She smiled. "But it helped us win a war."

"What do you mean?"

"My father used to tell the story all the time. In the War of Independence, when our men had to escape from the British at Ticonderoga. The American troops blocked the road with felled trees, so the British were pushed into the woods. It took them nearly a month just to go fifty miles!"

"Because of the witch-hopple."

"That's what everyone says."

He grinned. "The British must have been city slickers like me."

Her heart melted. She hadn't seen him smile like that in weeks. She thought: Maybe I don't have to trick him. Maybe I can just tell him how I feel, the way Uncle Jack said. "Drew," she said softly, "you're going home tomorrow. I'd be very pleased if . . . if you'd kissed me good-bye."

His black eyebrows arched cynically. "Really? And could I get a warranty beforehand that my kiss wouldn't make you cry?"

She was feeling desperate. "I didn't meant anything by my tears. Truly! It was just a bit of silliness that day. I was *funning* you! I laughed about it the moment you were gone."

"I didn't think you were a liar on top of everything else," he growled. "I walked back to the river five minutes later that day. The girl who didn't want me to kiss her anymore was still crying her heart out!" He pulled off his hat and threw it to the ground. "Oh for God's sake, Marcy, leave me alone. I want to paint. If you stay here, keep your mouth shut and don't let me see you!"

Dang you, Drew Bradford! she thought miserably. You just brought it on yourself. "I'll go fishing now," she said. "I'll build a fire on the beach and bring you the cooked fish along about noon. Do you have enough water in your canteen?"

He nodded. "And a small tin of biscuits."

"All right. It could be afternoon before I get back. It depends on the fish."

From his satchel he pulled out a pad of paper and his box of watercolors, then opened his canteen and poured a bit of water into a small cup. Setting his brushes into the water, he put the cup down on the rock, positioned himself facing Owl's Head, and sat cross-legged with his paints spread out in front of him. "I'll manage," he said coldly, and bent to his sketch-pad.

Though she caught enough fish for lunch—and supper besides—in the first half hour, Marcy stayed out on the water a long time. She wasn't eager to return to Drew: If lunch was late, he would lose track of the time, and linger till amost dark on the rock. And her conscience was gnawing at her for her underhanded scheme. If she spent too much time with him, he would surely sense her uneasiness.

I love him, she thought. I've got to keep that in my head.

She beached the boat and carefully unloaded their supplies: The provision basket, extra clothing and blankets, their rifles and gear. She made a small fire and cleaned and cooked up several of the fish, set some coffee to boiling. She packed a few utensils in a knapsack, then scattered the fire so it would go out.

She took a deep breath and turned to the beached boat. "I'm sorry, Drew," she whispered, and set the boat adrift, pushing it far enough into the current so it wouldn't return to the island. Then she picked up the coffeepot and the skillet of fish, and went off to give Drew his lunch.

After he had eaten Drew returned to his watercolors. He had already done half a dozen views of Owl's Head, and was now concentrating on Clear Pond and the surrounding hills and trees. Some of the pictures he finished to his satisfaction, putting in the final details with a delicate brush and nearly dry paint. But other pictures, Marcy knew, were meant only as studies for paintings he would later enlarge in his studio, working them up in oils. These pictures were lightly sketched, the colors merely suggested with dabs of paint, the margins filled with notations in his neat, precise hand.

Marcy watched him paint, trying not to disturb him, fascinated equally by his skill and the solemn intensity he brought to his work.

At last the light began to fade. Drew looked up with a start. "Good grief, it must be nearly eight o'clock! We'd better be getting back to the others." While Marcy gathered their lunch supplies, he packed up his equipment, carefully tucking the finished paintings into the center of the sketchpad. The trek back to the beach was laborious; the leafy gloom had already begun to obscure the treacherous hobblebush.

The beach was still lit by the sun's afterglow. Drew looked around and frowned. "Where the devil's our boat?"

"Tarnation!" she said, trying to sound surprised. "Maybe I didn't pull it in far enough when I came back from fishing! It must have drifted away."

"Damn! Is there any way we can signal them back at the camp?"

"What do you mean?"

"A bonfire, maybe."

"They won't see it from here."

"What about on top of the rock?"

She shook her head. "No. Too many trees on the other side of the island."

"I don't suppose we could fire off a rifle."

"We're too far away. They wouldn't know where the sound was coming from."

He dropped his hat and satchel to the beach, and began to

rebuild the small campfire. "I guess we're stuck here for the night. And no supplies." He struck a match to the kindling.

"Don't worry about it, Drew. They'll find our boat adrift on the lake in the morning. And Uncle Jack will figure out what happened. I caught enough fish this morning for our supper. I'll have a mess of flapjacks going in no time, to go with them. While there's still some light left, why don't you see if you can find a few big logs to keep the fire going all night?"

"Right." He stood up and headed for the edge of the clearing. "I just hope it doesn't get too cold tonight."

She pointed to the mound of supplies. "We'll be as snug as can be. Look. Blankets and everything. I'll get supper started right away. Mind you don't trip on that witch-hopple."

He returned a few minutes later with his arms full of wood, which he set near the fire. Marcy looked up from the pancake batter she was mixing and smiled at him. She was surprised to see a scowl on his face. He had seemed in good spirits, not at all put out by their being stranded. She put aside the batter and stood up. "Do you want to help me set up our supplies near the fire?"

"I want to talk to you first."

"About what?" She felt her heart fluttering nervously.

"I've been thinking. It was mighty lucky for us you unloaded the boat."

"Well, I had to. I took out the provision basket to make lunch."

"And the rifles?"

"I figured they'd be safer out of the boat." Drat! Her voice was shaking.

He peered into her eyes. "Safer from whom? We're on an island. If you were concerned, you would have brought them along to the rock. And what about the blankets?"

She turned away from him, fearful of his searching gaze. "Tarnation!" she said belligerently. "What's all the fuss? It makes the boat lighter for fishing! Now let me get back to my flapjacks."

He grabbed at her arm and turned her back. "We've fished

from a loaded boat many times! What's in that crazy head of yours, Marcy?"

"Let me go, Drew."

"Was it deliberate?" He put his hand on her other shoulder and shook her. "*Was* it? Did you let the boat go on purpose?"

She laughed, a forced, silly giggle. "Drew Bradford! What a thing to say!"

"My God, it was! I can see it in your eyes."

"Bosh!"

"How would you like a good spanking?" he said through clenched teeth.

Her eyes widened in horror. She tried to pull away from his steely grip. "You wouldn't!"

"Then I want some answers. And pretty damn fast! Did you let the boat go on purpose?" She nodded. "Why?"

"Please, Drew..."

"Was anything supposed to happen here tonight?"

"I...don't know...I..." She felt her cheeks burning.

"Good God," he breathed. "I don't believe it. Am I to be accused in the morning of being a cad? Is that it?" His hands tightened on her arms. "*Is* it?"

"Yes." The word dragged out of her.

He let her go, fighting to keep his control. "And Old Jack. Is he in on the game?" he asked in disgust.

She nodded, wishing the earth could swallow her up.

"And what was to be my punishment?"

"Marriage," she whispered.

"Damn!" He ran his fingers through his hair. "Prodded along by your uncle's shotgun, of course." His blue eyes were like ice, burning and chilling her at the same time. "Why?"

She gulped. "Because your name is Bradford."

"Ah." Silence. "But my name was always Bradford," he said at last. "And you looked right through me. When did 'Bradford' begin to have the chink of gold about it?"

"When...Mr. Collins told me..."

"Yes. Of course. The afternoon I went fishing with Alonzo. I should have guessed when I saw you bathing at the falls—

I *was* meant to see you, wasn't I?" She looked away, fighting back her tears. "Answer me!" he barked.

"Y—Yes."

"And all those coquettish scenes . . . like a clumsy, cheap seductress . . ." He laughed bitterly. "You never saw me as a man." He turned away, his shoulders sagging. "At first I was your chum, helping you nail your rich man, amusing you with my kisses. Then I was a pile of greenbacks. You never saw me as a man." He turned back to her, his eyes glowing with hurt and rage. "And now I'm to be tied and spitted in the morning. The reluctant bridegroom. It's like some shabby melodrama."

"Drew . . . I didn't mean . . ."

His lip curled in a cruel grimace that made her tremble. "How much am I supposed to do? Is there a limit to my debauchery in Old Jack's eyes?"

She backed away, fearful of what she read in his face.

He reached for her. "If I'm to be skewered in the morning, I won't settle for a dumb show. We'll play out the act tonight, so you can look convincingly violated when Old Jack turns up tomorrow!"

Terrified, she turned and raced down the beach. She was no match for his long strides; he pounded after her and swiftly overtook her. Swinging her around by one arm, he threw her to the sand and fell on top of her. "Now . . . is *this* what you want?" His hand clutched painfully at her breast. "And this?" His other hand plunged between her legs, pushing upward at the juncture of her trousers. She whimpered and tried to push him off her, but he grabbed her wrists and forced her hands down to the sand. "Damn you, Marcy," he growled, and closed his mouth over hers. She struggled vainly against him. Her lips hurt from the savagery of his kiss. When he raised his head at last she could taste blood in her mouth.

"Drew, I beg you . . ." Her voice was a pitiful cry.

He stared for a moment, then released her and stood up. He bent down and scooped up a blanket. "I'll sleep on the rock," he said tiredly. He stormed into the woods; she could hear his crashing progress toward the center of the island.

She sat up shaking, too frightened, too horrified at her own behavior even to cry. She thought: What have I done? She'd been playing a child's game with a man's life. A man she loved. She moved unsteadily to the campfire and knelt down, mechanically building up the fire, continuing with her supper preparations, cooking the flapjacks and frying the fish. She made enough for two; he'd never find his way to the rock in the dark. She felt numb, as if her heart had turned to ice.

She ate a bit of supper, though she had no recollection of the taste; then sat, staring dry-eyed into the fire, until Drew stumbled back into the clearing. She was afraid to look at him directly, but she could see out of the corner of her eye that his sleeve was torn and his arm had a long scratch.

He marched to the fire and angrily threw down his blanket, then knelt beside her and reached for some food. He wrapped a fish in a flapjack and ate it silently, washing it down with a cup of coffee.

And then her tears started. She had promised herself she wouldn't cry: it would only add to her shame. But the tears came anyway. She sniffled quietly—she'd die if he knew she was crying. She sat very still and watched a large teardrop slide down and perch on the tip of her nose. She twitched her nose slightly. The drop remained. It was beginning to tickle. She was afraid she'd sneeze. Very slowly she raised one hand to her nose, poking out a cautious finger to dab at the offending tear. Finger to her nose, she looked up. Drew was watching her.

"Oh God," he said, and burst into laughter.

"Stop laughing," she said, sobbing.

He shook his head. "What am I going to do with you? Don't cry."

"I'm not crying!" she wailed, and fell into his arms. She stayed there, warmed and comforted by his strong embrace, until the fit of crying passed. Then she pulled away, sniffling and wiped her eyes against her sleeve.

"Don't use your shirt. Here." He pulled out his handkerchief, mopping at her eyes and wiping her nose. He smiled ruefully. "My funny, foolish Marcy, with your cocked-hat schemes. You never needed them. All you have to do is look at a man"—he devoured her with his eyes, "and he can't help falling in love with you." He bent his head and kissed her softly.

"But you kept saying you didn't want to marry. I didn't think you cared about me."

"*Cared* about you? My God. You make me laugh, you make me feel alive, like there's nothing I can't do when I'm with you."

"Oh Drew..." She lay back on the sand and pulled him down to her, caressing the silken softness of the hair that curled at his neck.

"Marcy," he whispered. He kissed her again, his soft tongue caressing the edge of her lips so she trembled at the sensation. He trailed kisses across her cheek, then gently turned her head with his hand so he could kiss her ear. She smiled to herself, remembering that first day when he had blown in her ear and ruined Uncle Jack's hunting. It was nice to recall that he had wanted to kiss her ears even then. She closed her eyes, enjoying the feel of his mouth, then gasped aloud as a shiver ran through her body. He had plunged his tongue into her ear, and was now moving it in small circles, tantalizing and teasing with every gentle stroke. She could feel her heart beating wildly and a strange tickling had begun in her throat.

"Oh, please..." she breathed, and pushed him away. It was almost too agonizing to endure.

He laughed and sat up. "I always knew your ears were beautiful. I didn't think they were that sensitive! I can't imagine what the rest of you is like!"

She looked at him through half-closed eyes. How beautiful he was. His face in the firelight was strong and angular, elegant with its patrician nose and wide mouth. She had never wanted anyone or anything as much as she wanted him. She sat up in her turn and smiled, slowly unbuttoning her shirt. "Why don't you find out?"

He watched her, his eyes smoldering, as she pulled the shirt free of her britches and tossed it aside. Then he reached out and stroked her bare shoulder. His hand was hot, burning her flesh. His long fingers traced a path from her shoulder across her collarbone to her other shoulder, and then down her arm till it reached her hand. He lifted her fingers to his lips and kissed them one by one. She trembled and quivered with each kiss and caress, her body on fire with a longing, a need she hardly understood. And each time he touched her, it made the longing harder to bear, more intense and painful, yet oddly seeming to bring her closer to the release of those feelings. With gentle hands she pushed him away and un-fastened the two small buttons of her chemise, wriggling out of the top of it so it bunched around her waist.

"Wait," he said. He rose and picked up a blanket, spreading it out on a smooth patch of sand farther away from the fire. He knelt to her and gathered her in his arms. She hadn't realized how strong he was; she felt very small and fragile as he carried her to the blanket and laid her gently down. He pulled down his suspenders, then stripped off his shirt and undervest. His body was smooth and sleek, the skin like taut silk over surprisingly muscular arms and shoulders. The broad expanse of his chest was broken only by a large hairy patch in the middle, black and thick like the hair on his head. The thought of that chest pressing on her naked breasts gave Marcy a jolt down to her toes. She stretched out her arms to him, eager to feel his strong body on top of her own. Instead, he laughed softly and lay down beside her. "No," he said. "I want to find out first how sensitive you are." His hand reached out to caress one breast, cupping the firm orb in his palm while his thumb traced lazy circles around the nipple.

She sucked in her breath. "Dang you," she choked, strain-ing against him. "That drives me wild!"

He chuckled. "Good." His hand moved to her other breast. "I always suspected you were a hot little creature. I intend to drive you wilder before I'm through!"

She twisted away from his hand. "You lop-eared devil! Maybe I won't let you."

He grinned. "You're not going to have any say in the matter, you little tease! I reckon I owe you for that scene at the waterfall. You haven't minded teasing *me* this past week.

Now the devil is going to get his due." Despite her struggling, he pinned her hands to her sides and bent his mouth to her breasts, kissing, nipping gently with strong teeth until she thought she would go mad.

She writhed in delicious torment. "Oh Drew ... stop ..." But of course she didn't want him to stop. And of course he knew it. It seemed a wonderful extension of all the games and teasing of the past weeks. But this was a grown-up game. With the man she loved. And now he was loving her back, turning her insides to jelly with his mouth and hands. "Stop ..." she breathed half-heartedly.

He released her hands and smiled at her. His eyes glowed by the light of the fire. "I haven't even begun to explore all your sensitive spots. For example ..." His hand slid down her belly and moved to the inner edge of her thigh, scratching tantalizingly at the soft juncture. Even through two layers of clothing the sensation was exquisite. She shuddered.

"You varmint," she gasped, "you timber wolf ..." She reached for him and curled her fingers into his hair, tugging at his head until his face was poised above hers. She slid her hands about his shoulders and pulled him down to her. His chest was hot against her naked breasts, and when she moved beneath him she could feel the delicious tickle of his coarse hair on her flesh. He kissed her hard and she responded, stroking the firm skin of his back and shoulders, glorying in the feel of his muscles rippling just below the surface. But when he softened his kiss, his lips parting gently, she attacked, thrusting her tongue determinedly between his teeth, savoring the sweet moistness of his mouth. His body stiffened in surprise, and then he wrapped his arms about her, half lifting her as she lay, holding her tightly to his heaving chest while his mouth responded to hers. When at last their lips parted and he released her she could see that he was trembling. He struggled to his knees, then stood up; he stood for a moment, breathing hard, before reaching down and pulling her to her feet. His torso was covered with a thin coat of sweat and his eyes glittered with passion. He raised one mocking eyebrow and smiled, his glance sweeping her body. "Now, you imp,"

he growled, "how fast can you get out of those britches before
I have to tear them off you?"

She giggled. They eyed each other warily, savoring the
game. Her hands went to her belt at the same moment he
began to unbutton his own trousers. They never took their
eyes off each other as they pulled off trousers and under-
drawers, then removed their boots and stockings. In a moment
they were standing naked together, laughing like carefree
children.

Drew stepped back to look at her. The grin faded from his
face. "My God," he whispered. "You're glorious." He knelt
in front of her and put his hands on her hips, burying his
face in her bosom.

Her trembling legs refused to support her for another moment. She pulled away from him, dropped to the blanket,
and stretched out, waiting. She wasn't sure what he would
do next, but she trusted him. She loved him. When he pushed
at her thighs to separate them she responded willingly, feeling
his hard shaft on her leg as he covered her body with his.
He began to rock his hips gently, moving up and down so
his member rubbed against the delicate softness of her. She
felt a throbbing, a wild pulsing that seemed to begin where
he touched her, radiating a warmth that surged through her
whole body. She felt his hardness pressing, demanding entrance, though he seemed to hesitate.

"Yes, Drew. Please," she murmured. "I'm not afraid." He
pushed gently, then thrust hard, sending wild sensations
shooting through her. She had thought her night of clumsy
groping with Zeb had prepared her for the feelng; but, dear
God, she thought, it had been nothing like this! Zeb had
merely touched her; Drew possessed her, filled her with his
throbbing manhood, making her feel helpless and captured—
and strangely triumphant all at the same time. She sighed and
wrapped her arms tightly around him, enjoying the hot fullness of him within her. "Oh, Drew," she sighed again, "that
was wonderful."

He laughed, his voice shaking oddly. "Now I'm *sure* you're
a virgin." Her eyes blinked open in surprise to find him

smiling down at her. "I'm not finished yet," he explained gently.

"Are you teasing me again?"

"It seems to me I haven't teased you enough! Now close your eyes like a good little girl." He kissed her mouth and pressed her lids shut with tender fingers.

Obediently she relaxed beneath him. Whatever came next couldn't be more wonderful than this feeling of being warmed and protected by him. His hips began to move slowly: His hard shaft was suddenly alive, thrusting, gliding, plunging deep so she moaned in pleasure, then withdrawing and waiting, barely touching her. Just when she thought she would scream in frustration, he would enter her again, sometimes with a maddening slowness that caused her to pound at his bare shoulders, sometimes with such force that she cried out for sheer joy.

She began to lose all sense of time; there was only his mouth, his hard body, his throbbing possession of her. His movements quickened. He grasped her shoulders in a grip that was almost painful, plunging into her again and again. She arched her back, meeting him thrust for thrust, then gasped aloud as a deep shudder ran through her body.

"Oh, God, Marcy!" he said, quivering violently. He thrust once more and collapsed against her.

They lay entwined for several moments, then he raised his head and pushed the damp curls back from her forehead. He laughed softly. "Now I'm finished."

She opened her eyes and looked at him. Beautiful Drew. He was still within her. She put her legs together, unwilling to release him. "That *was* wonderful," she breathed.

"I was afraid I might hurt you."

"No. Not at all."

"Not many virgins are so lucky the first time."

"Yes. I guess so." She twitched uncomfortably beneath him.

"Now what? Do you want me to move?"

She put her arms tightly around him. "No!"

"Then what's the matter? Come on, Marce. I know you

well enough to know when something's going on inside that funny little head of yours."

She was glad he couldn't see her blush in the fire's glow. "It's just that . . . dang it, Drew! I'm not sure I *was* a virgin!"

He shook his head. "I can't really believe you've been with a man before. Not this way."

"No. Never! But Zeb . . . he's sort of been my friend in Long Lake, and . . . well, I let him touch me . . . once."

He clucked his tongue. "Did you now? Wicked Marcy."

"Don't laugh. I think something must have happened, because . . . oh, I can't tell you!"

"Did it hurt?" She shook her head. "Well," he continued, "were you bleeding?"

"A little bit, I think."

He stroked the side of her cheek. "Poor Marcy. But I think you can consider yourself still a virgin. At least until tonight. Did you ever tell anyone?"

"I was too embarrassed. But Uncle Jack found out about it anyway."

"What happened to Zeb?"

"Uncle Jack tanned his hide."

"And you got off scot-free, I suppose."

She nodded, filled with guilt.

He grinned. "You're a dangerous female to make love to!"

She gulped, filled with sudden anguish. He hadn't realized how true his words were. Zeb had got a beating. Drew was going to be forced into marriage. She shivered beneath him. "I'm getting cold."

He rolled off her. "I'll bet the water is warm. Come on. Let's go for a swim." He jumped up and hauled her to her feet. They ran, hand in hand, to the dark water of the lake and waded in, enjoying the delicious warmth of the water as it closed around their bodies. They swam for a bit, then Drew stood up, the water reaching his shoulders, and pulled Marcy into his arms. "You know I never can get enough of kissing you," he said hoarsely.

She went to him willingly, giving him her lips, but after a few minutes it was clear that kissing wasn't the only thing he had in mind. She giggled, feeling the insistent hardness poking at her under the water. "If we could only make love in the water," she said. "It would be so cozy."

"Why not?" He pulled her into the shallows and urged her down into the water, then lay on top of her, as the warm current lapped softly over their bodies. This time when he made love to her it was with a tender gentleness that almost made her cry. She had never felt so happy in all her life. When his body had quieted they still lay together beneath the softly rolling waves, until at last Drew roused himself. "Good grief," he said. "If we fall asleep, we'll drown like this. Still joined. And what would poor Mrs. Marshall think then?"

They laughed at the thought, clinging together while their bodies shook with merriment. Still laughing, they stood up and splashed out of the water. Drew fetched a towel from his valise and rubbed Marcy's body briskly, then toweled himself dry while she quickly donned her clothes and pulled their blankets closer to the fire. When Drew was dressed again they lay down side by side, pulling the blankets around them. Drew reached out his hand. Marcy slipped her fingers into his. He smiled tenderly.

"Beautiful Marcy," he whispered. Closing his eyes, he slept.

The smell of coffee woke him. He opened his eyes. Marcy knelt by the fire, tending her skillet. She seemed absorbed in her work, a small frown creasing her forehead; he was able to examine her, through half-closed eyes, without her being aware of it. It astonished him—as it had since that first day—how breathtakingly beautiful she was, and how little she realized it. It was one of the things he loved about her, her naturalness, her innocence of her own charms. She gave her beauty freely to be scrutinized and enjoyed, because it never occurred to her to be coy. Most of the women he had known had far less beauty—but far more conceit about their looks.

And she gave her body freely. He felt himself growing hot, just thinking about their magical night of love. All these weeks he had loved just being with her, laughing and kissing, but last night . . . He closed his eyes, remembering. He had not thought it was possible to feel such passion for a woman.

No, he thought ruefully. Not a woman. A scheming devil. An imp, who probably should have been spanked for her little game. And now he was trapped, forced into a marriage that was wrong for both of them. He had nothing to offer her, no prospects, no real guarantee that he could make a go of it as a painter. He could offer her nothing but the dregs of his own confused search.

And she wanted money. He'd almost forgotten that. She'd only turned to him when she'd found out about the Bradford money. Well, she was in for a rude awakening. He wasn't ready yet to give up his painting and become a dutiful son— Brian Bradford's reluctant partner! Still . . . He felt strangely flattered. It might have been the Bradford name that attracted her, but she could have chosen Heyson or Ed Collins as well. And the passionate creature in his arms last night hadn't been thinking about money. His beautiful Marcy . . .

Don't be a fool! he thought. It was all wrong! A forced marriage. All his reason, all his logic told him it was all wrong. He should be furious with her for ambushing him into this.

Then why did he feel like crowing for joy? Like a child about to take his first ride on a locomotive?

He opened his eyes and sat up. She looked up from her cooking. "If you want a shave, I've boiled some water," she said.

"Not even a good morning?" He moved around her and put his hands about her waist, kissing her gently on the neck.

"Tarnation, Drew! I'll burn the flapjacks," she snapped.

He frowned and let her go. Was she regretting last night already? A girl was a virgin only once. She had come to him willingly, true enough. But she was so young, so naive. Had she really known what she was doing? He cursed his own hungers. He hadn't really thought about it last night. Only his aching love, his need for her. "Where's that hot water?" he said gruffly.

He shaved in silence, eyeing her in the reflection of the

small mirror he had hung up on the broken branch of a tree. Her expression was closed and guarded. Damn! he thought. What's going on in that head of hers now?

"There are no more fish left," she said. "I hope pancakes will be enough for breakfast."

"Look in my knapsack," he said, toweling dry his face. "I still have a bit of plum conserve left."

They ate in silence, looking at their food. But once, when he happened to catch her eye, he saw her blush to the roots of her hair. "Don't look at me like that," she whispered.

He smiled gently. "Someday I'll paint a picture of you— just as you look now. I'll call it 'Marcy blushing.' If I can ever do justice to that color. To that face. You blushed the first time we met. Do you remember? On the path to the boardinghouse. When you called me 'greenhorn.'"

"Please, Drew . . ." she choked.

"What is it?"

"We have to talk. About last night."

Yes, he thought. She had to understand how things really were. "And about my being a Bradford."

"Marcy! Heaven be praised—you're safe!" Old Jack's voice boomed out from the lake.

They looked up. Five boats were coming toward them, four with occupants, one in tow. Marcy stood up and began to pack away the provisions and blankets, keeping her face averted from Drew and the nearing boats. By the time the party had landed and moved up the beach to where they waited, she had extinguished the fire, dumping out the last of their coffee into the sand.

"Of course we're safe, Uncle Jack," she said briskly.

Mrs. Marshall smiled, the mother hen come to collect her lost chick. "We were so worried about you, my dear. And then when we found your boat adrift . . ."

"There was no way of signaling you. But I was quite safe with Mr. Bradford."

Mrs. Marshall snorted and looked with suspicion at Drew. "I have not found Mr. Bradford the sort to inspire confidence!"

Oh, God, thought Drew. Here it comes. He felt like a silent spectator at a familiar play, waiting for the actors to speak their well-known lines. It was time for the outraged uncle.

"And I sure as blazes don't like it!" said Old Jack. (Right on cue!) "You've played mighty free with my niece's affections all summer, young man! And now you've spent the night with her, *alone*!"

Drew felt completely removed from the scene. His fate was already sealed—he had accepted it. With some uneasiness, but accepted it. Now all he had to do was watch the actors play out their parts.

"Alone under questionable circumstances!" said George Heyson primly.

Well done, thought Drew. Another actor in the melodrama.

"It's hardly to be expected that you wouldn't take advantage of Marcy's tender years," said Stafford, his suave voice holding just the edge of venom.

Jealous bastard, thought Drew, fighting the urge to smash his fist into the man's face.

Mrs. Marshall inhaled majestically, pointing a quivering finger at Drew. "It seems to me, Mr. Bradford, that there's nothing left for it except to do right by this young woman!"

Drew nearly laughed aloud. She was stealing Old Jack's line!

He looked at Mrs. Marshall with what he hoped was a sincere and contrite expression. "Are you saying I should marry the girl, ma'am?" He was suddenly tired of the play. Let it end.

"You're darn tootin' you should!" cried Old Jack, throwing down his hat. "And the sooner the better!"

"Stop it! All of you!" Marcy's eyes were blazing, her cheeks two bright spots of angry color. "I won't have this! Mr. Bradford has nothing to be ashamed of!"

Old Jack looked shocked. "Marcy, girl. He's *got* to marry you!"

"No!" She turned to Drew, her blue-green eyes like mountain pools, dark and liquid. "No," she said more softly. "Nothing happened, Uncle Jack. Mr. Bradford is a gentleman."

"But Marcy..."

"Nothing happened, I tell you."

Drew stared at her. What was the little fool saying? "Marcy..."

"No, Drew. I won't have it."

"I should marry you. It's only right."

"I quite agree!" Mrs. Marshall said in a high quaver.

Marcy shook her head. "I won't have you telling lies to be noble, Mr. Bradford. She turned to the others, her chin jutting in stubborn defiance. "Mr. Bradford's a gentleman. I'm not about to ruin a man's reputation and future over something that never happened."

"But Marcy..." Old Jack's voice was a bewildered bleat.

"*Never happened*, Uncle Jack! Now I won't listen to another danged word on the subject!" She snatched up her knapsack and the provision basket and marched to the boats. "If we don't get back to camp soon, we'll never make Long Lake before nightfall!"

Drew watched her go, feeling an odd mixture of relief and disappointment. He thought: I don't understand you, Marcy Tompkins. I don't understand a bit of you!

He stared at her in the boat while she averted her eyes from his, watched her at their base camp while they packed up the last of the supplies, searched her face as they loaded up the boats and prepared to return to Long Lake. At the last moment, she remembered she had left her knife in the lean-to. He mumbled an excuse to the others and followed her back, cornering her in the lean-to before she could escape him. He wrapped his hand around her wrist, pulling her close, and peered into her eyes. "Why, Marcy?" he asked hoarsely.

She smiled up at him, her eyes filled with tears. "Because I love you, Drew," she murmured. "I know you don't want to get married. Rich or poor, you don't want to get married." She gulped and blinked, and the tears ran down her cheeks. "I didn't think love could make you feel so sad...and so happy. And terribly old." She laughed, a tremulous little laugh. "What a child I was, with my silly plans."

His heart was aching. "Oh, God." She was right, of course. He couldn't marry. Not right now. It would be a disaster.

She forced a bright smile, brushing the tears from her cheeks. "Tarnation, Drew! If we don't get back to the boats soon, Mrs. Marshall will start clucking again, the old hen!"

It was twilight when they drew up at the landing of Long Lake. He had sat in a daze the whole way, thinking of her words. She *loved* him! If it had been torture to love her in silence, it was doubly agonizing to know she loved him in return. Nothing could come of it. Not right now. Maybe . . . if he could get to Paris, come home a success . . . he could marry her. He groaned inwardly. But how could he ask her to wait? He sighed. Thank God he was leaving tomorrow morning. Maybe, away from the North Woods, he could begin to forget her.

The boats were unloaded at last. The guides had been paid and, one by one, had said their good-byes and gone home. It was dark. Drew stood on the veranda of Sabattis's Boardinghouse and gazed out at the evening star. Marcy had wept at the evening star, he recalled with longing. *Fool!* If he had any sense, he'd be inside with the rest of them, changing into his "city" clothes, preparing for supper. There was a movement in the bushes. Marcy stepped into the glow of the lantern that hung from the veranda roof.

"What are you doing here?" he asked. Hadn't she tormented him enough?

"Mrs. Sabattis always closes up at nine. I'll come to your room at ten. You're in the end room, aren't you? I'll be there at ten."

"Good God, Marcy! No!"

"Yes." Her voice was firm and quiet.

"I can't marry you now. You know that."

"I don't care."

"I can't support a wife. I'm not even sure I can support myself. If you still want that rich husband, you ought to search elsewhere. Look, my name may be Bradford, but I've no money of my own. Only a father who's reluctant to support me as long as I'm involved with the foolishness of my painting."

"I don't care!"

"Dammit, you're not listening! I have no prospects beyond what my paintings might bring, and I'm not sure they're worth anything. But they're important to me. Try to understand. All my life I've had love, approval, acceptance . . . all unqualified, anything I wanted. Not just because of my father's money. I don't even know why. I never had to *earn* anything! Do you understand? But the painting is mine. It's not money or mills or businesses that I'll inherit from my father. It's *mine*! And I'm not sure right now that I have room in my heart for anything else. Even you."

"I don't care!"

He wanted to shake her. "You're the most stubborn . . . Look. I've made up my mind. I'm going to Paris, just as soon as I can make my arrangements."

"Drew, I don't care," she said softly. "I love you. If you go away tomorrow and I never see you again, if I live and die in these mountains, I want tonight. I want one more memory."

"Oh, God," he groaned. "What have I done?"

"You didn't do it. Love did. I'll come to your room at ten."

He shook his head. "Marcy . . . no. No."

She smiled gently. "Yes," she said.

The moon hung high that night, turning the Sabattis's veranda to silver. The breeze was cool, blowing Marcy's skirt and waist. She shivered. What would Uncle Jack think if he knew she'd come out without her drawers and shift? She opened the front door of the boardinghouse, moved quietly up the staircase, and tiptoed down the long, moon-lit corridor. Drew's room was at the end, next to the Sabattis boys. But Tom had taken his summer earnings and gone off to see his girl at North Creek tonight, and the other two boys were out guiding a party of sportsmen. No one was nearby. She passed a room that still showed a light under the door, then two rooms from which snoring emanated, then the empty room;

Drew's room was dark. She felt a moment's panic. If he were asleep, she could wake him. But what if he were gone... the room empty? She took a deep breath and opened the door.

Drew stood by the window in the darkened room, his tall form bathed in moonlight. He turned as she entered. "I was hoping you wouldn't come," he said. "I've only got to send you away."

"What makes you think I'll listen to you?"

"You're a stubborn little..."

She cut him short. "I'm going to love you tonight, Drew Bradford, whether you want me to or not."

"Damn you, get out of here!"

She shook her head. "And I'm going to kiss you, for starters!" She marched across the room, backing him into a corner, and put her arms about his neck. She pulled his head down to hers and planted her lips firmly on his. He yielded for a moment, his lips soft and warm, and then he went rigid. He pushed her away from him and cursed under his breath.

"Marcy...don't..."

She unbuttoned his shirt and slid her hands across his chest, feeling his nipples grow hard even through his woolen undervest. "I will, Drew. And there's nothing you can do about it."

"What if I holler?"

She could hear the laughter in his voice, though he tried to hide it. He was weakening. She giggled. "Do you want Mrs. Marshall to have a conniption fit?" Her fingers had begun to work on the buttons of his undervest.

"Good God, don't you have any sense of decency?"

"Not a lick. At least not when I'm in love." She unfastened the last button, pulled open his undervest, and kissed his hard chest.

He drew in a rasping breath. "You devil." He closed his eyes and dropped his head back, fighting hard to resist her enticements. "Marcy, please..."

She pulled off his shirts and ran her fingers across his sleek shoulders, scratching at the patch of hair on his chest, feeling his muscles stiffen and twitch with each caress. He kept his

hands clenched at his sides while she explored every inch of
his beautiful torso with hands and lips, tasting the salty moistness of his burning flesh. She could feel him trembling, a
throbbing that surged through her fingertips to quiver and
pulsate within her own bosom. Her mouth went dry and she
gulped madly, desperate for his touch. "Tarnation," she said,
her voice a soft croak. "Must I do all the work?" She reached
for his hands and placed them on her buttocks over the thin
skirt she wore.

He groaned in agony, then surrendered, pulling her close
against him, kneading her firm young flesh through the skirt.
He kissed her wildly, his mouth seeking her neck, her ears,
her downy cheeks. At last, hands shaking, he stripped the
few garments from her body and carried her to the bed.

Through lids grown heavy with passion she watched him
pull off the rest of his clothes. He stood silhouetted in the
moon-lit room, his beautifully formed body—broad-
shouldered but narrow in the hips—making her heart catch.
He lay down beside her, but made no move to touch her. "If
I had the strength," he said hoarsely, "I'd tell you to go this
very minute. This is madness!"

She smiled. Even in the dim light she could see how much
he wanted her. Her eyes traveled his body—the black thatch
on his chest repeated in the black patch below that harbored
something that waited, proud and overbearing. His brain might
want her to leave; his body surely didn't. It gave her an odd
sense of power. He was tall and strong, in command of his
world, sure of himself. And yet, lying beside her, he was
helpless and enslaved. She liked the feeling. She'd too often
felt like a child with him. A child he teased and kissed and
loved—but a child. For the first time she felt like a woman.
His equal. Someone he truly needed. She hesitated for a
moment, then reached out and touched him, that part of him
that was still so new and thrilling to her.

He gasped. "*Jesus*, Marcy..."

She withdrew her hand at once. "Is that wrong?"

"No more wrong than your being here tonight," he growled.
He was still fighting it. Well, she'd fix him! "I said I was

going to love you tonight, Drew. No matter what. And I will!" She began to caress him again, feeling a quivering, a swelling in her hand with each soft stroke. The feel of his hardness, the hot dry flesh, was like a spark to her own flame, igniting within her, turning her insides to liquid fire.

He made a strangled sound deep in his throat and wrenched away from her. "Damn you." He rolled out of bed and stood up; grabbing at her ankles, he hauled her violently to the edge of the bed. He separated her legs, slid his hands up to her thighs, and plunged into her, pulling her hips forward to meet his violent thrust. Again and again, as if he would force his way right through her. She had never felt anything so exquisite. She writhed on the bed, holding her forearm to her mouth to stifle her cries of ecstasy, and wrapped her legs around his waist. She felt her insides explode in a drenching rush, then Drew shuddered twice and collapsed against her, falling forward onto the bed to cover her body with his own.

"God, I love you, Marcy," he mumbled, burying his face in her neck. They lay quietly together for a long time, arms wrapped around each other, until finally Drew stirred and sat up, peering down at her in the gloom. "What am I going to do with you?" He shook his head. "Coming to my room half naked."

She laughed softly, her voice still shaky. "It appears to me you already answered that question!"

He sighed and gathered her into his arms. "What *am* I going to do, Marce? I'm off to Paris as soon as I can. How can I ask you to wait for me?"

"Take me to Paris with you." The thought popped into her head as though it had been waiting there.

"No. I can't marry you. It wouldn't be right. It wouldn't be fair."

"I don't *want* marriage, Drew. I don't want to be a burden to you. If we're not married, and . . . it doesn't work out, I can leave. It's better that way—don't you see?" She kissed him gently "Say yes, Drew. If nothing else, I can be your unpaid model!"

Silence. Then "Why the devil not?" he muttered at last.

"All right. I figure it'll be about a week or so before I can get enough money together for the trip. Then I'll come back and get you. Oh God!" He held her more tightly to his chest. "Are you *sure*, Marcy? I don't want to bring you unhappiness. Are you really sure?"

"Do you love me, Drew?"

"You know I do."

"Then I'm sure," she answered.

Her eyes flew open with a sudden realization. Good gracious! she thought. Her scheme had come true! That long-forgotten foolish scheme! She'd be leaving the mountains, the treacherous mountains that had killed her parents. And leaving with the man she loved.

She snuggled more firmly into Drew's warm embrace. She'd be safe at last.

After hours on the train, his mind torn between memories of Marcy's sweet body and anxiety about their future, Drew arrived at home in the city.

"Nice to see you again, Parkman." Drew handed his hat to the butler and indicated his luggage, which waited on the stoop.

Parkman nodded. "I'll have Brigid bring it to your room, Mr. Drewry. I trust your summer went well?"

"Very well. Is my mother in the parlor?"

"No. She's upstairs in her sitting room. A sick headache."

"Damn! I wish I could get her to throw out that tonic. She's poisoning herself."

"Quite so, sir." Parkman eyed Drew's travel-stained clothes. "Shall I draw you a bath, sir?"

"In a little while. I'll ring for you. I want to see my mother first." He mounted the broad staircase slowly, trying to collect his thoughts. She wouldn't like it. She'd become terribly possessive these last few years, clinging, trying to tie him to her with bonds of sentiment. Bonds of the past. He hadn't minded. It had seemed a small thing to indulge her. He had known that sooner or later he'd have to make the break, but put off thinking about it. Until now. And now he needed her. Brian had always been tight-fisted about money, bestowing his monthly allowance with ill grace, muttering darkly about "my artist son" as though the words disgusted him. He'd never agree to subsidize the trip to France. Not even as a loan. But if Isobel talked to him . . .

Drew's heart sank at the sight of his mother, reclining on her chaise. She looked terrible. She was pale and drawn, her hands fluttering toward him like nervous birds. And when he bent to kiss her on the forehead, he saw that her pupils were small pinpoints. Damn! he thought. She might have done without her tonic for one day, knowing he was returning.

"Hello, Mum," he said gently. "How's my girl?"

"How good to have you back, Drewry." She sighed. "I've had the vapors all day. But you look wonderful. So healthy and robust. The country air must agree with you."

"Yes." He sat down beside her and held her hand, launching into an abbreviated account of the summer's adventure, the fishing, the hunting, the painting. Yet all the while he was conscious of her nervous prostration, the edge of tension that might explode into tears or hysteria. It was not the best day to tell her his plans.

"And now you're home," she said at last. "I've missed you so. It's been so lonely here, and Arthur . . ."

"What about Arthur?"

Her eyes filled with tears. "I'm afraid I've grown tiresome to him. I haven't seen him very much this summer. But never mind. Now you're home, dear boy. Home to stay."

He frowned and stood up. "Not for long, I'm afraid." She gave a little gasp. "I hate to tell you like this," he went on quickly. "I know it's sudden. But my summer of painting has shown me how much I *don't* know. I must study . . ."

"Of course! You'll return to the National Academy. I'm sure we can arrange to have you study under one of the masters."

"No. I don't like the way they're teaching. It's all studio work. Even up in the mountains, I couldn't paint what I saw. I kept amplifying my palette, darkening my colors, over-working everything. Transforming what my eyes saw into what I'd been taught to paint in the studio. I might have been working from sketches by candlelight, for all the good it did me to be out-of-doors."

"But where else can you study?"

"Paris. They're working *en plein air*, somehow managing to put sunlight onto their canvases."

She put her hand to her mouth, rubbing her dry lips. "Paris? How long would you stay?"

"I'd like to study for a year, at least."

"A year!" Her voice was sharp with accusation. She took a deep breath. "I don't see how it can be done. You might as well put it out of your mind. Your father will never allow it. He'll cut off your allowance entirely."

"I know that, Mum." He knelt down and held her hand. "That's why I've come to you. If you could persuade Father to lend me enough money to live on for a year..."

"But how could you pay him back?"

"After a year in Paris I should be able to earn a living from my paintings." He laughed ruefully. "Or else I'll have learned that I can't paint worth a damn. In which case, I'll give the whole thing up and become Father's partner."

"No! I won't have it. Your painting means so much to you." She pushed the hair back from his forehead. "Your father *might* listen to me. But even if he did, he would see to it that you felt beholden to him. How could you work under those circumstances?" She hesitated, then smiled. "Now I'll tell you a little secret, my dear boy. I have a few bonds put away... nothing extravagant, mind you. Perhaps three thousand. You could live quite handsomely. And study as well."

"Three thousand! Oh, Mum." He thought of Marcy living comfortably, with the pretty dresses she wanted, the easy life. Perhaps he could even afford a servant for her. He kissed his mother exuberantly on the cheek.

She smiled wanly. "Though it will grieve me to be parted from you, I shall let you go if you promise to write me often. Now, I must see my banker. How soon do you intend to sail?"

"Two weeks at the outside."

"Why then, I'll even have time to arrange a small soiree

to send you on your way. Saturday. That should give me enough time to make my plans."

He cleared his throat. "I won't be here on Saturday."

"Whyever not?"

He hesitated. "I'm returning to North Creek on Friday."

"North Creek? Haven't you had your fill of the wilderness?"

"There's someone there. A girl."

She laughed—a small, nervous laugh. "You've had girls before. I would have thought you'd have said your farewells before you left the mountains."

"I'm going back to get her. To take her with me to Paris."

Isobel colored, two patches of angry red blotching her pale cheeks. "No! I won't have it!"

"I love her, Mum," he said gently.

"Love!" Her voice had become shrill. "What do you know about love, breaking my heart this way?"

He frowned. "What are you saying?"

"You're all I have, Drew! Your father is gone. And I'm losing Arthur . . . I can't bear to lose you too."

"I'm your son. I'll always be your son. What does that have to do with Marcy?"

She sneered. *"Marcy.* Common little country girl, no doubt."

"Stop it, Mother!"

"Give her up, Drew," she whined. "Don't take her to Paris."

"I *love* her."

"I might even be able to manage four thousand. *If you give her up*."

"Don't push me, Mother," he growled.

She half rose from her chaise, her eyes burning. "You ungrateful boy! You can starve, for all I care! If you think I'm going to hand over a single penny of my money so you can go traipsing all over Europe with some *trollop* . . ."

"Dammit! Stop it!"

"You wretch!" she shrilled. "Now you've taken to swearing at your own mother. Go to Paris with your whore! Go to the devil!"

"As far away from here as I can get!" He stormed out of her room, slamming the door behind him, and marched down the corridor to his own room. He pulled open his bureau drawer, grabbed a small velvet box. Snapping it open, he withdrew half a dozen diamond studs that normally adorned the shirt of his dress clothes. He turned and tugged furiously at the bell pull. Parkman appeared at his summons.

"Are you ready for your bath, sir?"

He could still taste the bile in his mouth. That vindictive old woman . . . "No. Pack my things. I'm going to the Astor House."

"The *Astor House*?" The disapproval was strong in Parkman's voice. "The Astor House is scarcely a suitable accommodation . . ."

"It's all I can afford." He thrust the diamond studs at Parkman. "Do you know a good pawn shop?"

"Of course, sir."

"Then see what you can get for these." A thousand or so, if he was lucky. Out of which he'd have to pay a hundred and fifty for their passage to France. "Oh. And one more thing, Parkman. I want you to get a message to the telegraph office." He sat at his desk and scribbled out a note to Marcy.

"Arriving by night train North Creek, 6:30 A.M. Saturday, with passage to France and wedding ring. Meet me. Bring a preacher. We're getting married."

Chapter
Six

T he buzzing fly droned in a lazy circle over Willough's head, landed briefly on the glass shade of the kerosene lamp, then flew out of the open window behind Brian Bradford's shoulder. Willough sighed. She was sorry to see it go. Its droning had been a distraction from the droning of Mr. Rutherford, who seemed willing to talk about the fine points of banking all afternoon.

She sighed again, and fanned her face with the Chinese fan. It was no use. Nothing seemed to help against the stifling August day. She could feel the bones of her stays digging into her rib cage, and the rivulets of perspiration that ran down from her knees under their layers of stockings and petticoats and skirts. She had put on a pale blue piqué walking suit with a short-sleeved Swiss muslin waist beneath, and a ruffled V-shaped neckline; if they hadn't had guests at the luncheon table, she would certainly have removed her basque jacket.

They'd been here in Saratoga for three days now, she and Daddy and Nat, and their company. In all that time, Daddy had avoided talking business, allowing Mr. Rutherford to bore them with his interminable monologue, and flattering Mr. Seneca at every opportunity. Daddy must want a large loan from their bank, she thought.

She permitted herself to relax her proper carriage, leaning back into the cushions of her chair. Grandma Carruth would have been scandalized had she been alive, but Willough was too hot and uncomfortable to care. She stared up at the beamed ceiling and frowned, seeing a string of cobwebs that traced a pattern in one corner. She didn't know why her father didn't get more help in his house.

Her father's house. Her mother had never set foot in it, all these years. And never would. Yet her mother always referred to the town house on Gramercy Park as the residence of Mr. and Mrs. Brian Bradford. It was never called simply her mother's house, though of course it was. In the city, at least, the fiction was maintained for the world at large. The servants were instructed to say that Mr. Bradford was merely out of town on business, seeing to his holdings in the Adirondack Mountains. And there were long letters exchanged between her parents, detailing the running of the household, her mother's constant pleas for more money for some extravagance or other. And every few months Brian would come for dinner, or a social occasion. When the Astors or Belmonts or Goelets gave a ball, of course, Brian Bradford would escort his wife, bending attentively to Isobel all evening. If the cream of New York society gossiped at all about the Bradfords, it was to envy them for a devotion that seemed to survive separations that would have put a strain on any other marriage.

Willough glanced around the room. Mother would hate this house. It was certainly grander than the boardinghouse at MacCurdyville, but a far cry from the elegance of the town house in the city. It was a country lodge, with its large stone fireplace soaring the twenty feet or so to the beamed ceiling of the parlor in which they sat. The room itself was two stories high, dominated by the fireplace and the sweeping staircase that led to a balustraded balcony overlooking the parlor. The bedrooms led onto the balcony. Beneath the balcony, on the main floor, were the dining room, the kitchen,

and a small wing that housed a local couple—the only servants. Brian had had the place furnished in a simple but elegant
country style: handsome chintzes cushioning the comfortable,
well-padded chairs and sofa, frosted-glass kerosene lamps in
brass sconces, a brightly patterned Oriental rug. A wall lined
with books, and a bearskin hung on the stone fireplace. It
was a cozy house; Willough had always felt more at ease
here than in Gramercy Park.

She stirred in her chair. She was becoming less and less
comfortable as the afternoon wore on. Surely Daddy would
be growing drowsy from the large luncheon they had eaten,
and would dismiss them all to take his nap. She looked up.
Nat was watching her, his piercing eyes half shaded by his
shaggy blond brows. She was feeling too restless to care about
her manners. Brazenly, she stared back at him. What was it
about him that always made her so conscious of his masculinity? His clothes were ill-fitting; but she suspected that,
even in fine tailoring, he would look as though his hard-
muscled torso was about to burst the constraining seams of
his coat. Perhaps it was the way he sat and moved, never
quite relaxed, like a poised tiger about to spring. Or the square
set of his jaw, the determined line of his mouth. Still, it was
a nice mouth . . .

She started. Merciful Heaven! She'd been gazing at his
mouth like a brazen hussy! She felt her cheeks redden; when
she stole a glance at his eyes, she read amusement in their
amber depths.

"Yes, I quite agree!" Brian's booming voice cut through
her thoughts, halting Rutherford in midsentence. He made a
face, rubbed at his stomach. "I don't know why I can't find
a cure for this dyspepsia!"

"Perhaps you should see a doctor, Daddy."

"Nonsense, Willough! What do they know? When I want
to cut an open-pit mine into a mountain, I don't ask a book-
trained engineer! What the devil can a doctor tell me?"

"Quite so, Brian." Rutherford smiled benignly.

"A good nap. That's what I need." He wagged a finger at
Rutherford. "But I want to talk to you at dinner tonight. I've

got a new piece of land over near New Russia. It seems a shame, with all the charcoal I can get from that lumber . . . it seems a shame to send my pigs to some other man's finery to be turned into bars or cast iron, or even steel. Brian, my lad, I said to myself, why can't you open your own finery?" He laughed expansively. "And the answer that came back was . . . money!" He laughed again. "Well, we can talk about it at dinner."

Willough bit her lip. "I didn't know you were considering that, Daddy," she said quietly. "Perhaps we can discuss it later this afternoon. I'd surely like to hear your thoughts on the matter."

Brian smiled indulgently. "Would you now, lass? I don't know why you bother your pretty head about these things. I'll discuss it with Nat. He can give you the details."

"But, Daddy . . ."

Brian stood up and scowled. "Not now, Willough! If you really want to be useful, you'll have Martha send up a glass of mineral water to my room." He turned to the bankers. "You might enjoy a stroll into town while I'm napping."

Mr. Seneca nodded. "Excellent suggestion, Brian. Is there a lady's shop in Saratoga? I promised my wife a lace cap this trip."

"Yes. Right near the American Hotel on the Broadway. I just took Willough in, day before yesterday. Spent a fortune! But a daughter's worth it. I keep telling her I don't want her to dress like an old maid! Find yourself a husband, lass, I tell her. That's the way to go! Forget about this nonsense with the business." He laughed and started up the staircase. "Unless you intend to be one of those emancipated females in bloomers!"

Willough felt the blood drain from her face. She kept her mouth frozen in a tight smile as Brian disappeared into his bedroom. She nodded mechanically at Rutherford and Seneca, who picked up their hats and walking sticks and departed for the town. She wanted to die. She sat quietly in her chair, wishing that Nat would go away and leave her to her private agonies. She didn't know how long she could keep from crying.

Nat crossed to the cold fireplace and tapped at the andiron with the tip of his shoe. "Don't you ever let go, Willough?"

She gulped, looked up at him. "What?"

He smiled gently. "Scream, throw things, have a tantrum?"

She *was* going to cry. She jumped up from her chair and went to stand at the window, staring sightlessly at the heat-soaked lawn. "Don't be ridiculous, Nat," she said stiffly.

"Oh, I know it's not genteel. I wasn't raised with your fine manners. But a good holler sometimes makes you feel a hell of a lot better!" His voice dropped to a murmur. "Do you want to cry on my shoulder?"

She turned around to look at him. He was smiling in under-standing. She hadn't known this man long, but she knew he wouldn't have shamed her, the way Daddy had. She took a calming breath and returned his smile, feeling warmed by his kindness. "What do you do, Nat, when you feel . . . oh, pent up?" A small laugh. "No. I'll answer that. I've seen it often enough. You pace the floor." She laughed again as he looked abashed. "We've worked so closely these last two months. It's hard to have many secrets."

He grinned. She liked his dimple. "But sometimes even the pacing isn't enough," he said. "I miss the work at the furnaces. For God's sake, don't tell your father, but some-times I go out behind Mrs. Walker's at MacCurdyville . . . long about dawn . . . and help her boy chop wood. Matter of fact, I offered to help Robert repair a wagon wheel today— he can't get a man from town to work in this hot weather. I figure I'll work up a good sweat, then go for a swim in the lake."

She sighed, still feeling bitterness toward Daddy. "I envy you. Perhaps I should have learned to chop wood."

"A brisk walk might do you as much good. Tell you what— I'll beg off with Robert. You go fetch your bonnet and par-asol." He laughed. "If the walk isn't vigorous enough, I'll teach you to climb trees!"

"I'd like that." She stopped. "Oh! No, I can't. Arthur

Gray's in town to take the waters. He sent his card around and invited me to stroll with him this afternoon."

His face went hard. "The oily Mr. Gray?"

She frowned. "Don't you dare take that tone, Nat. Don't you *dare*. Arthur's a friend. I intend to invite him to come to supper on Monday night. You'd better not forget your manners!" She glared at his cold eyes. "And . . . and I intend to go strolling with him today!"

He bowed mockingly. "Have a good walk. And guard your virtue."

"Oh!" She picked up a paperweight from the table and hurled it at him. It missed him and left a dent in the dark pine paneling.

"Good!" he said, turning toward the door. "Now, if you could manage to do that when your father makes you angry, you might finally grow up!"

"*Dammit*, can I have a little quiet in this house?" Brian's voice bellowed from behind his closed bedroom door.

Willough glared up toward the balcony, bit her lip in anger . . . but said nothing.

"Just so," said Nat softly. As he walked out toward the stable, she went to her bedroom to get ready for her stroll with Arthur. He arrived promptly and they stepped out from the relative coolness of the house into oppressive heat. Taking her arm, he guided her along a path under the trees.

Willough smiled and dabbed at the dampness along her upper lip. "Tell me, Arthur, is the Congress Hall Hotel as fine as they say? I've been in the reception room for musicales, of course, but how are the rooms?"

Arthur Gray pulled off his straw skimmer and fanned at his face. "What a scorcher!" He glanced down at the flower in his lapel, already beginning to wilt. He unpinned it and threw it away, replacing the small straight pin on the inside of his lapel. "The rooms are nicely appointed. Bells and gas and water in every room. Primitive, of course, by New York standards, but quite satisfactory for this neck of the woods. And the mineral baths can be refreshing." He replaced his hat and tucked his hand under Willough's elbow. "Let's try this path. It looks shady and much cooler than the one we've just come from."

She nodded and closed her parasol. "You haven't given me an answer yet. Will you come for dinner on Monday?"

"You make it very difficult to refuse. But my house on Fifth Avenue is finished. I'm deep in the preparations for my party. Did you get my invitation?"

"Of course."

"I didn't really want to send it." Playfully, he lifted her hand to his lips and kissed the soft flesh. "I wanted to urge you to come in person. Will you?"

She giggled. "Will you come to dinner on Monday?"

"I can't refuse you. I'll change my plans and go back to the city on Tuesday morning." He bent and plucked a daisy from the side of the path. "A flower for the pretty lady. May I pin it on?"

She hesitated. Her heart-shaped neckline came to a deep V in front; Arthur would have to put the tips of his fingers into the bodice of her dress to fasten the flower securely. Don't be a fool, Willough! she thought. This is Arthur! Had he ever been anything but proper and polite? Once she had thought of him as Uncle Arthur; now he seemed a warm and friendly big brother. "Of course," she said.

He slipped his hand into the neckline of her dress and pinned on the flower; he was distant, deferential, quick. She didn't feel a moment's uneasiness. "It looks charming on you," he said, and withdrew his hand. "Isn't there a cooler place around here?"

"There's a lodge near the lake."

"Doesn't your groundskeeper live there, above the boat-house?"

"Not anymore. He married a widow with three children last summer, and moved in with her. Daddy turned the upstairs into a sitting room for me. It's very pleasant, with the breezes coming off the lake. I often go there to read. Come on." She smiled. "Sometimes Martha thinks to put a pitcher of lemonade on the table."

The lodge was a two-storied boathouse set among the trees

on the edge of Saratoga Lake. The lower floor was given over to the gear and tackle of the several boats that Brian Bradford owned, boats which now bobbed in the water next to Brian's private dock. The room above was airy, with windows on all sides, and fresh-looking white wicker furniture. On one of the tables was a stone crock covered with a damp square of cloth. Arthur lifted a corner of the cloth and sniffed. "It's lemonade, or I miss my guess." He looked about the room. "Are there glasses?"

Willough pointed to a small cupboard. "There." She took off her English straw hat and put it on the settee with her folded parasol, next to Arthur's hat.

Arthur opened the cupboard and took down two glasses. He laughed softly at the sight of a small decanter filled with a deep red liquor. "I didn't think you were a secret drinker," he teased.

She felt herself blushing. "Oh, Arthur, that's just for when Daddy comes down here occasionally. He finds lemonade a bit tame for his taste."

"To be sure. Lemonade is a child's drink."

It almost seemed like a challenge. "I *do* drink claret lemonade. I'm old enough!"

"My dear, you're old enough to do whatever you want to do."

It *was* a challenge. It was really too hot a day to drink wine, but she could scarcely back down now. "Then why don't you put a bit of that wine into our glasses before I pour the lemonade?"

Arthur smiled and brought the decanter to the table, placing it next to the crock. He poured carefully; the finished concoction was a lovely shade of pink. They sat facing each other across the table, sipping slowly, while Arthur told her a funny little story about the last time he had been in New York.

What an agreeable man, she thought, admiring his refinement, his courtliness. She regretted all the years she had avoided his company. Guard your virtue, Nat had said. How absurd! She had never felt safer with any man. And Nat, of

all people, warning her . . . Nat, with those eyes that seemed
to strip the clothes from her body . . .

"What say we go for a boat ride?" asked Arthur suddenly.

"You'll have to do all the work. Won't it be too hot for
you?"

"I'll stay in the shade, along the edge of the lake. And
you'll have your parasol."

Willough stood up. "I should have brought my fan. *Nothing*
will make me cool today." She was sorry she'd had so many
glasses of claret lemonade. It only made her feel more flushed.

"I have an idea. You can trail your feet in the water as we
go along. That'll keep you cool."

She hesitated. "How am I to manage that? With my stockings and all?"

"Why don't you take off your shoes and stockings here?
Then I can carry you down to the boat." He smiled disarmingly. "It will be very romantic. Like a princess being carried
to her barge."

She giggled. "Oh, Arthur. What a fanciful thought!"

He tried to look serious. "Fair damsel, may I be of assistance?"

She perched on the edge of the chaise and bent to unbutton
her shoes. "You may, my liege. If I'm not too heavy for you."

"Wait. Let me." He knelt at her feet and slipped her shoes
off. He looked up and smiled. "You'll never fight your way
through all those petticoats and frills to reach your garters.
Let me do it."

She stared at him with wide eyes. Could Nat be right?

Arthur looked hurt. "Willough," he chided. "You can't
possibly think . . ."

Silly goose! she thought. A man didn't seduce a woman
in broad daylight! What was she making such a fuss about?

"Pretend I'm your maid," he said. "Lean back on the chaise
and relax. I'll do the rest."

"You're being silly, Arthur."

"Then indulge me. Your maid gets to pamper you. Let me
pamper you for a little while. For all the times when I didn't

see you, growing up. When I couldn't buy you an ice cream, or show you a magic trick, or dandle you on my knee."

How could she say no? He had pinned the flower on her bosom without offending her. She sighed and leaned back against the cushions, allowing herself the pleasure of feeling waited upon. Carefully, he stripped back her overskirt and its contrasting underskirts, then folded up her several petticoats just below her knees. Her garters were fastened above her knees, under the lace edge of her drawers. He reached up under the petticoats and unhooked her garters with delicate fingers; she scarcely felt his touch on her flesh. When he pulled off her stockings she had a pang of embarrassment, that her limbs should be exposed to his gaze. But how ridiculous! she thought. She'd gone wading many a time at the seashore—with her skirts held up—and *strangers* had seen her bare legs. Why should she be embarrassed with Arthur?

She closed her eyes and wiggled her toes. "Oh, that's so cool, with the breeze on my limbs!" She was content to let her skirts stay just at her knees; she was too comfortable to be concerned about the niceties.

"Such a hot day," he murmured. "I don't know why you wore a jacket over your waist. Come. Out of it. Out of it!"

She could feel his fingers beginning to work on the buttons of her jacket. She opened her eyes and smiled lazily at him, laughing as he sat her up and pulled the jacket off her. Without the long heavy sleeves, she certainly felt more comfortable. So comfortable that she'd almost forgotten why they were there. "The boat ride . . ." she began.

He pushed her back against the pillows, fluffing them behind her head. "The boat ride can wait. You look cooler than you have all afternoon." He picked up his straw skimmer and began to fan her feet.

She sighed and closed her eyes again. "I feel like a Sybarite!" She giggled. "You've no idea how warm one's knees can get under all these petticoats!"

"Poor knees. We must make them more comfortable." Carefully he pushed her skirts just above her knees and continued fanning. She sighed contentedly, then gasped. Some-

thing was touching her bare skin. She opened her eyes to see
that Arthur had bent to her, and was kissing her leg.

"Merciful Heaven! Why did you do that?"

He looked at her and smiled, a gentle, benevolent smile.
"Because they're such charming knees. And so distressed
under all those petticoats."

She felt herself blushing. But he was dear Arthur, after all.
Dear, safe Arthur. Isobel had always said it: *If you're in
danger from a man, you'll know it*. She had no fear with
Arthur. "How can limbs be charming?" she demurred, with
a shy laugh.

He gazed at her, his eyes warm and sincere. She had never
felt so flattered by a look in all her life. And his words brought
more flattery. "You have beautiful legs—what I can see of
them. It's a pity a woman must keep her beauty hidden under
so many layers of clothing." She felt deliciously wicked,
surprised at her own enjoyment of his frank admiration. She
had never thought it could feel so wonderful, to have a man
praise you with his words and his glances.

He unbuttoned his frock coat and took it off, then loosened
his collar and cravat. "You look so comfortable. I hate to
disturb you to go boating."

She stifled a yawn, then giggled. "I think the claret lemonade has made me sleepy."

"Then why don't you take a nap? There'll still be time to
go boating in the cool of the afternoon." He leaned over her
and smiled. "Why don't you close those beautiful eyes? Let
me see if I can make you more comfortable."

"Are you still determined to be my maid?"

He grinned and sat beside her on the chaise. "Of course!
Now close your eyes. And when you wake this maid will
still be here, not stealing a sweet in the pantry."

Still giggling, she closed her eyes. Such a silly game! She
was certainly not used to such giddy behavior. Who would
have thought Uncle Arthur could be so amusing? She felt his
hands go around her waist, shifting her body to a more hor-
izontal position. With the heat, and the claret lemonade, and
his kind ministrations, it would be very easy to fall asleep.

"Am I interrupting something?" Nat's voice, hard as granite.

Arthur jumped up and whirled around. "What the devil are you doing here, Stanton?"

"I came for a swim. I thought I heard voices."

Willough sat up. She didn't know whether to be angry or humiliated. It was one thing to play with Arthur; it was quite another to be found in such a state of undress by a man like Nat! Quickly she pulled her skirts and petticoats modestly over her bare legs. "Haven't you any manners, Nat?" she said. Her voice was quivering. "Of all the rude behavior..."

"I didn't know I was expected to knock," he said. He looked at Arthur, his amber eyes burning with fury. "But then, *I'm* not a gentleman!"

"You'd better get out, Stanton."

Nat crossed his arms against his chest. He was wearing only a dark work shirt—the sleeves rolled up, the front half unbuttoned; it was blotched with sweat. He clenched and unclenched his teeth, so his jaw twitched angrily. "You'll leave first, Gray. Either by the stairs...or the window."

"Now see here, Stanton..."

"Mr. Bradford always struck me as a somewhat old-fashioned father. He might be interested to hear *my* interpretation of this little scene."

Arthur's glance wavered. He managed a thin laugh. "Brian and I have always enjoyed a comfortable association, both privately and in business. I'd hate to see that jeopardized." He bent to retrieve his coat and hat.

Willough struggled to her feet, smoothing out her skirts. "Arthur, you don't have to..."

He smiled. "I would do nothing, my dear, that might damage your father's esteem for either of us." He indicated Nat with a contemptuous jerk of his chin. "*Honi soit qui mal y pense.* You have my profound sympathies, Willough, that you're forced to work with this coarse lout! I'll see you at dinner on Monday." He pushed past Nat and hurried down the stairs.

Willough whirled to Nat, her lip curled in disgust. "Would you like a translation?"

"Don't bother. I can guess."

"It means *Shamed be the man who thinks evil!*"

"I only think what my eyes tell me," he growled. "What is he—forty? The lecherous bastard! Playing his little games with you..."

"He's thirty-eight," she snapped, wondering why she had to defend Arthur.

"And you?" His eyes swept her coldly. "Twenty-one, at the most, I'd guess. And so young and green that a man could soft-soap you into anything!" He jerked his chin in the direction of the wine decanter. "Even without *that* to lull you into complacency!"

"You *do* have a vulgar mind! Arthur was fully dressed, and I"—she felt herself blushing, remembering her shameless skirts—"I... was never in any danger!" she finished hastily. "Whereas you—look at you! Don't you even button your shirt in the presence of a lady?"

He laughed sardonically. "He was fully dressed? Christ! Do you think sex is like those pretty pictures in the museums—all those handsome naked bodies so tastefully arranged? My God, Willough, he can have his cock in you without unhooking his gaiters!"

She gasped in horror, her hand going to her mouth. She scarcely understood what he meant. But there were dark shadings in his words and his eyes. Frightening. Mysterious. "Stop it, Nat!"

"No! I want you to listen and understand, so you won't let it happen again! He wouldn't even have to undress you! You ladies with your split drawers make it very easy for a man like that."

She was beside herself. "How *dare* you speak of my underpinnings!"

"Oh, God!" He ran an impatient hand through his sandy curls. "They're your *drawers*, Willough, and damn little protection from what Arthur had in mind! He would have hurt you, Willough. Hurt you badly."

She was shaking like a leaf. "You're disgusting."

"I'm sorry," he said gently. "I suppose I'm *trying* to frighten you. I want you to be on your guard with men like that."

She could feel the tears starting to burn beneath her lids. "Disgusting," she repeated. "Disgusting and horrible and vicious and..." The words choked in her throat.

He stepped closer. "Willough..."

She looked up. Without her shoes, she was far shorter than he. He seemed to loom above her—the broad shoulders and barrel chest, the shirt falling open to his waist. She could smell his sweat, a musky headiness that was frightening and repelling and strangely seductive all at once.

She thought: I don't care what he says. Arthur is a gentleman. But *this* creature... with his masculine scent, his overpowering body... this is a... (she found it hard even to *think* the word)... a sexual animal.

"Willough..." he said again, and put his hand on her bare arm.

Her eyes widened in panic. She sucked in a terrified breath and cringed away from him, feeling her flesh burning at his touch.

His amber eyes registered pain. Then anger. "Christ," he muttered. "You little fool." Turning on his heel, he pounded down the stairs.

She sank to the chaise, trembling, and let the tears come at last.

In the days that passed, Nat could not get the incident out of his mind. There was no one he could discuss it with until his weekly visit with his grandfather. As they sat at the table, Nat cut another piece of cake and handed it to his grandfather. "And there she was, Gramps, with her skirts up, giggling like a schoolgirl."

The old man took a bite of the cake and licked his lips. "They do make a fine cake on that Lake George steamer."

"That's why I brought it to you. I enjoyed it myself during luncheon..."

"So he had her skirts up." The old man shook his head. "He sounds like a scoundrel."

"Yes." Nat had begun to pace the small cabin. "I don't even think she realized what he was up to. But I swear he would have had her in another minute, if I hadn't come in. Her eyes were half closed. She didn't see the look on his face. Like a leering satyr."

"And now you've got to be decent to the man?"

"She's invited him for supper tomorrow. And he's Bradford's friend as well. Or at least his confederate." He smacked his palm angrily against the arm of his grandfather's wheelchair. "I don't know if I can prevent myself from throttling the bastard! But I intend to keep my eye on him the whole evening. There'll be no repetitions of that boathouse scene, by God!"

His grandfather chuckled. "I don't care what you say, boy, I think the girl's got under your skin."

He looked at his grandfather. Could it be so? Willough— with those melting eyes? *"No. No. It's just that she's so damned gullible. She thinks if a man talks like a fine gentleman, he can be trusted."*

"Does she trust *you*?"

"Hardly. I don't have the gift of gab. Not like that snake. And I touched her. Put my hand on her arm. You should have seen her face then." He sighed. "I can't decide whether she was disgusted at my effrontery—and my low station—or afraid of me. Or afraid of all men," he added thoughtfully.

The old man snorted. "They're raising them that way nowadays. Helpless little creatures who don't know the first thing about a man, and take a fit on their wedding night!"

Nat laughed. "How do *you* know?"

"Remember that nicely padded baggage I had for years? Mary-Rose? She worked as a housekeeper at the Lake George Hotel. The stories she told me about what went on in that bridal suite . . . !" The old man rolled his eyes to the ceiling.

"Maybe that's why she's afraid. Maybe that's what she's been taught. Or *not* taught. But she must have longings. We're all Nature's children under the skin. I wonder how she explains away her feelings." He had a sudden vision of Willough's tender mouth. "I wonder if she's ever been kissed." He laughed harshly. "But she's afraid of me."

The old man watched him, his pale eyes shrewd and searching. "Is she right to fear you?"

"She's safer with me than with Gray!" He began to pace again, his heels clicking on the old floorboards. "Dammit!" he burst out. "Sometimes I want to shake her—I've got half a mind to..."

"Do you have feelings for the woman, Nat?"

"Of course not! It just makes me angry, that's all. That man fawns all over her with his smooth talk, and she falls for it. He's a hero to her." He frowned, remembering the terror in Willough's eyes. "I touch her in friendship," he said, "and I'm a villain, clearly out to ravage her. But I swear, Gramps, he would have talked her out of her virginity. Just with the right words."

"And she doesn't see that."

He laughed bitterly. "Maybe it's her snobbery. Rich men are safe. Poor men aren't."

"You could always seduce her with words—like a rich man would—just to prove your point."

Nat laughed. "Don't think I haven't thought of it! But I'd have to be damned mad at her first!"

"Why?"

Why did her face keep rising up before him, with those beautiful eyes that opened onto her soul? Her fragile, vulnerable soul. "Because it would be too easy," he said softly. "And so unfair." He ran his fingers through his hair. "Oh God, Gramps, why is life so complicated? Isn't there any peace anywhere?"

Marcy waved to the stationmaster of North Creek. "Morning, Tom," she called. "Is the night train from New York City due in on time?"

"Morning, Marcy." He nodded and pulled out his large

watch. "She left Saratoga right on time. I reckon she'll get
here on the dot. You meeting a hunting party for Old Jack?"

"No." She blushed, feeling suddenly shy. "Just a . . . a
friend." She turned away. It was too wonderful, too exciting
to share with anyone just yet.

They knew in Long Lake, of course. The Plumleys had
thrown a big party, and all the neighbors had wished her well.
Even Zeb Cary had managed to smile and shake her hand,
though he allowed as how that city slicker hadn't seemed like
much to *him*.

She smiled and looked around at the flower-trimmed depot,
the sunny street. What a beautiful day for a wedding. She
smoothed the skirt of her gown, a dark green wool with a
plain bodice and small lace collar. It was her best dress, but
she wished she had a prettier one to get married in. Foolish
Marcy, she thought. As long as the groom was her own Drew,
what did it matter?

There must be a rich swell in town, she thought. On a
siding at some distance from the station there was a private
railroad car. As she watched, two young men in gray linen
stepped down from the car and crossed the dusty road, heading for the hotel. As they passed her, one of them slowed his
steps, appraising her in the early morning sunshine.

Not today, *greenhorn*, she thought, laughing to herself.
Today I'm getting married!

She examined the railroad car more closely. It was very
nice, with its polished mahogany and brass, but it no longer
held the fascination it once would have. It represented a silly
dream. She heard the toot of a locomotive in the distance.
The reality was coming down the track, with Drew.

She felt her heart begin to pound. Drew! It had been more
than a week. She hadn't thought she could miss anyone as
much as she missed him! She waited, filled with anticipation,
as the train chugged into the station, and waved excitedly
when she spotted him. He was down the steps and pulling
her into his arms before the engine had squealed to a halt.

"You're more beautiful than I remembered," he said, and
kissed her exuberantly. She clung to him and returned his

kiss with all the aching passion in her. She would never tire of his kisses! She watched him with hungry eyes as he directed the removal of his luggage from the train. He seemed to have a great deal of baggage, valises and carpetbags and large boxes tied up with ribbon. He grinned and put his arms around her waist. "Did you stay at the hotel last night?"

"Yes. I took a bedroom with a small parlor." She felt herself blushing. "I told them . . . my husband would be joining me tonight."

His mouth twitched in a lopsided smile. "You were mighty sure of me!"

"Dang you, Drew Bradford. What made you so sure *I'd* be here?"

He bent and kissed the tip of her nose. "That last night in Long Lake," he said, and laughed as she blushed again. He arranged to have his baggage put into their room in the hotel, then insisted on finding a restaurant that could serve him the largest breakfast in town. "For my strength tonight," he said, his eyes twinkling mischievously. While Marcy worked on toast and jam, Drew dug into venison steak and eggs and flapjacks, washing it down with strong coffee. And all the while he bombarded Marcy with questions.

"Did you get the preacher?"

"Reverend Carpenter. The church is the other side of the depot. He said he could marry us at four o'clock today."

"And Uncle Jack?"

"He went out with a fisherman at dawn. But he'll be here at four."

"Did you ask any friends to come?"

"No. It's a hardship for them to make the trip from Long Lake. Ten hours by stage, and then back again as soon as the wedding is over."

He grinned wickedly. "Didn't you even invite that young man who debauched you?"

"Drew Bradford! You polecat! I don't even know what that means, but it just plain sounds awful!" She giggled in spite of herself. "But I didn't invite Zeb." She watched him as he

finished his breakfast. Her eyes could never get enough of
him. "What about *your* family?" she said at last.

A small crease appeared between his eyes. "I didn't have
a chance to track down Willough."

"Willough?"

"My sister. I thought she was at MacCurdyville, but she's
not. She may be at Saratoga, but I wasn't about to march in
on her—and my father—when my train was passing through."

"You don't get along with your father?"

He shrugged. "We're not enemies. We're just . . . strangers.
He doesn't like my life, and I don't much like his."

"And your mother?"

He gulped the last of his coffee. "I'll write to Willough
before we leave, and tell her about our wedding. She'll enjoy
breaking the news to Mother."

"Drew . . ." Marcy said softly, seeing the pain in his eyes.
She had grown up with love; somehow she had thought that
all families were happy.

"No. No serious talk. It's our wedding day. Tell me, Mrs.
Bradford that is to be, do you get seasick?"

She bit her lip. "I don't know!"

He laughed. "Well, we'll soon find out. We'll take the train
for Boston tomorrow. Our ship sails from there. And then,
nine days later, we'll be in Le Havre. That's a port in France.
We'll take the train to Paris from there. I have a few letters
from some artist friends in New York. With their help, we
should be able to find cheap rooms in the Latin Quarter."

She smiled in delight, her eyes shining. "Oh Drew, it sounds
so wonderful and magical!"

"Come on," he said, counting out the cost of their meal
and dropping the coins on the table. "I want to walk off this
breakfast, and then we'll go back to the hotel."

"What for?" she purred seductively.

"My God, you're becoming a hussy already!" He reached
out and pinched her sharply on the behind, managing to look
innocent when she squeaked loudly and every other patron
in the restaurant stopped eating to stare at them. "You know
very well what for," he said, taking her by the elbow and

steering her out into the sunshine. "And then, maybe, if you're good, I'll show you your wedding dress."

She gasped in delighted surprise. "Wedding dress? But how could you . . . how did you know what size . . . ?"

He stopped and put his hands around her waist. He nodded in satisfaction. "Uh-huh. I was right."

"What about the . . . other measurements?"

"I studied the clerks for a while, until I found one who looked about your size and shape." He grinned. "Of course, I had to hold her in my arms to be sure she felt just about the way you did."

"Did you kiss her, too, you slack-jawed wolf?"

"Only her ears, to get the proper measurement for the earrings."

She frowned in mock seriousness. "When we're married remind me to measure a rolling pin for your head!"

He laughed and swung her around in his arms, then bent and kissed her on the mouth.

She trembled down to her toes. "You can't keep kissing me on the street like this," she said breathlessly.

"No." His eyes enveloped her in their warmth, blue and clear as a summer sky. "Damn the walk," he whispered. "I want to make love to you right now."

In their hotel room he lay on the bed—shoes and frock coat off, hands comfortably behind his head—and watched lazily as she undressed. It didn't take her long. The green dress, all one piece, unbuttoning from collar to hem; her muslin petticoat; flannel drawers and short-sleeved chemise. Plain black stockings, high laced black shoes. She undressed in a leisurely manner, enjoying his eyes on her body.

"You're tanned all over," he said. "How do you manage that?"

She smirked. "There are dozens of waterfalls to bathe in . . ."

"If I ever thought you'd played that scene for anyone else . . ." he growled.

Her smile faded. He wasn't joking. There was the edge of jealousy in his voice. She ran to the bed and leaned over him. "Drew. I'm yours. Always."

"Marcy." He pulled her down to lie beside him, caressing her with gentle hands, praising with his kisses her face and bosom and soft neck. He kissed her until she was quivering, then he rolled off the bed and began to remove his own clothing, his fingers working impatiently at his waistcoat buttons. She snuggled against the soft bed, stretched voluptuously, her arms over her head, and watched him. "Oh, God," he said, his hands poised on his cravat. His voice was husky with passion. "Someday I'll paint you like that, a beam of sunlight setting fire to your hair, your breasts rosy with love and anticipation."

She sat up and put her hands on her hips. "Tarnation! You can be the painter tomorrow! Will you please hurry up and be the lover today?"

He laughed at that, and shed the rest of his clothes quickly, but when he held her in his arms, it was with a tenderness that made her want to weep. He kissed her breasts, her flat belly, her neck and ears, then turned her over and kissed her shoulders, the hollow at the small of her back. She moaned in pleasure and rolled back, reaching for him. Their bodies fused, came together, warmed by their passion and the bright sunlight that streamed across the bed. It seemed a glorious eternity, while she soared like a bird in the heavens, her body trembling and pulsing, her heart and soul joined to his as surely as was her flesh. At last he sighed and moved away, sated. He leaned on one elbow and gazed lovingly at her. She smiled at him through half-closed eyes, too content even to speak.

"You *are* Nature's child," he said. "So natural. So wonderful."

She frowned at him, mystified.

He laughed and indicated her soft nakedness. "Look at you. In full daylight. Before lunch!"

"Dang you, is that meant to be an insult?"

"Hardly. But most women nowadays wouldn't even make love to their *husbands* except at night. And in a darkened room."

"Is it wrong of me?"

"Wrong? Good grief, I can't believe my luck!" He smiled. "You look sleepy. And I know I am. I couldn't close my eyes for a minute on that train, just thinking about you. We have time for a nap." He helped her climb under the quilt, then pulled her into his arms.

She snuggled against him; her eyes were growing heavy. She giggled softly. "Sleeping while the sun is shining. Now *that's* wrong!" Feeling deliciously wicked, she closed her eyes and slept.

She awoke to find him gone. The sun had shifted while she slept, and now shone on a patch of carpet. She thought: It must be well after noon. She jumped out of bed, hurriedly wrapping the quilt about her, and went into the adjoining small parlor. Drew was there, already dressed in an elegant suit of clothes. She was dazzled by his handsomeness, regretting again the plainness of her green gown. Then she remembered he had spoken of a wedding dress.

"It's about time you woke up," he said. "I've had my bath already, and lunch should be arriving at any moment." He indicated a small tub that had been placed in a corner of the room. "Get in. I'll scrub your back."

Giggling, she dropped the quilt and climbed into the tub. "Am I never going to see my gown?"

"In time. Here." He handed her the soap. "Do your front. Because if *I* do it, we'll never get to the wedding." There was a knock on the door. Drew looked at her full bosom and stood up, smiling benignly. "Come in."

"Tarnation," she whispered, sinking down to a more modest level under the water. A young bellboy had appeared, carrying in a large tray that rattled and clattered under its linen covering.

"Over here, boy." Drew tossed the lad a coin, trying not to grin as the boy gulped, stole a hasty glance at Marcy in her tub, and vanished out the door.

"Drew Bradford! You might have warned me!"

"And denied that young man a look at your beautiful shoulders?" He pulled the linen covering off the tray and picked up a bottle. "Have a glass of champagne."

"While I'm still in my tub?" This was surely the most extraordinary day in her life! "I've never had champagne."

He knelt beside her and handed her a glass. "I intend to spoil you as much as I can," he said, and kissed her softly.

She sipped at the champagne, making a face when the bubbles tickled her nose. It tasted a bit sour to her, but after it had gone down, it left a nice warm feeling in her throat. She took another sip and smiled at Drew. By the time they had—together—washed her all over, she had finished that one glass and was starting on a second. She climbed out of the tub, feeling a bit wobbly, and allowed Drew to towel her dry. Reluctantly, she put down her glass (surely she had been mistaken to think it sour!), and turned toward the bedroom. "I'll just get my shift and drawers"—she looked at him with accusing eyes—"and then you *better* show me my dress!"

"No. Stay here. I intend to dress you from the skin out!" He brought out several large boxes and began to untie their ribbons. "Including your underpinnings."

"Drew! You didn't get me a corset . . . ?"

"Of course I did."

"I've never worn a corset!"

"You've never been married before, either! Here. Put on this chemise." He handed her the prettiest garment she had ever seen in her life, a beautiful wisp of fine muslin, sleeveless, knee-length, extravagantly trimmed with lace at the neckline and hem. She slipped it over her head, enjoying the slide of the delicate fabric against her skin. The drawers came next, of the same muslin as the chemise, and trimmed with the same lace. She gasped when he pulled the corset out of the box. That beautiful thing was surely not meant to be hidden! It was of deep pink silk, lined and padded, its whalebones held in place with decorative quilt stitches and embroidery.

Drew laughed delightedly at the look on her face. "You'd better eat some lunch first. You may not want to eat once I lace you in!"

Lunch was cold chicken and ham with a mustard sauce. And ice cream and sweet cakes and fresh grapes. She wolfed down her food impatiently, eager to see the rest of her finery, and topped off the meal with a little more champagne. She was beginning to feel giddy. She stood up and sighed, holding her arms straight out at her sides. "Now, Drew, do your worst!" He put the corset around her, fastening the large hook in the center front, then hooking the smaller ones above and below. The corset reached just from the tips of her breasts— cradling and lifting them—to several inches below her waist, dipping down in the front to flatten her already trim abdomen. "It feels a little queer, but not at all what I expected!"

He laughed and went to stand behind her. "That's because I haven't pulled the laces yet! Tell me when it's tight." While she sucked in her breath, he tugged at the tapes until she felt she couldn't breathe.

"Tarnation! Stop! I'll never be able to bend over and lace my shoes!"

"You're not supposed to. The ladies who dress like this usually have servants. I'm afraid you'll have to rely on me." He looped the corset tapes, brought them around to the front, and tied them in a bow. He pulled out the next garment, a white cotton-and-lace fitted bodice that buttoned down the front, and looked very much like a chemise except that it was waist-length.

"What's that?"

"A corset waist. So the lines of the corset won't show through the dress." He put it on her, stopping to kiss her as he fastened the last button, then produced a pair of gray silk stockings and frilly garters. "I didn't buy you shoes. I didn't know what size. Sit down." While he put on the stockings and fetched her shoes from the bedroom, she poured them both another glass of champagne. The bustle came next, a little half skirt of stiffened and ruffled horsehair that tied around her waist. This occasioned a delay in her *toilette* while she danced around the room, sitting on one chair and another, trying to find the most graceful way to sit, without the bustle slewing around and sitting beside her on the chair.

"It can't be done," she said at last. "I'll have to stand for the rest of my life!"

He laughed and kissed her. "You can always lie down. Let's get your petticoats." White muslin trimmed with lace, and tied on with a tape, followed by gray silk with a pleated ruffle at the hem and pale green embroidery. The gray silk fastened with a button on one side. "Damn," he said, struggling to close it. "I should have pulled your corset tighter."

She looked down at herself. All these layers of clothing, and they hadn't even reached the dress yet! She would surely need some more champagne to fortify her! And as long as there were a few more pieces of chicken...

At last she was ready for the gown. Drew presented it with a flourish, his arms filled with yards and yards of pale gray taffeta. When he held it out she saw that it was trimmed with fringes and pleatings and puffings of the most delicate shade of pink she had ever seen.

"Oh, Drew," she gasped. "It's beautiful! But so extravagant. All these things. Can you afford them?"

He laughed ruefully. "Probably not. And when we're starving in Paris, we may both regret this day." His forehead creased in a sudden frown. "Dammit, Marcy," he muttered. "I wish I had more to spend on you."

"No serious talk today. You said so yourself. Open that other bottle of champagne and then show me how to get into this wonderful dress!"

"The skirt comes first. Of course, it's really two skirts together." He slipped the double skirt over her head, arranging the long train of the underskirt, then showing her how to pull the hidden tapes of the overskirt so it bunched up in graceful poufs over her hips and bustle.

"I'll never be able to move. What about the top?"

"Not yet. This model comes with a *tablier*. It's a kind of apron. Here. Let me." He wrapped the *tablier* around her waist and hooked it in the back. It draped beautifully in front, its graceful curve trimmed with a thick pink fringe.

"*Now* the top?"

He shook his head. "No. I decided to be practical. You'll be able to wear this gown for daytime and evening. If we fill in the low neckline with a chemisette..." He produced a sleeveless, high-necked garment of fine pleated batiste, which tied on under her bust, and was finished with a frill of lace at the neckline. At last he helped her into the short basque jacket that fit snugly and accented the slim grace of her figure. Only when he had given her a matching pink parasol and hat, and pale green kid gloves, did he allow her to return to the bedroom and look at herself.

She gaped in astonishment. Who was that woman there? She pirouetted around the room, returning again and again to the mirror to stare in disbelief. "I look at *least* twenty-one!" she said.

His mouth twitched. "Indeed. At the very least."

"Don't laugh at me. Oh Drew!" She threw her arms wide for sheer joy and flung herself flat on the bed, grinning up at him.

He smiled in pleasure. "I'll give you the ring in church, but come into the other room for your earrings."

"Drat!" she whispered, biting her lip.

"What is it, Marce? Is something the matter?"

Her eyes were wide and filled with dismay. "I can't get up! I can't even move!" She wriggled helplessly on the bed, trying in vain to bend in the middle. "We'll have to get married in this bedroom. I'm not joking, Drew. Truly, I feel *buried* in all these clothes."

He threw back his head and roared with laughter. "I think you've just had too much champagne." He reached down and pulled her to her feet, steadying her against himself when she wobbled slightly. "I think you're a bit tipsy."

"I am not!" Her voice sounded strange to her ears.

"Tipsy or not, I love you." He kissed her softly, then deepened his kiss, his mouth moving on hers, his arms pressing her tightly to his hard chest.

Panting hard, she pulled away from him and began to giggle. "I'd like to say you take my breath away, but I think it's this blamed corset!"

Laughing, he pulled out his watch. "It's time to go to church. Come get your earrings, then we'll go."

She put on the earrings, lovely gold filigree balls, turned

about once more for a final inspection, and declared herself
ready. "No. Wait," she said suddenly. "There's a bit more
champagne."

"You've had enough."

"I'm fine, Drew. And we can't leave the rest. It will only
go to waste."

"No. It'll go to your head. And get that stubborn look off
your face. It's foolish to drink any more."

"Oh, bosh! I'm fine. Look." She poured out the rest of the
champagne and drank it quickly. Just let him try to stop her,
she thought. She drew herself up, straightened her hat, opened
her parasol. "You see? I'm perfectly fine!"

He sighed in resignation. "It's your head. Come on, bride."

They set off for the church. She thought: I really *do* feel
fine. We must have champagne in Paris whenever we can!
She took Drew's arm. It felt more secure. The road was
suddenly wavy and difficult to walk on. And the arm that
held her parasol refused to stay up, but kept drooping so the
parasol dipped down and bumped against her knees. She stole
a sidelong glance at Drew. She wasn't sure, but he seemed
to be chuckling under his breath.

"Why don't you close the parasol?" he asked. "You can
loop the ribbon around your wrist."

"I think I shall," she said grandly. "It's very heavy."

Old Jack was waiting at the church, down in front with
the Reverend Carpenter. "I'll be jiggered," he said. "You look
like a mighty fine lady, Marcy."

She smiled and sailed down the aisle to him, though her
knees gave way in mid-sail and Drew had to support her with
his arm. By the time the Reverend Carpenter had opened his
book and begun the service, she was frowning in bewilderment. Who had let loose the swarm of bees in the church?
She couldn't see them, but she could certainly hear them,
buzzing so loudly in her head that they threatened to drown
out the reverend.

I can't breathe, she thought. I've eaten too much. And this
danged corset . . . ! She wriggled in distress, looked helplessly
at Drew, and hiccoughed loudly. The Reverend Carpenter

stopped, his mouth twitching in a weak smile, and cleared his throat.

"Shall I go on, Miss Tompkins?"

"Of course," she said, and hiccoughed again. Beside her Drew made a sound that was like a snorting horse.

"Go on, reverend," he said solemnly.

Marcy blinked her eyes, trying to clear her head. Good! That seemed to have chased away the bees. But the hiccoughs remained, and were getting worse, bubblng up from her chest every minute or so. Drew didn't seem to mind; in fact, he was now chuckling softly, but the reverend looked scandalized.

The smile faded from Drew's face. "Please go on, reverend. Pay Miss Tompkins no mind. An unfortunate physical condition. She can't help it. It runs in the family."

Old Jack began to sputter. "Consarn it! Family condition? She's been drinking!" The reverend dropped his missal.

"Uncle Jack!" cried Drew in horror. "How can you say that? You know I'm 'Temperance.' Marcy is as sober as I am. I wouldn't marry her under any other conditions. Now please, reverend, hurry with the ceremony. You can hear how the poor child is suffering." He turned mournful eyes on Marcy, whose hiccoughs had now become so violent that she felt in danger of snapping the hooks of her dress.

I want to die, she thought. Something is the matter with my head, and my eyes, and my ears. And the room, which doesn't want to stop spinning. And these blamed hiccoughs...

"*Do* you, Miss Tompkins?"

She jumped. The Reverend Carpenter was staring at her. What an unpleasantly loud voice, she thought. "Do I what?"

"I've just asked you if you take this man, and ... etcetera."

She nodded vigorously and hiccoughed again. "I do," she said. "And etcetera too."

"Then I pronounce you man and wife."

She grinned and threw her arms around Drew's neck. There was a loud pop. She looked down and saw the button of her gray petticoat slide from beneath her skirts and wobble across the floor. There was a rustling sound, then the petticoat itself lay about her ankles.

"Oh hell!" said Drew, and burst into laughter. He handed the reverend his fee and thanked him profusely as the poor man, white and shaking, escaped to the safety of his parsonage. He turned to Old Jack. "I'd thought to ask you to have a bit of wedding supper with us, Uncle Jack, but I don't think Marcy can quite manage it."

Old Jack shook his head. "You dang well better keep a tight rein on that girl! I have friends in North Creek. Don't fret for me. I'll see you in the morning." He jerked his chin toward Marcy, who was now swaying precariously. "What are you going to do about her?"

Marcy stared at her left hand in bewilderment. "When did you give me the ring, Drew?" The words were oddly slurred.

Drew laughed again. "She sure as hell can't walk back to the hotel, Uncle Jack! With or without her petticoat around her feet. Come on, Mrs. Bradford. Step out of that petticoat and hang on to your hat."

She frowned at him, but did as she was told. At least the hiccoughing had stopped.

"Good night, Uncle Jack." Drew reached out, grabbed Marcy around the waist, and slung her over one shoulder. "See you in the morning."

Dang him, she thought, clutching her hat for dear life as she bobbed upside-down on his shoulder. She really ought to tell him to put her down. But she was suddenly too tired to care.

She woke to find herself in bed, and the hotel room in darkness except for one small kerosene lamp. Drew was sitting and reading, his tall form covered with a long white nightshirt. Her hands went under the covers, feeling for her clothes. He'd left her the chemise, at least. She sat up. Her head still felt light. "What time is it?"

He looked up and smiled. "Only about nine." He put down his book and crossed to the bed. "How do you feel?"

She groaned. "Good grief. Was I really drunk?"

"Gloriously. I don't think the reverend will ever be the same."

"And I hiccoughed? And said those things?"

"What things?"

"About the bees in the church."

He chuckled. "No. Thank God you didn't tell us about the bees."

"And my petticoat?" Maybe she'd imagined that, too, she thought hopefully.

"I had to go back later and fish around in the dark for the button."

"Oh-h-h. I'm sorry, Drew."

"Sorry?" He began to laugh. "I thought it was the best wedding in the world!"

She giggled. "The reverend was lucky I didn't lose my drawers!" They began to laugh together, clinging to each other in helpless merriment until Marcy began to feel the tears pouring down her cheeks. "I can't . . ." she gasped. "I can't! If I don't stop, my face will crack! And I'm dying of thirst."

"There's a big pitcher of water in the parlor." He kissed her, patted her softly on the rump. "Hurry back. I'll be waiting for you."

When she returned from the parlor he was stretched out on the bed. It all seemed so unreal, so wonderful, this whole incredible day. And now her love, her *husband* was waiting for her. She marched over to the bed and stared down at him. "Tarnation, Drew Bradford! I do love you!"

She let out a whoop and leaped on top of him. There was a loud crash as the bed slats gave way and the mattress fell through to the floor. They sat up together, roaring with laughter, their bodies tangled in the sheets and quilt.

Marcy threw her arms around his neck, feeling a sudden sharp pang at her heart.

"Oh Drew," she whispered. "Let's never stop laughing."

Chapter
Seven

Willough poured the coffee and handed the cup to Nat. I wonder what he's thinking, she thought, staring at me with those eyes. Golden brown, with dark flecks in them. A tiger's eyes. She knew what he was thinking when he looked at Brian—the eyes were cool, polite, with just the edge of distaste for the rich industrialist. I'll work for you, I'll work with you, the eyes seemed to say, but I don't have to like what you're doing.

She certainly knew what he was thinking when he looked at Arthur. He had watched Arthur like a hawk all during dinner, frowning each time Arthur bent to her with a soft compliment, a gentle touch of his hand on hers. And when they had moved into the parlor for coffee, Nat had positioned himself in the middle of the sofa, so there was no way Arthur could sit next to her. She had glared at Nat, and drawn up a small chair to the serving table.

After that humiliating scene in the boathouse, she thought, he must think that I'm a fool as well as a snob. I behaved so badly, forgetting all I've been taught of how a lady should behave. The game went too far. Not because of any impropriety on Arthur's part, but because I encouraged him. I'm sure nothing would have happened, but it was frightfully indiscreet nonetheless.

"I'll have more coffee, lass." Brian held out his cup to her.

"Are you sure, Daddy? You didn't sleep well last night. I could hear you tossing and turning when I came down here for a book."

He laughed softly. "Hell, lass, I should be getting drunk!" His voice had a lilt to it. "We've something to celebrate tonight. Eh, Nat?"

"I'm still concerned."

"Humbug! What's to be concerned about? Rutherford and Seneca practically guaranteed my loan before they went back to the city this afternoon. By winter I should have the new finery built and ready for operation."

"Where are you going to get the men? We're short at the furnaces now because you've started a crew cutting wood and making charcoal over at New Russia."

"That's right, Daddy. And when winter comes, you'll lose more of the laborers to the lumber camps."

Brian snorted. "Lumbering! It's dangerous work. Why should a man choose that, if he can work in a finery?"

"It pays well, sir. And it doesn't take too much skill."

"Dammit, Nat! Neither does hauling charcoal, so why should I lose my best teamsters and fillers to the lumber camps?"

"Because you don't pay them enough, Daddy. We're already short-handed. You take your furnace men and put them in the new finery, and you'll have to find new men someplace!"

Arthur reached forward and put down his cup and saucer. "There's been a lot of talk, Brian, down in Albany . . . not openly, you understand . . . but Clinton Prison is bursting at the seams. There's some talk of using the prisoners to help out. Not as teamsters, certainly. Somewhere they could be watched . . ."

Brian scratched his chin. "Maybe in the mines . . . I wouldn't

have to be concerned about wages..." He eyed Arthur
shrewdly. "How much would it *cost* me?"

"It's just in the talking stages right now. It would depend
on who's up for reelection. And it might take some new
legislation, to get round all those ladies' humane groups...
But it would mean a lot of free labor."

Nat frowned at Arthur and turned to Brian. "I'm not so
sure it would be a wise idea, sir. If it meant that just one
man around here was put out of a job, there could be trouble."

Arthur looked at Nat with contempt. "You're remarkable,
Stanton. All this sentimental concern for the men, and the
land. I wonder you don't join the ministry. You seem to have
missed your calling."

Nat smiled tightly. "I dislike all plunderers, whether they
exploit men, or land, or"—his eyes flicked briefly to Willough—"anything else."

Willough looked from one tense face to the other. "There's
no point in discussing it," she said quickly, "unless it becomes
a reality."

"Quite so." Brian rubbed his belly and nodded to the servant who had come in to the parlor, and was standing attentively at his side. "Is everything in order, Martha?"

"Yessir, Mr. Bradford. Robert has set up a bed in the
boathouse, and I've left you a sleeping powder on the table,
and laid out your nightclothes."

"Well then, if you'll excuse me. Willough? Gentlemen?"

Willough frowned. Daddy looked drawn. "Are you sure
you're all right?"

"Certainly, lass. I know I didn't sleep last night because it
was too warm. The boathouse gets the breezes from the lake.
It should do for me very well. We'll see you in the morning,
Arthur? Before you go back to the city?"

Brian went out into the night, to the boathouse and his
bed. Willough stared pointedly at Nat. Why doesn't he retire
also? she thought. It was intolerable to sit here with the two
men glaring at each other. Doesn't Nat have any sense of
propriety? She was scouring her brain, trying to think of

something to say that would send him away, when he rose from his chair.

"If you'll excuse me," he said. "I have some work to do." He nodded to them both and went up the stairs to his room.

Thank heaven! she thought. She smiled at Arthur. "More coffee?"

"Please." While she poured, he moved over to the sofa and patted the seat. "You look uncomfortable in that stiff chair. Here."

She handed him the coffee and sat beside him. "I hope it's not too warm in the city," she began. She stopped, glanced up at the balcony and the bedrooms that overlooked the parlor. Nat was sitting at his desk in his bedroom, a book open before him, his head bent to the pages. He had left his door open. She thought: The impertinence of the man! She tried to ignore his presence as she chatted with Arthur, but she was acutely aware of her own voice each time she murmured a response or laughed at a harmless pleasantry; she wondered how it sounded to Nat, spying from his room.

Except for a sharp edge to his voice, Arthur seemed unaware of Nat. At last he put down his unfinished coffee and turned to Willough. "Come for a walk in the moonlight. I find our . . . chaperone intolerable."

They strolled under an August sky filled with moonlight, scented with honeysuckle—and talked of nothing in particular. He's such a gentleman, thought Willough. Not a word about what had happened in the boathouse. She was grateful for his sensitivity to her feelings. She would have died of embarrassment if he had spoken of it. At last she sighed. "It's been a lovely evening, Arthur. But you've a train to catch in the morning. And Daddy wanted to see you before you go."

"And it's dangerous for us to be out here together," he said softly.

"What do you mean?" She felt her heart skip a beat.

"I think you know, Willough. I shan't press you tonight. Not under the spell of this moonlight. But I want to see you when you return to the city. Not in your mother's house. I wouldn't want to call on you there. Perhaps supper. Del-

monico's. A private dining room. Someplace where I can
have you all to myself." They had reached the back door of
the house. Arthur laughed sharply. "I hope, for your sake,
that your watchdog has gone to bed." He took her hand in
his. "May I kiss you good night? A very chaste kiss," he
added, as she hesitated.

"Of course." She lifted her chin. He bent his head and
brushed his lips softly against her cheek.

"Till the morning," he said.

She let herself in at the kitchen door. The back of the house
was in darkness. Not even a light showed under Robert and
Martha's door. She passed through the kitchen and the moonlit
dining room. A faint glow of light came from the parlor
beyond. Martha must have left her a kerosene lamp to see
her way to bed. She stopped, feeling a sudden chill of fear.
With the exception of the servants, sleeping in their quarters,
she was alone in the house with Nat. The bankers were gone.
And Daddy was in the boathouse, insensible till morning
because of his strong sleeping draught. She laughed at her
foolishness. Nat had surely gone to bed by now. But just to
be on the safe side, she'd lock her door for protection.

She frowned in perplexity. Against *what*? The things Nat
had said in the boathouse had frightened her, but she hadn't
really understood. Oh God! Why hadn't her mother ever told
her anything? Surely that "fate worse than death" had nothing
to do with the delicious giddiness she had felt with Arthur
in the boathouse, or just now, when he had spoken softly in
the moonlight. She was sure it had more to do with the
trembling, the breathless terror she felt when Nat looked at
her.

Nat was in the dimly lit parlor, pulling down a book from
the bookshelf. Willough felt the anger boil within her. How
dare the man! He had waited up for her, like a suspicious
parent, like a disgusting snoop! "You're beneath contempt,"
she said.

He turned mild eyes to her. "I came down for a book.
Nothing more."

"And your open door? And your spying on us?"

"It seemed a sensible idea. To keep an eye on you."

She smiled in sarcasm. "Don't you want to know what happened outside, with Arthur?"

"I'm sure nothing happened. Your father has usurped the boathouse. And I fancy your Mr. Gray likes his comforts."

"Especially for a *seduction*?" she asked, mocking him.

He sighed. "I don't want to quarrel with you tonight."

But I want to quarrel with you! she thought. Oh, how she itched to tell him what she thought of him! "Is it because he's rich and you're not?" It was cruel, but she suddenly wanted to hurt him.

A small muscle twitched in his jaw. "Money's only important for what you can accomplish in the world. Not for its self-indulgence."

"But surely you envy him," she persisted. "His refinement. His polish. His obvious familiarity with the finer things. That you can only dream about." He flinched at that. Good! she thought. She'd drawn blood. He turned and replaced the book on the shelf. "Doesn't it disturb you that he's so much finer than you are?" she purred.

He whirled on her, his nostrils flaring in anger. "Go to bed, Willough," he said tightly.

"*Miss Bradford*, if you don't mind. I wonder Daddy doesn't insist you sleep out in the stables with the carriage horses!"

The storm burst from him. "You little bitch," he spat. "You rich man's daughter! Do you enjoy playing with fire? You're tempting me beyond endurance!"

Her eyes widened in fear. What had she done?

He took a menacing step toward her, his teeth clenched in fury. "*Run!*" he said. "Run to your safe little room and lock the door behind you. Or I just might do something that your father should have done years ago!"

She stumbled toward the steps, quivering in fear and something else—horror at her own cruel words that had unleashed the storm.

"No. Wait."

She stopped and turned, eyeing him uneasily.

"Willough. Miss Bradford." He took a deep breath. It was

clear he was struggling to control his anger. "Forgive me.
For what I just said. And for ... playing the spy. That was
uncalled for." He crossed to a window and turned, half sitting,
half leaning on the sill. He seemed to be choosing his words
with care. "Don't go up just yet. I've behaved badly all
evening. All week, actually. Since that unfortunate day in the
boathouse. Forgive me."

She stared at him, at his strong face softened by the glow
of the single lamp. She'd never heard that tone in his voice
before.

"I can't blame you for being angry," he said. "I've been
a fool. The truth is ... I *do* envy Gray. Not for his money,
or his advantages, or all the rest of it. But for you."

"He's just a friend. I've told you that before." My God.
Why was she shaking?

"But he wants you. And you smile at him." His voice was
filled with despair. His eyes swept her costume. "And you
dress in your prettiest gowns for him. You wore that lavender
bow for him. You haven't worn it since the first day you
came to the furnace. You should always wear it. It matches
your beautiful eyes."

She gulped. "I didn't think you'd noticed."

He smiled gently, bringing the soft dimple to his cheek.
"I notice everything about you. You look especially charming
in your new gowns. Your father may be many things, but he
has an instinct for what makes a woman look ... like a woman."

Her heart was beginning to thump madly. His words were
like caresses, gently touching her very soul. "Nat ..." she
whispered.

"And when you sit at your desk ... so solemn, so serious
... you chew at your pen, and frown. You're so adorable, I
can't get any work done, watching you." He cursed softly,
glancing around the parlor. "It's too dark in here. Come
closer. Will you? So I can look at you?"

I must be mad, she thought. Her feet seemed to carry her
across the room to stand before him. Leaning against the sill,
he was no taller than she. She felt no fear, only a wonderful
tingling to be so near him.

"Why do you hold your mouth so primly? When you forget, and your lips part, they're full and ripe, like a summer rose." He groaned. "Oh, God. I don't dare to touch you. You're so beautiful. You can't be real."

"Oh, please . . ." she breathed. It was too sweet, too magical to be endured. She was trembling from his words, from longings she could barely understand.

"I dream of kissing you," he murmured. "Like the enchanted princess in a fairy tale. But I'm not a very worthy prince. I'm afraid you'd vanish. The kiss of a mere mortal who worships you . . . *Would* you vanish, Willough?"

"I . . . I don't know . . ."

"Touch your fingers to your lips, Willough," he whispered. She *was* enchanted. Drawn into his spell, incapable of anything but obedience to his will. She caught the intoxicating scent of honeysuckle through the open window. She felt drugged—by its perfume, by his words, by his soft eyes that glowed with ardor. She put her hand to her mouth.

"Now touch my lips," he said. "Let me taste the sweetness of your mouth on your fingertips."

She reached out with her quivering hand and placed it on his lips. At her touch, he drew in a tortured breath and closed his eyes. He kissed the ends of her fingers; his hot breath burned her flesh, sending jolting tremors through her body.

He opened his eyes, those amber eyes that seemed to plumb her very depths. "My beautiful princess."

She smiled shyly. "The prince is satisfied with very little."

"What else can I hope for?"

"This." Moving closer, she kissed him full on the mouth. She rocked unsteadily on her feet. She hadn't thought a man's mouth could be so sweet. It couldn't be wicked! No matter what Isobel said. It couldn't be wicked to kiss a man and feel this way. His lips were soft, yet firm, and when he moved his head slightly, they stroked her mouth in a gentle caress. At last she drew away, breathing hard. His hands were tightly held fists on the windowsill. She smiled. "Aren't you afraid I'll run away?" Merciful heaven, how she ached for his touch! "I won't vanish if you hold me. I promise you."

He hesitated, then spread his legs where he sat, and drew her in close to him. She put her arms around his neck; it seemed the most natural thing in the world. "Willough," he said, and kissed her hard, his arms pulling her tightly against his hard chest.

She clung to him, feeling as though she would swoon.

"Wait." He lifted his mouth from hers and reached up to her hair. "I've been longing to do this all summer." He pulled the pins from her hair, uncoiling the thick black chignon, and stretched out the long tresses till they rippled down her back and shoulders and breasts. He held a lock to his face, inhaling its fragrance, rubbing its satiny smoothness against his cheek. "Oh God, Willough," he choked, and swept her back into his arms.

Her knees were turning to rubber, incapable of holding her up for another minute. Already positioned between his opened legs, she leaned against his inner thigh, seeking support.

He started violently, and stood up with such haste that she nearly toppled backward and had to cling to his forearms to keep from falling. "Christ!" His voice sounded strangled. He shook his arms free of her grasp. "Go to bed, Willough. For God's sake, go to bed!"

"What... what is it? What have I done?" She was still trembling from his kiss.

"It's not you. It's *me*! Look at yourself. Your hair all over the place... Christ! I could have had you out of your gown in another minute!"

"I don't understand..."

"Must I spell it out? You've allowed me to seduce you! And I'm not nearly as slick as Arthur!"

She gasped, her hands going to her burning cheeks. "Oh my God! Is that why...? The only reason you..."

"Willough, I..."

"You planned it!" she cried. "You kept warning me about men who flatter women. You planned it, didn't you? *Didn't you?*"

"I don't know. Yes! You were such a little fool..." He ran his hands through his hair. "No. No, I didn't. God, I don't know. I thought about it. But I swear to you I didn't mean for this to happen..."

Her voice was a shriek of grief and frustration and humiliation. "Damn you! You *planned* it! You bastard!" She went at him with her fists, pounding at his face, his shoulders, his chest. He took her blows without moving, his eyes cast down in shame. "I'll ruin you! You bastard. I'll see you never work again!" She had begun to weep, her words coming out in little choking gasps. Finally, overcome, she turned away from him and buried her face in her hands, sobbing bitterly. How could he? Oh, God. How *could* he? At last, with a deep shuddering sigh, she calmed. She wiped the tears from her face and, filled with hatred, turned to look at him. He was still standing by the window, staring shamefacedly at the floor. His cheeks were red from her blows.

All those soft words, she thought bitterly. Meant to lure her, to make a fool of her. But his kisses ... she had never felt that way before. He *couldn't* have pretended. His kisses had to be genuine. Hadn't he trembled, his voice shaking as he pulled her into his arms? Yes. He'd started out just to humiliate her, to show her how easy it would be to seduce her. But somewhere along the way, his baser nature had emerged. His lust had translated itself into kisses he himself couldn't control. She shuddered. It was true, what Isobel had often said. All men were savages, lustful animals governed by their passions, selfishly thinking of their own pleasures.

And she had been more than willing. Oh, yes! She might have let him ravage her, whatever that entailed. She would certainly have allowed him to go on kissing her. She felt a pang of guilt, remembering: she had longed to feel his hands on her body. She'd been clay in his hands, a helpless female at his mercy.

She frowned. An instinct she didn't know she had—perhaps a woman's intuition—had sparked a sudden thought. *At his mercy.* But then ...

"Why did you stop?" she said softly.

He looked uncomfortable. "What?"

"If you were so sure you could have taken what you wanted, why did you stop?"

He scowled. "I'm not a cad!"

She pursed her lips in annoyance. "Yes, you are! That was a caddish thing to do . . . to shame me . . . to make me a fool in my own eyes. You had no scruples about that. So why did you stop?"

He lowered his eyes, unwilling to look at her. "I couldn't take advantage of you," he mumbled.

"Why not? You're not a gentleman. You've said so yourself."

"But you're a lady," he growled.

"But helpless and willing at that moment. You knew that. I wouldn't have stopped you. So why did *you* stop?" She had the oddest feeling. The more uncomfortable he seemed, the more a strange joy seemed to flower in her heart. There could be only one reason. A man who cared for a woman would protect her innocence. *Did* he care for her? "Why?" she insisted. She was on the attack now.

"Dammit, I'm not a complete villain!"

"But you're a man," she said softly, and felt a thrill when he blushed. She put her hand on his arm. He flinched at her touch. She smiled seductively. "Perhaps you didn't enjoy kissing me." She wet her lips, running her tongue across the fullness of her lower lip. "Didn't you like to kiss me?" she whispered.

He groaned. "You jezebel! You have the sweetest mouth in the whole world." He was beginning to tremble.

Did she dare hope? "Maybe you didn't like my figure. Though I felt very comfortable in your arms." She dropped her head and looked up at him through the veil of her lashes.

His hands shot out and clutched her by the shoulders. "Damn you! Do you *want* me to rape you?"

She stared at him, steady-eyed. "No. I just want an answer. Why did you stop?"

He let her go and turned to the window, staring out at the night. "Because I happen to be in love with you."

She caught her breath, feeling waves of joy and wonderment break over her. Love! "Are you?" she asked softly.

"Yes."

She wanted to laugh and cry all at the same time. "Then you meant what you said . . . all those sweet words?"

He turned back to her, his face twisted with remorse and misery. "All those. Yes. And words my heart couldn't even begin to express. Oh, Willough. I'm so sorry. I had this crazy notion—Arthur is very wrong for you. I thought if I could make you see that—But the minute I began to talk, the minute I had you in my arms, I knew I must have been in love with you all along. I didn't give a fig about Arthur, or anything else. I just wanted to hold you, to love you forever." He looked down at his waistcoat, unhappily buttoning and unbuttoning one small brass disc.

He loved her. The wonder of it bubbled up in her breast. He *loved* her! No man had ever said the words to her before. And with a ring of sincerity that made her tremble with joy. She smiled tenderly at his bent head. "Does that mean you wanted to kiss me?"

"*Kiss* you? God knows I ached to take you right that minute! But half an hour later you would have hated me. And I would have hated myself."

"Oh, Nat!" She threw her arms around him, welcoming his impassioned kiss, and straining against him with all the passion in her own being. Denied passion, repressed for so long in her heart. Even after their lips parted, she remained locked in his embrace, her face tucked into his collar, feeling the scratch of his chin against her cheek. "*Would* I hate it?" she asked hesitantly.

"To be made love to? God, I hope not. But not now. Not like this. There's a right time. And for you, I think that time will be on your wedding night. With your husband."

She drew back and looked at him. "Arthur?"

His voice trembled in his chest. "Do you want it to be Arthur?"

She smiled and ran a gentle finger along the edge of his chin. "No," she whispered.

His eyes searched her face. "Willough? By all that's holy
... *Willough*? Can it be so?" She nodded. "And would you
marry me, if I ask you?" She nodded again. He laughed softly,
relief and astonishment washing over his countenance. "I
can't believe it. Willough ... beautiful Willough ... that I love
so ..."

"Merciful heaven, Nat! Will you *please* kiss me again? I'll
be an old maid before you kiss me, let alone by the time
we're married!"

He kissed her softly, then released her and led her to the
sofa, sitting down and pulling her onto his lap. She felt very
small, nestled against his brawny chest, enveloped by his
arms. "I used to watch you too," she said shyly. "You're such
a *good* person. It showed in everything you did. The way
you cared about the Wilderness, your concern for the men.
They think so much of you."

"But I frightened you."

"I don't know why. I thought about you so much. I missed
you terribly on the weekends, when Daddy and I would come
to Saratoga." She sighed. "Perhaps I was afraid of my own
heart."

"Are you afraid of me now?"

"No. It's only ... I don't know how to put this. I'm not
sure I understand myself. I'm not afraid of you—as Nat. But
you ... the man ... I'm always aware of how small I feel
beside you. So ... so helpless. It's frightening."

"And does this frighten you?" He tipped up her chin and
kissed her softly, then deepened his kiss when she responded
willingly to him. She threw her arms around his neck and
tangled her fingers in his soft curls. Could this be happening
to her? To be sitting on a man's lap, kissing him like a hoyden,
like a wild abandoned creature?

He stirred suddenly and grunted, drawing back from her
kiss. His eyes were dark and smoldering. "Now you'd better
go to bed," he said. His voice was a deep rasp in his throat,
and his chest was heaving as though he had been running.

"What is it?" she began, then sighed in dismay. Without
really knowing, she understood. And it was all her fault. She

rose from his lap and struggled with her loose tresses. "I'm sorry. I seem to bring out your base nature."

He stood up and took her hands in his. "My God, Willough, you make me feel like a *man*. There's nothing base about that. It's healthy and natural." His eyes swept her lush curves. "You have the most beautiful body . . ."

"Nat, please." She tried to pull away.

"I won't touch you. I promise you. But why should you be ashamed?"

"Because it's shameful."

"No it's *not*," he growled.

"Let me go," she whispered.

"No. I told you I won't touch you. But I *want* you, Willough—as a man wants a woman. Don't forget that. And don't be ashamed of it either." He released her hands and cradled her face in his palms. He kissed her softly. "Now go to bed. I'll see you in the morning. If it's all right with you, I want to speak to your father."

"Of course." She moved toward the stairs, wondering how she could be parted from him even until the morning.

"Willough?"

She turned, waiting.

He was smiling gently. "You haven't said it yet."

She felt herself blush, her normal reticence returning. "I've let you kiss me in more ways than I could have imagined! You know how I feel."

"I want to hear you say it."

"It's very difficult for me, Nat." Her eyes were begging him.

"I know. There's a high wall around you—built of ignorance and inhibitions. And snobbery too. I've got to break it down, brick by brick, or you *will* hate me on our wedding night. That's why I want you to say the words, no matter how embarrassing it seems."

"Nat . . . please . . . I . . ."

"Say it, Willough."

"I love you," she whispered, her face burning. She smiled in relief. That wasn't so difficult, after all! Nat was right.

All the conventions, all the genteel propriety—a confining
wall to be breached, with the help of a tender tutor. She
grinned. "I love you, Nat Stanton!" she exulted. She sailed
up the stairs to her room, feeling giddy with happiness. The
moonlight streamed through her windows; Martha had neg-
lected to pull the shades. She undressed without lighting her
lamp, then stopped, her clothing around her ankles, her hand
poised on her nightgown. She stepped out of the circle of
garments on the floor and stood in front of her cheval glass,
staring at her nakedness. She'd never in her whole life had
the courage to look at her own body this way. Her breasts
were firm, her hips rounded and sensuous. And the moonlight
turned her naked flesh to silvery velvet.

She laughed softly. A beautiful body. That's what he'd
said. Reluctantly, she turned away from the mirror, slipped
into her nightdress, and crawled into bed. She thought of the
paintings in the museums. For the first time, she found herself
wondering what a *real* man's body looked like. Nat's body.
She laughed again. Mother would be scandalized. She hadn't
even felt a pang of shame at such thoughts.

Nor had she a thought for Arthur Gray who cursed softly
and cracked his whip over the head of the chestnut mare as
he drove a rented carriage the next morning. He was in a foul
mood. The carriage was old and shabby—the best the hotel
could supply—and he hated driving himself. The sooner he
got home to his own elegant coach and driver, the happier
he'd be. But he needed to get those papers from Brian before
his train left today. And the name of that alderman who was
interested in buying some land up in the Clinton area. Brian
had met the man in Saratoga last week. Arthur smiled grimly
to himself. He could work out some arrangement with the
man. Brian didn't have to know all the details. No point in
cutting him in for more money than he had to.

Arthur cursed again. Damn last night! It had been perfect—
the honeysuckle, the moonlight, Willough trembling beside
him, virginal and innocent. And no privacy! With Brian sleeping in the boathouse and that oaf watching the parlor, what
the hell was he supposed to do? It was years since he'd tried

to take a woman out of doors, or in the backseat of a carriage. And then they were usually the experienced whores from Mulligan's Hall on Broome Street. They didn't make a fuss at the discomfort, and they didn't have nearly as many skirts to contend with!

But he wanted Willough. God, how he wanted her! All the years, all the frustrated passion with Isobel had suddenly focused on her daughter, till he was obsessed with her, mad to find satisfaction in her warm and young body. Yes. Supper at Delmonico's. Upstairs. It was very private, with a comfortable settee in the corner, and soft lights and champagne. And a door that locked.

He drew up to Brian's house and was ushered onto the veranda, where breakfast had been set out. Only Stanton was there, drinking coffee. Arthur nodded coldly, and was surprised at the cordial greeting he received in return. He helped himself to eggs and bacon, wondering what could have put Stanton in such a good mood. Somehow it only added to his own black humor. When Brian appeared he concluded their business quickly, eager to be on his way home. He'd just wait to see Willough, and then he'd leave.

He heard a rustle at the door, and turned. Willough was there, floating out on a cloud of pink silk foulard, and looking like an angel. He frowned, examining her more closely. Something was different. It wasn't just her hair, arranged in soft curls and ringlets that cascaded down her back, or the spray of flowers she'd tucked behind one ear. Her whole *attitude* seemed changed, the way she moved, smiled, carried her head.

"Good morning, Daddy." She kissed Brian on the cheek. "Arthur . . ." She smiled fleetingly in his direction—friendly, impersonal, indifferent—and turned her attention to Stanton. "Nat." The voice was soft and melting. Stanton crossed the veranda to her and stared deeply into her eyes before leading her to a place at the table.

Damn! thought Arthur. Something's happened between them! He should have come back into the house with her last night, made sure Stanton had retired. He cursed his own stupidity. He should have taken her, no matter what. The thought that she might have lost her virginity to Stanton last night enraged him more than anything else. He studied them both again. No. It wasn't likely. Stanton didn't seem the type. And Willough still had that air of fragile innocence. If Stanton had educated her in the ways of sex last night, she'd either be brazenly bold this morning or blushing with remembered shame. He smiled in satisfaction. It gave him a certain comfort to think she was still in the dark. *He* would enlighten her when she came to New York City for his party.

Brian looked up from the plate of food he'd been shoveling into his mouth, and motioned to the servant. "Ah. Martha. Is that the mail?"

"Yes, sir."

He riffled the few letters. "Bills!" he sniffed. "When they want to be paid, they can find you. A letter from my dear wife. She needs more money, I don't doubt. Here's one for you, Willough."

Willough had been picking at her food, exchanging shy glances with Stanton. She looked up in surprise. "For me?" She took the letter and ripped it open, smiling delightedly as she read it over. "It's from Drew!"

Brian snorted. "My artist son? What's he up to now?"

"Oh, Daddy! It's wonderful! He's got himself *married*, and now they're both on the way to Paris, France, where he plans to paint."

"Dammit, he's no son of mine," Brian growled. "Martha, what the hell did you put into that coffee? Bring me a glass of mineral water!" He turned to Willough with a scowl. "I don't want to hear you mention your brother's name again."

Willough looked up from the letter. "Her name's Marcy. He sounds very happy," she said softly.

"Wife or no wife, he's no good to me unless he's working beside me at the ironworks."

Arthur said, "I'll have to send him a wedding present. I was always very fond of Drew."

Brian smiled in malice. "So was Isobel. I wonder what she thinks of this news?"

"She doesn't know," said Willough. "Drew has asked us to tell her."

Arthur arose from his chair, put on his gloves, picked up his hat. "I'll tell her. It will be easier to take, coming from me." He said his good-byes, reminding them once more about his party, and hurried out to his carriage.

The train ride to the city was intolerable, the clacking of the wheels echoing his impatience and frustration. He had to have Willough. *He had to have Willough.*

He frowned, thinking of his upcoming interview with Isobel. It wouldn't be easy telling her about Drew's marriage. She had always doted on the boy. But wait a moment! He sat up stiffly. Drew was in Paris. It was clear he meant to make a career of his painting. If Brian had pinned any hopes on his son succeeding him, he would have to think again. The succession, if not the total inheritance, would now fall to Willough. He laughed softly. And Willough's husband.

It wasn't just the money, of course. He could have married half a dozen heiresses, if all he wanted was the money. And he did well enough for himself. The Fifth Avenue house would make that clear to New York society. But Boss Tweed was in trouble, and all his alliances were crumbling. There were too many aldermen and commissioners who would be ready to "sing" if it came to that. And some of them might even remember Arthur Bartlett Gray from the old days. He needed the power that would come from a controlling interest in the MacCurdy industry.

And a socially connected wife, with a name like Carruth . . . It was almost as good a name as Astor, and more respected in some quarters; the Carruths had been the cream of New York society while John Jacob Astor was still selling furs. With a wife who counted the Carruths in her family tree, he could move beyond Tammany Hall and sordid politics. Yes. To seduce Willough might satisfy his passions (and he had always found something exciting in corrupting an innocent), but *marriage* would guarantee his future.

But what to do about Stanton? There was certainly an attraction between the two of them. It might just be a passing

fancy on Willough's part; sheltered young girls often enjoyed
flirting with the danger of crude men like that. But surely
she wouldn't marry him. Still, he would do well to hasten
her disaffection. He had a sudden thought. He would invite
Stanton to his party. In the city, the man would look like the
bumpkin he was; Willough's rustic sweetheart would soon
lose his charms when viewed next to a Fifth Avenue gentleman.

Arthur stroked his mustache thoughtfully. The job could
be done. But he'd need an ally. He couldn't appear to challenge Stanton directly. He would seem too much like a jealous
rival.

Isobel. She had a way of making even a second-generation
heir appear an upstart. She could cut Stanton to ribbons. But
he'd have to be careful. The news of Drew would devastate
her. If she thought for a moment that he, Arthur, wanted
Willough for himself, she'd die. He chuckled under his breath.
He'd appeal to her snobbery, suggest that Willough's infat-
uation might lead to marriage. The thought of Stanton as a
son-in-law would horrify her. And—more subtly—he would
appeal to her dislike of Willough. If he phrased it in just the
right way, he could get her to destroy Stanton.

He thought: Sweet, cruel Isobel. She would do anything
to prevent her daughter's happiness.

In Saratoga, Willough stared out at the sun-dappled lawn,
pressing her hands nervously together. It had been hours since
Arthur had left, hours since Daddy and Nat had retired to the
dining room. She could hear the murmur of their voices,
broken occasionally by the sound of Brian's laughter. Good!
Whatever Nat was saying of his intentions toward her, Daddy
was not displeased. But why didn't they hurry? She had
already been into the kitchen twice to see to the picnic basket
Martha was preparing; she couldn't pester the poor woman
again! She took a deep breath, filled with a sudden longing.
Please hurry, Nat, she thought. She ached to have him kiss
her, to hold her in his arms. He had brushed his hand across
her shoulder as he had seated her for breakfast—a tantalizing
thrill that had left her hungering for more.

She heard the sound of heavy footsteps, then Brian slid open the dining-room doors. "Well, lass, it seems you're to be married!" he boomed.

Her eyes flew to Nat's face. He was smiling broadly, the dimple in his cheek more pronounced than ever. "November sixteenth," he said. "It will give you less than three months. But I wasn't about to wait a moment longer!"

"It's a good time," said Brian. "We usually close down Three and Four for repairs then. That way, we won't miss Nat while you're on your honeymoon."

Willough felt a pang of dismay. Why did he think of the business first? "But aren't you happy for *me*, Daddy?"

"Of course I am, lass! Nat's a fine man. You couldn't have done better. You're giving me a *man* to run the ironworks, the way it should be run. That damned brother of yours..."

Nat stepped forward and took Willough's arm. "I'm marrying your daughter, sir. Not the business. And right now, if you'll excuse me, it's your daughter I want to spend the afternoon with. If she's got that picnic ready."

"Waiting for ages." She smiled shyly. His eyes were on her lips. She shivered in anticipation. "Will you announce our engagement at once, Daddy?"

"No. We'll wait a couple of weeks. Until I'm in the city and I can discuss it with your mother."

"I'd prefer not to wait."

"No, Willough. My mind is made up."

Her lips pursed in annoyance. "But Daddy..."

"Dammit, Willough! One headstrong child is enough! A son who runs off and gets married, and now a daughter who thinks to tell her father what to do!"

Would she ever be able to please him? "I'm sorry," she said. "Whatever you say, Daddy."

"Where's that picnic?" asked Nat. There seemed to be a sharp edge to his voice. He steered Willough through to the kitchen to pick up their basket, then led her out into the sunshine, taking a path that meandered along the shore of Saratoga Lake. When they came to a grassy bank sheltered by a large yellow birch he stopped. "This is a lovely spot."

She shook out the lap robe that Martha had packed and spread it on the grass. "Are you angry with me, Nat? You've hardly said a word since we left the house. And you haven't even kissed me today."

He gathered her in his arms. "I'm sorry. I must be a fool. I'm not angry at you. I'm angry at him, I suppose. When he talked about a *man* to run the business. As though you hadn't worked beside me all that time. I saw the look on your face." He frowned. "Come to think of it, I suppose I'm angry with you too. You're still the good daughter obeying him without question. Dammit, Willough. You've got more spunk than that. Why can't you stand up to him?"

She sighed unhappily and stirred in his embrace. "I've never felt free. I've always tried to please him. And my mother, too, I suppose. Though it never seemed to help."

"Why don't you try to please yourself, for a change?"

"I'm not sure I know *how!*"

"Do you feel free with me? I don't want you to be like so many women today, who go from being their father's little girl to their husband's. Do you feel free with me?"

She felt his hard-muscled arms wrapped tightly about her, imprisoning her. "I still feel frightened," she said. "Yet not frightened. It's so confusing. But I *want* to be free with you, if you'll be patient and gentle."

His eyes were warm with concern. "How are you frightened?"

"When you look at me, when you hold me..." She took a shuddering breath. "Since that first day, I don't think there's been a moment when I haven't trembled when I'm with you. It's so strange. I've never felt this way. It has to be a kind of fear."

He smiled tenderly. "Or passion."

"That's a *terrible* word! A lady doesn't think such things!"

"What damn fool told you that?" he growled. "Passion is something all women should feel, if they allow themselves! Now put your arms around my neck," he ordered, "because I'm going to kiss you until you can tell the difference between passion and fear!"

He bent his head to her, his mouth hot and eager as it covered hers, pressing and insistent, moving against her lips with a hungry intensity. The trembling, which had been a small flutter in the pit of her stomach, now crept upward, setting her heart to thumping madly. Surely he must feel my heart beating, she thought. They were pressed breast to breast. *Breast to breast.* At the thought of the proximity of their bodies, despite the layers of clothing, she felt the most extraordinary feeling sweep over her. She stiffened in panic and pushed him roughly away.

"What is it?" he said. "Are you afraid?"

She found it hard to control her voice. "I . . . I don't know."

"What did you feel?" he asked gently.

She knew her face was burning. "Oh, I can't . . ."

"Try."

She put a trembling hand against the flat of her belly. "Here . . ." she whispered. "And here." She averted her gaze as she allowed her hand to drop lower.

He laughed softly. "You're a perfectly normal woman. At least your body is normal. I don't know what they've done to your head."

"What do you mean?"

"You pushed me away. But how did your body feel? I'm not talking about what you think is proper, or right. Or whether you think you *ought* to feel that way. Did you enjoy the feeling? Did you want me to keep kissing you?"

She bit her lip. "Yes. But . . . it's so wicked."

"No it's not." He grinned broadly. "We've answered one question, at least! It's not fear. It would be a strange kind of fear that left you so eager for more!"

She felt as if she would cry. He was so gentle and understanding. "Oh, Nat, I do love you."

"I intend to see that you never stop. But for the time being, how about feeding me? Let's see what Martha packed in that basket."

She giggled and sat down on the blanket, spreading her skirts around her. "I told her I wanted something special. We planned the menu together," she said, unpacking cold roast capons, pickled melon rind, and an artichoke pie, already cut into neat wedges.

Nat sat beside her, frowning at the pie. "What's that?"

"Why, it's artichoke!" She stared at him in surprise. "It's really very good. It's just the hearts, sliced up and cooked with onions, then put into the crust."

He scooped up a wedge and took a tentative bite. "Well, it's good, I suppose. But I'd prefer honest food."

"How ridiculous! This is perfectly lovely food! Why I . . ." She stopped, seeing the look on his face.

"I didn't have your advantages," he said quietly. "You'll have to get used to a plain man. With plain tastes."

"Oh, Nat, I'm sorry," she said, shamefaced. "I did sound like a snob again, didn't I?"

He smiled. "A bit. But the pie is good. I'll take another slice. And something to wash it down."

"I'm afraid it's just fruit punch. I still have a lot to learn about you. When I think of it, you probably would have preferred a bit of rum in it."

"You'll learn." He laughed, helping himself to half a capon. "Just so you don't plan a wedding I can't eat!"

She wrinkled her brow. "You really didn't give me much time."

"I don't want a fancy wedding."

"But I must decide whether to have it here or in New York City."

"Where would your parents prefer?"

She sighed. "It's not as simple as that. They . . . don't really live together. Daddy visits Mother in the city occasionally, but . . ."

Nat grunted. "Yes. That would explain it."

"Explain what?"

"Nothing."

"No. Tell me!"

"I'm not sure you'll want to know," he said gently. "Your father and Mrs. Walker . . . in MacCurdyville . . . last year . . ."

She gasped. "I don't believe you! Not Daddy!"

"He's not a god, Willough. He's just a man."

How could he say such things about Daddy? "I don't want to talk about it," she said sulkily.

He stared at her for a long time, then, "What's your mother like?" he asked.

"We don't get along very well. Drew has always been her favorite."

"My mother died young. I was only eight. We lived near Ingles then. Near Gramps. It's funny, I don't remember my mother without thinking of how beautiful the land was then. They hadn't stripped all the trees, or cut into the hills. We used to walk in the woods, she and I." He sighed. "She loved the woods."

"Why didn't you stay?"

"Gramps did. He had his work. He was a trapper. But my father was heartbroken when she died. He couldn't stay. And my little sister was sickly. She needed hospitals, medicine. We moved to Troy, so Dad could work in a manufactory. Ugly city." He shrugged. "My sister died anyway."

"Oh Nat . . ."

He smiled in reassurance, leaned over to kiss her. "Don't look so sad. It was a long time ago. Now, is that cake I see in the basket?"

"It's hazelnut. I hope you like it."

"My favorite!" He laughed. "We used to go out gathering hazelnuts, my kid brothers and I. And one time . . ."

While she cut him a piece of cake and poured another glass of punch, he told her stories of his childhood. A loving childhood. With brothers, and parents. There was a gentleness, a serenity in him when he talked of those days. The tension, the quiet frustration that she had so often sensed in him, seemed to drop away. Perhaps that's what she'd seen from the first, all unknowing—the warmth and concern, the goodness in his heart.

And the masculinity. Shamelessly, she let her eyes travel the length of his strong body, taking in every detail. The hard-muscled legs beneath his trousers, the outline of his thighs, his narrow hips. And something dimly perceived, and dimly understood—a shape, a roundness revealed when his frock coat fell open. She gulped, and forced her eyes to move upward. His chest was broad; she remembered the mat of golden hair that drifted across its hard expanse. She wondered if he still owned the leather vest she'd seen him in, the first day they'd met. His shirt fit badly, the sleeves too short for his arms. But they left her that much more of him to look at. His arms were almost as hairy as his chest had been, a dusting of golden curls that poked out beneath his sleeves and glinted against the dark tan of his hands. His hands were strong-looking. Short fingers with a wide palm. Wonderful hands, she thought. Powerful, yet tender, gentle. She shivered in pleasure, imagining those hands on her arms, on her face, on her . . . She couldn't even begin to picture where. She had only a vague image of those hands on her pale skin.

"What are you thinking about?" His voice was deep and filled with laughter.

Startled out of her reverie, she glanced at his face, then looked away, feeling the blush of shame color her cheeks. "Nothing."

"Your thoughts couldn't be any more wicked than mine, so there's no use blushing! Wouldn't you like to know what I'm thinking?"

"I don't think so."

"I'll tell you anyway. We're getting married on November the sixteenth. I just realized it's my birthday. Thirty-one," he added, in answer to her unspoken question. "And you'll be my birthday present. I've been imagining the scene. You'll be wrapped in your bridal gown, like a beautiful birthday gift. It will be a cold night. With a fire burning in the fireplace. No other light. I'll unwrap you in front of the hearth, and watch the firelight flicker on your soft body, and see the glow of love in your eyes. And then I'll carry you to the bed, and then"—he closed his eyes and laughed shakily—"and then it won't be my birthday. It will be the Fourth of July."

She bit her lip, feeling herself trembling again. And then what? she thought. What would he *do* to her? Something that made Isobel cringe in horror, and the servants whisper and snicker. In the boathouse, he had said that Arthur would hurt her. Would *he* hurt her? And yet, the trembling was not just fear. It was thrilling when he spoke that way, his words caressing her. "Nat," she said softly.

He opened his eyes. "I love you, Willough." He reached out and curled his hand around the back of her neck, pulling her close to him. "You look beautiful in pink. I meant to tell you this morning." He kissed her softly, his fingers stroking the nape of her neck. She sighed and let herself lean back so she was bent across his arm. His lips left hers to brush fleetingly against her throat; then he lowered her to the blanket. He stroked her chin with gentle fingers and kissed her again, his mouth sweet and undemanding.

I'll never be afraid of him again, she thought, closing her eyes and savoring the joy of being kissed, of being loved by him. Her eyes blinked open. What was he doing? His finger on her chin had begun to press down, separating her lips, pulling open her mouth. She tried to move beneath him, to turn her head, but he was now leaning so firmly over her that she could feel his heart pounding in his chest. *What was he doing?* My God! She felt the tip of his tongue brush against her opened lips, and then he had invaded her mouth! Her hands became angry fists, pounding at his shoulders.

He sat up and frowned at her. "Willough..."

"Stop it!" she panted. "That's disgusting!"

"How do you know?" he growled. "Have you ever been kissed like that?"

She struggled to her feet, smoothing her skirts and patting her tousled curls. "Yes! One of Drew's friends. I hated it! And I hated him!"

He stood up in his turn, but made no move toward her. "Do you hate me?"

"Oh, Nat. Of course not."

"Then why don't you let me kiss you first? If you don't like it, you can tell me afterward. But give yourself a chance, Willough." He held out his arms. She hesitated for a moment, then moved into his embrace, putting her arms about his neck. When his lips came down on hers she returned his kiss, close-mouthed, until—prodded by his probing tongue—she gave him access. This time his tongue played a tantalizing game, circling the edges of her lips, darting in and out, stroking and caressing. Allow yourself to *feel*, he had said. She relaxed against him, concentrating on her mouth, and his, and the wonderful sensations he was arousing in her. When his tongue moved upward to slide against the roof of her mouth, she thought she would swoon, feeling the earth spinning beneath her feet. When at last he released her she sank to her knees, quivering.

She smiled weakly, her heart filled with an odd mixture of elation and dismay. "Now I'll surely be damned in Hell for enjoying *that*!"

He laughed softly and dropped down beside her. "We'll be damned together, then." He pulled her into his arms, and this time, when he kissed her, she didn't hesitate for a second. His kisses were so wonderful that she protested only when he rose and pulled her to her feet.

"I think we'd better go back now," he said. "I'm enjoying myself far more than is good for you."

It still mystified her, some of the things he said, but she no longer cared. She found herself smiling every time he looked at her, and the sunniness of the next few days echoed the joy in her heart.

She smiled up at him as they strolled to the boats late one afternoon. Even as they settled themselves for a leisurely boat ride, her mouth curled up involuntarily. Not until Nat told her he'd be going alone to Ingles did her smile change to an unhappy frown.

"I don't see why I can't go with you, Nat. I'm so longing to meet your grandfather."

Nat let go of the oars, and rolled up the sleeves of his shirt. "Not this week, Willough. Gramps will need some time to get used to a *female* in the family. We'll go together next Sunday." He loosened his neckerchief, then resumed his rowing.

Willough tilted her parasol to block the sun as the boat moved on the smooth surface of the lake. She settled herself more comfortably against the mound of pillows. "He sounds a bit forbidding, your grandfather."

"Not really. A bit grumpy because his stroke has left him so helpless. He's just seen too much, gathered in too much bitterness through the years. He doesn't seem to be able to find much good in people anymore."

"He sounds a little like his grandson."

Nat stared in surprise. "I never thought of that." He leaned on the oars, let the boat glide. "It's just that . . . the war . . . it was such a horror . . . I don't understand the cruelty of people, the greed. It all seems so petty beside the war."

"You said once that your grandfather was the only family you had. I remember you said your father passed away. What about your brothers? You were telling me about them the other day. As little boys. But what happened to them?"

He blinked and looked down at his hands, tense and knotted against his thighs. "Dad was killed the second year of the war. In 'sixty-two. The three of us were all on leave back home when the news came. After that we were separated. Jed and Pete were together in the Twelfth New York Volunteers—my division didn't get to Gettysburg until the third of July." He stopped and rubbed his hands across his eyes. "I didn't find them until the next day, when Lee abandoned Culp's Hill. It looked like Pete had stopped to help Jed when . . ." He gulped. "Pete was only eighteen. Oh, hell!" he growled, and bent again to the oars, slashing at the water so the boat shot forward with a sudden jerk.

Willough watched him in silence, allowing him the privacy of his grief and anger. It made her love him all the more, the tender devotion to his grandfather that was partly love and concern, partly a desperate need to cling to the remains of his shattered family. "It's a wonder you're not a recluse like your grandfather," she said at last.

A wan smile flitted across his face. "I didn't have to be. The last eight years . . ." He sighed. "I slept, ate, worked. It's remarkable how people can live without feelings, if they set their minds to it."

"Oh, Nat . . ." She leaned forward and touched his arm.

He grabbed at her fingers and brought them to his lips. "I might have spent the rest of my life that way." He smiled and the tension drained from his face. "But I was undone by a pair of misty violet eyes."

She found herself blushing. "I'm glad it was I."

He grinned and steered the boat toward a shadowy inlet on the edge of the lake. "What could I do? You were the prettiest girl around. And you looked sturdy enough to raise a mess of children!"

The blush had become a crimson tide, creeping over her whole body. Sometimes his frankness could be distressing. "*Do* you want lots of children?" she asked timidly.

"As many as we can. I want a house full of laughter." He steered the boat into the shallows and put up the oars, then smiled at Willough, reclining on her pillows. "Now, my violet-eyed love, if you'll close up that parasol and make a little room for me . . ." Carefully, he moved to the stern of the boat and lay beside her, draped one arm possessively about her, and leaned her head across his shoulder. He breathed deeply, his broad chest rising and falling. "God, I love the peace of the woods." He pointed above them to a large maple tree that shaded their retreat. "Look. A robin's nest. You don't see many of them around MacCurdyville. Or any of the furnace towns. And now the land over at New Russia is being stripped . . ."

She frowned. "How *did* Daddy manage to get it? If it was state land, as you said."

"My guess is that he used Arthur to bribe a few legislators into changing the law. I'm sorry. He's not the only one. But he *is* your father."

She found talk like that upsetting. He didn't much like her father, or the way they lived, or the way they ran the business. "*Why* do you love me?"

He anchored her more firmly in the crook of his arm. "I told you. Because you have beautiful eyes." There was laughter in his voice.

"No. Really."

He raised himself up so he could look down on her. His

amber eyes had become serious. "Because you're strong. Clear-headed. Yet so fragile. And sad, I think."

She didn't like to meet his gaze. "Don't be silly."

"Yes. Sad. You don't like to talk about yourself. Your family. Your growing-up. You keep your distance. It's part of that damned propriety that keeps a wall between us."

She pursed her lips primly. "I've always been taught that a person respects another's privacy."

He shook his head. "That's just false modesty between people who love each other. I want to know you. All about you. When we kiss there's no distance between our lips. And when we're married there'll be no distance between us— your naked body pressed to mine. I want our souls to be the same, joined as our lips are joined, as our flesh will be joined—until I know every corner of your heart."

She thought: You ask too much. Naked bodies. Naked souls. It was too frightening. She laughed brightly. "What more is there to know? I'm what you see. Don't look for more."

"I can be patient," he said gently. "It's taken years for you to build that wall. I don't expect it to come tumbling down in a day. Now kiss me, and show me what you've learned."

She smiled and put her hand on his shoulder as he leaned over, covered her mouth with his. She strained against him, responding with a passion that still surprised her. She didn't wait for him to demand, but parted her lips to his searching kiss, even managing to meet his tongue with her own. What heaven, she thought, feeling her senses reeling.

And then he put his hand on her breast.

She pushed him roughly away. "What kind of woman do you think I am?"

He scowled, his shaggy blond brows veiling his eyes. "Dammit, Willough! I told you. You'll be a virgin until the day we marry. That's a promise!"

"But in the meantime, you don't mind touching me," she said accusingly. "As though I were a . . . Oh! I can't even say the word! What makes you any different from Arthur? *You* talk about naked bodies, about . . . about *virginity*. It's disgusting. *He* never did. I don't love him. I love you. But you'll never make me understand why I should be frightened of him . . . and not of you."

He stared at her, his golden eyes filled with pain. "I touch you because I love you," he said quietly. "Because I want to bring you pleasure. And it *should* be pleasurable, no matter what you've been taught. But I can't make you trust me if you don't. Perhaps we should be getting back to the house."

"No. Wait. I *do* trust you, Nat." She smiled shyly, took his hand in hers, and placed it over her breast. She shivered at his caressing touch as he bent again to kiss her. "Be patient with me," she whispered. "I'll learn."

On Sunday evening Willough sat on the veranda, listening to the chirp of the crickets. The waning moon had set hours ago. The only light came from the one kerosene lamp that still burned in the parlor. It must be terribly late, she thought. But Nat was coming back from Ingles; she couldn't sleep without seeing him first. After Daddy had gone to bed she had crept downstairs to wait for Nat. She felt her skin prickle in anticipation. She was getting quite shameless in her behavior. Since that wonderful afternoon in the boat, she had let him touch her body every time they kissed, his hands running over the bodice of her dress, her back and shoulders, even her hips in the front, where she seemed to feel the heat of his skin through all her skirts and petticoats. But tonight, waiting for him, longing for him, she had put aside her corset and her bustle and her second petticoat; tonight, when he put his arms around her waist, he would feel a real woman beneath the fabric, not a stiff barrier of whalebones.

She heard the creak of a carriage wheel, the soft clip-clop of hooves on the dirt road. In the gloom, she could just make out the carriage and two men. She waited, breathless, while the carriage pulled up in front of the house and Nat climbed down, paid the driver, waved the man into the night. She waited until Nat had stepped up onto the veranda, and then she went to him.

"Willough," he said in surprise. "It's so late. You should be asleep."

"I haven't seen you all day. You left so early in the morning. How was your grandfather?"

"Quite pleased with the news, as a matter of fact. He's looking forward to meeting you next week. And though I'm not supposed to tell you, he's busy writing an inscription in his favorite book to give to you."

"Why aren't you supposed to tell me?"

He chuckled. "It goes against the grain for him to admit that he's eager to meet you. You seem to have conquered the men in my family in a remarkably short time." He reached out and folded her into his embrace. "God, I missed you!" He stiffened in surprise as his hands explored the yielding softness of her waist, then he pulled her close to him and kissed her willing mouth.

She trembled in ecstasy. Released from its confining prison, her body felt and responded to the length of him, his hard-muscled chest against her breasts sending shocks through her, his hips pressed to hers with a hardness that was wonderful and strange all at once. When he released her and led her to the wicker settee she thought she'd die of longing. He sat down and pulled her beside him, turning her so she was cradled against him, bent back across his arm. He kissed her softly; she wanted to cry out her impatience. She thought: Why doesn't he touch my breasts? O God, why did I wear this heavy gown? I'll never feel his caresses! She had a wild urge to tear off her clothes, to press her naked flesh against him. And then—wonder of wonders!—his fingers were unbuttoning the bodice of her gown, slipping inside to grasp the firm roundness of one breast. She gasped in pleasure and clung to him while his hand explored first one breast and then the other, fingers teasing her nipples until she could feel them pucker and harden in response. There seemed to be a pulse that beat deep within her, aching, yearning for fulfillment, a throbbing that intensified with every kiss, every stroke of his fingers. "N-Nat..." she whispered at last. "I'm shaking all over. I never dreamed..."

He laughed, his own voice unsteady. He sat her up and began to rebutton her gown. "You don't know what it does to *me*! My birthday can't come soon enough to suit me!" He kissed her gently. "Now off to bed with you. I'll stay out here awhile and cool off."

"But, Nat . . ."

His voice was a little less gentle. "I intend to keep my promise, Willough. But don't make it any more difficult for me!"

She floated up to her room in a cloud and undressed in the dark, still feeling his hands on her naked flesh. When she crawled into bed she lay for a long time, stroking her own breasts, and wondering why it felt especially exciting only when Nat touched her.

In the morning the cloud was dispelled. In the clear light of dawn her behavior shocked her. She stared at a patch of sunlight on the ceiling above her bed. Self-abuse, she thought, feeling her face burning with shame. That's what it was. Touching her own body that way. Every proper mother lived in horror of such depravity in her children. She remembered a childhood scene—of Isobel slapping her hand, her governess giving her a frightening lecture on the evils that would befall her—because they'd found her touching a part of her body that was forbidden.

And Nat. Every time she was with him, she seemed to lose ground. He took advantage of her willingness to wrest concessions from her. The shameful kisses, the libertine hands that touched her all over. And now last night. He had practically undressed her! And she had let him! She could never forbid him again. She groaned in misery and rolled over in her bed. And the worst of it was . . . she had enjoyed it. Every kiss, every caress. *Only wicked women enjoy a man's coarse attentions*, Isobel always said.

She sat up angrily and swung her legs out of bed. If I'm wicked, she thought, it's because he's making me so! She frowned. What was that? On the table next to her bed was a rolled-up piece of birch bark. She uncurled it and stared at the words in Nat's handwriting.

"I love you, my sweet birthday present," it said.

That's all he can think of, she thought sulkily. Our wedding night, and his own lustful pleasures. She dressed quickly and went down to breakfast. Daddy wasn't there yet.

Nat rose from the table and grinned at her. "Did you get my note?"

A sudden thought struck her. "How did it get to my room?"

"I put it there. This morning."

"While I was asleep?"

He smiled again. "Sleeping like a fairy princess. I nearly kissed you."

She frowned at him. "Have you no sense of propriety? Coming into my *bedroom* like that? What will people say?"

"Oh, hang propriety," he growled. "Unless I assaulted you in your bed there's nothing the matter with it!"

"Is that the next step? The kisses, and the ... the ... undressing me ... And now my bedroom is no longer to be inviolate?"

"Dammit!" he said. "What the hell's gotten into you? I thought we'd conquered those inhibitions by now. I'm sorry about last night. I thought you wanted me to do that. I thought that's why you took off your corsets."

She felt the blush burning her cheeks. "I don't know what I wanted," she whispered. "I'm so filled with confusion."

He tipped her chin up with one finger. His eyes were warm with love and tenderness. "My poor sweet Willough. It will all be set right when we're married. I promise you." He brushed his lips against hers in a sweet and innocent kiss.

There was a loud cough behind them. "If I can disturb you two lovebirds ..." Brian's rumbling voice.

Nat winked at Willough and turned about. "Sir?"

Brian waved a piece of paper at them. "I've just heard from Arthur. He seems to have guessed from your behavior that something's in the wind. His reception is to be held on Sunday. He thought, since Willough will be there, that you ought to be invited as well, Nat. He's asked me to tender his invitation, and to urge you to come."

Nat shook his head. "I don't see how I can. I usually visit my grandfather on Sundays. He depends on me."

"Can't you arrange for someone to look after him?"

"It can be done, but Gramps wouldn't like it."

Willough smiled hopefully. "Oh, Nat. I'd love to show you off at Arthur's party."

He raised a skeptical eyebrow. "I'm surprised Arthur would invite me to begin with."

"What the hell's that supposed to mean?" growled Brian.

"We're not overly fond of one another, if you don't mind my saying so, sir."

"Dammit, I *do* mind! If you're to be my son-in-law, I want you to get along with all my business acquaintants. As a matter of fact, this would be a good opportunity to introduce you around in the city. You can spend two or three weeks, meet the right people. I might even announce your engagement at Arthur's party. Make quite a splash, eh, lass? What do you say?"

Nat turned to Willough. "What do you think?"

"You'll have to meet my mother sooner or later."

"Christ," he muttered. "I don't even own a dress suit."

Brian clapped him on the back. "You'll get it in Saratoga. Have them send me the bill. There'll be time to get a good custom-tailored one before the wedding. You'll have a few days here to arrange for someone to look after your grandfather while you're away. We'll leave here on Thursday. Give Isobel a chance to look you over before Arthur's party."

Nat shook his head. His eyes were dark with uneasiness. "Why does that sound like running the gauntlet?"

Willough laughed. "Don't be silly, Nat. It'll be fine."

"I hope to God you're right, Willough. I hope to God you're right."

Chapter Eight

"We ought to be going in now. I'm sure they're waiting for us." Willough brushed a leaf from her lap and stood up, looking across Gramercy Park to her mother's house.

Beside her, Nat reluctantly rose to his feet. "Let's hope your mother can make it through luncheon *today*. I'm rather tired of her scenes five minutes after we sit down to table."

"Oh, Nat, that's unkind! She can't help it if she's been feeling poorly every day since we arrived. I'm sure Drew's going away has been a terrible strain on her constitution. We're fortunate to enjoy better health."

He shook his head. "I'm surprised you'd defend her. Since her fainting fits—quite conveniently—seem to be brought on by something that you say to her."

She pursed her lips in annoyance. "Mother and I don't get along, true enough. But it's cruel to suggest that her vapors are of her own making."

"Her 'vapors,' as you so delicately put it, are helped along by her addiction to that tonic she takes."

"Nat! What a thing to say!"

He frowned. "You'd better get used to my plain speaking. I don't intend to curb my tongue. That tonic of hers must be half opium. And then if she takes laudanum at night to help her sleep..."

"Oh, Nat. She's been very kind to you. I wouldn't have expected it, knowing how she feels toward me."

"We haven't exchanged five words since I arrived. I wonder what she *really* thinks of me?"

Isobel seemed in good spirits when they sat down to the table. Willough felt an unexpected pang of sympathy for her. The news of Drew's marriage had been a devastating blow. Willough was pleased, of course, that Drew had managed to escape Isobel's clutches; still, she couldn't help but pity her mother, who had made it clear that her son was now dead to her.

Yes, thought Willow, Isobel was in fine form, showing the Carruth breeding that still won the admiration of New York society. Gracious to Brian, civil to Willough, and positively lavish in her attentions to Nat. And after the unkind things he had said about her!

Even the luncheon table reflected her good taste. She had spared nothing. The best silver, the finest china. And Grandma Carruth's delicate crystal goblets, perched fragilely on the Battenberg lace cloth. She smiled warmly and indicated the place of honor to her right. "Mr. Stanton, if you please." She waited until they had all been seated, and Parkman had poured the wine, then she lifted her goblet. "I understand, Willough dear, that your father will be announcing your engagement tonight at Arthur's party. May I take this opportunity to wish you both well? And to welcome you into the bosom of the family, Nat. I may call you, Nat, mayn't I?"

"Of course, Mrs. Bradford."

"Oh, but you must call me Mother."

One golden eyebrow shot up in surprise. "Isn't it a bit presumptuous before the wedding?"

She smiled sweetly. "My mother used to say that people of taste may presume anything they wish. But if it will make you more comfortable, you may wait till after the wedding.

Which can't happen too soon for my daughter, I should guess. She's positively glowing." She chatted amiably with Brian while the soup was served, a cold jellied consommé. The caramel-colored aspic shimmered and trembled in its delicate china bowls.

Willough frowned across at Nat, watching the expression on his face as he struggled with the jelly and lifted a quivering spoonful to his mouth. She thought: He might at least *pretend* to enjoy it!

Isobel was perfection itself. The moment Nat put down his spoon and gave up in disgust, she signaled to Parkman to remove the soup plates. She sipped delicately at her glass of water. "Do you like artichokes, Nat?"

He smiled in relief. "As a matter of fact, yes."

No! thought Willough, but it was too late. Parkman had already placed before him a whole artichoke, swimming in a shallow bowl of hot, buttery broth. Nat stared at it in consternation as the others were served, then looked up to catch Willough's eye. There was something close to panic in his glance. He had obviously remembered the pie; the green globe before him bore no resemblance to it. As nonchalantly as possible, Willough broke off an outer leaf of her artichoke, dipped it into the broth, and scraped the inner surface against the edge of her lower teeth, extracting the delicate gray-green flesh. She discarded the inedible portion of the leaf in the empty bowl that had been placed at her elbow. She smiled encouragingly at Nat. He hesitated, then imitated her action, biting off too much of the leaf. She watched in dismay as he chewed in vain on the coarse leaf, unable to swallow it. At last, with a murderous glance at Isobel, he pulled the piece out of his mouth and tossed it into his discard bowl. Heartened by the sight of Brian, who had already worked his way through half of his own artichoke, Nat tried again. He managed to deal with about three more leaves, but it was clear that his temper was on the edge.

Willough smiled uneasily. "It's as good as the pie that Martha made, isn't it, Nat?"

"Yes," he said tightly, and pulled off the next leaf with

such ferocity that the artichoke sloshed through its buttery broth and leaped out of the shallow bowl, knocking over the delicate crystal water goblet. There was the sickening crack of breaking glass. Willough sucked in her breath.

"Dammit to hell," muttered Nat.

"Nat! Your language!"

"Don't be a fool, Willough," snapped Isobel. "Nat had a perfect right to be angry. Parkman!"

"Ma'am?"

"Remove this course at once and clear away the broken glass! I will not have this sort of thing! What's to be the next course?"

"Ortolan, ma'am."

"Merciful heaven! Who planned this menu? Aspic, and artichoke that's impossible to eat! And now songbirds? Take it away, and tell cook not to send out anything else like this!" Isobel was warming to her indignation. "I want food on this table that a *man* can eat! A man with simple tastes! Plain roast beef. Even if cook must serve it cold." She smiled at Nat. "Will that be agreeable to you, Nat?"

"Very agreeable," he said through clenched teeth.

Willough thought: Why is he angry at Mother? She's doing everything she can to make him feel comfortable.

"Oh, dear." Isobel leaned forward and placed a delicate hand on Nat's sleeve.

"What is it now, Mrs. Bradford?"

She smiled apologetically. "It's only that the artichoke seems to have splashed rather badly on your frock coat. Well, it could have been worse. If you put on another coat this afternoon when you go for a stroll with Brian, Parkman will see that this coat is cleaned."

Nat stared at her steadily. "Except for my dress clothes, this is the only frock coat I own."

"Oh, dear. How thoughtless of me. Well, we'll see if we can find something for you to wear out of Drewry's wardrobe. A nice coat. And a few shirts also. I'm *sure* you can use them."

Nat grunted in anger, ignoring her, and bent to the roast

beef that had been placed on his plate. What's gotten into him? thought Willough. Mother was being unusually gracious and kind. Could there be such a difference in their backgrounds that he failed to see how rude his behavior was? She ate in troubled silence through the rest of the meal.

Isobel tried once more to engage Nat in conversation, then gave up, contenting herself with discussing Arthur's party with Brian. When the plates had been cleared, and ice cream put before them, she tried again. "Are you related to the Boston Stantons, Nat?"

He put down his spoon. "I doubt it very much. I'm sure the Boston Stantons are a fine old family. However, *we* were the *Troy* Stantons. And before that the *Ingles* Stantons. And before that . . . God only knows. Though I'm sure there must have been a bastard or two in there." He slapped down his napkin. "If you'll excuse me . . ." He rose from his chair and stormed out of the dining room.

Isobel looked concerned. "I seem to have upset him. Go after him, Willough dear. Take him into the parlor. We'll have coffee there in a few minutes."

"Yes," said Brian. "There's something I want to talk to him about."

Willough hurried out, catching Nat in the vestibule. "Come into the parlor," she said sharply. "Mother's serving coffee in a minute. And Daddy wants to talk to you."

He hesitated, then followed her into the parlor. His eyes searched her face. "Well?"

She was reluctant to meet his glance. "How could you?" she said at last. "Your rudeness was unforgivable. And Mother was trying so hard to be nice to you."

He snorted. "I think she did it all deliberately. The questions about my background, the false concern for my clothing—which obviously offended her sensibilities. And that *damned* meal! That was her doing, too, or I'm hanged."

"Nonsense! Why do it?"

"To make me appear a crude and clumsy fool. An upstart. A cat who dares to look upon a queen."

"Oh, Nat! How cruel of you! Why should she do such a thing?"

He laughed sadly. "So that you'd look at me the way you're looking at me now—with a little dismay, a little uneasiness, a little horror at your choice of bridegroom."

"Never," she whispered, near tears.

He softened, and pulled her into his arms. "Perhaps I'm the one who's so conscious of our differences, imagining that you must hate me." He kissed her gently, then laughed. "But I think I'll refuse to take coffee. Your mother is apt to give me a cup that leaks!"

The coffee service went well. Isobel poured with her usual grace, and Nat even managed to smile and pay her a small compliment. At last Brian belched loudly, put down his cup, and turned to Nat.

"I'll be announcing your engagement tonight, but I think you ought to know of some decisions I've made. Clegg is retiring. As soon as we get back to Saratoga, you'll take over as resident manager."

Nat smiled in pleasure. "That's very good of you, sir!"

"I'm not doing it for you. I'm doing it for me! I'm not getting any younger, you know. And then, after you and Willough are married, you'll become my partner."

"I'm . . . overwhelmed!" Nat grinned at Willough.

Brian stuck his hand in his pocket and absentmindedly jingled the coins. "I'll give you five thousand for a wedding present. After that she's your burden, lad."

Willough frowned, a stray thought sticking in the corner of her brain. "If Nat's to be your manager and partner, who'll be your clerk?"

Brian shrugged. "I've been watching Bill. He looks good for the job."

"But Daddy, *I* . . ."

"Don't start that again, Willough," growled Brian. "You'll be a married woman. You'll be able to stay home where you belong."

Willough opened her mouth to protest. Just then Isobel sank back into her chair. "Oh dear! Such a spell of weakness.

I'm quite overcome. Willough, will you see me to my bed? Perhaps you could read to me for a bit before I sleep."

Willough looked desperately at Nat. "But I . . . we . . ."

"Nonsense, lass!" boomed Brian, rising from his chair and clapping Nat jovially on the back. "Nat's coming with me. To my club. I want him to meet Bigelow. Besides, you're looking a bit peaked. Do you good to rest up, take a nap before Arthur's party."

If I'm looking a bit peaked, she thought bitterly, it's his doing. Bill as clerk. *Bill!* And though she hated to admit it, she had felt a pang at the announcement that Nat was to be his partner. Bradford and Stanton. Never Bradford and *Bradford.*

Isobel seemed to be disturbed by the same thought. As Willough helped her to her room and rang for Brigid to undress her, Isobel railed against her husband. "It would have been Bradford and Bradford. If he hadn't driven Drew away years ago. But I suppose *Nat* is delighted. It isn't every day that a man can get to own a business just by marrying the boss's daughter!"

Willough gasped. "Nat would never . . . !"

"Of course not, my dear." Isobel patted her daughter's hand. "I'm sure Nat is genuinely fond of you. Still, it doesn't hurt a man's ambitions to marry well."

Oh, God, thought Willough, remembering. That first day, Nat had told her that he wanted to be manager when Clegg retired. That was why he had taken the clerk's job—to stay on her father's good side. How much better a position he was in now, by dancing attendance on the daughter! No! She couldn't let herself think such unkind thoughts. Nat loved her. He *loved* her!

Isobel sighed wearily as Brigid went to turn down her bed and fetch her tonic. "I'm sure you're doing the right thing, Willough. If marriage is what you want." There was an odd note in her voice. It gave Willough a chill of uneasiness.

"Why shouldn't I want it, Mother?"

Isobel looked flustered. "This is a delicate subject, my

dear. And one best discussed with your husband after you're married."

Why would no one talk about these things? she thought desperately. "But if I wait to discuss it with my husband, it will be too late to change my mind!"

"You needn't take that sharp tone! I find this very distressing. But if you insist on frankness, despite my sensibilities ... It's only that ... a man's demands can be very ... frightening."

"In what way?"

Isobel put her hands to her burning cheeks. "Please. No more. I'll only add that I wouldn't go through it again, if I'd known then what I know now. But you must follow your own dictates, Willough. Now please leave, and let me take my nap."

Willough stood in the corridor outside her mother's room, willing her heart to stop its mad thumping. Was marriage the horror that Isobel suggested?

"Shall I turn down your bed for you, Miss Willough? For a nice little nap?" Brigid emerged from Isobel's room.

Willough jumped in surprise. "No. I'm too restless to sleep."

Brigid clucked her tongue in sympathy. "'Tis a shame Mr. Bradford took that nice Mr. Stanton for a drive. He'd be good company this afternoon. You'll pardon my saying so, miss, but you're mighty fortunate."

"Do you like Mr. Nathaniel?"

Brigid smiled archly. "That I do! He'll make you a fine husband, you mark my words. A big strapping lad like that ... Me brothers used to say, with a man like that a girl couldn't walk for a week after—well, you know what I mean!—and be glad for it!"

Willough felt her mouth go dry. "Perhaps you'd better see to my gown. It needs a bit of pressing."

Brigid bobbed politely. "Very good, miss," and hurried down the corridor to Willough's room.

Willough thought: I mustn't think of such things. I'm being foolish. Yet Nat had said in the boathouse that Arthur would have hurt her. Was that what it was? Pain and grief?

A book. She might divert her fevered brain with something light to read. Daddy had some books in his study. There was no point in going downstairs to the library. She picked up the first book that caught her eye. *The Undeveloped West, or Five Years in the Territories*. It didn't look promising. She flipped it casually, noting the advertisements for other books by the same publisher. *Human Science, or Phrenology*. Definitely not. *Sights and Sensations of New York*. That might be interesting to order. *Sexual Sciences; including Manhood, Womanhood, and their Mutual Inter-Relations; Love, its Laws, Power, etc*. She scanned the list of topics; maybe there were answers here. She groaned. No. Only more frightening mysteries. "How young husbands should treat their brides to avoid shocking them." "How to increase the joys of wedded life, and how to increase female passion." She pushed the book back onto the shelf. There must be something that would be more helpful! She saw the word "Wife." On a little brown book tucked into a corner of the last shelf. This was more like it. *An Obedient Wife*. Smiling in relief, she pulled down the book and opened it.

"Oh my God," she whispered. Trembling, she replaced the book and stumbled out of the study, seeking the safety, the sanctuary of her own room. And all the while, before her eyes, she still saw the pictures. Of naked women tied to bedposts. Of leering men with whips. She had heard there were books like that. She hadn't imagined that *Daddy* would read them!

She sank onto her bed, her mind whirling in confusion. Was she a fool to marry Nat? Quite aside from the more terrifying aspects of the man—Brigid's "big strapping lad"— there were other doubts in her mind, doubts she'd tried not to face. His behavior at luncheon: Feeling out of place, he had accused Isobel of deliberate malice. Yet it was very clear to *her* that her mother had never been less snobbish, more democratic toward her social inferiors. Would he always be defensive about his background?

And the partnership in the MacCurdy enterprises. Putting aside her own bitter resentment—and, yes, *jealousy*—she was still left with a question. Was he marrying her for Daddy's money, for her inheritance?

And the last, most frightening question. Was it love he felt for her? Or lust? She'd seen the power of his hands, crushing his pipe in anger, pounding a table. Would that lust, that powerful anger translate itself into something horrible after they were married? Like the pictures in Daddy's book?

She curled up on the soft quilt, fighting back the doubts, the fears that threatened to overwhelm her. Sleep, when it came, was a relief.

She was awakened by Brigid's soft shake. "Miss Willough. I've drawn a bath for you." She struggled upright, blinking her eyes. Evening had fallen. She watched as Brigid scurried about the room, pulling the shades, turning up the gaslight. Her gown was laid out neatly across one side of the bed— a frothy concoction of pale blue silk and pink tulle festooned with garlands of silk flowers. Beside it were fresh underpinnings: drawers and sleeveless chemise, a blue silk corset, and several petticoats, including one with a stiff bustle. "I've brought you a cup of tea," said Brigid. "And then I'll just get you into your tub. But Mrs. Bradford..."

Willough sipped her tea. "I understand. I can manage the bath quite nicely. I'll wait for you in my wrapper. When you've finished with my mother you can help me with my gown and hair."

"It should be a lovely party. Mr. Gray has been telling your mother about it for weeks."

"Yes." Willough smiled. She was beginning to feel the excitement. Arthur's elegant new house, her beautiful ball gown, and Nat at her side. She laughed softly. After her nap the terrors of this afternoon were gone, like a bad dream.

She bathed slowly, luxuriating in the scented tub, then dried and perfumed and powdered herself. She donned the lace-trimmed chemise and drawers and hooked on her corset, leaving the back lightly laced. Brigid would tighten it for her later. She slipped into a lace and dimity wrapper, tied it loosely in the front, and sat at her dressing table to brush her hair. There was a soft tap at the door.

Brigid must have finished with Isobel already. "Come in."

Nat was there, in his shirtsleeves and black dress trousers, a helpless expression on his face. He waved his starched collar and tie. "I can't manage the damned things."

She smiled and stood up, taking the collar from him. "Why didn't you ring for Parkman?"

He kissed the tip of her nose. "He's not as pretty as you."

She giggled and put the collar around his neck, buttoning it to his shirt band. She tied the tie with deft fingers, frowned at the results, pulled it loose, and started again. "How was your meeting with Bigelow?"

He shrugged. "He's a good man to know, but I would have preferred to spend the afternoon with you. You smell delicious." He slipped his hands under her wrapper and pulled her close, then bent his head to the patch of exposed flesh at her bosom.

"Nat. Don't."

"Why not?" He brushed his mouth against her bare skin.

"Because I'm in a state of undress, and this is my bedroom. And you shouldn't even be here!"

His lips had moved up to her neck. "You have the softest skin . . ."

"You're not even listening to me. All you want is . . . is my body!"

He stopped kissing and grinned at her. "Yes indeed, ma'am."

"And you probably just came here tonight to try and talk me into bed," she said sourly.

His amber eyes were dark with bewilderment. "My God, you're serious! Willough, how many times do I have to tell you? I *won't*! Not till we're married."

"That's what you always say," she accused. "For your birthday. As if you can hardly wait! But you take what you can in the meantime. Like some lustful pirate!"

He ran his hand through his sandy curls. "Goddammit! Are there only two kinds of men to you? The 'gentleman' who won't even touch a woman, and the animal who's filled with lust? Well I'm not either one. I'm a man who loves you, honors you, respects you. But I want you too. Your body! And *that's* part of love!"

"Stop it! I don't want to hear such talk!"

He put his hand on her bare arm. "Willough . . . please . . ."

She shook off his fingers. All the horrors of the afternoon had come crowding back. "Don't touch me!" she cried. "You're so . . . disgusting sometimes. So . . . so . . . *male*! Don't touch me! I don't like to be pawed!"

"Pawed?" His eyes were like amber fire. His strong arms shot out and clamped about her shoulders. "I'll touch you, all right! By God, I've got half a mind to take you across my knee! I'm so sick of being treated like a ruttish swine because I love you. Because I *want* you—in a healthy, normal way. Maybe a good spanking will bring you to your senses!"

She blanched in fear, overwhelmed by his physical strength and presence. The thought of him spanking her, the intimacy of his hand on her buttocks, even in anger . . . She gulped. And when they were married no part of her body would be safe from his touch. Her lips began to tremble.

He exhaled slowly and dropped his hands. "Willough, I'm sorry." He turned to the door. "I'd better finish dressing. I'll meet you in the parlor when you're ready. All right?"

She tried to smile. She *did* love him. "I'll hurry."

Arthur's new house on Fifth Avenue was an elegant marble mansion in the Italian style—far different from the sedate brownstones of Gramercy Park and Washington Square, which represented the "old" society of New York. The "new" society, like the Astors, with money to spend, were building ornate palaces on the avenue above Madison Square at Twenty-third Street. Boss Tweed himself had built his home uptown at 511 Fifth Avenue, at Forty-third Street.

Willough could see that Arthur had spared no expense. Alighting from their carriage, they were ushered into the front hall, a magnificent foyer paneled in rich dark wood, elaborately carved, and hung with massive tapestries. A large chandelier, its gaslit globes blazing brightly, illuminated the hall and the red-carpeted staircase that descended majestically to the upper floors. At one end of the hall Willough glimpsed, through wide double doors, a blue and gold paneled room from which emanated the lilting cadences of a waltz. At the other end of the hall, matching double doors revealed a red-brocaded room massed with potted palms. In the center of the red room was a large buffet table crowded with platters of food, blazing candles, and silver bowls filled with scarlet roses. Besides the dining room and the ballroom there seemed to be several smaller rooms off the foyer; from the tinkling sound of a piano, Willough guessed that one of them must be a music room.

Arthur greeted them cordially as the servants took the ladies' wraps. He looked extraordinarily handsome, from the distinguished flecks of gray at the temples of his brown hair to his smoothly manicured mustache and the shine on his patent-leather shoes. His dress suit was superbly cut, a dapper contrast, Willough noted with dismay, to the badly fitting suit that Nat had managed to buy in Saratoga. "Isobel," Arthur said, kissing her hand. "Brian. And Stanton. Good of you to come. I hope we can be friends." He held out his hand, which Nat took reluctantly.

Brian laughed. "And business acquaintances, perhaps. I might have a little announcement to make later in the evening, Arthur."

Arthur's brown eyes flickered in sudden curiosity. "Really? Well, wait until our musicale, when everyone is assembled." He turned to Isobel. "I took your advice, my dear, and engaged those opera singers from the Academy of Music."

Isobel beamed. "Your home is lovely, Arthur. May we look around?"

"Please do. I'd show you myself, but there are still guests to greet." He smiled warmly at Willough. "But I haven't forgotten that I had invited *you* especially to take a glass of champagne with me. As soon as I can break away, I intend to hold to my promise. In the meantime, make yourselves at home. Stanton, there's some good whiskey on the sideboard in the dining room." His casual glance took in Nat's ill-fitting suit. "You look like a hard-drinking man."

Nat smiled, though a small muscle worked in the side of his jaw. "I can hold my liquor."

"Well, I want to see the house," announced Isobel. While Arthur moved off to his other guests, Isobel took Brian's arm and began her inspection, exclaiming in delight at every painting and vase and piece of furniture. Nat went to take Willough's arm, then changed his mind when he saw the look on her face.

"I want that drink," he muttered. "Are you coming?" She nodded and followed him into the dining room, watching in silence as he tossed down a glass of whiskey. "What is it?" he said at last. "Are you still angry with me?"

"No."

"Then what's wrong?"

How could she tell him of her doubts and fears? *She* was to blame, not he. For allowing other people's words to upset her. "Nothing's wrong," she said miserably, "and everything's wrong. I don't know."

His eyes were dark and troubled. "Shall I tell your father not to make that announcement tonight?"

She bit her lip. "No," she whispered.

"Ah! There you are, Willough!" His face wreathed in a broad smile, Arthur moved through the dining room, nodding at his other guests. He led Willough and Nat to a large table in the corner of the room that had been given over entirely to the service of champagne. He handed them both a glass, and raised his own champagne flute in a toast. "To the fulfillment of all our dreams," he said softly. They drank, and then he turned to Nat. "Are you enjoying New York City, Stanton?"

"Enjoying is not quite the word I'd choose. It's a handsome city, with beautiful homes and avenues—if one is able to ignore the ugly squalor and poverty of the side streets. Unfortunately, I'm not."

"I said it before. You should have been a minister."

They smiled tightly at each other. Oh, dear, thought Willough. Let them not quarrel! "What a lovely epergne!" she said quickly, indicating the centerpiece on the table, a large glass cornucopia brimming with grapes and small apples.

"Thank you. I bought it in France. The summer of 'sixty-three, I think. Lord, it was hot on the Continent that summer!"

A soft laugh from Nat, low and bitter. "It was hotter in Pennsylvania that summer. Particularly at Gettysburg."

Arthur didn't blink. "So I heard. I was fortunate. I had the money to buy a replacement."

Nat's jaw tightened. "Or the cowardice."

Willough was horrified. "Nat! You're a guest in Arthur's house!"

He glared at her, his eyes burning. "But I'm not a gentleman. Remember?"

A suave smile from Arthur. "Fortunately, I am. I'll consider the source and ignore your remark. Willough, would you care for a dance?"

She was burning with shame at Nat's behavior. "Yes. Please!"

Arthur led her to the ballroom, where the musicians had just begun a polka. But after a few turns around the floor, Arthur stopped and guided her to a shadowy alcove between the windows. "You don't really want to dance." They sat together on a blue-brocaded sofa. Willough was too ashamed even to look at Arthur. "You look magnificent tonight," he said. "I don't suppose that fool Stanton has told you so."

"Arthur. Please . . ."

"I don't know what there is between you and Stanton. But I want you to know I'd be honored if you'd be my wife." She stared at him, her eyes wide with surprise. "I don't expect an answer now," he continued. "But I want you to know that I'd treat you as you deserve to be treated. With modesty, and gentleness, and respect. I know there's a difference in our ages, but that only makes you more dear to me. I could spoil you and pet you, my sweet Willough. I don't know what hold Stanton has over you, but who could love you more than a man who has watched you grow from a shy and reserved girl to a beautiful woman? You'd rule my home . . . and my heart . . . like a queen."

"Arthur . . ." she whispered, feeling overwhelmed.

"My love for you is pure and honorable. Only you can decide if your happiness lies with me." He smiled gently. "Shall I take you back to Stanton now?"

She shook her head. "No. I'd like to be alone for a while."

"I'll leave you then. Perhaps you'll save a waltz for me later."

She sat in her quiet alcove, as the dancers swirled about the room, and thought of what he had said. A pure and honorable love. She didn't love him, but the kind of love he offered her was infinitely less frightening than the unknown future with Nat. What shall I do? she thought, agonized.

She made her way at last back to the dining room. Nat was trapped in a corner with a dowager who clutched at his arm every time he tried to break away. She was hard of hearing, and kept insisting that he repeat himself into her ear trumpet. Willough deliberately avoided his desperate glances while she helped herself to a plate of oysters and wandered back to the foyer to inspect the smaller rooms.

Nat found her at last in the music room with its murals of cupids and goddesses, aimlessly picking out a tune on the paisley-draped grand piano. He waited until two gray-haired ladies had left the room and they were alone. Then he turned to her, his gold-brown eyes filled with uncertainty. "Am I still in the doghouse?"

"How could you call Arthur a coward?"

The eyes had turned to hard amber. "What would you call it?"

"Oh for heaven's sake! Lots of men didn't serve, if they could pay for a replacement! And the war's been over for eight years. It's no reason to be rude to Arthur. And in his own house."

"It's one more reason to dislike the man," he growled. He took a deep breath, relaxing his tension. "Willough, let's go home," he said softly. "I don't belong here." He tugged uncomfortably at his tight collar. "I'm sorry we even came to New York. In Saratoga, I only had your reserve to deal with. Now the wall between us is twice as thick. I'm not sure why

... or what ... But all this"—he indicated the lavishly appointed room—"it's just so much more clutter getting between us."

"Go home? The evening's barely begun! How would it look?"

"Dammit!" he exploded. "I don't care how it would look! When are you going to stop worrying about appearances in that priggish world of yours?"

"*Oh!*" It was too much! He was rude, insulting. Impossible. Tearing off her glove, she whirled on him and slapped him across the face. As hard as she could.

His head snapped back for an instant, and then he grabbed at her wrist, his fingers like a steel band, pulling her close. His eyes glowed in fury.

"Let go of me!" Her voice was shrill with fear.

"What's going on here?" Arthur stood in the doorway.

Nat turned, his hand still grasping Willough's wrist. "Get out of here, Gray. This doesn't concern you."

"I think it does. I'm not about to let a stupid clodhopper like you terrify a guest in my house!"

"You son of a bitch!" Nat released Willough's hand and swung at Arthur, his powerful fist landing a blow that sent Arthur sprawling, blood gushing from his split lip.

"Arthur!" Willough was on her knees, dabbing at his mouth with her lace handkerchief. She looked up at Nat, towering above them. "You coarse oaf!" she spat. "You crude animal!" (Could that be her own voice? Her own words?)

Nat's face turned white, though the marks of her fingers still glowed red on his cheek. "And you're a spoiled child," he said coldly. "Twisted by your fancy society into a snob and a prude. I don't know who that woman was in Saratoga, but she's not the rich man's brat I'm seeing tonight!"

She glared at him. Her fury had carried her far beyond the point of reason. "This rich man's daughter is going to exercise her prerogatives. You're no longer working for the Bradfords!"

"*Good!* I was just about to quit. I wasn't sure you wanted me in the business anyway." His lip curled in a sarcastic sneer. "But what will you do for kisses, now that you're used to them?"

Damn him. *Damn him!* She looked at Arthur, still lying on the floor, trying to staunch the blood from his mouth. "Mr. Gray has asked me to marry him."

There was a gasp from the doorway. Isobel was there, her eyes wide with horror. "Arthur! You . . . you Judas!"

"Then why don't you marry him?" Nat challenged. "Arthur won't *paw* you. He won't assault your fine sensibilities with his crude lusts!"

"No." Her voice dripped with contempt. "*Arthur's* a gentleman."

He laughed, a harsh, mirthless sound. "What you really mean is that Arthur's *safe*. He'd expect separate bedrooms!"

"I find you disgusting, Mr. Stanton." And frightening, she thought. Her heart had thumped in alarm when he'd said the word *bedrooms*. Nat would expect to sleep in the same bed with her. She'd never thought of it before. Now it filled her with fear, and a cold dread of the unknown.

"If you find me so disgusting, then marry Mr. Gray."

She looked up at him, at her mother still clasping a hand to her bosom in dismay. She felt an overwhelming urge to hurt them both, for all the doubts and miseries she'd suffered because of them. "I *shall* marry Mr. Gray!" she said, on the verge of tears.

Nat sucked in his breath between tight-clenched teeth. "May you be damned to hell," he said quietly. He turned on his heel and headed for the door.

Sobbing, she struggled to her feet and pointed a shaking finger at his retreating back. "You're not to come round to MacCurdyville, do you understand? I'll ruin you!"

Arthur stood up beside her and put a comforting arm around her shoulders. He ignored Isobel, who seemed about to faint. "Now, now, Willough dear. You mustn't disturb yourself. Leave it to me. I'll do whatever I must to see that Mr. Stanton doesn't upset you again. Not ever again."

* * *

"Combien?" Marcy pointed to the deep pink rose nestled in the basket of white blossoms.

The flower seller eyed her with suspicion, poked at a pot of yellow tulips, glanced up at the gray sky. *"Vingt-quatre centimes, Madame."*

Tarnation! thought Marcy. She knows I'm an American, all right! Five cents for a rose! She shook her head and moved on down the boulevard. She'd get her flower from the Place de Clichy, as usual. Old Jacques never had the freshest blossoms, but his prices were more fair. And sometimes he even managed to give her a bit of greenery to go with the single flower she had bought every day since they'd come to Paris. It was only that the pink rose had caught her eye, reminding her of the bush she'd planted in front of Uncle Jack's door.

She frowned up at the sky. It was going to rain. She'd never make it back to the studio. If it hadn't been for that danged Mr. Stewart . . . silly old goat, with his long gray side whiskers and his funny English accent, and his big teeth that made him look like a rabbit. But he was a successful painter, Drew said. His paintings were accepted at the Salon every year, and he earned a nice living with his brushes. They'd met him at the gallery of Père Martin, a dealer who had shown some interest in the young painters just coming up. While Drew, who spoke fluent French, had gotten into his regular debate with Pissarro and the others, Marcy had chatted with the portly Englishman, glad of someone to talk to. She was *trying* to learn French, and Drew was a patient teacher, but sometimes she found the foreignness, the loneliness of the city almost unbearable. If it hadn't been for Drew, and the occasional artist, like Stewart, who spoke English . . . She sighed. It was odd. She'd never felt lonely in the Wilderness, even when she'd spent weeks at a time tramping the solitary trails, or paddling a canoe over some vast lake.

She felt the first drop of rain on her head. Resting her basket of groceries on a low iron fence, she draped her shawl over her bright hair, and clutched it firmly at her neck. Dang Mr. Stewart, she thought again. She'd be home by now, brewing up a cup of hot tea, if he hadn't seen her at the *charcuterie* buying sausages for supper. He'd chattered away forever. And then to offer her that position! She giggled aloud. She didn't think he had an evil thought in his head. Still, to pose for him, for pay . . . and in the nude! She didn't mind posing for Drew. That was different. But she doubted she'd even want to pose for Mr. Stewart with her clothes on!

She shivered. It was beginning to rain harder now. It was the fourth time this week. A cold drizzle that crept into the bones, chilled the studio, no matter how much coal or wood they threw into the small stove. She gazed down the wide boulevard with its rain-slicked pavement reflecting the flat gray sky. Except for the occasional chestnut tree that still retained a few dull brown leaves, there was nothing to indicate that it was fall. The seasons were formless, the days were formless in this city. For all its dazzle and bright lights and manicured parks. She gulped, feeing the pain of homesickness. Where was the glorious show of color, the shining days and crisp nights of autumn, the beauty that made a person glad to be alive? It's in your blood, the Wilderness, Uncle Jack had said. Perhaps he was right.

But she had Drew. And the love and laughter they shared. And that was more important than the Wilderness.

It was raining too hard to stop for a flower now. She turned onto the rue de la Condamine. They had been fortunate to find the studio. Most of the Realist painters had left the Latin Quarter to be here in Montmartre in the Batignolles district. The rents were cheaper, and they were near the Gare Saint-Lazare. It was very convenient on a sunny Sunday to take the train to St. Germain or Argenteuil so Drew could paint in the open air. Drew was hoping that in the spring they could rent a house in one of those charming outlying towns.

She nodded to the *concierge* and made her way up the three flights of stairs to the studio. It was a single high-ceilinged room with a soaring window that let in the northern light. Just right for painting, Drew had said. The furnishings (added to by the tenants through the years) were sparse: a small round table that wobbled slightly, three unmatched chairs, one red velvet armchair that had seen better days, and a battered old sofa covered in faded chintz. A small work table—spotted with paint—for Drew. An iron stove for heat and cooking. Several folding screens served as partitions—for the "kitchen," which consisted of a marble-topped cabinet filled with pots and crockery, and a porcelain basin with a cold-water faucet; for the "bedroom," a narrow brass bed, an armoire without doors, a three-legged stool for a night table. And a space hidden away, for more intimate functions, with its chamber pot and bidet. There were two hanging kerosene lamps, half a dozen candle holders, and—set near Drew's easel at the window—a cracked but still magnificent candle stand, a discard from the Church of the Madeleine. The walls of the large room were covered with Drew's work, dozens of watercolor sketches, drawings of Marcy done in black and red *conté* crayon, a few pastels, and three paintings he'd completed since they'd come to Paris. They were scenes of boulevards, of boats and boaters on the Seine, of dancers at the opera. Like Degas was doing.

He'd left his Adirondack Wilderness pictures and sketches at his house in New York City. She would have liked to see them. To make comparisons. She didn't know much about art, but she knew that what he was doing here in Paris was far different from what he had done before.

Marcy set down her basket, shook the rain from her shawl, and hung it on a hook near the door. She touched a match to the kindling in the stove, put on the kettle for tea, and began to unpack her purchases. The sausages looked nice and fresh, and the sweet brioche was still warm from the baker's oven. There were a few potatoes left from yesterday—she'd fry them with the sausages and an onion or two. Two oranges, a big bunch of grapes. A bottle of *vin ordinaire*—they were really becoming quite French in their ways!

But no flowers. She was sorry now she hadn't stopped, rain or no rain. Crossing to the window, she removed a few dead blossoms from the geranium plant in its chipped cachepot, then put it on the table. It would have to do. She fussed about, drinking her tea, setting the table, as the evening shadows lengthened.

She smiled. Drew's footsteps, pounding exuberantly up the stairs. She threw open the door and stood there grinning, waiting for him. He bounded into the room, picked her up and swung her around, ending his greeting with a hearty kiss. Putting her down at last, he went to the open door and called out. *"Ici, mon petit!"*

At once a sweet-faced little boy appeared, nearly hidden by a large bouquet of flowers, from whose multicolored depths poked a bottle of champagne tied in a purple ribbon. The boy bowed to Marcy as best he could, handed her the flowers, and began to sing a song, piping out the notes in a clear, squeaky voice, somewhat off key. Tarnation! thought Marcy. How do they learn to speak French at such an early age? It never ceased to amaze her, though Drew always laughed at her fanciful idea. "But really, Drew," she'd say. "It must be much harder for them to learn French than it is for our American children to learn English!"

"Merci!" She beamed when the lad was through, kissed him on the forehead, and handed him a piece of toffee. "What was he singing?" she asked, after Drew had tossed him a coin and seen him out the door.

Drew's blue eyes twinkled. "It was a very bawdy song, all about how nice it is to sleep with my beautiful woman!"

"Drew Bradford! You devil. You ought to be ashamed! Corrupting that poor child!"

He chuckled. "He comes from a family of fifteen children. Three of his sisters are prostitutes. I don't think there's *any-thing* he doesn't know!"

She shook her head. "I'll never get used to the wickedness of this city!"

His mouth twisted in a wry smile. "They're all the same. But you're the one who wanted to live in a city."

"You're not wet. Has it stopped raining?"

"I left my umbrella downstairs. I'll fetch it when it dries. It's a foul night out. That's why I decided we should stay home. In spite of the occasion."

"What occasion?"

He frowned. "The flowers and the champagne. And the song. What did you think they were for?"

Her heart was filled with joy and love. "I thought they were just because you loved me."

"And so I do, Mrs. Bradford. But the gifts are in honor of our anniversary. Two months today."

She gasped. "Oh, Drew! I forgot!"

"I'll make you pay for it. Tonight. In bed." He leered wickedly. "Now find something to put those flowers in. They're a gift for you today, but *I* want to paint them tomorrow. And while you're getting supper ready, I'll pour us some wine."

"What about the champagne?"

He laughed. "Remembering what happened the *last* time you had champagne, I think I'll wait until you've finished cooking before I open the bottle! Now you have to help me decide the rest of your present. I thought we'd go to the theater on Friday night. Shall it be a *café-concert* at the Folies Bergère? Or the Comédie Française to see Sarah Bernhardt?"

"Oh, I don't know. What do you think?"

"You'd probably prefer the Folies. Let's save Madame Bernhardt until your French is better."

"Isn't it awfully extravagant, Drew? The stateroom on the boat was far finer than I expected."

His blue eyes clouded. "It was hardly first class. And hardly what I wanted for you. But I suppose we had better cut down." He handed her a glass of wine, took a sip from his own glass. "I had a letter from my sister Willough this morning. I met the postman on my way to class. Willough's getting married." He shook his head. "To Arthur Gray!"

"You know the young man?"

"That's the thing of it! He's not young. Arthur must be nearly forty now."

"Lots of girls marry older men." She giggled. "You're *ages* older than I am!"

He pinched her bottom through her skirts. "Imp! A seven-year difference is a far cry from a seventeen-year gap." He frowned. "But that's not what I find so curious. For the past ten years or so, Arthur has been . . . my mother's friend. We used to call him Uncle Arthur, as a matter of fact. I know there was never anything between them. Oh, perhaps years ago, a few kisses. But nothing more, though Mother liked to pretend a romantic attachment. It made her feel young again. She must be grief-stricken. She said she was losing him. The last time we . . . spoke. I'm sure she never thought it would be to Willough! Poor Mum."

Marcy caught the note of pity in his voice. This was the first time he'd spoken with sympathy for his mother. "Why don't you write to her?"

"No!" He glared at her, then turned away. "No," he said more gently. "We have nothing to say to each other."

She had a funny feeling. "Is it because of me?"

"Don't be foolish. It had nothing to do with you." He strode to the window and stared out at the rainy night.

She sighed. Of course it did. Whatever had happened between Drew and his mother, she knew with certainty that she was the cause. She folded back the screen to her "kitchen," and pulled out a skillet, which she placed on the top of the small stove. "How was your class?" she asked at last.

He shrugged without turning. "Confusing. Monsieur Julien teaches one thing, and all the artists I know paint another. Père Julien admires Leonardo. We troop to the Louvre and copy Leonardo! Muddy colors and all. But Monet, Renoir . . . all the Realists . . . The colors they use are *alive*! Even the old guard, Corot and Boudin, who manage to impress the Salon jury every year and get to show their paintings, have begun to use a lighter palette." He turned about in disgust. "But Monsieur *Julien* admires Leonardo's palette."

"But all the Realists are starving. They can't sell a single painting. Only yesterday, Camille Monet came by to borrow a bit of sugar. We spoke as best we could, but I'm sure she's worried. Perhaps Monsieur Julien's ways are best."

He snorted. "*Old* ways. I refuse to believe it!"

She hated it when he began to talk like this. She knew how much he suffered. And yet she felt useless. Powerless to help, to reach out to him. "Why don't you find another

teacher? There must be other places to study besides the
Académie Julien."

"I don't think I can afford it. I'd like to take a class in
anatomy as well. And Monsieur Julien's prices are the lowest
around. Even then, he's charging me ten francs a month for
rent and model fees. If I can pass all the exams, I might be
able to get a free tuition to the Ecole des Beaux-Arts. But I
don't know. There are too many obligatory courses and pe-
riodic exams. And the masters teach in rotation. I'd still want
to take a few private classes. And that takes money."

She giggled, remembering. "I could get a job."

"What?"

"I met that funny Englishman, Mr. Stewart, today. He
offered me a job as his model. Oh Drew! You should have
seen his face. Blushing like a sunset, while he told me that"—
here she affected an exaggerated British accent—"he would
rawther have me pose unclad."

"Dammit, Marcy! Don't you dare!"

"Drew, I was only joking. Of *course* I wouldn't! Even if
I decided to model for him, I wouldn't take my clothes off!"
She put her hands on her hips. "But if I decide to do *that*,
Mr. Drew Bradford, I'll do it! And you won't stop me!"

He laughed. "I always forget that stubborn streak of yours.
Maybe if I produce enough pictures of you, all of Paris will
be so tired of seeing that face that no one else will want you!"
He pulled her away from her pots and kissed her on the mouth,
his arms holding her close. "Though I can't imagine that
anyone could ever tire of that face," he whispered.

While she continued with supper, he pulled out a crayon
sketch he had done in the Bois de Boulogne, ruling it lightly
with a penciled grid. He produced a canvas he had prepared
with an undercoat of burnt siena, drew a similar (though
larger-scaled) grid on the canvas, and proceeded to transfer
the smaller drawing, square by square, to the canvas. He
worked quickly. Satisfied with the results, he put the canvas
on his easel and began to squeeze out some paint onto his
palette. "I saw the most astonishing picture today. In Père
Martin's window. Claude Monet painted it. I must have stared

for half an hour. All the shadows had *color* in them. He didn't just use a bit of bitumen to darken in the shaded areas. The shadows were entirely different colors. Extraordinary! I wonder if it can be done, without using black or bitumen."

"Don't get too involved," she said. "Supper will be ready soon." She smiled, watching him. This was where she wanted to be. In this drafty old studio. In this damp old city. With her love.

The smell of the sausages and onions finally pulled him from his work. Supper was a merry affair, with champagne and much laughter. Afterward, she stripped down and bathed, standing up in a large basin placed near the warm stove. Drew watched her, his eyes roaming over her body. She wasn't sure whether he was seeing her as a lover, or as an artist. But when she helped him undress for his own bath, she felt an odd sense of triumph. It was clear, from the angle of his hard shaft, that she had defeated his art tonight! While he dried himself, she moved impatiently about the studio in her flowing nightgown, extinguishing the kerosene lamps, locking the door, putting away the last dried dish.

"Tarnation!" she said at last. "Are you ever going to get into bed?"

He toweled himself slowly, his blue eyes filled with laughter. "I might."

"Dang you!" She marched purposefully toward him, pulling off her nightgown just as she reached him. She snatched his towel from him, threw it to the floor. Grabbing his hand, she dragged him behind the screen and pushed him flat on the bed. "Now you just stay there until I get the candles blown out!"

He chuckled. "Yes, Mrs. Bradford. No wonder you were such a good hunter in the woods. You know how to go after your prey!"

"And I know how to capture it too." In the darkness she perched on the bed beside him and leaned over, brushing her lips gently against his. His hands came up to stroke her back, tracing a line down her spine. She shivered.

"You have the nicest back," he murmured. "And the pret-

tiest little tail." His hands caressed her firm bottom. "I used
to walk behind you in the woods, watching how you moved
in those trousers of yours. I had such wicked thoughts!"

"Did you now?" She left his lips and moved down to his
hard chest, her tongue circling his masculine buds, as sensitive to teasing as were her own breasts. He twitched in
pleasure, then inhaled sharply as her head moved lower. She
nipped gently at the fold of flesh at his narrow hips, then
hesitated for only a second before bending her lips to his
quivering shaft. He was soft and warm; she felt her own
senses quickening with the excitement of touching him, of
kissing him there.

"Oh, God, Marce. Stop..."

She was growing hot and moist, eager for him. She couldn't
wait a second longer. She straddled him quickly, lowering
herself onto him, feeling the delicious fullness of him within
her. He lay on his back, eyes closed, his handsome features
tense with passion. "You have a very willing prey," he said
hoarsely.

She giggled. "Tarnation. *Too* willing! It's like jacking a
deer at night with a lantern. It's no fun to bag the critter when
it just stands there!" Before he could stop her, she jumped
off the bed, danced around the screen, and went to stand at
the window. Down the street, the gaslights made little puddles
of gold in the rain-soaked pavement.

"Get over here." Drew stood in the center of the room,
breathing hard.

She laughed. "No."

"Then it's time *I* was the hunter."

"You'll find you've got yourself a she-wolf!" She squealed
as he lunged for her, just managing to elude his grasp. He
cursed good-naturedly. Like a child would, to taunt its friends,
she waggled her arms derisively in his direction. Drat! A
tactical error. His long arms reached out, clutched at her
fingers, pulled her in close. While she wriggled and struggled
against him, he pinned her arms behind her and kissed her
hard on the mouth. She melted for a moment; then, remembering their game, strained against his imprisoning arms.

"She-wolf be damned," he said. He swept her up in his embrace and carried her to the bed, flinging her across the coverlet. Before she had time to plan her next strategy, he was upon her, his hard shaft finding the soft entrance, plunging deep.

She gasped and clung to him, moving with every wild thrust, arching to meet him in hungry joy. They rode out their storm together, cresting in a rush of feeling, of dazzling sensation, that left her breathless.

He laughed softly. "That's the best trophy I ever came home with!" He sat up and looked at her. "Come to think of it . . . that scene at the waterfall. Which one of us is really the hunter after all?"

They crawled under the covers together, falling asleep in each other's arms, as they always did.

It was hours later when Marcy awoke. She could still hear the sound of the rain pattering against the windows. Drew was not beside her. Beyond the folding screen, she saw the light of a candle flickering on the ceiling. Quietly she slipped out of bed. Drew, his trousers and smock pulled on carelessly, was at his easel, painting by the light from the candle stand. His forehead was creased in a frown, but the tenseness of his body, the way he slashed at his canvas with short strokes, spoke more of desperation than of anger.

Marcy sighed and crept quietly back to bed. It was not her place to intrude, though she ached with helpless misery. The more works Drew saw, the more painters he spoke to, the more he seemed to lose his confidence. Lying in bed, she felt the hot tears rolling down her cheeks.

Oh God, she thought. She loved him so much. And there wasn't a danged thing she could do to help him.

"Oh, Miss Willough, you made a beautiful bride."

Willough glanced in the mirror, seeing the smile of pleasure on Brigid's face. And well *she* might be pleased! Hadn't Arthur hired her away from Isobel—at double the salary, twenty-four dollars a month—to be Willough's personal maid? She stared at her reflection. A beautiful bride. Around her the room hummed with activity as the two young chambermaids lovingly folded the lace of her bridal veil, hung up the white tulle and satin gown, turned down the sheets of the large bed. A beautiful bride. It was astonishing that her seamstress had managed to finish the gown in time, each silk orange blossom painstakingly tucked into a tulle flounce.

But Arthur had been impatient, setting an early date for the wedding. It was still only October. She stared at her pale face, paler against the white of her dressing gown. In less than a month she should have been Nat's bride. On his birthday.

Brigid began to brush out her black hair. What have I done? she thought. It was as if, from the night of Arthur's party and the announcement of their engagement, she had climbed aboard a speeding locomotive. Powerless to get off, to stop its headlong flight, she had watched—as though from a great distance—her life hurtle toward a future she neither wanted nor welcomed. But the round of parties had begun, the social world of New York finally taking Arthur to its bosom. There had never been a moment when she was able to tell him that somehow she had made a ghastly mistake.

And, after all, how would it have looked? Grandma Carruth would have cursed her from the grave, and the family would have died of shame.

Arthur had been a perfect gentleman, of course. That's what had made it all the more difficult. He had kissed her a few times. Very respectfully. Not at all frightening. But she had felt none of the thrill that being in Nat's arms had given her.

Nat. She gulped, fighting back her tears. She had hoped, until the last minute, that she'd hear from him. Then, pride in hand, she'd written to Mrs. Walker at MacCurdyville. Would she ask around for him? The letter had come only this afternoon, half an hour before the ceremony. Nat seemed to have vanished.

Daddy had been furious, of course, the night of Arthur's

party. "Quit?" he'd roared. "What do you mean the son of a bitch has quit? What the hell am I supposed to do for a manager with Clegg retiring?" In the end, Bill had been named manager, and Daddy had pulled one of the founders from the ranks to be the new clerk. There had never been a question of offering it to Willough. Wasn't she getting married? She sighed unhappily, fingering the perfume bottles on her vanity. Perhaps he had *never* wanted her as a partner. And how could she fight Daddy? She didn't want him to hate her.

But Isobel certainly hated her. In the past, though Willough had felt her mother's animosity, Isobel had treated her with a certain amount of restraint. Now Willough had stolen *her* Arthur, and Isobel was not about to let her forget it. They had clashed over everything. The flowers, the guest list, the attendants—until Willough felt herself reeling with the waves of hatred.

Strangely, though Isobel made it clear that Arthur had hurt her by his actions, the two of them still spoke to each other. Indeed, Willough had overheard a mystifying conversation between them only the other day.

"You owe me a favor, Arthur," her mother had said. "I did what you wanted me to do, though you lied about your intentions."

"Isobel, my dear. You don't understand."

"I think I understand more than you know." Her mother's voice had been sharp with bitterness. "You owe me a favor. I'll expect payment in return some day."

Willough sighed, shook her head impatiently. "That's enough, Brigid."

"Yes, ma'am." Putting down the brush, Brigid began to plait the black tresses into a long braid. She cocked her head to the sound of horses' hooves clip-clopping down the circular drive of Arthur's house. "It sounds like Mr. Bradford is finally going home."

"Yes." The wedding party had broken up more than an hour ago. Isobel, in her element among the cream of society, had received them in her flower-banked parlor at Gramercy

Park after the service at Grace Church. Daddy had had Delmonico's cater the banquet for two hundred and fifty guests. When the bride and groom had finally left the Bradford home, Daddy had followed in his carriage. He had closeted himself with Arthur in the downstairs study while they discussed the terms of the marriage.

It was a formality, of course. The terms had long-since been agreed upon. A bankbook of ten thousand dollars, stock in the MacCurdy enterprises to go to Willough when she turned twenty-five. Held in trust by Arthur until then. It was the best that Daddy could do. He'd lost a great deal of money when the stock market had closed on the nineteenth of September. "Black Friday," they were already calling it. There'd been too much building and speculation in the spring, particularly in railroad stock. The railroad panic had triggered a panic in the general financial markets, and dozens of banks had been ruined. Rutherford and Seneca had called in their loan—money that was already committed to the building of Daddy's new finery. But Daddy had been lucky. Two out of three iron mills were now idled. He might be cash poor at the moment, but at least the MacCurdy Ironworks was still running.

"'Tis a pity you can't have a proper honeymoon, ma'am." Brigid nodded her head solemnly. "My friend Kathleen's mistress went to Hot Springs for a whole month, she did."

"After Saratoga, Hot Springs would have little charm, Brigid."

"Well, Europe, then."

"No. Mr. Gray doesn't think it's worthwhile at this time. The Season is just beginning. He doesn't want to miss any of it."

Brigid sniffed. "Especially as how the Carruth name seems to have opened up a slather of doors to him!"

"Brigid! Don't you like Mr. Arthur?"

"Well, he's not Mr. Nat, if you'll pardon me saying so. And that's a fact!"

Willough felt a pang at her heart. "Leave me now." She

waved an impatient hand at the two chambermaids. "And take those chattering magpies with you."

She was alone. In this big, empty room. She looked around at the bedhangings, the fine carpets, the lace curtains at the windows. Arthur had spared no expense, redoing it just to suit her. He certainly treated her well. She sighed. She'd be a good wife to him. No matter how her heart was aching. Hadn't she trained for this all her life? The social graces, the proper behavior. Grandma Carruth's pride and joy. Isobel's dutiful pupil. And Daddy's obedient daughter. She supposed it would be that way with Arthur. *An independent woman is a disgrace to her sex*, Grandma always said. Only Nat had encouraged her to talk back to Daddy.

She extinguished all but the lamp near the large bed. It looked comfortable, with its clean white linens, and she was tired. The Goelets were giving a reception tomorrow. She wanted to look rested. She frowned. She wondered if she ought to say good night to Arthur first. He must be in his own room by now.

There was a knock at the door that connected their two rooms. Arthur came in, dressed in a red silk dressing gown. "I thought your father would never leave," he said.

She smiled. "I was about to come and say good night to you."

He smoothed his mustache. "Not yet. Not on our wedding night."

She felt herself beginning to tremble. "But Arthur . . . I thought . . . You said you'd treat me with respect . . ."

One eyebrow shot up in surprise. "My dear Willough, you didn't think that meant I intended to be a celibate bridegroom!"

She didn't know what she thought. Only that she hadn't expected *this*. "Arthur, I'd really prefer . . ."

"Now, now, my dear. There's no sense in postponing it. It won't make it any easier if we wait." He pulled her into his arms and kissed her. His mustache tickled her nose.

She thought: Perhaps it won't be so bad after all.

He unfastened her wrapper and slipped it off her shoulders.

He kissed her again, a little less gently this time, and began to unbutton her nightgown.

"No, wait!" She felt the beginnings of panic. "Put out the light."

He smiled thinly. "Of course. Get into bed first, so you don't trip in the dark."

She did as she was told, crawling under the covers and pulling the sheet up to her chin. He turned out the gas lamp next to her bed. In the darkness she could hear the soft sounds of his hands fumbling with the silk tie of his dressing gown, then another sound. Oh God! Had he taken off his *nightshirt*? She felt the bed shake as he sat down; then he was under the covers with her.

"Take off your nightgown, Willough," he said.

She closed her eyes. It made the dark even blacker. "No."

"You're very dear to me, Willough. I promise you I'll be as gentle as I can. Take off your gown."

"No."

His voice held the edge of impatience. "Very well. You don't have to take it off until you're ready."

She felt his hand in the dark, groping under the covers. She stiffened as he touched her breast, then forced herself to relax. She had let Nat touch her that way. Why not Arthur?

"Dearest Willough. How I've wanted you." He murmured soft words, loving words. And all the while his hand caressed her breasts, stroked her shoulders through the thin lawn of her nightgown.

She sank more deeply into her pillows, allowing the tension to leave her. He *was* gentle. He leaned over and began to kiss her more passionately, his mouth hard and insistent on hers. Still, she wasn't afraid. She started to touch him once, then withdrew her hands when she felt his bare shoulders. *That* was frightening, to think he was naked. His lips closed on hers. At the same time he rolled on top of her. She felt a strange hardness poking at her belly. She tried to cry out, but his mouth on hers prevented her; her parted lips seemed to fire his ardor. His tongue sought her mouth, plunging deep until she thought she'd choke. Oh, God! What was he doing now? His hands were tugging at her nightdress, pushing it up, above her hips, her waist. She pounded at his shoulders with her fists, struggling to free her mouth, her trapped body, from his possession. Pressed down by his hard chest, she thrashed beneath him, legs spread wide; too late she realized her folly. *That* was what he had wanted all along, the vulnerable core of her that her frightened struggles had exposed. She started to draw her knees together; at that moment something tore her apart, forcing its way into her with such savagery that her fists became claws, scraping against the flesh of his shoulders. With a desperate toss of her head, she freed her mouth from his. "Arthur! *Stop!* You're hurting me!"

"In a moment, Willough," he panted. "Sweet, sweet Willough!"

She bit her lip, fighting back the tears. Not content with ripping her open, he was determined to rub her raw. Again and again he thrust into her, until she thought she couldn't bear another second. He gave a sudden gasp, twitched violently. And then it was over.

He rolled away from her and sighed. "Dear Willough," he murmured. "How I needed you!"

Damn him! she thought. He sounded *contented*! He had shamed her. Hurt her. Used her! And he was content!

"I'm sorry I hurt you," he said gently. "It's always that way the first time."

In the darkness, she stumbled out of bed toward her dressing room with its galvanized tub and its modern plumbing. Closing the door, she lit the gaslight with shaking hands, staring at herself in horror. Her nightgown, her white thighs. Spotted with blood. She wanted to vomit. She peeled the gown from her body, ran a little warm water into the basin, and sponged herself as best she could. There was no washing away her shame.

"Willough."

She extinguished the light and opened the door.

"Willough," he said again. "Come back to bed."

She could hardly keep from crying. "I want to get a fresh nightgown."

"Not yet. Come back to bed."

Reluctantly, she moved toward him. "Not again, Arthur. Please!"

In the dimness, she could see that he had made room for her. "Get in. You're behaving like a schoolgirl."

"But it hurt!"

He reached out and pulled her down beside him. "It won't hurt as much this time. I promise you." He moved on top of her, spreading her legs with strong hands when she resisted.

He was right. It didn't hurt as much. But it was just as terrible. When he had gone back to his own room she found a fresh nightgown in the dark, and crept back to bed, curling up on a corner of the mattress that was as far away as she could manage it from the spot where they had lain together.

In the morning she sent word to him by Brigid that she was not well and intended to spend the day in her room. She soaked for a long time in her tub, trying not to think of the pain, the disgust she had felt for him. For what he had done to her. It was just as Isobel had warned her. She picked at the food Brigid brought. When she looked in the mirror she saw a stranger who would never be the same again.

Late in the afternoon, Arthur appeared at her door carrying a tea tray. He smiled and set it down on a small table. "I thought we'd have tea together. I hope you're feeling better."

"I don't want tea."

He shrugged and helped himself to a cup, watching her as she stood at the window and stared at the carriages that moved up and down Fifth Avenue. "Come here," he said at last, putting down his cup. When she obeyed he pulled a diamond and ruby bracelet from his pocket and fastened it about her wrist. "I thought this might cheer you up, my sweet."

"It's very handsome," she said dully.

"Look, Willough, I know you're still feeling a bit embarrassed. It's natural. All young brides feel that way. It's your upbringing. Your natural reticence. But now that you're married, you can allow yourself to change, to welcome feelings that you've kept in check until now. Do you understand?"

"Yes. Of course." Why didn't he just go away and leave her alone?

"Oh for God's sake, Willough, don't sulk!" he burst out. "It'll be better the next time. You'll see. It just takes getting used to. It'll be better the next time."

She felt anger in her heart—for him, for herself, for the whole sorry business. "There's not going to be a next time!" she said defiantly.

"Don't be ridiculous," he growled.

Why don't you please yourself for a change? Nat had said. Well, perhaps she was Brian's daughter after all. "Never again, Arthur," she said firmly.

His eyes glowed with fury, a frustrated passion that bubbled to the surface. "Damn you! I'll show you who's in charge here!" He swung at her with his open palm, striking her so hard that she fell to the floor. Dazed, she struggled to her knees, clinging to the leg of her chaise. He knelt before her, his hand like steel about her wrist. "You're my wife, dammit! *In every respect!* You'll remember your wifely duty if I have to tie you to the bed! One frigid Bradford woman is all I'll put up with!" He rose to his feet, calmed himself, straightened the cuffs of his frock coat. "And may I remind you we have a reception at the Goelets this evening," he added, his voice as cold as ice. "You'd better be dressed and ready. I don't intend to be made a fool of by my wife." Turning on his heel, he strode from her room.

You made your bed. Now lie in it. She could almost hear Grandma Carruth's voice. She was Arthur's wife. It was her duty to obey him. Even if it meant she must let him...

She shivered. Nat had said all men were the same in bed. It might have been just as awful if Nat had done that terrible thing to her. But she had never felt alone or empty when Nat was with her. She couldn't imagine he could be so thoughtless—in or out of the bedroom.

She got shakily to her feet, rubbing her hand against her still-stinging cheek. The Arthur she had married was a stranger. A cruel, lustful stranger, with no warmth or compassion. She saw the scene in the boathouse with new eyes. He had manipulated her feelings, played on her childish sense of romance, to get what he wanted. And would have, if Nat hadn't been there.

Nat. She saw his dear face before her. He had been gentle, sensitive, denying his passion in deference to her feelings. She had let her foolish fears destroy their love. And now it was too late.

You made your bed. Now lie in it. "Oh, Nat," she whispered. "What have I done?"

Chapter Nine

Marcy shivered under the coverlet and reached sleepily for Drew to warm her. Drat! He was gone already. She yawned and blinked, pulling the covers more tightly about her. She'd really slept longer than she'd intended; but it was so cold and the bed so cozy. She laughed softly. It had become a game between them: Concerned with the cost of wood, they had begun the winter by letting the stove die out each night before they went to bed; now, with winter half over, it was a game, the toss of a die deciding who would warm the bed each night. She laughed again. Drew had lost last night—she wondered if the loser was obligated to keep the bed warm until the other got up in the morning. She'd discuss it with him tonight. But only if *he* lost the toss!

She frowned suddenly. And only if he wasn't worried about money. They were still getting on, of course, but it was a little tight. Drew had finally managed to persuade Père Martin to hang two of his canvases, but the dealer had made no promises. He'd been buying from the Realists for a few years now, for forty or fifty francs a painting, and they hadn't sold well. Drew was a newcomer, a foreigner on the scene.

Of course, Père Martin had said, if Drew could get a painting accepted by the official Salon, it would be a different story. If an artist attracted the public's attention and favor by exhibiting in the yearly Salon each spring, he could command higher prices. But *Monsieur Bradford* would have a difficult time getting accepted by the jury, *malheureusement*. He had not found his style; his paintings were too formal, too self-conscious; his palette alternated between the somber tones of the Renaissance and the bright colors of the new Realists. And with the worldwide banking panic last fall, the market had gone down. At the last minute, Père Martin had taken— on speculation—a few pen and ink drawings of Marcy.

Marcy sat up, and stared unhappily at Drew's work table. He must have gotten up again last night to paint. There was a painting of a tree that seemed to have been smeared deliberately, a broken crayon, several torn sketches. And an empty wine bottle.

She wanted to cry. She was failing him. There were too many nights like that—where all her love was not enough to bring him comfort. She wondered how soon it would be before he remembered that he hadn't wanted to marry.

Well, at least she could be of practical help. She jumped out of bed and dressed quickly in the cold room, then wrapped her pink corset and best gray silk petticoat in a piece of muslin, which she tucked in her market basket. It was too cold to have breakfast in the studio; she'd get a small brioche and some coffee at the snug café around the corner. That way, she wouldn't waste precious coal lighting a fire.

It had snowed last night. She made her way down the slippery pavement, struck—as always—by the ugliness of a city after a snowfall. In the mountains it would be shiny-clean, the snowbanks dazzling to the eye, the dark evergreens capped with white puffs. Here, the carriages had already churned up the roads, leaving snuff-colored ruts dotted with refuse thrown from an occasional window. Along the sides of the road, the soot from thousands of chimneys had turned even the untrampled stretches of snow to a dull gray. Ugly, she thought again, wrapping her shawl more tightly about her thin cloak.

Just as she was crossing the street at the rue de Londres, a fiacre came bearing down on her; the coachman, his bright red scarf flapping in the crisp air, shouted her out of the way. She leaped back to the sidewalk, slipped on a patch of ice, and landed on her back, managing to hang on to her shawl and basket as she fell. She took a moment to catch her breath, then struggled to her feet, waving off the concerned passersby who had gathered around. She smiled weakly, and went on her way. That danged coachman! she thought, rubbing the small of her back. She'd ache for a week.

She turned into the rue St. Lazare. Number Ten. She nodded to Mr. Stewart's housekeeper—busy sweeping the snow from the walk—and mounted the steps to his *hôtel particulier*, his private house. It must be nice, she thought, to be a successful enough painter to afford a house like this. Stewart greeted her at the door.

"Good morning, m'dear. You're late."

"Sorry. I took a tumble on the ice, and had to walk slowly."

Stewart grimaced in concern. He looked more like a rabbit than ever. "Oh, but it's not serious, I trust."

"No. I'll get into my things right away." She followed him into his well-appointed studio. It was always a pleasure to pose for him, and never more so than on such a chilly day. The large stove near the model's platform radiated warmth. He rang for some tea, "just to take the chill off, don't you know," while she stepped behind a large screen and climbed out of her green gown, pulled off her plain petticoat. Over

her lace chemise she hooked on her pink silk corset, tying it
as tightly as she could, then followed it with her good gray
petticoat. She threw her shawl about her shoulders for a
temporary cover, and crossed the room to the platform.

While he fussed with the shades of the skylight, adjusting
them for the proper light, she took off her shawl and drank
her tea, sitting on the pale green sofa. She was always amused
by what came next, as he checked her pose against the painting. He really *did* look like a plump little rabbit, scurrying
back and forth from his large canvas to where she sat; fluffing
out a bow on her petticoat; moving the position of an arm,
patting a wayward curl on her head. "Lift your right shoulder
a bit." "No. That's too high." "Pull down your chemise. You
showed a little more bosom yesterday." At last, declaring
himself satisfied, he picked up his palette and brushes and
began to paint. He frowned, his eyes on her waist. "How
long have I been working on this picture?"

"About a month, I think."

"Damme, if you don't seem to have put on a bit of heft,
m'dear."

She smiled. "Perhaps I have." And likely to put on more,
my English rabbit, she thought. If what she suspected was
so. She was glad now she'd decided to take this job as Stewart's model. If there *was* a baby on the way, they'd need the
extra money. She hadn't told Drew, of course. About the baby
or the job. He'd only make a fuss. She'd tell him about her
condition after she'd been to see a doctor. As for the posing,
since she and Mr. Stewart had agreed that her current state
of *déshabillé* (he liked fancy French words) was as undressed
as she intended to get, what was the harm?

"How is your husband's painting coming along, m'dear?"

"Well enough. He's working hard."

Stewart squinted at her, his thumb held out at arm's length.
"He'd do better to stay away from that mad crowd of painters.
They're dotty. I've heard them talk. Light and shadow. The
'virgin *impression* of nature.' A lot of claptrap!"

"Drew doesn't think so."

Stewart snorted. "He should have been here when they

started showing their paintings ten years ago. At the Salon des Refusès. Because the Academy was wise enough to reject their new ideas. That critic Wolff at *Le Figaro* has made his reputation just by mocking their works. Incomplete perspectives. *Visible* brushstrokes, ye gods! Those strange angles they claim to have borrowed from Japanese prints. And the colors! Like children's artwork."

"I like them," she said defensively, half rising to her feet.

He shook his head. "Well, they're too modern for my taste. Settle back in your chair. And tilt your chin up. I want the color of your eyes to show."

The session today seemed interminable. Her back had begun to ache from the fall on the ice. When Stewart's cook brought lunch she picked at her food, her appetite strangely gone.

At last Stewart put down his palette and brushes, and took off his painting smock. "We'll stop a little early today, m'dear. You seem tired." He crossed to the platform, reached into his pocket, and pulled out two franc notes, pressing them into her hand.

She looked up, startled. "That's twice what you usually pay me."

He smiled, showing his big front teeth. "I thought maybe you'd stay a trifle longer, m'dear." Abruptly he plunged his hand down the front of her chemise.

She gasped and scrambled away from him. "You dirty old man! You're old enough to be my father. My *grandfather*!"

"Now, now, Marcy . . . a friendly chat. I'm a lonely man." He lunged for her. He was surprisingly agile for his age and bulk.

Tarnation! How was she going to get out of here? She had to get her clothes. But they were on the other side of the room from the door. And by the time she reached them, he could have the door locked and the key in his pocket! She had a sudden wild thought. Evading his hands, she headed for the large canvas in the middle of the room. She snatched up a brush, poised it in front of the picture. "Do you want to lose a month's work?"

He stopped dead in his tracks. "You wouldn't!"

"Danged if I would! The very idea!"

His gray side whiskers seemed to droop mournfully against his cheeks. "I didn't mean anything by it. I just thought you'd let me touch you for a bit."

She waved the franc notes angrily. "For money?"

"Why not? All the women do. How do I know you're Bradford's wife, and not just his mistress? I don't want to *do* anything. Just touch your breasts. And paint them, perhaps."

He was getting a stubborn look around his mouth. She made a move for the door. "I'm leaving."

He blocked the way. "No."

She inched her way back to the painting, picked up the brush again. "Bring me my things from behind the screen. And put them on the floor near me. *Do* it, dang you, or I'll ruin this painting! And when you're done, go and sit on the sofa." She began to undress down to her chemise and drawers, watching him carefully to see he didn't move from the sofa. She knew she could destroy the painting before he reached her, but still . . .

"You're being very unfair," he sulked. "I could tell everyone you've been coming here to sell yourself to me."

What a nasty little man. She dressed in her plain petticoat and green gown, wrapped up her other clothes in the basket, put on her cloak and shawl. She held up the money. "One franc is for my modeling fee." Her lips curled in disgust. "The other is for looking. And touching!" Deliberately she dipped the brush into a dab of black paint on his palette and, with two quick strokes, painted a mustache on her likeness. "Au revoir. M'dear!" she said, and swept from the room.

She giggled all the way down the street. But after awhile it didn't seem so funny. She'd been counting on the money the modeling would bring in. And he was the only artist she knew who was rich enough to pay.

At the Place de Clichy, she picked up some bread and cheese and herring for supper. And her daily flower from Jacques. A lovely blue hyacinth today. She stared at a packet of narcissus bulbs. She'd love to get another potted plant. Something she could grow herself. But her poor geranium plant had long since died in the cold studio.

She shivered. She really didn't want to go home to that chilly room yet. Not while her back was still aching so. Drew would be at the Café Guerbois. All the painters gathered there. After their classes. After their lonely hours in a studio. And the Café Guerbois was *warm*. She turned off the place, hearing the sounds of music and laughter long before she reached the café.

It must be crowded today. Drew had been telling her about the new association they'd formed—Monet, Renoir, Sisley, Degas, and the rest. Tired of the rejections from the official Salon, they had decided to stage an exhibition of their works. Manet, having finally achieved a big success at the last Salon, had declined to join them. It had cost Drew sixty francs to join the association, and he had only a few completed paintings, but he was determined to show in April with the others.

Renoir was laughing when she came in, leaning across the marble table to slap Drew jovially on the back. He looked up and waved, his liquid brown eyes appraising her. An artist's eyes, in an artist's face, with its sharp nose and sensuous lips. He was thirty-three and still struggling, but at least he didn't suffer as Monet did with a wife and child to support. *"Ah! La belle Marcy!"* he cried. It always sounded different when they said her name in French.

She smiled and nodded back, endeavoring to catch a word or two of the greetings from the men around the table. Drew made room for her on the red leather banquette beside him, but as twilight came on and the wine and absinthe flowed, she found herself bored with conversation she could scarcely understand, with the painter's realm that was barred to her, even if she'd known the language. And the ache in her back was now a low, throbbing pain. "Let's go home, Drew," she said at last.

He turned to her with a frown. "My God, Marcy. We've got to decide how we're to hang the paintings!"

"I'm getting a cup of coffee," she said, pushing past him

on the banquette. Already deep in conversation with Degas, he scarcely heard her. She stood up and went to the bar to order coffee.

"With a beautiful face like that, one should not be sad. *N'est-ce pas?*"

Marcy turned. One of the young artists. Degas's protégé. "Oh, Leopold. I'm just tired. *Fatiguée.*"

"And a little . . . how do you say . . . *triste*? Sad?"

"I don't understand what they're talking about."

He shook his head, his eyes searching her face. "It isn't the words that puzzle you. It is the passion, *n'est-ce pas?*"

She gulped back her tears. She was tired, and her body ached, and he had touched the sorest part of her heart. "It's just that I can't reach him. We don't laugh much anymore. If it is a passion, as you say, it doesn't make him happy."

"I am fortunate. I know my limits. I am . . . ah! *comme on dit* . . . ordinary. Mediocre. I do not suffer as the others do."

"Is Drew a good painter? *I* think so. I try to tell him so. But . . ."

"It is what one thinks of himself that matters."

"What can I do?" she whispered.

He shrugged. *"Rien*. Nothing."

She returned to the table and stood above Drew, her hand on his shoulder. He turned his head, smiled that funny smile of his, kissed her fingers. "Claude wants you to sit for him. He says you're very beautiful." He said something to Monet in French. Renoir laughed, and offered a comment. Marcy caught the words *l'Anglais*, and *Stewart*.

Drew rose to his feet, his eyes like blue ice. *"Are* you, Marcy? Are you sitting for Stewart?"

"Not anymore."

"But you did," he said accusingly. "And didn't tell me."

"I *said* I might."

"Though I asked you not to."

She stuck out an angry chin. "And I told you I'd make up my own mind!"

"My dear stubborn Marcy," he said. His voice was as cold as his eyes. "And he paid you?"

"Of course."

He smiled bitterly. "Do you have so little faith in me?"

"No, Drew. I . . ."

He reached into his pocket, pulled out eight francs. "Here," he said, slapping the coins into her hand. "Père Martin sold the drawings. I'd almost forgotten you were the girl who wanted to marry a rich man."

His words were like a knife to her heart. "Dang you, Drew Bradford," she whispered. "I'm going home."

He caught up with her halfway down the street. "Marcy, I'm sorry." He swung her into his arms, kissed her until she was breathless.

She snuggled against him. All was right with the world. She giggled. "Oh, Drew. You'll never guess why I've stopped posing for Stewart." All the way back to the studio she told him the story, skipping only the part where Stewart had actually touched her bosom.

Drew laughed uproariously. "A mustache! You imp! You didn't really spoil his painting!" They had reached home. While Marcy lit the lamp, Drew started a fire in the stove. "All the same," he said, pulling her into his arms, "I don't want you to pose again for money. In or out of your clothes!"

She reached up, brushed the wayward black curl from his forehead. "What if we need the money?" Should she tell him about the baby?

"We'll manage."

"What about your parents?"

He released her and turned away. "I don't think my mother intends to lift a finger, no matter what happens."

"And your father?"

"My father has made conditions I can't possibly accept."

"But Drew . . ." She stopped and gasped, her eyes wide with shock. The ache in her back had become a terrible wrenching pain. She felt as though her insides had given way in a great rush that was suddenly becoming a bloody pool upon the floor. "Oh, no. Oh, no," she moaned. She reeled and would have fallen but for Drew's strong arms.

She heard the anguish in his voice, just before darkness

closed over her. "Marcy," he said. "What in the name of God am I doing to you?"

The open barouche made its way slowly up Broadway, passing City Hall Park. Willough shivered in the chill winter air, and tucked the fur lap robe more snugly around her. Fumbling in her handbag, she pulled out a handkerchief and held it to her nose. The smells of the city were nauseating her again: The horse manure from the drays and carts and carriages; the filthy, squealing pigs that roamed the street and rooted around the trees in the park; the stink of burning coal from shops and factories. She found herself thinking of Nat— he would have wondered what this part of the city looked like before "civilization" took away its beauty and charm.

On the corner of Reade Street she saw a tattered beggar, clutching the remnants of a uniform around him. A forgotten casualty of the War between the States. We use up everything in this country, she thought. Men, and land, and resources. Without a backward glance. All in the name of Mammon. She pulled a coin from her purse and turned to the footman behind her. He nodded, took the coin, and leaped off the back of the coach to press the money into the old soldier's hand. The footman ran alongside the moving coach for a moment; when they stopped to let a horsecar pass he swung himself up to his perch again.

Willough watched him brush a bit of mud from his livery. Livery! she thought in disgust. Arthur did everything but put a crest on the servants' uniforms! *He* worshipped Mammon completely. Oh, he hid it well. Under a veneer of casual indifference. But she knew that every friendship they made, every social engagement, was designed to further his fortunes. She sighed. That was probably the reason he'd married her. He didn't need Isobel's connections any more, that back-door entrée into the world of New York society. Now he had a Carruth on his arm when he swept in at the front door.

Not that Mother would have anything to do with them.

Nursing her grievances. They'd hardly seen her since the wedding. They'd seen Daddy a few times. He'd come down from MacCurdyville to talk business with Arthur. Willough was worried about him. He looked ghastly. Drawn and tired. Constantly complaining about his digestion. He'd decided it wasn't dyspepsia—more likely an ulcer or chronic colitis—but he still refused to see a doctor.

And he was concerned about the business. He'd had to stop the construction of the new finery, but he was still looking for ways to save money. He and Arthur were talking again of using the prisoners from Clinton Prison as free labor. Willough wasn't sure how it could be arranged—she had an uneasy feeling that something illegal was involved. But every time she tried to sit in on their discussions, or ask a question, Daddy would shoo her away.

"Go on about your business, lass," he'd say.

In the carriage, she brushed away tears of anger. Her *business*. She'd never dreamed that her business would be a life of idleness, of uselessness. With a man she didn't love, a man she was coming to despise. She fought back a sudden wave of nausea. And now, with Dr. Page's news . . .

At Madison Square, the carriage turned into Fifth Avenue, moving at a brisker pace now that the traffic had thinned out. She frowned in distaste as Arthur's house came into view. She had found it dazzling at first, but now its glories were beginning to pall. There was a lack of restraint in the elaborate stonework, the overabundance of gilt and velvet and plush. Like Arthur. Handsome and well turned-out. But with a certain lack of class that showed around the edges. She sighed. She had treated Nat badly, finding him unpolished. But Nat had a dignity that Arthur would never match, for all his liveried servants and fancy clothes. If only she'd realized it in time.

She thought: I mustn't think of Nat. I have a life. I have a duty.

She smiled at the parlor maid who opened the door and helped her out of her velvet and fur pelisse. She took off her hat and gloves, rubbed her cold hands together. She had to talk to Arthur.

"Lillie, is Mr. Gray at home?"

"In his study upstairs, ma'am. But he's expecting Mr. Davis."

Willough nodded. One of Arthur's many business friends. They came and went at all hours. She didn't know what they did. She didn't even know exactly what *Arthur* did. But he was always giving her large sums of money, sometimes in the form of a bank draft, more often in cash. And then, a week or two later, he'd ask her to make out checks in payment for various expenses around the house. And there were papers to sign. She never bothered to read them. Just business, Arthur said. She never questioned him. It was part of her duty as a wife—to hold her tongue.

After Lillie had gone Willough hesitated in the foyer. She couldn't quite decide whether to take a cup of tea down here in the small drawing room or go upstairs to her sitting room. Perhaps she'd ring for Brigid to unlace her corsets. She heard a low cough from the music room. She pushed open the door and peered in.

Brigid was there. With a man. The maid gasped in surprise and curtsied quickly. "Oh, Mrs. Gray. I know we shouldn't be in here."

Willough frowned. She didn't think Brigid was keeping company with anyone. And certainly not with a man who seemed old enough to be her father. She eyed him more closely. He didn't appear to be at all well. His face was pale and beaded with sweat, and his cough, though soft, was continuous. "What is this, Brigid?" she said gently.

The girl looked ready to cry. "Oh, ma'am. This is me big brother Kevin. We just had a nice visit, and he was leaving. And then he started to cough and I didn't know what else to do. So I brought him in here to rest a bit."

"Can I send for a doctor?"

Kevin smiled wanly. "That's very kind of you, ma'am. Me being a stranger and all." Unlike Brigid's, his voice held scarcely a trace of an accent.

"Brigid talks about her brothers often. But I don't think she's mentioned you."

"That's because I'm the black sheep of the family, so to speak. The prodigal son. I left the old country in 'fifty-five to come here. The rest of 'em didn't come over till three, four years ago. I think they expected me to be a rich swell by now. But I'm just a longshoreman at the docks." He coughed again, his face reddening with the effort.

"We really should send for a doctor."

He shook his head. "It won't do no good, ma'am. It's just the T.B. I reckon it will take me some day, the way it took my wife and boy."

"Oh, but there must be something..."

He shrugged. "When you suck in the air of this foul city from morning till night, it's bound to rot your lungs." He put his cap back on, tugged politely at the brim. "I'll be going now, ma'am." He kissed his sister on the forehead. "See you in Church on Sunday, my girl." He walked to the door of the music room, then stopped, watching—a frown on his face— as Lillie let in Arthur's business friend and showed him up- stairs. Kevin jerked his thumb at the man's retreating back. "If you don't mind, ma'am. Who was that?"

"That's Mr. William Davis, an acquaintance of my hus- band's."

Kevin snickered. "Davis, be damned, if you'll pardon my language, ma'am! I remember him when he was just Tim O'Leary, stealing apples from the carts on Broome Street. Unless my eyes are playing tricks on me." He scratched his chin. "Eighteen years ago! I lost track of him finally. But I always thought he'd come to a bad end. He belonged to a gang on Broome Street. They hung around Mulligan's Hall. Lifted purses, mostly. But I heard they were fencing goods now and again. And... arranging for women, ma'am. If you know what I mean. I never met their leader. Artie Flanagan, he was. Worked as a bouncer part-time. At Mrs. Soule's establishment, Thirty-three Mercer Street. They said he was always putting on airs. Reading law books and talking big. Just as if he wasn't a mick like the rest of us."

Brigid clucked her tongue. "It takes a lot of brass for a man to get by with nothing but his charm."

And good connections, thought Willough. *Artie Flanagan.* Could it be? She shook her head. What a ridiculous idea. Of course not! "I'll be in my room when you've said good-bye to your brother, Brigid."

With Brigid's help she changed into a loose tea gown, glad to discard her corsets. She was just sipping her second cup of tea when Arthur knocked at her door and strode in. He carried a fat envelope and several folded sheets of paper.

"The usual," he said. "Ten thousand in cash."

For the first time she was curious. She thought: From William Davis. Alias Tim O'Leary. "What does Mr. Davis do?"

Arthur didn't blink. "He's in investments. The money is a legal fee. For some advice I gave him."

She took the envelope from him. "Do you have papers for me to sign as well?"

"Yes."

She moved to her desk and picked up her pen. While he wasn't looking, she pressed the nib against the leg of her chair. "Oh, dear," she said, holding up the pen as Arthur came toward her. "It's bent. Have you a pen on your desk?"

Impatiently he tossed her the papers. "Yes. I'll get it."

As quickly as she could, she scanned the documents. Merciful heaven! They seemed to indicate that she was a partner in a real estate company! Zephyr Realty. Picking up a pencil, she scribbled the name on a scrap of paper, just managing to hide it under her blotter as Arthur returned. She signed the papers with her usual indifference, handed them back to him. "Anything else?"

"I need a couple of checks. The first one to Senator Martin. One thousand dollars. It's his birthday tomorrow. I thought it would be nice to give him a contribution in honor of the occasion. He's up for re-election this year."

She pulled out her checkbook and wrote the check as he directed.

"The other is for Charlie Verplanck. He's the one who put

up our iron fence last month. Make the check out for five-hundred and fifty dollars."

She looked up in surprise. "I thought I saw the bill on your desk for twice that!"

"You must have been mistaken," he said evenly.

"I noticed, when I passed City Hall today, that it was the same fencing."

"Yes. Verplanck did the job as well."

"How fortunate. That's a big fence. It must have earned him a pretty penny. I wonder who arranged for him to get the contract?"

He eyed her coldly. "You're awfully curious today."

She smiled. Was he actually beginning to squirm? "I thought it might be amusing to start another Tweed-type scandal. Now that Tweed himself has been put away in the penitentiary."

He was trying hard to keep his composure. "I find you very *un*amusing today. As a matter of fact, I've resigned from the Tammany Society. Broken all my connections with that reprehensible man."

"You're coming up in the world, Arthur. The Astors have replaced the Tweeds." Just as the Tweeds had replaced the Broome Street gang? she thought idly.

He stroked his mustache. "You're all vinegar, today, my dear. Oddly enough, I find it heightens your attractiveness. It's been rather awhile. I think I'll come to your room tonight."

She stood up from her desk and crossed to the window, pulling aside the lace curtains to gaze out on the street. She always hated those times. Once a week or so he came to her room. To her bed. It was always pitch dark, and she was still too horrified by the whole thing to do more than lift her nightgown. She could never decide if he came to satisfy himself, or to humiliate her. There was never any love in it. But it was her duty. "Don't you have someone else to amuse you tonight, Arthur? One of your charming mistresses?" She turned and smiled thinly at him. "And I assume you have someone in Albany as well. For those times when you must be in the capital."

"I've never made a secret of it." He crossed to her and put his hand on her arm. "But I want *you* tonight."

Her heart was filled with bitterness. "Why? Is it your revenge on my mother? Because she didn''t succumb to your oily charms?"

"Damn you," he said softly. His hand shot out, striking her across the face.

She took a moment to recover, then stared at him, her violet eyes blazing with hatred. "In any event I'll sleep alone tonight."

His smile was cold and dangerous. "I don't think it would be wise."

"I've just come from Dr. Page. I'm carrying your child. The doctor thinks it best for my constitution that you ... abstain ... until after the child is born."

His expression softened. "A child! That's wonderful news, Willough."

"I despise it already, Arthur. As I despise you. I suspected it weeks ago, but I didn't want it confirmed. I didn't want to know. The child will be born in July, in case you're interested."

"Willough, my dear. I'm delighted. You'll find me a very attentive husband in the next few months. A woman's confinement can be tiresome."

"I don't intend to be confined. I'll go about my business as long as I can."

"Not if you show! It wouldn't do to be seen in public under those circumstances."

She laughed her contempt. "Oh, Arthur. How frightfully middle-class you are." If he truly was Artie Flanagan, he hadn't quite transformed the sow's ear into a silk purse after all.

He picked up his papers and walked to the door. "You're getting to be a regular virago. It's a pity you've never been able to carry a little of that fire into the bedroom." He brushed a bit of lint off his frock coat. "I won't be in for supper." Then he was gone.

To spend the evening with one of his women. She sighed

and sank into her chaise. What a sham her life had become. More painful than that was the sting of his appraisal of her frigidity. Was she predestined to it? Was it every woman's sexual nature to be cold? Or only hers?

"Frankie, you look cold. Why don't you go back to the bunkhouse and see if Cook will give you another cup of hot java?" Nat tied his scarf more snugly about his neck and tucked the ends into the collar of his heavy woolen shirt. He stamped the accumulated snow from his boots and smiled at Frankie, a shivering lad of about thirteen. The boy's face was pale, even by the light of the kerosene torches planted at intervals along the narrow forest road. "Maybe he'll give you some more pork and beans. You look like you could use some. Tell him I said so. Go on," he urged, as the lad hesitated. "You have time to go back. It'll be another hour before this load is ready to move." He jerked his head in the direction of the large flat sled and its team of horses.

As the boy scampered off, Nat looked up at the night sky. The moon was beginning to set. One of the horses shook its mane and snorted. Nat laughed softly. "I don't blame you, dobbin. I don't like getting up at one in the morning either!"

From the top of the skidway, one of the other lumbermen called to him. "Come on, Nat. Lend a hand."

He nodded his head and clambered up the side of the steep, snowy bank to the top of the skidway, a crude loading stand built against the slope. All during the fall, Ordway's lumbermen had chopped the soaring trees around Eagle Lake, sending the giants crashing to the forest floor. They started in the fall when the farmers and tourist guides, putting aside their summer occupations, could swell the ranks of the lumbermen. Besides, it was best to wait until autumn, when the sap was down. Summer-cut wood, especially pine, tended to attract woodworms as the logs lay waiting to be moved; and city folk didn't fancy wormy lumber.

Nat had become quite adept with his ax, managing to fell

forty trees a day in decent weather. He certainly had the strength, after all his years of pounding iron. And the old-timers in the lumber camp had shown him how a man could notch and aim a tree to fall just so. No one wanted to be responsible for a "widowmaker," a badly aimed tree that lodged in another as it fell, risking the life of every man who had to untangle the mess.

Nat had almost enjoyed the back-breaking work. It made him so bone-tired, so sapped at the end of a fifteen-hour day, he had no energy left to think of Willough. To curse her.

The autumn had been a busy one at the Ordway tract. When a tree was felled it was trimmed of its branches with the duller side of a double ax, then hauled—skidding along the leafy floor of the forest—by a team of oxen until it reached one of the many skidways scattered through the tract. After the wood had been stacked by the lumberjacks, who jacked the logs onto the skidway with the help of a spiked pole, the logs were measured to standard (thirteen feet in length and nineteen inches around) and marked on the ends with an embossing hammer, which identified the owner of the tract. Ordway's mark was the number 34.

Now, deep into winter, it was time to take the logs to the banking ground. They'd had to wait until enough snow had fallen so the roads could hold the weight of a loaded sled while easing the burden for the horses. A light sled had been sent on ahead to pack down the snow and provide an even path. On the straight stretches they had sprinkled water, which froze and turned the ruts into smooth ice to facilitate the haul; but on the often steep hills, the problem was reversed. Here they needed sand or straw to slow the progress of the sled. And the job had to be done at night. If the sun melted a patch of snow, the horses could stumble, the sled tilt and slide dangerously.

The banking ground, where the sleds were headed, was a frozen lake that Ordway's men called simply the Flow. It was damned at the outlet to the Rock River. In the spring, when the Flow melted, the dam would be removed, and the floating logs, borne on the flood, would travel down the Rock River to the Cedar River, and finally into the Hudson, where they joined the cuttings of hundreds of other logging operators in the mountains. The white pine and spruce and fir, which made up the bulk of the trees that were cut in the Adirondack Wilderness, were light enough to float easily on the current. Their ultimate destination was Glens Falls, where nearly four thousand sawmills were in operation.

Nat stood beside the skidway, pike in hand, and helped to roll the giant logs onto the sled. Glens Falls. Ordway had his sawmill there. Nat cursed softly, remembering. And so did Brian Bradford.

Bradford! Damn the lot of them! Once he'd thought that the war was the only evil that man was capable of. It had taken his involvement with the Bradfords to show him that evil came with power. "Sorry, Stanton," he'd been told. At every ironworks in the region, from Crown Point to Essex, from Ticonderoga to Lake Henderson. "We can't use you." Eight years. *Eight years* he'd put into learning everything there was to know about iron. And there wasn't a job to be had. "Not for *you*, Stanton." He'd finally got at least a partial answer to his baffled questions. From some flunky at Port Henry who'd been given "instructions." He wasn't high enough up on the echelon to know the whole story, but the word had come from MacCurdyville, presumably Brian Bradford himself. And there were whispers about *Miss* Bradford—now Mrs. Arthur Gray—and insults of a personal nature.

Mrs. Arthur Gray. The cold bitch wasn't content with walking out on him. She wanted to rub his nose in it as well. I'll ruin you, she'd said, that last night at Gray's house. Nat laughed bitterly. She was doing one hell of a job trying!

In the end, he'd been lucky. He couldn't leave the region— because of Gramps—go out to Pennsylvania where they were operating furnaces and forges. But Ordway was still hiring late in the season. Nat didn't know a damn thing about lumbering, but he'd learn. And Ordway paid well, at least. Thirty dollars a month. And room and board. It wasn't what he'd been earning as Bradford's manager, of course. But it was enough to keep Gramps in food and firewood.

Gramps had been a real problem. It had been difficult to get down to Ingles and back every Sunday. He'd arrive back at the lumber camp exhausted, and have to put in a full day's work. And once or twice he'd failed to get a ride back to Ordway's tract, and had been docked a day's pay. At last, though his grandfather had made a bit of a fuss, Nat had worked out an arrangement that provided for Gramps, and salved his own conscience as well. One of the lumbermen, Joe Corinth, lived in North Creek. Every Saturday night he left the lumber camp to be with his wife. If Nat saw that he wasn't going to be able to get away to see Gramps, he'd give Corinth an envelope with some money in it. Corinth would pass it on to Tom, the stationmaster at North Creek, who'd send it on the first train to Crown Point. The stationmaster *there* would give it to Ed Harold, who had agreed to buy food and firewood for Gramps and take it out to Ingles.

It was complicated, but it worked. Nat still managed to get to Gramps fairly often. When there was no envelope everyone on the chain went about his business because that meant Nat was making the trip himself.

Nat threw down his pike and wiped the sweat from his forehead. They'd finished loading the logs onto the sled. About fifty or sixty logs, which was about all that the team of horses could manage. Using heavy chains, they fastened the lumber to the sled, twisting a small log through the chain as a binder at the last, to pull up the slack.

The burly drover who was to take this load jammed his knitted cap more tightly to his head and looked around the clearing. "Where the hell's my road monkey? Where's Frankie?"

"Take it easy, George," said Nat quietly. "He'll be here in a minute. I sent him on an errand."

"What the hell'd you do that for? You're not running this show, Stanton. You're just helping me. Check that goddam chain one more time. And if that kid don't show up soon, I'm going to beat the tar out of him."

"Christ! He's only a kid."

"He's doing a man's job. And pulling down a man's pay! So he better get here."

Nat smiled tightly. "You're a prince, George. You could make a stone squirt lemonade. Here's your road monkey." He pointed as Frankie came panting up to the sled and team. "Get your tools, lad."

Frankie nodded and slung an ax and a shovel over his shoulder. George climbed up to the top of the logs in the front of the sled, grabbing the horse reins that Nat tossed up to him. Nat clambered aboard the stack of lumber and took his position near the fastening chain in the middle. While George maneuvered the sled on its runners—avoiding the deep ruts in the road—Nat's job was to keep an eye on the load itself, to be sure that a chain didn't loosen or a log slip. Frankie went on ahead to make the road smooth, stopping every few yards to chop at an icy bump or fill in a deep rut with snow.

The first couple of miles was fairly level; Nat found his glance and his thoughts wandering. The land around here had been worked over long since. By the light of the flickering torches, the tree stumps looked like stubble on a giant's beard. He remembered Brian Bradford and the land at New Russia. How many more government tracts, he wondered, had been leased over to greedy men like Bradford? And all quite legally.

Way off in the distance, an owl hooted. Nat thought: Enjoy your night, you bird. While you can. While there's still a tree left to perch in. It had started off with man pitted against Nature. The pioneers in the Wilderness. The age-old struggle. But lately the odds seemed to be changing.

"Look alive," said George. "We're coming to a slope." He hauled on the reins and stopped the team. Nat checked the lumber, twisted the binder log one more turn to tighten the chain, and fastened down the binder with its own small chain. The hill was quite steep. Using his shovel, Frankie dug into the mounds of sand that had been left at the side of the road, and sprinkled it on the icy ruts. When Frankie had just about reached the bottom of the long hill George started the team again. The sled creaked under the strain of its load, seemed to pause for a second at the crest of the hill, then began its cautious descent, The iron-clad runners of the sled scraped on the sand; the horses snorted, their hot breath suspended in the frosty night air. In spite of George's hold on the reins, the sled began to pick up speed, propelled by the heavy load. One of the horses stumbled in a hidden rut. The sled tipped dangerously, wobbled once, then righted itself. Nat clung to the rocking logs, checked the binder log again. But that sudden lurch had been enough; the heavy sled was now traveling at its own pace, picking up momentum as it hurtled down the slope. Faster, and still faster, while the icy wind whistled past their ears, and the horses trotted furiously. "Jesus!" said George hoarsely. "The son of a bitch is going to go!" His face was white. "Jump!" he yelled, and threw himself off the logs into a snowbank.

Nat scrambled to his feet, prepared to leap. The horses were now galloping in fear, manes streaming, in a mad contest to outrace the careening sled to the bottom of the hill. "Frankie!" shouted Nat. The boy looked up, his eyes wide with terror, to see horses and sled bearing down on him. He cried out; tried to run; slipped and fell, hitting his head on his own shovel. He lay in the middle of the road, dazed. Without a moment's hesitation, Nat sprang to the edge of the logs and leaped onto the flank of one of the racing animals. He leaned forward, grabbed the horse's bit in his fist, pulled with all his might. The horse screamed in pain and terror. But he turned—rearing violently so Nat was thrown from his back— and ploughed into a snowbank on the side of the road. The sled, stopped short in its headlong flight, shuddered and lurched sideways. There was a sharp snap as the chain gave way, and then the rumbling of the logs as they tumbled off the sled.

Nat looked up. He saw the logs falling. He saw Willough's face. And then he saw nothing.

He awoke to the scent of flowers. They smelled like Willough's hair. That silken glory, black as a raven's wing. "Willough," he whispered. It didn't sound like his own voice.

"There, there, Mr. Stanton. Don't try to move."

He opened his eyes and blinked. He seemed to be in a

room full of flowers, bright pink roses that danced across the walls, yellow lilies that hovered above his head. He blinked again. The lilies were attached to a bosom, the bosom to a gray dress, the whole giving off the strong odor of flower-scented perfume.

"Are you feeling better?"

He allowed his eyes to stray upward from the lilies and the bosom. A cheerful-looking woman, with bright cheeks and a snowy head of hair, was beaming down at him. "Where..." he croaked, then cleared his throat and started again. "Where is this?"

"You're reposing in my house, Mr. Stanton. In my sister's room." She laughed, a birdlike chirp. "Though Mabel would be as amused as I am to see a big strapping fellow like you in the pretty little room where she spent so many happy hours. And never will again."

He frowned. Was she expecting sympathy? "Has she... passed on, ma'am?" he asked delicately.

"Bless my soul, no! She's just married and gone to live in Boston! So when my nephew—that's Dr. Mortimer, you might just remember him, though I'm not certain you were lucid when they brought you in..." She drifted off, her bright eyes on his face. "You must be thirsty. Would you care for something to drink?"

"Please."

"Don't try to get up." She took a glass of water from the bedside stand, lifted his head with one hand, and brought the glass to his lips. "As I was saying... when my nephew wanted a place for you to stay—he has such a tiny house, and far too many children—I naturally thought, why not Mabel's old room?"

He closed his eyes and turned away from the glass. There were things he had to remember. "But where is this house?"

"Why, in North Creek. They brought you here after that dreadful accident in the woods. Mr. Ordway was quite beside himself. He seemed to feel that the boy, and the team of horses, too, would have been done for, but for your quick action. He said you were not to worry about a thing. He will pay you your wages during the period of your convalescence, and until you are completely recovered."

He stirred restlessly under the quilts. He ached all over, and his left leg felt strangely stiff and numb. "Recovered from what? I remember the logs falling on me. That's all."

She looked uncomfortable. "Well, of course you had rather a lot of cuts and bruises about you. A very nasty blow to the head, and several broken ribs..."

He felt a coldness in the pit of his stomach. "And...?"

"You were pinned under the logs for a long time and lost a great deal of blood—we'll set that to rights in no time, now that you're yourself again." Her snowy head bobbed vigorously. "A few weeks of my calves' foot jelly will have you fit as a fiddle in no time."

"Is that all?"

"You must face these things with pluck," she said. "God sends us trials..."

"In the name of God, woman," he burst out, "what is it?"

"Your leg... it was very badly crushed..."

His eyes widened in horror, anxious hands searching under the covers. "My God, have I lost it?"

"Oh, no, Mr. Stanton. Not at all! My nephew—Dr. Mortimer—set the bones as best he could. But he fears that you'll limp for the rest of your days."

He exhaled in relief, managing a small smile. "I never was one for dancing, ma'am. Ma'am...?"

"Mrs. Mortimer. Mrs. Grace Mortimer."

He was suddenly very tired. "I'd like to sleep again, ma'am, if I may." No. There was something he had to remember.

"That's wise of you, Mr. Stanton. And when you wake up again I'll give you a nice sponge bath, and perhaps a shave. I used to do it for Mr. Mortimer all the time when he was alive."

He rubbed at his chin. It was a very heavy growth. One might even call it... the beginnings of a beard. He looked at Grace Mortimer with fresh panic. *That's* what he had to remember! "How long have I been here?"

"Oh my. Well, let me see. This is Friday..."

He frowned. The accident had been on Tuesday. The eleventh. "Today's the fourteenth?"

"Oh, no. The twenty-first."

"God!" He struggled to sit up. "Sweet Jesus . . . how could I have lost so many days?"

"Mr. Stanton! Do try to be calm. You were in a great deal of pain. Your leg was quite shattered. Dr. Mortimer thought it advisable to keep you heavily sedated. You had lost so much blood. You would never have had the strength to endure such suffering . . ."

"You don't understand! I've got to get a message to Crown Point! There's someone who depends on me . . ." He had begun to shake.

"Of course. I'll have a telegram sent at once."

"To Mr. Ed Harold." He dictated the telegram, fighting the terrible weariness that was creeping over him. He had to stay awake until the reply came in. He had to. He had to . . .

He opened his eyes. It was night. Grace Mortimer was sitting in a little gold chair beside his bed, a small Bible on her lap. She smiled at him, her eyes warm with concern. "Do you wish a cup of tea, Mr. Stanton?"

Her expression told him everything. "I think I'd prefer a glass of whiskey. He's dead, isn't he?"

She bit her lip. "I'm so sorry, and so is everyone else. They all assumed . . . when you didn't send any money on Sunday . . ."

"That I'd gone to see him myself."

She nodded. "Mr. Harold said . . . it looked like he'd run out of fuel. He'd burned most of the furniture. When they found him he was on the floor near his stove. He'd been trying to burn his invalid chair."

"Oh my God . . ." He covered his face with his hands.

"If you'd like, I'll get that whiskey now."

"No. Just leave me alone for a while." He stared up at the ceiling, where the kerosene lamp made a pool of light. He had no memory of when the tears started. It seemed somehow that they'd always been there just behind his eyes, in his heart. He wept for Gramps, and Jed, and Pete. And all the wasted lives. He couldn't even turn his broken body to bury his face in the pillow. He lay on his back, the tears sliding down his temples, and mourned the loss of his family.

After awhile, the tears were replaced by anger. And a cold hatred. All the evils of civilization—the cruelty that set one man to destroying another, and all to despoiling God's earth; the carelessness of the powerful; the greed and snobbery— had become focused on one person. One person who had come to represent all that he'd learned to hate.

"I'll pay you back, Willough," he whispered. "By God, I'll get my due."

Chapter Ten

"Please, madame. Take it." Old Jacques smiled at Marcy and held out a large pink peony. His French was sharp with a provincial accent.

She shook her head, answering him in the simple French words she had learned. "No, I thank you. One cannot afford what one cannot afford."

"But every day, for nearly nine months, you buy a flower from me. And so I say to myself, if she does not buy a flower today, it is because she has not the money. Jacques, I say, today you *give* her the flower. Please, madame. Take it."

Relenting, Marcy took the flower from him, thanked him, moved on down the boulevard. She sniffed the fragrant peony. *Pivoine*, Jacques had called it. She must remember that. At least if she could ever afford to buy one again.

She glanced up at the soft twilight sky. The first star. When she looked up at the heavens she could almost forget the city swirling around her. She blinked back her tears, aching with longing for home.

She sighed. She had one more errand. Drew had given her enough extra money to buy a little firewood. But it was a warm evening, a lovely June night. They didn't need firewood for heat. And she could heat supper over the spirit lamp. But Drew needed paints. If Monsieur Tanguy, the color-grinder, was still in his shop on the rue Clauzel, she'd pick up the blue and the yellow that Drew lacked. Firewood could wait. If need be, she'd buy some tomorrow on credit. She already owed the *boulanger* and the greengrocer; one more debt didn't matter until Drew sold his next drawing.

She sighed again. If only he were able to sell a *painting*. Not for the money, but for his confidence. He'd been despondent since the association of artists—the Café Guerbois *habitués*—had opened their group exhibit in April on the boulevard des Capucines. For a whole month they had endured the derision of the critics and the public; and when the exhibit had closed and they had tallied up their expenses against their receipts for entrance fees, catalog sales, and the commission on the few paintings that had sold, there was not even enough left to pay back each artist the sixty francs in dues he had advanced. One by one, the artists, Pissarro, Renoir, and the rest, had packed up and left Paris, relying on the hospitality of wealthy friends in the provinces to see them through the dry spell.

And still the criticism continued. Sarcastic articles appeared in *Le Figaro* and *Charivari*, mockingly alluding to the group of painters as "Impressionists," because of Monet's painting of Le Havre, which he had, at the last moment, titled *Impression, Sunrise*.

Drew's two works that he had exhibited—dancers at the opera, and a scene of the rue de la Condamine, painted from their window—had been dismissed by the critic Albert Wolff with a few terse words: "Constipated little pictures, with sudden bursts of bizarre color. It would appear our American friend gained nothing by crossing the Atlantic."

She bought Drew's paints, and a bit of alcohol for the spirit lamp, then hurried down the street for home. She hoped the landlady wasn't around. They were three weeks behind in the rent now, and it was getting very hard to make up excuses. Drew had already sold his watch.

The studio was dark. Drew wasn't home yet. She tried to ignore the finger of uneasiness that scratched at her insides. They'd quarreled this morning. About money, of course. She'd had an offer from one of the instructors at the Ecole des Beaux-Arts. They were willing to pay her three francs a day to model in the classroom. In the nude. Drew had been livid with rage.

"You're my wife, Marcy! I won't hear of it!"

"But it's a good job. And there's not much else I can do. My French isn't good enough to work in a shop."

"All those men staring at you . . ."

"Oh, bosh! How can you be jealous? They won't be looking at *me*! Just at my body! Like a flower you paint, a tree in the Tuileries, a china cup. That's all I'd be to them."

He had looked at her sharply, his blue eyes filled with mistrust. "Perhaps you're aiming to catch the notice of some young man whose father is rich enough to pay his tuition."

She had been near tears. "Dang you, Drew Bradford! Why won't you let me *help* you?"

"If you're so eager to make money—and don't care how the hell you get it—you can go back to modeling for that lecher Stewart. Or join the Montmartre ladies in their evening strolls!"

She'd felt the blood drain from her face. "At least it would be nice to be wanted by a man. For any reason."

He had bowed to her, a twisted smile on his lips. *"Touché."* Snatching up his hat and sketchpad, he'd stormed out of the studio, slamming the door behind him.

Now it was getting late. And he wasn't home yet. She ate a cold supper, washed the dishes, mended a pair of stockings. Paced the floor. What was happening to them? He didn't make love to her these days. Not since her miscarriage. In bed he stayed as far away from her as possible; but when he slept, he pulled her close. It was the only time she felt needed anymore.

She heard the chime of a clock on a distant church. Midnight. She picked up the flower Jacques had given her, brushing its soft petals against her cheek. She was useless to Drew. It wasn't the lack of money that bothered her; it was the thought that she was failing him. All the love she had in her wasn't enough to balance out his disappointment in his work.

They shouldn't have married. She'd trapped him into it; he hadn't wanted it. But she'd been so sure it was right. Because they loved each other.

Still holding the flower, she sank down onto the bed. He hadn't told her that he loved her in a very long time. Perhaps he no longer did. Perhaps he never had. She'd managed to ruin his life. To estrange him from his family. She was a burden to him in this city.

This city. How could she ever have thought she wanted to live in a city? There was no joy, no life. And no safety either. She'd had nothing but grief. And now this city was taking her love from her, turning him into a stranger with haunted eyes.

She slept, the peony still clutched in her hand, and dreamed of sunny meadows and Drew laughing.

Drew did not laugh as he stumbled across the dawn-lit cobblestones; his head ached. He passed the lamplighter extinguishing the gaslights on the rue de la Condamine. Oh, God, he thought. He hadn't meant to drink so much, hadn't meant to stay out all night. But every time he remembered the awful things he'd said to Marcy, he felt such a pang of guilt he hadn't the courage to face her.

He knew she was upset because they didn't make love anymore. But how could he? He thought of all the weeks she'd lain in bed after her miscarriage—bright and cheerful, hiding the grief that any woman would feel after such a loss. He groaned. And *he* had done it to her. It was inevitable, with the life they led. That cold and drafty studio, not enough food or warm clothes. And the constant worry about where the next meal would be coming from. His sweet Marcy. Once so tanned and robust. Now thin and pale, almost fragile. How could he make love to her now? How could he risk her carrying—and losing—another child? He loved her too much for that.

He stopped at a shop near the studio, and gazed into the window. There was a straw bonnet there, bright with pink ribbons and silken flowers and a butterfly perched on its crown. He'd pretended not to notice when Marcy had admired it the other day; he couldn't bear to see the longing in her eyes.

He stared at his reflection in the glass. He thought: You're a failure, Drewry Bradford. To begin with, a failure as an artist. Oh, it wasn't because of the criticism from that ass Wolff, who wouldn't know good painting if he ran into it. He wouldn't have given a damn about Wolff's comments, if that sort of thing didn't influence the buying public. Wolff destroyed only his commercial success; the critic who destroyed his soul was . . . himself. Something was wrong. He hadn't liked the work he'd turned out in New York. But painting like the Impressionists didn't seem to be the answer either. He wasn't Renoir or Degas. They were *good*, no matter what the world thought of them. Vibrant, real, pulsing with life. *His* backstage paintings, his scenes of boulevards, seemed like weak, spiritless imitations.

He sighed heavily. And he was a failure as a husband. He was dragging Marcy down with him, robbing her of her joy, poisoning her with his own despair.

With a heavy heart he climbed the stairs to the studio. Behind the folding screen Marcy lay across their bed, sleeping. Still in her gown. She must have waited up for him half the night. He leaned over her. To wake her. To hold her in his arms, cover her sweet face with kisses, beg her forgiveness for his cruel words.

And then he saw the flower, the pathetic blossom that rested in her hand, even while she slept. It was wilted and forlorn, like her bright hopes that had faded and died. When he'd met her she'd been young and innocent, bubbling with life, with her Cinderella dreams of finding a rich man.

Instead she'd found a struggling artist who couldn't afford to care for her as she deserved. No. As she needed and longed to be cared for. He laughed bitterly. He hadn't even been able to buy her more than a lace handkerchief when she'd turned nineteen in April.

Dammit! Somehow that pitiful flower was the last straw. He couldn't continue to bring her grief. It was enough! He made up his mind—a decision that seemed inevitable. If Brian wanted a son and partner, by God, he'd have one! He'd forget his ambitions, his stupid dreams of being an artist, and learn to be a businessman. But Marcy would have a house that was warm, and enough food to eat, and pretty things to bring the sparkle back to her eyes.

He thought quickly. The telegraph office would be opening soon. He'd get a cable off to his father right away. He didn't have enough money to pay for it, of course, but he could pawn his box of paints. He wouldn't be needing them anyway. Quietly, so as not to disturb Marcy, he gathered the paints together in their box, tossed in his brushes, his crayons. Everything.

There was no need to tell Marcy what he'd decided; it would only make her reproach herself. If she insisted on an explanation, he would simply tell her that his father had summoned him. He'd have Brian authorize his Paris banker to advance the money to pay for their passage home, and to clear up their debts. He'd pack his paintings and his drawings and take them home, to be displayed someday as a souvenir of his folly.

But never again did he want to see a sad flower in Marcy's dear hand.

He had been out and come back again when Marcy finally
stirred and opened her eyes. Something had wakened her. A
noise beyond the dividing screen. She sat up and stretched.
Tarnation! She must have slept the whole night away in her
gown. She stood up, smoothed her creased skirt, and moved
quickly around the screen. She'd have to hurry to make Drew
his breakfast before his class this morning at the Ecole des
Beaux-Arts. There was a little coffee left, and the loaf of
bread she'd bought for last night's supper, if it wasn't too
stale.

"Drew Bradford, what is this?" she gasped in surprise.
There in the center of the room was their little table, re-
splendent with a huge bowl of peonies and yellow roses.
Beside it was a basket of strawberries; a jug of thick, sweet
cream; the largest brioche she had ever seen, studded with
raisins. And a bottle of champagne.

Grinning, he gathered her into his arms. "This, my love,
is breakfast!"

"But how can we ... how can you ..."

He picked up a strawberry and popped it into her mouth.
"Don't you want it?"

She chewed and giggled at the same time. "You know I
do! But champagne for breakfast? What's come over you?"

His blue eyes peered intently into hers. "Do you love me,
Marcy?" he whispered.

She put her arms around his neck and clung to him. "Oh,
Drew. With all my heart." When he kissed her hungrily, his
arms holding her tight, she thought she'd weep. He was
suddenly the Drew of old, warm and loving and dear.

"Now, Mrs. Bradford," he said, popping the champagne
cork. "We're going to have our breakfast. And then, if you're
not too giddy from the champagne, I'm going to take you to
bed and make love to you all morning long." His eyes twinkled wickedly. "Whether your husband allows it or not. Do
you understand?"

She made a little curtsy. "Yes sir. But he's very jealous."

"And well he might be! Because I can steal you away with
presents. Open that box."

"This?" She picked up a round pasteboard box, its blue and white stripes sprigged with violets. She removed the lid, plowed through acres of tissue paper, and squealed in delight. Within the box was a straw bonnet, with pink ribbons and a butterfly. "But I don't understand, Drew. Why are you . . ."

"Have some champagne. And don't ask so many questions or we'll never get to bed. I thought the bonnet would look charming with your best gray gown. You'll be the most beautiful woman on the boat."

"The boat? What boat?"

He shook his head. "Questions again? I thought I answered that already."

"Tarnation, Drew Bradford! I'll kick your shins if you don't stop funning me!"

He laughed. "Oh, very well! It's just that you'd better start packing."

"Packing?" Dear God. She put her hand to her thumping heart, scarcely daring to hope.

He pulled her back into his arms, kissed her softly. "Dearest Marcy. We're going home."

Marcy bit back the questions "how?" and "why?" Even on the trip back she held her tongue, but she had sent him to visit his mother when they reached New York. He'd found them a small rooming house on Tenth Street. "Just for tonight," he'd said. "Tomorrow we'll go up to Saratoga to see my father."

Marcy'd taken off that funny little bonnet of hers, put her hands in his, gazed at him with those blue-green eyes that always melted him. "Go and see your mother."

He'd shaken his head. Argued with her. He couldn't ever forgive his mother for her ugly words about her.

Marcy had been adamant, her stubborn little chin jutting in determination. Whatever had happened between him and his mother, she'd said, it was time to make his peace. In the evening, if his mother was agreeable, the three of them could have supper together.

In the end, he'd laughed softly, given in. He couldn't fight her once she made up her mind to something.

At his mother's house he took the steps two at a time, eager to have this interview over and done with. Tomorrow's meeting with his father would be difficult enough; he had no idea what humor his mother was in. This was June. They had parted last August on a note of acrimony. And although he had found it impossible to forgive her insults to Marcy, he was nevertheless aware of how she had doted on him through the years. Irrational or not, she would have viewed his marriage as a betrayal.

He was dismayed to see how she seemed to have aged in less than a year. The hands she held out to embrace him had a slight tremor. Damn Dr. Page! he thought. He should have taken her off that tonic years ago!

"Drewry! Dearest boy! How I've missed you!"

"Mum." He knew she loved to be called by her pet name. He kissed her cheek, and sat beside her on a small settee as she directed.

"You don't know how I've reproached myself a thousand times because of our parting," she said sadly. "I kept hoping you'd forgive me, and write. Every day I watched for the postman, longing for a word from you. Longing to know you'd forgiven the hasty words of someone who loves you so." She smiled and blinked back her tears.

He felt like a villain. "Oh, Mum. I'm here now," he said gruffly.

"Where's your . . . where's Marcy?"

He noticed her choice of words. Not a good sign. "My *wife* is at Mrs. Oliver's Boardinghouse, over on Tenth Street. She's tired from the trip. She wanted to rest for a bit. But perhaps later, the three of us can dine together . . . ?"

Isobel stared at her fingers. "Perhaps."

"I love her, Mother. That hasn't changed. I hope you can begin to understand that and accept her."

"Of course, dear boy." A single tear dropped from her eye on to her folded hands.

Oh, God. "How's Willough?" he asked quickly.

"I'm sure I don't really know. What she and Arthur do is of little concern to me. I see them seldom."

"But is Willough happy in her marriage?" He thought: Or do you hate her so much you hope that she's not? Poor little sister.

Isobel looked uncomfortable. "She's . . . 'in the family way,' if you know what I mean. It's quite shocking, really, the way she exhibits herself around town, and in her condition. I gather she's due in just a few weeks. I can't understand why Arthur doesn't forbid such carryings-on!"

He laughed softly. "Perhaps little sister is finally letting go of her restraints. Good for her! We'll pay her a visit when we return from Saratoga. I think she and Marcy will get on famously."

Isobel pursed her lips. "You're set in your plans, then. I couldn't believe it when I heard from Brian that you were coming home. And to work for him! He must be very anxious to have you as his partner. He even sent his private car to take you up to Saratoga. It's waiting at the Grand Central Station."

"Good! I'd planned to take the train tomorrow. The day coach. But perhaps Marcy and I can go tonight. It'd be a pleasant trip. I'm sure Marcy's never traveled that way before. And we can sleep as easily on the train as at the boarding-house."

"But what about your painting, Drew?"

"I've given it up."

"Oh, how it grieves me to hear you say that. Because of Marcy?"

"I'm not bitter, Mother. So get that tone out of your voice. I'm just facing the truth. I have an obligation to my wife. An obligation I've accepted willingly. Because I love her."

"But you want to paint. You *need* to paint."

He pushed down the pain in his heart. "We all have to compromise with life."

"Drew. Listen to me. I still have that money set aside. I can afford to pay for a small studio for you. You can paint to your heart's content."

"And where are we supposed to live, Marcy and I?"

"You can stay here."

"Good God, Mother! What kind of a life would that be for Marcy? Even if you accepted her with all your heart?"

"I can't afford to pay for rooms for you as well. You'll have to stay here."

"No. I want to see Marcy happy. She's suffered enough this last year. I want to see her happy."

"At the expense of your own happiness?"

"I've made up my mind!" He rose from the settee and strode to the door.

"And you've let your father win you away from me!" she shrieked. She began to weep. "Oh, the ingratitude of children! The knife to the heart!"

He returned and knelt before her, frowning. "Stop it, Mum! You know I love you. But I must do this thing my way."

She sniffled, dabbed at her eyes. "You're right, of course. Don't be cross with me. I'm just a foolish old woman. I trust your judgment. Do what you think you must."

He smiled his relief. "May I bring Marcy for supper later?"

"Of course." She stood up and crossed to her vanity, fingering the cut-glass bottle filled with her tonic. She turned. "No. Wait. Will you indulge your Mum just one more time? I'm not at my best today. I hate to meet your dear bride when I'm languishing. When you return from Saratoga you'll come to dinner. The two of you. I'll have time to plan it properly. Perhaps we can have Willough and Arthur too. And your father."

"That might be very pleasant."

"But as for tonight..." The eyes she turned to him were dark and pleading. "I know I've lost you, dearest boy. It's a grief every mother with a son must face. But... will you take supper alone with me tonight? The way we used to? I'll put on my prettiest dinner gown for you. And you can change into your dress clothes. I've left everything in your room just as it was when you went away. Your clothes, your old drawings and paintings. Everything. You can take a hot bath, dear boy, and Parkman can help you dress..."

"But what about Marcy?"

"I'm sure she's worn out from the journey and would wel-

come an early supper and a good night's sleep. I'll tell you
what. The railroad car is at the station. And Keller's on board,
with a well-stocked pantry. I'll have someone escort your
Marcy to the car. Keller can feed her a good supper. And by
the time you get there, she'll be nicely settled in for the
evening."

"I don't know . . . it's her first night in the city . . ."

"And she's probably terribly nervous about meeting Brian
tomorrow. All the more reason for her to welcome a little
solitude tonight. To compose herself." She smiled in understanding. "We women are all the same. I'm sure that's how
I'd feel."

"I suppose so." He was torn. The thought of a hot bath . . .

Isobel's lip quivered. "For old times' sake, Drew. Please."

He capitulated. "All right, Mum. But, Marcy . . ."

"You go off to your room, Drewry. I told you, I'll take
care of Marcy."

Isobel watched her son's retreating back. It was good to
have him home. She intended to have him home forever. And
to see that he became a painter, if that's what he wanted. She
couldn't have him ruin his life by going into business with
Brian. Drew was *hers*! She wouldn't let Brian have him! And
some day, when he was a successful painter, he'd thank her.

She sat down at her desk, pulled out a sheet of paper. "I'm
doing this for your own good, dear boy," she whispered, and
began to write. The room was quiet except for the scratch of
the pen. When she had finished the letter she blotted it carefully, folded it, and slipped it into an envelope. Taking up
another sheet of paper, she crossed to her vanity and opened
a drawer from which she removed a large vial filled with a
white powder. She shook out a quantity of the powder onto
the paper, scrutinized the small white mound, and sprinkled
out a bit more. Carefully folding the piece of paper into a
neat packet, she added it to the envelope with her letter, then
sealed the envelope and rang for her maid.

She held out the envelope to the girl. "Have this sent round
to Mr. Gray. At once."

The maid bobbed, took the letter, and left the room. Isobel

looked at her hands. They had begun to shake violently. She unstoppered the bottle of tonic, put it to her lips, and took a large swallow. She closed the bottle, wiped her mouth against the back of her hand.

"Arthur, you faithless snake," she said to the empty room. "Don't fail me. *It's time to pay your debt!*"

As she waited for Drew to return, Marcy poured a bit of water into the china basin and splashed at her face and bare bosom. It was a warm evening. Even with her gown put aside, she felt uncomfortable. Perhaps when Drew came back from visiting his mother they might take a little stroll. The street couldn't be any warmer than this stifling room, and Drew had said that Washington Square Park wasn't too far away.

She prayed that he and his mother had settled their quarrel; it would make her joy in their homecoming complete. Well, almost complete. There was still the nagging doubt that something wasn't quite right with Drew. Oh, he'd been warm and loving, full of teasing and laughter. As he used to be. Their days had been filled with happiness—picnics in the Bois, carriage rides, flowers and champagne; their nights with hot passion. But sometimes, when he thought she wasn't watching, his face would take on a distant look that she found bewildering.

And there was the matter of the money. He had given her lavish gifts, trinkets and ribbons and bonbons; no matter how hard she tried, she couldn't make him understand that her joy—those last few days in Paris—had been because of *his* lightheartedness, not because of the things he bought her. And when she asked where the money came from, he was evasive. "My father's helping out," he'd mutter, then change the subject. But she remembered what he'd said in the past, that his father had made conditions he couldn't possibly accept. So why had Brian Bradford sent them money? And why were they going up to Saratoga tomorrow to see him?

"What about your painting?" she'd ask him. "What happened to your paintbox?"

He'd shrug. "I'll do a bit when we've settled in. Don't

worry." Either New York City or Saratoga, he'd said. He hadn't yet decided which would be more convenient.

And each time she tried to talk to him, to get clearer answers, he'd brush her aside with a laugh, a joke, a kiss. There was to be no talk of business, of painting, of money. Anything. In the end, there was nothing to do but trust in him and ignore her own misgivings.

There was a tap on the rooming-house door. Marcy threw her wrapper around her shoulders; a fresh-faced young maid entered at her bidding. "Mrs. Bradford, ma'am. There's a gentleman downstairs to see you."

Marcy frowned. "A gentleman? Oh. Perhaps he's come to see Mr. Bradford. But my husband isn't here just now."

"No, ma'am. He specially asked for you."

Who could it be? she thought. She didn't know anyone in this city. Perhaps Drew was teasing her again. She slipped out of her wrapper and reached for her gray bodice and skirt, murmuring her thanks as the maid helped her hook the waistband and fluff out the silk flounces. She was wearing her red-brown hair in the French style: a fringe of curls across her forehead, a simple ribbon that tied the two temple pieces up and back, the rest hanging loose. Far less complicated than the twisted and artificial styles she'd seen on the women of New York City. It took only a minute's brushing to smooth her coiffure. She followed the maid downstairs, crossed the rooming-house foyer to the small parlor.

"Marcy!" An elegantly dressed man walked toward her, holding out his hand in greeting. He certainly was the most nattily attired man she'd seen since they came to the city. He looked like a Parisian swell, with his spats and gloves and walking stick. Much older than Drew. About forty, she guessed. Clearly the "gentleman" the maid had said he was. And he had called her by name. Her Christian name! She eyed him with suspicion. After nearly a year in Paris, she'd learned how to take care of herself, but still . . .

He laughed and stroked his small brown mustache. "Forgive me. I've just realized how strange all this must seem to you! I'm Arthur Gray."

Arthur Gray. Was that supposed to mean anything to her?
It sounded vaguely familiar. A friend of Drew's, perhaps?

"I'm Willough's husband. I'm your brother-in-law!"

"Oh my!" She felt herself blushing. "Of course! I'm awfully sorry, Mr. Gray, I . . ."

"Please. Arthur. We *are* family. Matter of fact, that's why
I'm here. Drew's having supper with his mother tonight, and
they asked me to look after you."

"With his mother? Just the two of them?"

"Yes."

"Oh, I'm glad! It means that they're friends again."

He raised a quizzical eyebrow. "That's a very understanding
attitude for a wife."

She smiled. "We're very much in love. But then, you must
know what I mean. You and Willough haven't been married
as long as we have." She looked around the parlor. "Where
is Willough? Shall I get to meet her tonight?"

He looked uncomfortable. "Willough is . . . hardly in a proper
condition to meet anyone in the next few weeks."

She frowned; then her eyes widened in sudden understanding. "Oh! *Enceinte?*" She blushed. "That's what my *concierge*
would say."

He laughed. "Damned if Drewry hasn't found himself a
rare jewel. Yes. *Enceinte.*" His eyes were warm with approval. It made her feel terribly attractive and mature.

She thought: How fortunate Willough is to have such a
nice husband!

"Well," he said, "I'm to treat you to supper, while Drew
and Isobel become acquainted again. And since you'll be
taking the train to Saratoga tonight . . ."

"No. Drew said we're going in the morning."

He shook his head. "The plans have been changed. It seems
that Brian sent down his private car to take you up to his
place. I thought that, rather than going to a restaurant, you
and I could have supper on the car and wait for Drew to join
us later. Keller—that's Brian's man—makes a wonderful
clam chowder. You must be tired of fancy French food."

"That sounds very nice . . . Arthur."

"Come along, then," he said. "My barouche is waiting outside. Are you still packed?"

"Nearly. Drew and I didn't want to bother unpacking, just for the one night."

"Good. Then go and get your bonnet while I pay your bill and have the maid pack up your traps. We'll bring them over to the railroad car with us."

"Oh, no, I can pack..."

"My dear Marcy, if you're going to be a Bradford in this city, you'll have to get used to allowing people to serve you." He eyed her thoughtfully. "You *do* like being waited on, don't you? Like a French countess?"

"I don't know. I've never had..." She felt flustered. She'd never thought about it until now. But it had been nice, having the maid help her to dress.

"Come now. All young girls have dreams. In honor of your first night in New York, why don't we pretend that you are a countess?"

She giggled (it might be fun, at that!), and allowed him to commandeer the servants in the rooming house to wait on her. Her baggage was repacked for her, her hair was brushed and her bonnet tied on, her gown swept free of the dust of travel. She sailed out of the rooming house into the fanciest carriage she had ever ridden in, complete with two coachmen in bright green uniforms and silk top hats.

If the coach had been elegant, the railroad car was dazzling. It sat off on a siding at the Grand Central Station, with two large lanterns on either end illuminating the tracks and glinting off the bright blue and gold exterior. As they alit from Arthur's coach and mounted the steps to the railroad car, Marcy wanted to pinch herself. She truly did feel like a great lady. All the years she'd gazed with awe at these wonderful cars—and here she was, an honored guest, being ushered aboard to take supper in style!

The interior of the car was a wonder. The parlor was paneled in rich dark wood, carved in high relief with garlands of flowers and fruit. There were glittering mirrors, silver coat hooks, brass spittoons. Kerosene lanterns, backed by shiny reflectors, were fastened to the walls or hung from the curved ceiling. At one end of the parlor a desk had been built into the wall; at the other end, a bar, complete with cut-crystal decanters and rows of glasses behind a carved wooden railing. The carpeting was patterned in a lush floral design of cream and blue and red. The red of the carpeting was repeated in the plush of the comfortable parlor chairs, the gold-braided red velvet draperies at the windows, the large dining chairs that surrounded a paisley-covered table. At one end of the car, half hidden by a red velvet drapery, Marcy could see a galley kitchen, and beyond that a small door.

Arthur had followed her glance. "That's where you and Drew will sleep tonight. I'll show you the rooms later."

It was too wonderful for words! "Sleep?" she asked. "In a bed?"

"Of course! Did you imagine you were to sit up all night?" He laughed. "This car will be hooked onto the locomotive that's making its regular run. You'll leave here at about eleven-thirty. And you'll be in Saratoga in time for an early breakfast."

She sighed. "I didn't think people lived like this."

He smiled, took off his hat and gloves. "Unless you want to look around a bit more, sister-in-law, I'd as soon eat." He chuckled softly and bowed. "That is, if the countess permits!"

She felt wonderfully elegant and sophisticated. *"Madame la comtesse est agréable."*

"Very good! Very good indeed." Arthur summoned Keller, who took Marcy's hat and gloves and handbag, and directed the porter with the luggage into the back rooms. "Would you care for a glass of wine?" Arthur asked, as Keller covered the paisley with a white damask cloth and began to lay out china and silver.

"No. Wine makes me sleepy when I haven't eaten."

"A bit of champagne with supper, then."

She giggled. "Only a bit. I'm afraid that champagne goes to my head. I wouldn't want to be tipsy by the time Drew gets here!"

Supper was the most extraordinary meal that Marcy had ever eaten. Keller's clam chowder was creamy and rich, awash with bits of potato and chopped clams. It was followed by cold pheasant with mushrooms, rare roast beef and potatoes, spinach and carrots. Then came plum pudding, ice cream, fruit, and nuts. Marcy ate sparingly, eager to leave room for whatever delicacies might follow. She drank even less, though it was a joy to sip the champagne from delicately carved flute glasses; she certainly didn't want to embarrass Drew or herself with a repetition of her wedding day!

In spite of her restraint, however, the champagne seemed to be going to her head. She found herself laughing and giggling a great deal. And when she thought back on it, she could hardly remember what the pudding had tasted like, though she had a mental picture of Keller serving it flaming with brandy.

She put down her empty coffee cup and smiled at Arthur. "Oh, I'm so tired. Perhaps I should take a nap before Drew gets here."

"Nonsense. You just need to stretch your legs. Why don't I show you the rest of the car?"

She sat in her chair, too lethargic even to move, until Arthur came around to her side of the table and helped her up. Her legs wobbled for a moment. "Goodness! I think I drank more than I intended."

"You'll feel better if you don't give in to it. Come and see the bedrooms."

Meekly, she allowed him to lead her to the back corridor off of which the bedrooms were located. A small space for Keller—barely more than a closet with a settee that converted to a bed—a handsome guest room done up in olive green velvet, and Mr. Bradford's quarters.

"You'll be staying here," said Arthur, indicating the guest room. "I've had your luggage put in, but perhaps you'd like to see Brian's room. It has the very latest in modern conveniences."

Marcy nodded. Tarnation! She shouldn't have done *that*. It made her feel terribly light-headed. She found herself clinging to Arthur for support as he led her into Brian's quarters.

But the sight of the room revived her momentarily. It was

positively splendid! It scarcely looked like a room in a railroad car. The bed, covered in deep blue velvet edged with silver braid, was twice the size of her and Drew's Paris bed. It looked good enough to lie down on. She blinked sleepily. "Arthur, I . . ."

"Look," he said, pointing to a small room off to one side. "But perhaps you've seen indoor plumbing before . . ."

She chuckled. Her voice sounded strange in her ears. "Yes. Once I sneaked into a water closet in one of the fancy hotels in Paris."

"But I'm sure you haven't seen *this*. It's Brian's pride and joy."

Marcy stared in curiosity. It seemed to be a little box-shaped room—no wider across than two or three hand-spans—with a frosted glass door. When Arthur opened the door she peered inside. The other three walls were of marble, una-dorned except for brass pipes that ran down each side and were joined by crosswise piping studded with small holes. Marcy laughed. "It looks like a prison, with the bars on the wrong side! What in thunderation *is* it?"

"It's a rain bath. You stand in there, and warm water sprays over you. It's connected to its own boiler in a closet next door."

Marcy's jaw dropped. "It sprays you? All over your whole body?"

"You don't even have to sit down. And unless you duck your head, it doesn't get your face and hair wet."

"Oh-h-h!" It was surely the most wonderful thing she'd ever seen! "Do you suppose . . . in the morning . . ." She looked at him with hopeful eyes. "Do you suppose I'd be allowed to try it?"

"The Countess Bradford doesn't need permission, my dear. You can try it whenever you want. Tonight, if you wish. As a matter of fact, it being such a warm night, I thought you or Drew would like the refreshment of a rain bath. I had Keller turn on a very low flame under the boiler."

"Tonight? Now?" She really was beginning to feel very strange. "I'm not quite myself at the moment . . ." She rubbed her hand across her eyes and took a deep breath. "And the air has become so close."

"All the more reason to take a rain bath now. It will perk you up before Drew gets here."

"Yes." It was lovely to have him think for her. Her brain didn't want to function.

He smiled. "Then it's settled. Here's how you turn it on and off. You can disrobe in this room. I'll be in the parlor, waiting for you. Perhaps we'll even have time for a game of whist later." He left her alone in the bedroom, closing the door softly behind him.

Marcy unhooked the bodice of her gown and dropped it onto a chair. She blinked. Why was the light so dim? There was a small lamp on a bureau. She crossed to it, nearly stumbling on the way. Tarnation! What was the matter with her? She turned up the wick, then stared at herself in the mirror above the bureau. How odd her face looked. And her eyes, all blue-green and shining. Scarcely a dot of black showing in the middle! She dabbed at her forehead. It was so hot, so hard to breathe. Foolish gown! She pulled off her clothes and left them in a careless pile in the middle of the floor.

She blinked again. She couldn't think. Thunderation. What was she doing standing here with her clothes off? The rain bath. That was it. Arthur had showed her how to turn it on. She stepped into the little room and turned the faucet; the jets of water squirted her breasts and back and legs. She closed her eyes. The water was soothing on her bare flesh. It was like bathing in Buttermilk Falls. She could feel the warmth of the sun. It was so nice. So nice. She could stay here forever. So nice . . .

"Turn off the water, Marcy." The voice was soft, coming from somewhere beyond the mists.

"No," she said dreamily. It was an effort to open her eyes.

"Marcy. The water."

What could she do but obey the voice? She had no strength left. No will. She turned the faucet; stood there—in the little box—dripping. Why wasn't there a place to lie down here?

The door opened. She saw a thick towel. Hands. She allowed the hands to pull her out of the little box. Her eyes seemed filmed with gauze; nothing was clear. But the hands were tender, drying her like a baby. Gently they pushed her down onto the bed. She sighed and closed her eyes again, feeling the soft velvet beneath her back and hips.

Now the hands were touching her bosom. "Drew. My love," she whispered. Drew was kissing her. She opened her eyes and smiled at him. How funny! She didn't know that Drew had a mustache. She put her arms around his neck. How could he make love to her if he still had his clothes on? "Love me," she said. And then he was kissing her again.

But someone was at the door behind him. Through the gauze she could see *another* Drew. The Drew with the mustache stopped kissing her and stood up. The other Drew was shouting at the Drew with the mustache: "You bastard! If it weren't for Willough, I'd kill you!"

He was so loud. And her head hurt. It was too confusing. Sh-h-h-h! I can't sleep with all that noise! She put her hands over her ears. The Drew with the mustache was going away. Now the other Drew was shouting at her. Words. Noise! Her brain was fuzzy. She tried to speak; her tongue was thick, choking the words before she could say them. She thought she said: Drew, help me. Something's wrong with my head, my eyes. But there didn't seem to be any sound in the room. And when she looked again at the doorway, it was empty.

She ought to follow Drew. Talk to him. Find out why he was angry. But she was tired ... cold. She rolled up in the coverlet. "Why are you angry, Drew?" she mumbled. "Don't be." She should talk to him. But her limbs were like lead, and her head was buzzing.

She thought: I'll speak to him in a little while. Whatever he's angry about ... I know it will be fine when I talk to him. But sleep first, Marcy ... just for a few minutes ... close my eyes ... a few minutes ...

She woke with her head pounding. She opened her eyes. A red-hot poker pierced her brain. She groaned, squeezed her eyes shut again. Had it been a dream? She'd been lying in bed and Arthur had been kissing her. Arthur! Willough's husband! She laughed shakily. It must have been a dream! And then Drew in the doorway, saying all those things. Dreams were funny. While they were going on, you couldn't always understand them; but later, thinking it over, the dream became clear.

What had Drew been saying in the dream? "You wanted a rich man. You *always* wanted a rich man. But you couldn't even wait. Another day, and I would have sold my soul to give you what you wanted!"

What a funny thing to say! But the whole dream had been ridiculous. She—naked on the bed while Arthur kissed her! She gasped, her hand going to her breast. Oh my God! But she was naked now! She was afraid to open her eyes. If she should be in the railroad car...

She sat up in horror, seeing the blue velvet draperies of Brian's room. What have I done? she thought in a panic. Think! *Think!* What had Drew said? "It wasn't enough for me to give up my painting! You couldn't wait to have all your pretty things! For Willough's sake, you might have chosen another rich man to seduce besides Arthur!"

She was trembling violently now, remembering every angry word. *Had* she tried to seduce Arthur? Oh, God! Why was it she could remember what Drew had said, but she couldn't remember what she'd done? The last thing she remembered before the kissing was leaving the dining table. She didn't know how she'd gotten into bed with Arthur. Or why she was naked. She didn't think he'd actually made love to her; Drew had come in before anything had happened beyond kisses.

But how could Drew ever forgive her? What was it he'd said? He'd given up painting! Oh, God! How could he? It meant so much to him. And he'd sold his soul, he said. What did that mean? He'd mentioned once, a long time ago, that his father had wanted him to take over the business some day. Could that have been what he meant? The condition that he'd decided to accept? So that he could have money for Marcy?

She began to cry. Money for her. And she hadn't ever really wanted it. She'd only wanted to be able to help him, to love him. She hadn't wanted money.

Or had she? She had been a "countess" last night, enjoying Arthur's attentions, enjoying the rich surroundings, the servants, the food and wine. A part of her *must* have wanted Arthur to make love to her. He wouldn't have tried otherwise.

You're wicked, Marcy, she thought. No wonder Drew must hate you now.

She staggered out of bed, clutching at the chair to keep from falling. She dressed hastily, still trembling. She'd never felt so weak in her life. She stared at herself in the mirror. What am I doing here? she thought. With these people? In this life where I don't belong? Once she'd thought herself safe, away from the mountains that had killed her parents. She must have been mad. There was no safety here.

She hurried out of Brian's room. Keller was in the kitchen galley. "Good morning, Mrs. Bradford. Do you wish some breakfast?"

She shook her head. "No."

He reached over to a shelf, handed her a sealed envelope. "This came early this morning. By messenger. I didn't want to disturb you. The messenger didn't think an answer was wanted."

She stared at the envelope. Her name, Mrs. Drewry Bradford, was written on the outside. In Drew's neat hand. She tore open the envelope. A stack of greenbacks tumbled out. Fighting back her tears, she stumbled to a chair and sat down, her hand pressed tightly against her lips to keep from crying out in pain.

Keller was alarmed. "Mrs. Bradford! Are you sure I can't give you something?"

She took a deep breath. "No."

"I can call you a cab to take you to the Bradford house."

"No." She knelt in the galley and gathered up the money, replacing all but twenty-five dollars, which she put into her handbag. She handed the envelope to Keller. "Please see that Mr. Drewry gets this. And if you will, you can direct me to the ticket office of the Grand Central Station. Will I need a cab for that?"

"No, ma'am. It's just the other side of the platform and down the track. I'll take you there. Shall I bring your valise, ma'am?"

"Yes, please, Keller."

"Do you want to catch a train, Mrs. Bradford?"

"Yes. To the North Woods." I'm going back where I belong, she thought. Long Lake. Her mountains. Her sweet Wilderness.

"I'm going home."

The train whistle shrilled, sending a puff of steam into the afternoon drizzle. Drew pulled up his collar against the cold rain, and dashed into the waiting carriage. The whistle sounded again. Like a shriek of pain. Drew had an irrational urge to open his mouth and echo that mournful sound, wailing his grief to the impersonal sky.

No! He couldn't afford to give way to despair, couldn't allow himself to feel anything yet. There would be time to mourn Marcy, time to allow his numbed heart to acknowledge its pain. But first he had to deal with his father.

His father. He'd briefly contemplated writing a letter. A coward's way. As difficult and as painful as this meeting would be, he knew it had to be face to face. He had no illusions that Brian would understand, but he had to try. For his own peace of mind.

And there was something else. Perhaps it was losing Marcy that had done it. The thought of the lonely years without her. He felt pity for his father, an unexpected surge of feeling that made him regret the distance between them. Maybe it wasn't too late. If his father could swallow his disappointment, find forgiveness in his heart...

Martha met him at the door of his father's house and ushered him into the parlor. A cheery fire burned in the stone fireplace, dispelling the afternoon chill. "Would you care for something to eat, Mr. Drewry? A sandwich? Or some hot tea?"

"Thank you, no. I ate on the train."

Martha frowned. "You have no luggage. Won't you be staying over?"

"I'm not sure. I . . . left my traps at the depot. If I decide to stay . . ."

"I'll have Robert fetch them, in that case. Don't you fret. Now I'll just tell your father you're here, and then I'll set another place for you in the dining room."

Drew nodded as she left the room, then stood in front of the fire, warming his hands. He wasn't sure Father would *want* him to stay for supper. Not after he heard what Drew had to say.

"By God, boy, it's a pleasure to see you!" Brian Bradford strode into the room, hand outstretched.

"Sir." Drew answered the handshake with his own strong grip. The two men didn't meet eye to eye: What Drew lacked in brawn over the more muscular Brian he made up in inches, towering over his father. He sighed now, remembering. Brian had somehow viewed the height of his growing son as a kind of challenge. He wondered if they could ever be friends. Especially now.

"Where's that wife of yours? I thought I'd get to meet her."

"She's . . . gone."

"For good?"

"I expect so."

Brian frowned. "She didn't walk out on you, did she? Walk out on a *Bradford*?"

The pain was still too fresh. Drew turned away and stared out the window. Had it only been last night? Marcy . . . and Arthur? "Let's just say it was mutual," he growled.

"I'm sorry to hear that." Brian sounded genuinely sympathetic. "There's no chance for a reconciliation, I suppose." He sighed. "Well, as long as it doesn't affect our arrangements . . . You can take a few days off, pull yourself together. Then we can get down to work."

"No."

"What?"

Drew turned and gazed steadily at his father. "I'm sorry, Father. That's why I'm here. I can't work for you. I'm not suited. Never was. I'm a painter. I found that out in Paris. I may not be a *good* painter, but I'm a painter."

"But your message from Paris... coming into the business..." Brian's face was beginning to turn red. "Dammit, boy, what was that supposed to mean? Was it a goddam lie?"

"No. I meant it. But I was doing it for... Marcy"—he almost choked on her name—"not because I thought it was right for me."

"And now you intend to go back on your word? Like a damned turncoat?"

"That's a little harsh, Father," he muttered. "But... yes. I think it's best. For your sake as well as mine. My heart wouldn't be in it. You could give me the knowledge of the business, but I never could acquire your passion for it. I think that would distress you sooner or later. I'm sorry."

"You're *sorry*? And what about the money I sent to you? On false pretenses!"

"I'll pay you back. As soon as I can."

Brian sneered. "Can I trust you? Any more than I trusted your lies from Paris?"

Drew bit back the angry retort. "Send a lawyer around with a promissory note. I'll sign it," he said evenly.

"I'll send Arthur."

Drew exhaled through his clenched teeth. "If you send that son of a bitch, I'll kill him."

Brian looked surprised. "What has Arthur ever done to you?"

"That's between Arthur and me."

Brian shrugged. "Suit yourself." He crossed to a sideboard and poured himself a glass of whiskey. "So you'll pay me back." His voice was sharp with bitterness. "But what about the son I thought I had?"

Drew flinched. That hurt. More than he thought it would, after all these years. "You still have him. Try to understand,

Father. Painting is important to me. It's my life. I can no more give it up than give up breathing. I know that now."

Brian glared at him. "My 'artist son.'" His lip curled in scorn. "Malice, that's all it is. You've always resented me."

"It has nothing to do with you! If I could be the son you wanted—and still live with myself—I would!"

"*Malice!* I wanted a son who was a man, not a weakling who spent his days dabbling with paint!"

"Don't, Father." Drew's hands were fists at his sides.

"Have you learned to hold your liquor like a man?"

There was no point in staying. He'd only say things he'd regret later. And he was feeling too vulnerable. He'd lost Marcy. Perhaps it had been too much to hope that he and his father could make a new beginning, but he'd wanted it. God, how he'd wanted it! "I'll be going now," he said quietly.

"No!" Brian poured himself another glass of whiskey, then filled a second tumbler nearly to the brim and held it out to Drew. "Here!"

"Please, Father..."

"Are you afraid?"

"Don't do this."

"*Are you afraid*, my artist son?"

Drew swore under his breath and strode to his father, snatching the glass from his hand. "To your health, sir," he hissed, and raised the glass to his lips. He downed it in one long gulp and slammed the empty tumbler onto the sideboard. "I'm used to absinthe! Now, may I go?"

Brian's angry glance wavered; then he recovered himself. "Damn you, boy. Malice. Nothing but malice. You never wanted to come into the business because you're afraid you're not as good as I am!" He poked a belligerent finger into Drew's chest. "Admit it." Another poke. "Admit it!"

Drew was beginning to lose his self-control. All the hours of torment he'd suffered since he'd found Marcy and Arthur together were beginning to take their toll. He backed away from his father. "If you say so. Now let me go, for God's sake!" His voice was almost pleading.

"Malice!" roared Brian, and swung at his son. This time

Drew deflected the blow, grabbing at his father's arm. They wrestled silently for a moment, muscles tensed, hands clenched to hands. Then Brian grunted, his grip broken by Drew's young strength. He glared at Drew, all his frustration, all his anger in that one glance.

Drew felt as though he would cry. He thought: I need your friendship, Father! Not your hatred. Not now! With a groan, he clasped his father to his chest, wrapping his arms around the older man.

Brian wrenched himself free. "Get out."

Drew took a deep breath. His father was unforgiving—it was too late for there to be anything between them. "I'll pay back what I owe you," he said tiredly. "Every penny."

"I'll expect it."

He had to try one more time. "Father..." he said, and held out his hand.

Deliberately Brian turned his back on his son. "Get out," he said. "I never want to see you again."

Chapter
Eleven

"Brigid, see that the girls take down the mirrors in the drawing room. I noticed they were covered with fly specks."

"Yes, Mrs. Gray. Will you be wearing your mauve velvet gown tonight?"

Willough nodded, pulling on her chamois gloves. "I expect so. I'll need my lavender corset to go with it. And see that the dust covers from the ballroom chairs are removed with a minimum of shaking. I don't want the house filled with dust during the party tonight."

Brigid smiled. "And it wouldn't be healthful for the little one, ma'am, and that's a fact."

"Of course." Willough felt a pang of guilt. Why hadn't *she* thought of that? Cecily was her baby, sweet, helpless, and innocent. Why did she find it so hard to care?

I know why, she thought. Because Cecily was Arthur's child as well. All the months she'd carried her, she'd never forgotten that. And never forgotten the horror of Arthur invading her body on their wedding night, and so many nights afterward, to plant his conquering seed.

Perhaps if she'd been able to nurse Cecily longer . . . That first week, holding the infant to her breast, she'd felt an unfamiliar stirring of feeling, a rush of love for the tiny babe. But then the fever had followed, drying up her milk, racking her body with aches and pains and hot, swirling nightmares. When she recovered she found that Arthur had already hired a wet nurse, arranged for the christening, settled on the name— for *his* daughter. As though Willough didn't matter. Her blossoming maternal instinct had dried up as surely as had her breasts.

She stepped out into the September sunshine and breathed deeply. What a glorious morning! Crisp and sunny with a clear blue sky. It was so good to be out-of-doors again. She'd felt like a prisoner, all those weeks, lying in her bed. But she'd had a difficult delivery, and then the fever. And Dr. Page, who had encouraged her activity up until her confinement, was suddenly a tyrant, ordering her to stay in bed or within the boundaries of her own home until she was fully recovered. And then the weeks of rain that followed had kept her homebound. She'd been well enough to plan tonight's party, their first formal entertaining since Cecily had been born. But this morning, seeing the rain clouds gone at last, she had determined to spend the day outdoors, enjoying her freedom. Arthur wasn't expected until evening—business in Albany again. She wouldn't have to listen to him make a fuss over whether it was "proper" for her to be seen abroad so soon after her confinement. So soon! It had been nearly two months, but Arthur was forever concerned with the proprieties.

Dear Arthur, she thought with contempt. With his peculiar sense of what was right and wrong. Well, perhaps she shouldn't complain. They'd had a long talk the other night. Now that Willough had presented him with a child, he'd said, he was no longer interested in coming to her bed. Not for the time being, at least. When he thought the time was ripe for another child he would resume his conjugal visits. But she was passionless, he said, and he found her tiresome. As long as they kept up appearances, he'd seek his diversions elsewhere.

She didn't know whether to be glad she was free of her
burden or angry at his moral principles that didn't mind flaunting his mistresses. He'd even begun to spend time with Isobel
again, though without the same warmth they had shared in
the past. But at least they were now talking to each other.
And when Isobel visited her grandchild Cecily, she always
managed to exchange a few pleasant words with Arthur.
Strange. It seemed to Willough that the reconciliation had
occurred around the time that Drew had come home.

Drew. Frowning, Willough climbed into her coach and
opened her parasol. If only her pregnancy and confinement
hadn't kept her so isolated from what was happening. She'd
never been able to find out what had gone wrong with his
life and his marriage. Isobel was vague, Arthur was silent.
And Drew himself had refused to come to the house except
on the day of Cecily's christening. He'd spoken briefly to
Willough; wouldn't shake Arthur's hand; left quickly.

His wife was gone. Isobel seemed to think she'd returned
to her people. "Back where she belongs, the fortune hunter!"
as Isobel put it. Willough was rather sorry. She'd been looking
forward to meeting Drew's Marcy; his letters from Paris had
radiated love for his young bride.

He'd moved back into his old suite in Isobel's house, and
rented a room on Eleventh Street, where he could paint all
day. Isobel said he was happy. Willough wasn't sure of that.
She hadn't really talked to Drew. But it was clear *Isobel* was
happy. Her Drew was back under her roof. Back in her clutches,
thought Willough bitterly.

"Did you just want to drive down the avenue, ma'am? Or
are you paying a call this morning?"

Shaken out of her reverie, Willough stared at the coachman. "I'd like to go to East Eleventh Street, Jamison. Number
one hundred and four." It was past time to talk to Drew.

"Very good, ma'am." The coach headed down Fifth Avenue.

"No. Wait. Take me down to New Church Street." It was
a little out of her way, so far downtown, but she had all day.
And her curiosity was piqued. Since the day that Brigid's

brother Kevin had recognized Arthur's caller as a member of a notorious street gang of former years (and Willough's suspicions that Arthur himself was the former Artie Flanagan had been aroused), Willough had taken careful notice of Arthur's business transactions, his visitors, the amounts of money he gave over to her, the amounts he asked for in return in personal checks. And Zephyr Realty, of which company she had discovered herself a partner. Confined to her house, she hadn't been able to track down the other partners, or find any information on its affairs. But Arthur had handed her another paper to sign only the other day. She'd managed to peruse it quickly without arousing his suspicion. Zephyr Realty was selling a large piece of property on New Church Street, and for a considerable amount of money. She supposed that at some point Zephyr had bought the land, and cursed herself for not taking notice the very first time Arthur had brought documents for her signature.

She frowned as the carriage turned off Rector Street onto New Church. A street of tenements and rookeries, dilapidated old buildings with strings of wash hanging across courtyards where ragged children played and shouted. The cluttered sidewalks were broken, several of the gaslights were shattered, and here and there a sagging tenement wall was propped up by beams. She shook her head as they made their way down the street. She hadn't seen worse slums in the city of London! Yet Zephyr Realty had reaped a handsome sum from this land.

At one end of the street some laborers were at work, demolishing a three-story frame building. She had Jamison stop the carriage and escort her across the street. Picking her way carefully through the rubble, she accosted one of the men.

"If you please, my good man. What's going on here?"

"Ain't you got eyes, lady? We're tearing down this old rubbish heap."

"Yes. I can see that. But why? Will you build another? Perhaps something decent where a body can live?"

He snorted. "In this neck of the woods? It'd be a waste of time and money."

"Then the land must be quite worthless."

"Not to the right people, it ain't. This is where the Met-
ropolitan Elevated Railroad is putting their new line." He
scratched the dirty stubble on his chin. "It's a wise man who
knew when to buy this here piece!"

"But who would know the land was going to be worth
something? Aren't those things kept a secret?"

He shook his head. "Lady, go back to your fancy carriage.
And leave these things to the men."

"Just one more thing," she persisted. "Who decides where
the railroad will put its line?"

He looked at her as though she were a fool. "The Com-
missioner of Public Works. But of course everyone knows
that the aldermen from the district are in on the plans."

You can catch more flies with honey than with vinegar,
Grandma Carruth always said. She smiled in helpless innocence. "Why then, an alderman can make a great deal of
money by buying up the land before the plans are announced!"

"And wind up in the pen!" he snickered. "But a lot of 'em
manage to get around that. Hidden companies, someone else's
name. There's a heap of ways, and they ain't legal. But I
know a lot of men who got rich that way!"

"Thank you," she said, and went back to her carriage. My
God, she thought. Alderman Cadbury and his wife were among
the guests that Arthur had invited for tonight. She suddenly
wondered whether the party was a social affair, or a meeting
of stockholders and partners. Zephyr Realty celebrating its
killing.

"East Eleventh Street now, Jamison." She settled back in
the carriage and smoothed her skirts. Her first day out was
proving to be quite instructive!

Now if she could only get some answers from Drew . . .

In his studio, Drew put down his paintbrush and took a
bite out of a large cheese sandwich, eyeing it with distaste.
The bread was stale. And it made a miserable breakfast. But
at least it hadn't cost him anything. The Dutch beer saloon
downstairs had a free lunch counter; for the price of a five-
cent beer yesterday he'd got supper *and* breakfast.

He stretched. He'd been up for hours, but he was still stiff from that bumpy cot. He supposed he could have made it back to Gramercy Park last night, but he'd been so involved in this painting.

No. That's not the reason, he thought. He hadn't *wanted* to go home last night. It was easier to send a note round with a messenger boy telling Isobel he was working late and would sleep in his studio. He'd done it often lately. And Isobel was increasingly sharp and reproachful to him. He hadn't remembered his mother as being so autocratic, so demanding in her ways. She was beginning to try his patience. Oh, she'd been helpful, true enough. He couldn't have taken this room without her assistance—and her money. But he was starting to feel smothered. It was as though she felt her love and interest gave her the right to push and direct his affairs. He sighed. Marcy had encouraged him, supported him. But she'd never tried to usurp what was his.

Marcy haunted him so! It was a nightmare to think of her. Because, every time, the last tortured image in his brain was of Arthur bending over her naked body, her soft arms about his neck.

He heard a noise outside his door. Someone was coming up the rickety staircase. It couldn't be Isobel; she never managed to shake off the effects of her nightly laudanum until midmorning. "Come in," he responded to the light tap outside. He smiled uneasily at his visitor. "Willough! It's good to see you."

His sister smiled at him. "Is it, big brother? Then why have you been a stranger? You've been home from Paris for over two months. And I've only seen you once, at Cecily's christening."

Oh, God, he thought. Poor Willough. What could he tell her? That her husband was a man without honor? Seducing other men's wives? But . . . Marcy had trapped him—Drew— on Clear Pond Island to force him into marriage. Perhaps the blame was Marcy's. Perhaps *she* had seduced *Arthur*. And even that lecher Stewart, in Paris. Oh hell! What did it matter now? He was well rid of Marcy, he told himself. And he still couldn't tell Willough anything, no matter who had been to blame. "I've been busy, Willough. That's all."

"Too busy to visit me? When I was confined to my house? I thought we were better friends than that."

"Willough, I . . ."

Her violet eyes were thoughtful, searching. "Or is it Arthur? Has something happened between you two?"

He crossed to the window, staring out at the brick arches of the church school across the street. Several children were playing on the sidewalk; their happy laughter drifted up to him. Marcy always laughed. Oh, damn you, damn you, Marcy! he thought.

Behind him, Willough sighed. "How are you doing with your painting?" she asked at last.

He turned. This, at least, was safe territory. He waved his arm around the room, indicating the canvases stacked up against the walls. "I'm painting like a madman, every waking moment."

Willough pointed to the large canvas on his easel. "I read about the Impressionist show you were in last spring. Is this the kind of work they're doing?"

"No. That's the thing of it. I came back expecting to continue what I'd begun in Paris. The odd perspectives, the simplicity of the Japanese prints. But more and more I found myself going back to the field sketches and watercolors I did last summer in the Adirondacks. I'm working them up into large paintings now. But they're different. I've changed since last summer. Look!" He moved about the room, pulling out canvases, feeling again the excitement he'd felt when first he'd realized that his style had changed.

Willough peered intently at the paintings as he indicated them. "But you're right, Drew. Last year's pictures are good, but . . . they're small and dark."

"That's because I was using a canvas prepared with a brown undercoat. The way I was taught. Claude Monet paints directly onto his plain white canvas. I'd been trying that in Paris, on my street scenes. It gave me a fresher look, a brighter palette. I didn't think I could translate that to my mountain pictures."

"These are wonderful, Drew! Even your technique is different."

"Yes. Somehow the brighter colors almost demand a looser brush stroke. Though not as loose as what the Impressionists are doing. Not yet, at least. I have too many years of academic training to overcome."

Willough looked around the small room, with its single grimy window. "I don't see how you can paint such brightness in here! Can't you afford something better?"

"I'm afraid not. I owe Father rather a lot of money. A loan I must repay, when I sell a few paintings. And then I'm mounting an exhibit. I've a friend who owns a large studio. As long as I pay the expenses, he's agreed to show my works. I think I'm ready. God, I *hope* I'm ready!"

"When?"

"The show opens in a week or so."

"That's exciting! Send me the details. I'll be sure to come." She frowned. "Still, this dreadful place . . . If I had money of my own, I'd give it to you. But can't you borrow from Mother?"

"I already have. Frankly, I don't like being beholden to her."

Willough chuckled. "I don't believe it, big brother! You've discovered at last the dark side of being Mother's pet?"

He flinched. Her words cut too close to the bone. He laughed sheepishly. "We both have our blind spots. You said that once. And *you'll* still go running if Father calls you!"

That silenced her. She began to flip idly through his sketchbook. She stopped at a drawing of Marcy (why hadn't he destroyed them? he thought, anguished), studied it intently, then looked at Drew. "Are you happy, big brother?" she asked softly.

He nodded. "With my painting. Yes. For the first time."

"That's not what I meant."

"Are *you*, little sister? Happy, I mean?"

She shrugged. "I have my husband. And my child. And I

have my duty." Her eyes were dark with concern. "What happened to Marcy, Drew?"

His voice grated in his throat. "She made her choice."

"But . . . your letters . . . I would have thought . . ." She put a gentle hand on his arm. "You loved her. You needed her."

The bitter truth tore at his guts. Marcy the fortune hunter. "Perhaps *I* wasn't what *she* needed."

The conversation was desultory after that and Willough left with an invitation to Drew for a visit that she felt would not take place.

"Take me home, Jamison." Willough settled into her carriage. The bright morning had lost its glow. Drew was so obviously miserable. Her brother, who'd always been full of laughter. And she could do nothing. More than ever she was convinced that Arthur knew something. Something that had created a rift between him and Drew. Perhaps she'd press him a little harder. And if that didn't work, well . . . As far as she knew, Drew had met Marcy last summer, when he'd gone on that excursion. Who else had gone? Drew's friend, Ed Collins. She had his address somewhere. She'd write to him. This very morning. He must know where Marcy came from.

Willough nodded determinedly. Yes. Marcy. There might be some answers, some happiness for Drew, if she could talk to Marcy. She could spare enough from her housekeeping money to pay her fare to the North Woods and back. And maybe bring Marcy back with her.

Because it was as plain as day that Drew loved her desperately, no matter what he said.

She was greeted by the sound of wailing as she entered her front foyer. "Merciful heaven, Lillie!" she exclaimed. "What is that?"

"It's Brigid, ma'am. She just got the news. Her brother Kevin died."

"Oh dear. The one who had comsumption."

Lillie shrugged. "The T.B. takes a lot of folk, ma'am."

Yes, thought Willough. Especially the ones who (what was it Kevin had said that day?) breathe the foul air of this city.

And if he lived in one of those rookeries, with not enough
to eat . . . She was beginning to think more and more like Nat,
seeing the ugliness of civilization through his eyes. She sighed
unhappily. Dear Nat. They would have been so right for each
other. "Take Brigid off to her room, Lillie. See that she rests.
The other girls can manage her chores today. If she's feeling
a little better later and wishes to talk, tell her she can come
to my sitting room." Perhaps Arthur could be persuaded to
send some money to the family to pay for a proper funeral.

"Yes'm. Oh, Mrs. Gray. A telegram came for you just after
you went out this morning. I put it in the music room."

"Thank you." Willough crossed to the music room and
opened the door. She was struck with a fanciful thought. This
was where she'd last seen Nat, the night of Arthur's party,
when they'd quarreled. And this was where she'd seen Brigid's unfortunate brother, coughing his life away. She shivered. She was almost afraid to pick up the telegram.

It was from her father: *Lass. Come to Saratoga. Trouble
at MacCurdyville. I need you. Daddy.*

Oh, God, what could have happened? She knew, of course,
that the business was not as healthy as it had been. The Panic
of '73 had cut deeply into Daddy's cash reserves. He'd lost
a few good contracts for cast-iron stoves when some of the
manufacturers had gone under. And even though he was now
using prisoners from Clinton to save money, and had laid off
many of his longtime workers, there were still difficulties.
But she hadn't thought it was critical.

She thought quickly. It was still morning. If she left right
now, she could be up in Saratoga before nightfall. But the
party tonight—all those important people—Arthur would be
furious! He would come in from Albany at seven o'clock and
find himself without a hostess. She paced the floor, torn with
indecision. It was her *duty* as a wife. That was all she had.
Her duty. She didn't have Nat. She didn't have love.

"The hell with Arthur," she whispered, throwing down the
telegram. She was going to Daddy!

Daddy needed her. Daddy loved her.

She packed a few necessities and had Jamison take her to

the station. All through the trip she worried. And when she arrived at the house Martha walked with her to where Willough could see through the window onto the veranda. Brian Bradford reclined on the wicker chaise, a small lap robe across his knee, his eyes closed. "He looks terrible, Martha," she said to the servant.

"He's feeling very poorly, missus. Terrible colicky pains all the time now. Robert finally persuaded him to have the doctor. We're expecting him this evening. But I know it will cheer him to see you. It's been a long time since you've been here."

"Yes." Nearly a year, she thought. When she and Nat . . . She felt her heart catch with pain. Would she ever be able to forget him? And now to be in this house, so filled with sweet memories. Memories of a love that was gone forever. She'd strolled with Nat on that lawn, kissed him here in the parlor. Where was he now? she wondered. She stepped out onto the veranda. "Hello, Daddy."

Brian opened his eyes and struggled to sit up. "Lass. I knew you wouldn't let your old Dad down."

She perched on the chaise beside him. "Your telegram said there was trouble at MacCurdyville. Of *course* I came."

"It's a bad time, lass. A bad time." He grimaced in pain and clutched at his stomach. "And I'm not up to handling it. Bill's a fool of a manager, and that damned clerk of his isn't much better. They're ruining me. Every one of them. Clegg died last spring, or I would have had him back right away, retirement or not."

"What's the trouble?"

"You knew I had some of the prisoners from Clinton working the pit mines."

"I always thought it was a bad move, whether Arthur legalized it or not. Too many men were laid off to make room for the prisoners."

"Dammit, Willough, a man's got to save money where he can!"

"Not when it costs men their jobs. I can't believe money's *that* tight. I remember the books from last year. And unless there's no more wood on that New Russia tract, you still should be turning a profit on the charcoal."

"But I've had to drop my prices. Or that bastard Sam Doyle won't buy. And I figure the land'll be stripped in another six months. And I'll still be paying taxes on it. A worthless tract, by God!"

She thought of Nat and his anger at the destruction of the forest. That had been state land, meant to stay a verdant wilderness. "Why don't you start replanting? Put in new young trees. Then it'll be worth selling in a few years."

He waved an impatient hand. "The New Russia land isn't the problem," he growled. "I'd like to finish building the new finery, with or without a bank loan! I told Bill I wanted to see a better profit at the end of this year. I suggested he put it to the men—either we reduce the wages or we're obliged to close. The men aren't fools. They'd make the right choice. But they've been stirred up, dammit! There were a few rabble-rousers among the men who were laid off. Blaming it on the prisoners. And that damn fool Bill must have pleaded the case badly." Brian leaned forward to pick up a glass of water, drained it at a gulp, and belched loudly.

"What happened, Daddy?"

"Some of the men have taken over Number Three. They've shut down the furnace. Locked themselves in. They're threatening to smash the blast equipment."

Willough frowned in thought. "Wait them out. They'll come to their senses. As long as you're still turning out pig iron from the other furnaces..."

"It can't be done. The rest of the men have called a general strike in sympathy! No one will work—the furnaces are all dying down. Bill had to send the prisoners back to Clinton to keep the mob from killing them. And now the warden wants the governor to send in troops!"

"What do the men want?"

"Damned if I know! It's a stalemate, right now."

"Someone's got to go in there. Find out what they want. I think, to begin, we're going to have to promise them that the prisoners won't be back to steal away their jobs." She

was making quick calculations. They could wire Bill tonight
to keep things calm, do nothing, at least until morning. She
could get to MacCurdyville before midnight, look over the
books with the clerk, decide what concessions Daddy could
afford to make. If they could get more of the men working
again, they might settle for a pay cut. Everyone knew times
were hard. It was just important that the workers feel that
Brian Bradford was trying to be fair. "I think I can make the
men see that..."

Brian cut her short. "What the devil are you talking about?"

"Why, negotiating with the men. You'd have to trust my
judgment, of course, but..."

"*You?* Are you daft?" Brian lumbered up from the chaise
and moved to the veranda railing. He stared out over the
lawn, bathed in the late-afternoon sun. "I managed to get
hold of Nat Stanton. The men always trusted him. And he
has a head on his shoulders, not like that fool Bill!"

Willough's heart stopped. "Nat?"

"I had a devil of a time tracking him down. He's been
working as a gardener for an old lady over in North Creek."

"A gardener?" she echoed. The very mention of his name
had made her unable to think clearly. Nat. So near.

"He's become a hard man, Stanton has. A hard man! Still
unforgiving. He made me crawl to him. If I weren't backed
to the wall..." He winced in pain. "And I'm not well. I
know I'll be myself again as soon as that fool doctor can fix
me up, but in the meantime I need Nat. And that bastard
knows it!"

"You need Nat." She felt sick at heart. Daddy didn't trust
her to do the job. He still wanted a son.

"Yes. I need him. Or else I wouldn't have agreed to his
terms."

"Which are...?"

"Five thousand dollars. Right off the bat. In cash. He
wouldn't even continue our talk until I'd sent Robert to my
bank in Saratoga."

Five thousand dollars. That had been the dowry Daddy
had promised, long ago. Willough felt a pang of guilt. Of

regret. One way or another, Nat was determined to get what he thought was owed him.

"And then, if he succeeds in settling the troubles, he wants shares in the company. Twenty-five percent. And a voice in the running of the enterprises, including the sawmill at Glens Falls."

"He wants his partnership too." Perhaps she'd been right not to marry Nat. It was clear that the money and the partnership had been important to him. Oh, Willough, she thought, that's unfair. Hadn't Arthur had *his* reasons for marriage? The entrée into society, and perhaps the dowry as well. And there was the matter of Willough's stock that Arthur was holding in trust. No. She shouldn't despise Nat for what he wanted; her true anger should be directed at Brian for what he *didn't* want: his daughter's help. "Why did you send for me, Daddy?" she asked bitterly. "You didn't need me." It would still be Bradford and Stanton, not Bradford and Bradford.

"Nat insisted on it. He wants you in MacCurdyville. He thinks the negotiations will go better with a family member there."

She fought back her angry tears. "I suppose being a figurehead is better than nothing."

Brian smiled. "That's my girl. After all, it's only fair. I suppose we owe it to him. You can go up to MacCurdyville tonight. Matter of fact, you can leave right now. My railroad car is at the Saratoga depot. You can dine on board. It'll save time. In the meantime, I'll telegraph ahead to Nat. Let him know he can expect you tonight."

"All right, Daddy. That'll be fine." But it wasn't, of course. So many emotions at war in her heart: resentment of Daddy for setting so low a value on her worth, uneasiness at seeing Nat again, and yearning too. I still love him, she thought. Was *his* heart still the same?

Brian picked up a bell from the table and shook it roughly. "I'll have Robert drive you to the depot. Oh. And one more thing. Nat said I was to tell you. He said you'd understand. The day you arrive at MacCurdyville—that's his birthday."

Willough gasped. "Oh my God! His *birthday*?"

"Yes. I don't understand. When we talked about it I wasn't certain *what* day you'd arrive. But that's what he said. His birthday."

The words turned her blood to ice. She shook her head. "I won't go, Daddy! I can't possibly!"

Brian turned on her. His eyes were burning. "What do you mean, you won't go? Nat made it very clear the deal was off unless you went to MacCurdyville!"

"But, Daddy . . . do you know what he meant?" Nat wanted *everything* that was owed him. Including Willough.

Daddy's face contorted with anger. She was staring into the eyes of a stranger. "Goddammit!" he burst out. "I don't want to know! MacCurdyville is my life's work, my blood! It's worth anything to me to save it!"

She began to tremble. Out of fear of him. Out of horror for what had become of Nat's love. "Even your daughter's . . . sensibilities?" she whispered.

He whirled about and pounded his fist against the side of the house. "What the devil do your sensibilities have to do with it? We do what we have to in this life! Sometimes you win, sometimes you lose. And every man has his price. The only important thing is coming out on top! I want to keep that business! If you can't understand that, by God, *you're no daughter of mine!*"

Willough returned to the parlor car, her thoughts in turmoil. Food was prepared for her and grew cold on her plate.

"You've barely eaten a thing, Mrs. Gray."

Willough looked up at Keller and pushed back her plate. "I'm not really hungry, Keller. I'm sorry. The meal was delicious, but . . ."

"Can I get you something else?"

She left the table and settled herself into one of the parlor chairs. Another hour and they'd be in Crown Point. And another hour after that, MacCurdyville. She took a deep breath. "Yes. I think I'll take a small brandy." False courage. She thought: What am I doing? She still couldn't fight Daddy. It still mattered too much. To please him. She was a failure as a wife, as a mother. As a woman. How could she disappoint Daddy on top of everything else? Perhaps if she'd had the courage to tell him what Nat expected, to say it straight out: I'm to be his whore, for the sake of the MacCurdy enterprises. But even with her own honor at stake, her prudery had kept her from speaking plainly to Daddy.

Nat's birthday. That's what he'd said. And she was his birthday gift. It had always been their way of discussing sex. That *must* be what he meant. But, dear God, how could he shame her like that? Did he hate her so much? Those things that Daddy had said. They owed it to Nat. It was only fair. He was a hard man, still unforgiving. Unforgiving of *what*? Had it hurt him so terribly to lose her, to lose his future in the business, that he could do this?

Or did he still love her, want her? Did he think that this was the way to get her? To use Daddy to force her? But surely he knew that this sort of blackmail would do nothing but curdle her love for him. And she was a married woman. It wasn't right, what he proposed.

Oh, God, she thought, anguished. What did he feel for her? Was it love? Lust? Or hatred? The clacking of the train wheels beat a tattoo of fear in her heart. Her insides were trembling, cold dread clutching at her. How could she face him? How could she do what he demanded of her?

She took a deep shuddering breath, stilling her rising panic. She *had* to think clearly! Perhaps she'd misunderstood. Perhaps that's not what he'd meant at all. Daddy might have got the message wrong, she told herself. And then, even if Nat hated her—for whatever reason—he might still just be bluffing to frighten her.

She was beginning to feel better already. As long as she could remain rational, in control of her thoughts and emotions, she could see this through. Assume the worst . . . that he had meant just what she feared. Why then, she could appeal to his better nature, to the gentleness she had seen in him many times. Persuade him that nothing could be accomplished by his humiliating her.

And if he still insisted? She hardened her heart. She was

a Carruth. She'd been raised to conduct herself like a lady, no matter what the circumstances. If she was forced to it, she would submit (didn't she endure Arthur, though he disgusted her?); but she'd make Nat aware of her contempt, all the while he was debasing her. There would be no satisfaction for him, if he meant this as some sort of obscene vengeance.

She arrived at last in MacCurdyville in a state of relative calm. Despite the lateness of the hour, a carriage was at the platform, waiting for her; and when she arrived at the boardinghouse, she found Mrs. Walker herself still sitting up. "I'm glad you're here, Mrs. Gray. There's so much trouble. We're all counting on you and Mr. Stanton. I've put you in your old room. I left a lamp, and a pitcher of hot water, if you want to wash up a bit before you sleep." Mrs. Walker extinguished the last lamp in the parlor, leaving only a candle on the downstairs landing. She bent to Willough's small carpetbag. "I'll just leave your things in your room, Mrs. Gray, and then go to bed. Mr. Stanton wants an early breakfast."

"Thank you. You can wake me when you wake Mr. Stanton in the morning. I expect we'll go down to the furnace together."

"Very good, missus."

Willough said a silent prayer. She couldn't lose her courage now. "Oh, Mrs. Walker. Where did you put Mr. Stanton? I think, if he hasn't retired, I ought to speak to him tonight."

"I put him next to you, ma'am. In your father's room. I don't reckon Mr. Bradford is up to making the journey right now. Bill says he's not himself. We're all sorry to hear it."

"Yes. Thank you. Good night, Mrs. Walker." She waited until the woman had dropped off her carpetbag and retired to her own room, then she knocked softly at Nat's door. At his quiet response, she entered and closed the door behind her. He was standing at the window. "Mr. Stanton," she said. Her voice was cool, controlled.

He turned. "Mrs. Gray."

She caught her breath, feeling the old familiar jolt at the sight of him. The amber eyes, piercing even by the light of the small kerosene lamp; the powerful body—now clothed in a rather shabby frock coat—that still exuded male sexuality; the overpowering presence of him that was so frightening. Once, long ago, she'd realized that her feeling of fear was her own suppressed passion; now, remembering why she was here, it had become fear again.

"I wasn't sure you'd come," he said.

"Why not? I'm Brian Bradford's daughter. I'm needed here."

He laughed softly. His voice held a mocking edge. "That's right. I'd forgotten. A dutiful daughter. Doing what's *expected* of you. Are you a dutiful wife as well? To dear Arthur?"

She drew herself up and eyed him with scorn. "Nothing can be gained by acrimony. I've come here because I think I can be of help. It serves no purpose to resort to crude insults. Whatever has happened between us is in the past."

One blond eyebrow arched up, a question mark on the deep tan of his face. Daddy said he'd been a gardener this summer, she thought illogically. I wonder why? He's a founder!

"Do you really think the past can be dismissed so easily?" he asked.

"Of course," she snapped. "Only a fool clings to the past."

He smiled tightly. "Dear Willough, still the haughty grande dame when you want to be."

"Do you want to talk about tomorrow, or not?"

He inclined his head. "As you wish. To begin, I spent the day with Bill and the clerk, going over the books. I think the ironworks can afford to be a little more generous and still stay in the black. As I see it, we have two problems. First, to get the mob out of Number Three without damage to the furnace, and second, to negotiate a deal with the other strikers that they, and the business, can live with."

"What about the warden of Clinton prison? My father said he wants to have the governor send in troops."

Nat scratched his chin. "Yes. A few of his men were roughed up when the strikers forced them out of town. I'm not sure how we can handle that. The warden seems to feel that the troops should storm Number Three. There'd be hell to pay if that happened."

"I may be mistaken, but I don't think he has legal rights. Not unless Daddy asked for state intervention. This is private land. I'll send a wire tomorrow to Daddy's lawyers in the city. They can draw up the papers to insure that the authorities stay out of this."

"Good idea. As far as negotiating, I'm set on keeping the prisoners out for good. How do you feel about it?"

"The same way. I'd like to see as many men rehired as we can manage, even if we have to cut wages."

He nodded. "We'll go over the books tomorrow. I'll show you the figures I've come up with."

She felt herself breathing more easily. They still thought alike when it came to the business. Still worked as a good team. Perhaps that was the only reason Nat had asked for her here. She managed a small smile, turned, and headed for the door. She'd handled him well. Kept control of the situation. "I'll see you in the morning, then."

"Just a minute!" His voice was a sharp knife, cutting through her.

She turned, her chin set at a proud tilt. "Yes?"

His eyes narrowed coldly. "Didn't your father give you my message?"

"Of course. That's why I'm here. To represent the Bradford interests."

"*All* of my message?"

Maybe she could brazen it out. "Yes. But I wasn't sure you meant . . ."

"I did."

She flinched at the sudden hatred on his face. Keep control, she thought. Keep control! "I'm surprised. I didn't think revenge was your style."

"I told you once I'm not a gentleman." He rubbed at his leg and gave a bitter laugh. "But then I'm not sure that you're a lady."

She stifled the urge to hurl the cruel insult back at him. She must keep her composure. "I don't suppose I can appeal to your pity."

"I have no pity left, Willough," he growled. "I'm sick to

death of people, and what they do to one another. Well, damn you, it's my turn now!"

She made one last desperate try. "What if I refuse?"

He shrugged. "Right now, the lid is on. The men know we plan to deal in fairness tomorrow. But if you refuse me, I walk out. Then this whole damn town blows up—and your father's hopes with it."

"Why are *you* so important? Someone else can negotiate just as well."

"Not quite. The men trust me to be fair. Because they know how much I hate the Bradfords."

The venom in his voice made her recoil. *Why*, Nat? she thought. "You're determined to have your way with me, then," she said softly.

"Primly put, Mrs. Gray," he sneered. "As usual. The answer is yes."

Perhaps she could shame him. "I find you contemptible," she said coldly. "To take advantage of a woman this way. And when would you want your 'pound of flesh'?"

"Now."

She tried not to show the sudden terror that gripped her heart. No! She was a Carruth! She could submit without losing her pride, her honor. It was *his* shame, not hers. "Well, why not?" she said in her most businesslike way. "Let's get it over with. If you come to my room in ten minutes, I'll be waiting for you."

His voice grated like steel across a stone floor. "No! I said now. Here! I don't want a bridal scene. The prissy female covered up to her chin, discreetly lifting her chemise only as far as she must!"

"You're still as crude as ever, Mr. Stanton," she said with distaste.

He rubbed his left leg again and grimaced. "It's a little late to play the virginal innocent. Not when you've shown me you have claws."

She was still struggling to stay in command. "Nat," she said gently, "I think we should talk. I'm sure there's been some misunderstanding. . . . Think of the love we shared. If you . . ."

"I want you out of your clothes! *Now!*" he barked.

Her lip began to quiver. "N-Nat, I . . ."

"Now, dammit! Or I'll rip them off you!"

She took a deep breath. "If you'll turn your back, Mr. Stanton . . ."

"I'll not turn my back. And I'll not dim the lamp, so don't bother asking. I want to see what's left of your pride and your careless cruelty when you don't have your money and your silk gowns to protect you."

Damn him! She'd show him how a lady behaved in front of a boor! But in spite of her resolve, her hands were shaking. She tried not to let him see her nervousness as she put aside her hat and gloves and began to unhook the bodice of her gown. She shrugged out of it and laid it across a chair, then worked at the fastenings at the back of her skirt. She stepped out of it, removed her top petticoat. He was at the window; he hadn't moved since she'd come in. It was unnerving to have him standing there, watching her undress. She stared back at him with as level a gaze as she could manage, while she took off her bustle and unfastened her corset cover.

All she had on now were her chemise and drawers, her corset, and one petticoat. But the chemise was rather demure, with a modest neck and little sleeves. She'd felt more naked in a low-cut evening gown. She put her hands on her corset tapes and looked hopefully at Nat. There was no pity in his amber eyes. She sighed in resignation and unfastened her corset, pulling it loose from her petticoat. She turned to the bed and nearly lost her nerve. Oh, God. The bed. Her mouth was dry. She gulped once and looked at Nat. "I shall await your pleasure in bed," she said haughtily. "With my eyes closed. I trust you don't mean to insult my sensibilities further by forcing me to watch you disrobe."

"Spare me your virtuous prudery," he snarled. "You're not done yet. I want *everything* off!"

If she could only stop trembling! She drew on her last reserves of pride. "It is not my custom to prance around naked as a whore. Not even Arthur..." She stopped, feeling the hot flush on her cheeks.

He frowned. "I'm not interested in your domestic secrets. Arthur probably got what he deserved." His cold eyes raked her body with a brutal lust. "But you're *my* whore tonight. And I want you as naked as a jaybird!"

She was beginning to crumble. "Nat...please..."

He was unyielding. He folded his arms across his wide chest and glared at her.

Heaven protect me, she thought. Still trying to guard her modesty, she reached up under her petticoat and unbuttoned her drawers, letting them drop to the floor within the tentlike shelter of the full petticoat.

"Now the petticoat," he said.

Her hands were shaking violently. She could hardly grasp the ends of the petticoat tapes. "Nat," she pleaded, the words choking in her throat, "don't shame me like this!"

He stared at her—at her trembling form, her eyes filled with tears—then groaned. He passed his hand across his eyes. "Christ! what am I doing? I don't hate you enough for this."

She sobbed and wrapped her arms around her quivering body, gasping out her shame and grief. How could she ever have loved this man?

"Go back to your room," he growled. "I'll go down to the parlor to give you time to dress. Meet me in the office at seven tomorrow morning. We'll look at the books, then head for Number Three." He crossed the room to the door. She scarcely noticed that he was limping. At the door he turned. "Damn you and those melting eyes of yours," he said bitterly. "They make a man forget what a treacherous bitch you are!" Then he was gone.

She sank to the floor, weeping as if her heart would break. But her heart had broken long ago. The day she'd sent him away. The man she'd loved.

Why should she be crying now? Why should she mourn a cruel stranger?

Chapter
Twelve

Marcy dipped her bucket into the crystal stillness of Long Lake, then straightened, setting the dripping bucket on the sand. She gazed across the lake, where the hills rose in graceful swells, all the way to Owl's Head Mountain. The trees were really beginning to turn now, their brilliant color sparkling in the clear September dawn, and echoing in the shiny reflection of the water. Why can't the whole world be as beautiful as this? she thought. Why can't people's lives be as placid and serene as the water?

"Marcy?"

Drat! she thought. Why doesn't he leave me alone? She turned, forcing herself to smile. "Morning, Zeb."

Zeb Cary frowned, his eyes dark with accusation. "What happened to you last night, Marce? We were all set to go over to Merwin's Blue Mountain House—me and the other fellers. I *told* you I've been practicing my dancing. And then you up and disappear!"

"I didn't feel like dancing."

"Made me look a regular fool, in front of all those city

slickers at Merwin's. I reckon I was the only feller there without a girl!"

She sighed tiredly. "Zeb, I'm not your girl."

"Oh, I know you talk a lot about being married to that greenhorn you met last summer. But it don't matter to me *what* you done."

"Dang you, Zeb Cary! Are you trying to say what I think you're saying?"

"Look, I don't care, Marcy. But there's a lot of gossip in town. You're wearing that wedding ring, but no one's seen the groom! Even if we *did* give you a big send-off last summer."

"And I suppose if I go around with you, you'll make an honest woman of me?"

He seemed not to have noticed the gleam in her eye. "I'll treat you good, Marce. And I'd be right happy to marry you. No matter what."

"*No matter what?* Oh-h-h!" What was she doing, wasting her time with this . . . *child*? She threw herself against him and toppled him into the shallows of the lake. While he spluttered and splashed about, she stood over him, hands on her hips. "I'm married to a *man*, Zeb! Go and find someone else to pester!" The very idea! They all thought she was a ruined woman. Abandoned by her man before the wedding.

He waded out of the lake and glared at her. "Don't say I didn't warn you, Marcy. I've given you your last chance. When you didn't show up last night, I danced with Sillie Barker, the housekeeper's niece over to the Blue Mountain House. *She* didn't act like I was pestering her!"

Marcy picked up her bucket. "Get out of here, Zeb Cary. Or I'll douse you again! Go on! Shoo! Scat!" She turned her back on him and trudged up the incline to Uncle Jack's cabin. She carried the bucket into the house and dumped its contents into the large tub that rested on the cast-iron stove.

"You're up early this morning, Marcy. It's just about six, I reckon." Uncle Jack stood at the door to his room, scratching his ear.

"I couldn't sleep. I thought I'd get an early start on some wash."

"You need some more water?"

"No. This is my last bucketful. You sit down and have breakfast. The coffee's hot, and I left a stack of flapjacks warming on the hob."

He sat at the table, watching as she dumped soap into the hot water and began to stir the mixture with a large wooden paddle. "You just did wash three days ago."

"Well, but it's nice to have the sheets all clean and sweet-smelling. I'll bleach 'em in the sun and fold them away with lavender."

"Besides," he said softly, "it gives you something to do, don't it?"

"What are you talking about, Uncle Jack?"

"I'm not blind, Marcy. I've watched you mope around all summer long, since you come home, fussing with the cabin to keep busy. And I've heard you, too, pacing your room at all hours. When Merwin opened his house over to Blue Mountain Lake, you could have gone down to help. Not for the money. But just to keep busy, see people . . . even if they are a bunch of city folk. You used to like to be with folk, but not anymore."

"Oh, bosh, Uncle Jack!"

"Why don't you go back to that husband of yours? After two months, things should of cooled down between you by now!"

Her heart was stuck in her throat. "I can't go to him. It's too late. I expect he'll divorce me one of these days."

"You mean you *won't* go to him! You're as stubborn as ever. I should of warned Drew you'd need a good paddling now and then!"

"It's not as simple as that." She turned and entered her room, stripping the linens from the narrow bed, then went into Uncle Jack's room and did the same.

Coffee cup in hand, Old Jack followed. "It wasn't another woman, was it?"

"No. It wasn't another woman." She sighed. She had a

sudden vision of Drew at his easel, dabbing furiously at his canvas, ignoring the wayward curl that drooped on his forehead, ignoring everything but his painting. "But he had a mistress, all the same. And sometimes I think I was jealous of her."

Old Jack frowned. "Mistress?"

She gulped, fighting back the tears. "And then he gave her up. He gave her up for me! And probably hated me because of it."

"A mistress? And *he* hated *you*? I'll wring his fool neck!"

"No, Uncle Jack. I was the one who was to blame. I ruined everything. It was probably all wrong from the start. He didn't need me. He *never* needed me." She fished in her apron pocket for a handkerchief, and dabbed at her eyes. Carrying the sheets back into the kitchen, she dumped them into the tub and gave them a stir. She turned back to him. "Is that old hermit's cabin still standing on the top of Owl's Head?"

"I reckon it is. Why?"

"I thought I'd go up for a few weeks. I want to be alone. I'll take up some supplies, hunt and fish. I reckon I'll be better off if I don't have to talk to people for a while."

"And what do you plan to do about Drew?"

She covered her eyes with her hand. Why did the memory of him still hurt so? "I don't plan to do anything. He's better off without me. He can go back to his mistress with a clear conscience." She laughed sadly. "He warned me. And I didn't listen. She was his first love."

Willough stared at the furnaces of MacCurdyville, now cold and idled. Perhaps she and Nat could get them started again. She took a deep breath and opened the office door. Nat was sitting at his old desk, the books open before him. She had already decided that the best course of action was for her simply to pretend that the horror of last night had never happened. They were two people with a job to do. That was all. Still, she felt a certain uneasiness, wondering if his anger would get in the way of their business relationship. She wasn't prepared for the sudden blush that suffused his tanned face. Could he be feeling shame for his behavior? She decided not to risk finding out. It would be enough if they could get through the day with a modicum of civility. "Good morning," she said.

He nodded. "Mrs. Gray."

She thought: I don't hate you, Nat. God knows I should, after last night. But all she could think of was how it had felt when he'd held her, kissed her. So long ago. And the sudden realization that a part of her had never stopped wanting him; had ached with a strange longing. A part of her had prayed that he had forgiven her betrayal in marrying Arthur. She hadn't counted on his inexplicable hatred, his cold cruelty. He had called her a treacherous bitch. Terrible words. She yearned to throw herself at his feet: What have I done, Nat? What have I done to twist your love into this? But of course she couldn't. Proper ladies smiled and said the correct things. "Have you spoken to Bill this morning?"

"No. I thought it would be best if he stayed away today. There was too much ugliness the day the prisoners were sent back. I gather Bill only succeeded in pouring oil on the fire." He motioned her toward a chair. His eyes avoided hers. "Sit down. We'll go over these figures."

They worked steadily for more than an hour, discussing wages, the numbers of men that the ironworks could afford to rehire, the possibility of closing down one of the furnaces until the depressed iron market improved. Willough noticed that Nat's initial chagrin slowly gave way to the comfortable easiness that had marked their business dealings in the past. He even managed to smile as he stretched and closed the books. "I guess that just about does it. We'll still have to be flexible, of course, depending on the mood and the demands of the men. But at least we know how far we can bend. Jim Taggert is representing the regular strikers. I told him to meet us at Number Three at eight-thirty. I hope we won't have any trouble persuading the renegades to give us possession of the furnace. They've held it for more than a week now."

"What have they been doing for food?"

"The wives have been bringing in their meals. Bill tried to stop them the second day of the occupation, but the strikers backed them, and there was a small riot, with a few bashed heads."

"Good grief! And out of all this we've got to make peace?"

"That's about the size of it." Nat pulled out a large gold watch and flipped it open, checking the time.

How odd, thought Willough, noticing again the threadbare quality of Nat's coat. Yet he seems to have bought himself a fancy gold watch with Daddy's money. "That's a handsome watch," she said.

For the first time that morning he looked directly at her, his golden eyes hard and angry. "Do you think so? It belonged to Gramps."

She gasped in dismay. "Oh, Nat! Your grandfather. But then, he's not . . . ?"

He snapped shut the watch case; stood up abruptly. "Shall we go?" His voice was harsh and guttural. They made their way down the cinder path in a cold silence. It wasn't until they'd gone some way that Willough realized he was limping. Now she remembered that he'd limped out of the room last night. And he'd rubbed his leg—the same one he now was favoring—several times. As though it gave him pain.

"Why are you limping?" she asked.

His laugh was low, unpleasant. "I wasn't cut out to be a lumberman, I guess. But you didn't leave me much choice."

What was he talking about? "A lumberman? But . . . what happened to your leg?"

"My dear Mrs. Gray. I consider it a gift from you. The legacy of your malice. That, and my grandfather's death, of course."

"What do you mean? Your leg . . . and your grandfather?"

He stopped and stared at her, frowning in disbelief. "You didn't even know. Christ! When I couldn't get work in the forges . . . Didn't you ever wonder what I'd *do*? Or was it enough just to spread your poison, then walk away?"

"Poison? What are you talking about?"

He laughed bitterly. "The carelessness of the rich. You take what you want, and destroy what you don't. You despoil everything, so there's nothing left. *You didn't even know!*" He shook his head. "But if you're riding in your carriage, how can you see the mud in the street? Even if you put it there." He rubbed his hand across his eyes. "Oh, the hell with it. Come on. Let's get started."

They moved past a large crowd that had gathered—half the town of MacCurdyville. Nat acknowledged the waves and greetings from the people who recognized him; Willough tried to ignore the muttered curses that seemed directed toward a hated Bradford. They reached the large furnace house set into the side of the hill. At the top level, near the charging room door, Nat introduced Willough to Jim Taggert and two of his confederates, who represented the strikers. Taggert turned to the building and shouted. A man with a week's growth of beard peered cautiously out from the charging room, then stepped out to join them, his hands folded belligerently across his chest.

"We ain't taking nothing but full amnesty, Stanton," he growled.

"Agreed, Charlie. Unless you've done damage to the property. Then Mr. Bradford will expect to be reimbursed."

"No deal. Who's to say that skinflint Bradford won't come back to us later, saying we owe him?"

Willough stepped forward, her voice ringing clear and strong in the morning air. "I'll inspect the premises myself, with Mr. Stanton, as soon as you vacate. If there's no damage, you have my guarantee—as a Bradford—that you won't be held liable."

Charlie sneered. "Huh! Bradford! He said he wouldn't bring in prisoners, neither. But as soon as times got hard, we were out in the cold."

Nat's voice was edged with anger. "You have Miss Bradford's guarantee, Charlie! That still stands for something around here. And you damn well better respect it! Mr. Bradford could bring charges of criminal trespass against the lot of you, if he wanted. With or without damage to the furnace! I think he's being very generous."

Charlie grumbled and kicked at a pebble. "I don't know why *you're* so loyal to the family, Stanton. After what they done to you!" He snickered. "But maybe Miss Bradford there is paying you off ... and not in money."

Nat's face turned red. Stepping forward, he swung one huge fist into Charlie's jaw. The man dropped to the ground, clutching his bruised face. Nat glowered above him. "Miss Bradford is a lady. You'll keep a civil tongue in your head when you speak of her! Now get your men out of Number Three!" As Charlie scrambled to his feet, Nat's face softened. "Appoint a couple of your men to sit in on the strikers' negotiations. Maybe we can arrange to put you and some of your people back to work."

At Charlie's signal, the renegades filed out of the furnace house, carrying blankets and ragged quilts. Their eyes were cast down—men without hope. The women and children who detached themselves from the crowd to run to the men looked equally despairing, with pinched features and hungry eyes. What poor wretches they are, thought Willough sadly. She hoped that she and Nat could manage to find jobs for most of them.

Nat. How confused and mystifying it all was. He'd defended her honor! She couldn't believe it. Maybe it was just guilt, because Charlie had come close to speaking the truth. Perhaps that's why he'd blushed. He certainly couldn't be softening toward her. Not if he held her responsible for his grandfather's death! If that was so, it helped to explain his cruelty of last night. Poor Nat. What a dreadful loss his grandfather must have been for him. She bit her lip. How could he blame her for his grandfather? And yet he seemed to think that she should know why he couldn't get work in the furnaces. But that was absurd! Why wouldn't they hire him? He'd had more experience than half the men in the region! As a founder, as a clerk ... It made no sense. She sighed. After this was over she'd insist he tell her everything.

They moved into the charging room for serious negotiations. It was a large room, at the hilltop level so that barrows of ore and charcoal and limestone could be trundled in and dumped into the top of the furnace stack. Unused barrows were lined up against both walls, and near the platform-balance that weighed the loads was a tally board, like a giant cribbage board, for keeping track of the number of charges. Willough frowned, remembering the impersonal numbers. But the calculations took on a different meaning now. What was it Nat had said? Despoiling everything. Every twenty-four hours each furnace turned out two tons of pig iron. But to produce that took one barrow of charcoal eighteen to twenty times a day. She remembered more numbers. One acre of forest produced thirty to forty cords of wood, wood that was needed to make the charcoal. Nat had once told her that it took nearly fourteen cords of wood per day to feed just *one* furnace with charcoal. The numbers had meant little to her. Now, staring at the large charging hole that led into the furnace, she calculated what that hunger meant. Five thousand cords of wood a year. Nearly a hundred and fifty acres of forest stripped bare. *Every year!* For just one furnace. Good God, she thought, we *are* despoilers!

They began their discussions, sitting around a large table that had been set up hurriedly in the middle of the charging room. Taggert and his men were clearly more desperate than they wanted to appear; Willough couldn't help but notice that Nat was prepared to bend over backward to give them as much as he could. How like Nat, she thought. In a few days he would be a part owner of the ironworks, and yet his first concern today was for the men.

The negotiations went on for hours. There was so much to be decided. How many men could be rehired, how deep a pay cut they could afford to take, whether closing one of the furnaces would be best. Fewer men at more pay, or more men taking less pay. The arguments went back and forth. Again and again Willough reiterated the Bradford promise: no reprisals against the renegades, no Clinton prisoners to take away anyone's job. Mrs. Walker brought over a basket of sandwiches and hot coffee. While Taggert and his men, sandwiches in hand, stretched their legs, Willough and Nat sat silently eating at the table, carefully avoiding each other's eyes.

Willough couldn't bear the mystery any longer. "Nat," she said softly. "You said you couldn't get work in the forges."

He smiled, an ugly smile, his lip curling in disgust. "That's right. I'm a gardener now. For a nice little old widow in North Creek. I know more about compost piles than I ever thought I would!"

"But *why*, Nat?"

He leaned forward, his amber eyes burning into hers. "Because every door in every furnace was closed to me. You did a better job than you supposed!"

She was near tears. "Nat! I never knew what happened to you. I swear it! I thought you'd gone away for good." She swallowed hard, feeling the old pain. "I kept hoping . . . you'd come back."

He stared at her, a bewildered frown on his face. "I don't understand."

"Mr. Stanton, can we get back to our talks?"

Nat looked up. "Of course, Taggert." He turned to Willough. His eyes were cold again, his expression unreadable. "We'll discuss it later."

At last, after hard bargaining, they concluded the agreement. Number Four would be closed, but there'd be jobs for everyone. At reduced pay. There were handshakes all around, and Taggert and his men went out to tell the waiting workers, who greeted the news with glad shouts.

Nat stood up from the table and rubbed the back of his neck. He looked at Willough. He seemed almost friendly. "You did a good job. Your father would be proud of you."

She felt a twinge of bitterness toward Daddy. "Would he?" She rose from her chair, smoothed down her skirts. "Are you hungry? I'm sure Mrs. Walker can fix us a little something."

"I want to take a look around first. Make sure the furnace will be ready to blow in tomorrow. Why don't you go back to the house?"

"No. I did promise Charlie that I'd inspect the place for damage. I'd better come with you." They took the stairs down to the second level, walking out across the footbridge that overlooked the massive water wheel. The footbridge was narrow. Willough put her hand out to the railing to steady herself. Nat did the same, and their hands touched. She felt a thrill course through her body. She hadn't known she could still feel this way about him. *Why* did he hate her? She had to know!

"Nat. I want to talk..."

His eyes were on her lips. "I want to talk to you too," he said hoarsely. "About... last night."

Her heart was pounding. "Nat..." she whispered.

There was an ugly laugh behind them. "What a lovely scene!" They turned. Arthur was there, on the steps that led down to the walkway. He nodded to Willough. "My dear wife. It was bad enough you left me to deal with our guests alone. But to find you making sheep's eyes at this crude bumpkin..."

Cursing softly, Nat made a move toward Arthur, but Willough blocked him on the narrow footbridge. "Go away, Arthur," she said in a steady voice. "I came here to do a job for Daddy. I'll be home when the job is finished."

"I'll wait. There's a train for Crown Point in about an hour. I'd hate for there to be any... lingering farewells."

"You son of a bitch," growled Nat.

"Ah, Stanton. I thought you'd left the state by now. It's a surprise to see you back in an ironworks. I thought I'd got rid of you for good!"

Willough frowned. "What do you mean?"

Nat looked at Willough. His eyes widened in shock and sudden comprehension. "Oh my God!" He turned on Arthur. "It was *you*! You were the one!"

Willough wrung her hands. "What are you talking about?"

"The one who blackballed me! Saw to it that I couldn't work in iron. Ever again!"

A sneering laugh from Arthur. "Yes. Of course I made it very clear to Brian and the others that the request came from

Mrs. Arthur Gray, who was too much a lady to disclose the nature of her grievance against Mr. Stanton. And I hinted at other things. Irregularities in the books, et cetera. Mrs. Gray requested it, I said. Brian Bradford's daughter. It was a powerful combination. Those who didn't mind crossing me were afraid to cross Brian."

Willough gasped, her hand to her mouth. "You bastard, Arthur," she whispered.

He shrugged. "Why *didn't* you leave New York, Stanton? Though I can't say I was sorry to hear about the accident at the lumber camp. Pity it didn't kill you. Then I would have been sure that Willough wasn't still pining for you."

Nat clenched his jaw, his muscles twitching convulsively. "If you didn't think you could keep your wife, Gray, you shouldn't have married her. My grandfather is dead because of you. He froze to death—while they were still patching me up."

"Ah. A grandfather. I always wondered why you didn't leave the North Woods."

Nat's eyes narrowed in fury. "You'll regret I didn't leave, Gray. I'm going to kill you!" He pushed Willough aside and lunged at Arthur. But his crippled leg slowed him for a moment. In that second, Arthur had leaped aside, snatched up a heavy shovel, and swung it at Nat's head. There was a sickening thud. Willough screamed. Nat toppled backward over the railing, and fell into the spokes of the giant wheel. He lay twisted near the massive hub, some eleven feet below the walkway. There was blood on his head, and his eyes were closed. His skin had gone pale; he was breathing with some difficulty.

Willough gasped and rushed to the stairs leading down into the pit that housed the wheel. But Arthur was there, blocking her way. He clutched savagely at her arms. "Let me go, Arthur," she spat. "Damn you, let me go!"

His eyes burned with an unholy light. "No! You're coming home with me! You're my wife! You have a responsibility to me! And to our child! There'll be no more yearning for Stanton, or anyone else! You'll behave yourself, if I have to take a horsewhip to you! By God, I've worked too hard to get where I am to have it destroyed by the likes of you!"

She tore herself free of his arms and faced him defiantly, her bosom heaving in anger. "You're finished, Arthur. You bastard. I know about everything. The bribes to the legislators on behalf of your so-called clients, like William Davis. Or is it Tim O'Leary? The favors you've received from contractors to build your house, in exchange for city contracts. And Zephyr Realty, with its purchase of the New Church Street land, just before the city decided to allow an overhead railroad to be built there! I know all about what you've been up to!"

"Don't be a fool, Willough," he growled. "A wife can't testify against her husband."

"I don't have to. I've kept records. Every bit of money you've given me, along with a list of your visitors, and the checks you've had me write. A smart man can put that all together and come up with a pretty ugly picture of Arthur Bartlett Gray! Particularly if the smart man works for *Harper's* or *The New York Times*. In no time at all you'll be joining your old friend Mr. Tweed in the penitentiary!"

His face had turned white. "Willough, you wouldn't... Think of the scandal! Think of how it would look!"

"For the first time in my life, Arthur, I don't give a damn. About propriety or anything else! Nat's grandfather is dead, and he's crippled, because of you. You're the worst thing that's ever happened in my life."

He clutched at her wrist. "You can't do it! I won't let you! I'll kill you first!"

She sneered her contempt. "You should have stayed in the gutter where you belong, *Artie Flanagan*!" The look in his eyes told her she had guessed the truth. She shook off his grasp. "Now get out of my way. A *real* man needs me!"

"No!" His fist crashed into her jaw. She saw colors dancing before her eyes, then blackness. She felt her legs crumbling beneath her.

When she came to, Arthur was gone and she was lying on the walkway. She sat up and moaned, rubbed at her chin. Oh

God! Nat! She looked down. He was stirring, blinking and rubbing at his eyes. "Hold on, Nat, I'm coming!" she cried. There was no way he could climb back up to the walkway, even if he weren't badly hurt. And it was a good fourteen-foot drop from the top of the hub where he lay to the old creek bed at the bottom of the wheel. She raced down the steps, past the closed casting-room door. At the bottom of the wheel, she looked up. "Nat, are you all right?"

"Get help," he gasped.

It would take so long to get help. And she didn't want to leave him alone. But she'd seen the wheel in operation, when its steam engine turned it to force air out of the giant pistons. Air that kept the furnace burning at a white-hot pitch. The wheel turned smoothly, its gears well oiled. "Nat," she said. "If I could turn the wheel by hand, and bring you closer to the ground, could you get off?"

"I think so. I'm mighty dizzy, and my head hurts. But I think so."

She reached up and pulled with all her might. To her surprise, the giant wheel began to turn, its wooden beams making a soft creaking sound. As it turned over, Nat clung to a spoke, waiting until it was angled close to the ground before easing his way down its length and into Willough's helping arms. He stood alone for a minute, then stumbled to his knees, closing his eyes and clutching his head. "Jesus! I think the son of a bitch broke my skull!"

Willough sat down on the damp floor and pulled him into her arms, resting his head on her lap. She dabbed at the bleeding cut with her handkerchief. "Rest for a few minutes. I'll get someone to carry you back to the house. If it is a concussion, you should rest for a while."

"Damn," he mumbled, "I feel cold and clammy all over. Helpless as a baby."

She eased him out of her arms and onto the floor. "Stay here. I'll get help." But he had already closed his eyes again, and seemed unconscious. She stood up. My God, what was that? She lifted her head, sniffed the air. Damp, from the old creek bed. But something else besides. *Smoke!* Now she could

smell it distinctly. And see it too. Curling out from under the
casting-room door. The furnace house was on fire! She must
get help. The nearest outside door was in the casting room,
but it must be ablaze by now. The smoke was becoming thick
and billowing, and she could hear the crackle of flames beyond the closed door. She'd have to try the charging-room
door, up above. She hesitated, reluctant to leave Nat; but he
was unconscious, dead weight. There was no way to get him
out alone. She dashed up the rickety stairs to the charging
room. Racing to the door, she threw herself against it with
all her might. Oh God! It was *locked*. She smelled the smell
of kerosene, strong and pungent from outside the door. There
was a sudden whooshing noise, then flames shot up outside
several of the windows. She turned and grabbed hold of one
of the empty wheelbarrows; without a moment's hesitation,
she drove it through a window. She picked up a broom that
was lying in a corner and smashed out the last of the glass
shards from the window. Propelling herself through the opening, she dashed down to the bottom of the hill, where the
casting room was now a mass of flames. The casting house
bell was there. She grasped the rope and pulled with all the
strength in her. Let it bring help! she prayed. The men began
to appear, running down the slope, the man Charlie in the
lead. "Quick!" she gasped, pointing to the furnace house.
"Nat's in there! Below the wheel!"

It was impossible to get in through the door at the bottom
near the casting room. As they ran up to try the charging-
room door, Willough had a sudden thought. The creek had
been dammed and diverted years ago, no longer needed for
power after the steam engine had been brought in to turn the
wheel that created the air blast. But the dry creek bed was
still there, leading toward the furnace house. Willough turned
to Charlie. "Open the sluice gate!" she ordered.

Charlie nodded and raced to the sluice, turning the wheel
that held it shut. There was a rush of water, spilling and
tumbling down the slope until it struck the flaming furnace
house in a hiss of steam and smoke. It failed to extinguish
all the flames, but it created enough of a break in the fire so

the men were able to move in and drag Nat out. He was still groggy from the blow to his head, and the effects of the smoke. Willough gave directions for him to be put in Mrs. Walker's care, then turned her attention to the fire.

She barked orders like a commanding officer, directing a bucket brigade, sending someone back to the village to fetch more manpower, ordering carts of combustible charcoal moved from the vicinity of the flaming building. It felt natural to her—to take charge. As though she'd been waiting for this challenge all her life. And the men accepted her leadership without question. Not because she was Brian Bradford's daughter, she thought. Nor because she was a woman. But because she was *able*, and they knew it. In the midst of this destruction and chaos, she reveled in her triumph.

The sun was setting before the fire was finally extinguished. They'd lost the casting room, but the charging room was only burned around the windows and door, the giant wheel and its pistons had scarcely been scorched, and the stone furnace was intact. The furnace house could be rebuilt.

Willough slumped with exhaustion, feeling the strain at last. She trudged up toward the boardinghouse. She would see to it that the men all received a bonus for the work today. She'd insist on it with Daddy. She wasn't nearly as certain that she'd tell him what she suspected. That Arthur had set the fire deliberately. But the evidence was too plain. The locked charging-room door: It had been open when she and Nat had been up there. And the smell of kerosene. During the talks, she'd noticed the can of kerosene in the charging room, kept there to fill the lanterns that hung from the beams. But Charlie had found it outside when the fire was over.

More awful still was the realization that Arthur had tried to *kill* her. And Nat. She pursed her lips in determination. If it was the last thing she did, she would ruin him.

She was met at the door by Mrs. Walker. "Oh, missus! You just look plumb worn out! You go right up to your room and I'll have someone bring you a hot tub. And some supper. That'll set you to rights."

"Mr. Stanton. How is he?"

"It'd take more than a thump on the head to get him down. I recollect when he used to be up at the crack of dawn, helping chop wood before a full day's work at the furnace. And all on the sly, so your daddy wouldn't find out! He's a strong one. Don't you fret over him!"

"Yes, I know. But how is he feeling?"

"Well, I put a stitch in that cut of his. Just to be on the safe side." She shook her head. "I haven't done that line of work since my days as a cook in a lumber camp. I reckon I did enough patching and stitching in those times to last me a lifetime. Anyways, I stitched him up, and put a small plaster on the spot. And gave him a bit of laudanum. He was stubborn about that, but I told him it was for his own good. If that knock on the head shook up his brains, he needs to rest. He should sleep for a few hours. And then he'll be fit as a fiddle."

Willough sighed in relief. "Oh, I'm so glad." She moved toward the staircase. "I will have that bath now." She smiled at Mrs. Walker. What was it Nat had said once? That Mrs. Walker had been Daddy's mistress? She hadn't wanted to believe it then. Not in the days when she still thought Daddy was the most wonderful man in the world. She sighed again and climbed the stairs. At the top of the landing she turned. "By the way, Mrs. Walker, have you seen my . . . Mr. Gray?" She couldn't even bear to call him husband. Not anymore. Not after what he'd done to Nat.

"Land sakes, ma'am. He lit out of here hours ago. Just hopped into his carriage and skedaddled down to the depot. Just before the fire started. I reckon he caught the four o'clock train out of here. Now you just stop worrying about everything and climb out of that gown. I'll bring you a cup of tea before your bath, if you want."

It had been a long day. "No. I think I'll take a glass of whiskey." It wasn't ladylike, but she was sick of being a lady.

The bath was wonderful. Mrs. Walker had boiled up some herbs—lemon verbena, lavender, rose geranium—and strained the infusion into the bath water. She soaked in the scented tub, letting her mind wander, trying not to think of Daddy, or Arthur, or what she was to do with her life now.

She dressed in her nightgown and wrapper, brushed her hair in front of the small dressing table. She peered closely at her face. Her chin seemed swollen where Arthur had struck her, but perhaps it wouldn't bruise too badly. It was a small price to pay for her freedom.

She picked at her supper; she was too drained from the day's events to be hungry. But she wasn't sleepy either. She paced the floor of her room—long after her supper and bath things had been removed, and the house had stilled for the night—unwilling to face herself, the longings of her heart. At last she stopped her pacing and stared at herself in the mirror. "Are you a woman?" she whispered to her reflection. "Or are you still tied to all the stupid conventions?" Oh, damn conventions! They'd brought her nothing but grief! It was time to listen to her heart. She pulled Arthur's wedding ring from her finger and went into Nat's room.

He was sleeping quietly, his features soft in the light of a small night lamp that had been left burning on his night table. A small white patch of adhesive plaster on his temple was the only sign of injury. His color was good and his breathing regular; Willough muttered a fervent prayer of thanks.

Someone had taken off his shirt. His chest was bare. Willough's breath caught in her throat. He was beautiful, his tanned skin taut over swelling muscles. She remembered the first time she'd seen him in the furnace. How frightening she'd found his masculinity then. Now she yearned to have those powerful arms hold her, to feel herself crushed against that hard chest. She felt a surge of desire deep within her. She reached out a tentative hand, brushed her fingers across his hard-muscled shoulder. His flesh was silken and hot to her touch. He stirred restlessly in his sleep. The light sheet that covered him shifted, uncovering a portion of his legs, which were bare. The bottom of the furnace house had been damp and muddy. They must have taken off all his clothes.

Willough stifled a cry of dismay. His legs were strong and wonderfully formed, but along the left leg, from thigh to calf, was a line of ugly scars. Oh, Nat, she thought. How you've suffered. And I'm just as guilty as Arthur! I *should* have

looked for you. I should have wondered what had happened
to you. Perhaps if I'd known... No. She had no excuses
for herself. Half the North Woods, it would seem, had known.
About the blackball, about Nat's accident. Oh, God, why
hadn't she tracked down Nat's grandfather, his beloved
"Gramps"?

"Because you were a proper fool, Willough," she whispered. Concerned with the proprieties, with the niceties, with
her *duty* as a wife. To the exclusion of her common sense.
Her heart.

"I love you, Nat Stanton." She leaned over and kissed him
softly on the mouth, then straightened the sheet to cover him
more snugly. Walking quietly around to the other side of the
bed, she lay down beside him, turning so she could watch
him. The strong profile, the pale golden lashes that curled
against his tanned cheeks. She watched him until the very
last moment, when sleep closed her eyes.

She dreamed of Arthur—an ugly nightmare—and woke
with a start. Beyond the small window she could see the stars
and the silvery slice of the waning moon. Nat was still asleep,
his blond curls damp across his forehead. She eased herself
off the bed. It must be two or three by now. She was terribly
thirsty. The smoke from the fire had done it, no doubt. There
was a covered pitcher on a table near the door. And several
glasses. She slaked her thirst gratefully.

"Can you spare a glass of that?"

She turned. Nat was awake, struggling to sit up in bed.
"Of course." She poured a glass and brought it to him, watching with maternal concern as he drank it down. "Does your
head hurt?"

"No."

"Would you like something to eat? I'm sure..."

"Willough."

Avoiding his eyes, she took the glass from him. "Mrs.
Walker can..."

He closed his hand around her wrist, pulled her down to
sit on the bed. "Willough. Stop. How can I beg your forgiveness if you won't let me?"

She ached with remorse. "There's nothing to forgive. It was because of me that Arthur..."

"I must have been mad to think you had anything to do with it. All these months I've been burning up with hate, thinking it was your doing. Can you forgive me? How could I have believed it was you?"

"It could have been. I was spiteful enough to marry Arthur just to hurt you."

He smiled sadly and stroked the side of her face with gentle fingers. "Poor Willough. I wonder who was hurt more." His eyes were filled with pain. "And last night...oh God! I wronged you so. Shaming you like that. I was so filled with blind hatred."

"But even then, you relented at the last minute. You didn't force me to..."

He groaned. "I couldn't. It was easy enough to hate you when we were apart. And last night, when you defied me—proud and haughty—I could still consider you my enemy. Your pride only fed my hatred. But when your mouth started to tremble I was undone!"

She began to cry. "Oh, Nat! It was your hatred that hurt so. I didn't care about my shame. But your hatred cut like a knife, tearing me apart. I kept thinking you must have hated me from the moment we parted."

"No. That's what's so funny. I guess I never really did. I knew I should because of Gramps. I guess I hated myself more for still loving you."

"Your grandfather," she sobbed. "And your poor leg. I saw the scars..."

He lifted her chin with a finger and dabbed at her tears. "Willough. Don't."

"But your leg..."

"It's not as bad as it looks. The scars will heal. And the doctor thinks I should be able to walk more easily in another six months or so." He pulled her into his arms and held her close, stroking her hair until her weeping subsided. His arms were warm and strong; her face was buried in the furry softness of his chest. She felt protected, comforted.

And then, quite suddenly, it wasn't comfort that her body craved. She felt a burning ache somewhere within her, a hot flame that seemed to grow without her willing it. Her senses had never been more alive: the feel of his hairy chest against her lips, the sound of his heart beating close to her head, the wonderful masculine smell of him. She lifted her head and looked into his eyes. She was drowning in those golden pools. "Do you want me, Nat?" she whispered.

"I've always wanted you," he said hoarsely, and took her mouth in a burning kiss.

She trembled and parted her lips to his searching tongue. Her mouth had not forgotten its lessons. She met his tongue with her own, tasting the sweetness of his mouth. Her arms circled his neck and she pressed her bosom against his chest, filled with a passionate yearning that ached for release. Panting, she drew away from him, her trembling fingers working at the ties of her wrapper.

His strong hands closed over hers. "No. Let me do it. Let me make love to you, Willough, the way I've longed to. I've dreamed of this moment. Let me love you."

Her heart was melting. "You know I'm yours, Nat."

He peered deep into her eyes. "But will you trust me? Whatever I do? Will you know that I just want to please you?"

"How could I not trust you? I love you."

He smiled. She had forgotten about the dimple in his cheek. He got out of bed and stood up, pulling her up to stand before him. His naked body was firm and ridged with muscles, dusted with a light covering of golden hairs. She let her eyes travel the length of him, feeling her excitement grow as she imagined his hard chest pressed to her breasts, his legs entwined with hers. Oh, God. She stood transfixed. But there was still a part of him that frightened her. Arthur had hurt her often, rubbing her raw with something she had come to think of as a cruel weapon. And Nat seemed enormous.

"I do love you," she whispered. For his sake she'd be brave. Because she loved him she'd endure. Let him not read the doubt in her eyes!

He laughed softly. "I said trust me, Willough." He untied her wrapper and let it slide to the floor, then gathered up her nightgown and slipped it over her head. His hands reached out, closed gently around the soft globes of her breasts. His fingers stroked the velvety flesh, tracing tantalizing circles about her nipples; then his hands drifted down to caress her hips and cup her buttocks in his strong palms. "I could touch you forever," he said. "Beautiful Willough." He took her by the hand and pulled her to the bed, easing her down onto the pillows. He lay beside her and kissed her again, while his hands explored the hollows at the base of her throat, her breasts, her flat belly. His touch was gentle; she sank into the softness of the pillows, moaning in pleasure.

"I never knew a body could feel this way," she sighed, luxuriating in the delicious sensations that he aroused with his hands, with his mouth.

He stopped kissing her. "It's more than just quiet pleasure, Willough. Let yourself go. Give yourself up to your feelings, whatever they may be. I want you to be reckless and wild. Hold me tight. Scratch me!"

"Oh, Nat, I couldn't!"

He smiled. His eyes were heavy-lidded with passion. "Then I reckon I'll have to get rid of the proper lady once and for all." He bent his head to her bosom. She gasped as a wild thrill raced through her. What was he doing with his mouth? It was a feeling unlike anything she'd ever felt before. He sucked gently at one breast until the nipple swelled and hardened, then turned to the other breast and repeated the caress, his tongue circling the rosy fullness. She trembled and arched her back, straining against him, her body on fire with the feel of his hot mouth. She tried to say his name, but she was shaking too much to speak a word. His strong hands stroked her flanks, pulling her closer to him, until she could feel his hard body against the aching length of her. His insistent shaft pressed against her closed legs.

He kissed her hard, his tongue plundering her mouth, turning her insides to liquid fire. "Open for me, my love," he whispered.

She hesitated, suddenly fearful. It had been so delicious—
his hands, his mouth, his kisses. And now he'd spoil it: he'd
hurt her. But she loved him. How could she refuse? Dutifully,
she spread her legs and closed her eyes, unconsciously clenching her fists against his assault.

She waited, eyes closed, while he positioned himself above
her. But he wasn't doing anything! Then she felt his mouth,
trailing burning kisses down her belly. Lower, and still lower.
"Nat!" she choked. His mouth had found the intimate core
of her, kissing, nipping softly, sending throbbing shocks
coursing through her. She writhed beneath his hot kisses and
tangled her fingers in his curls. He shouldn't be kissing her
there! Surely it was wicked.

As if he sensed her thoughts, he raised his head from
between her legs. "Do you want me to stop?"

She *was* wild—a savage, abandoned creature reveling in
the pleasure he gave her. She raked her nails across his back,
her whole being filled with hot desire. "Oh, God. No!"

His body slid up the length of her, and he buried his face
in the tumbled curls at her neck. "I will, though." His hands
traveled down her hips, pushed her legs together beneath him.
She felt an aching disappointment; she had been ready for
him, waiting, hungering. But when she tried to separate her
legs, to welcome him, his strong hands forbade it. Instead,
he pressed his hard shaft between her closed thighs, gliding
back and forth, rubbing against her vulnerable softness. Tantalizing. Teasing. Again and again, while she gasped and
moaned in a frenzy. She felt herself growing hot and moist,
frantic for the feel of him within her.

She clung to him, thrashing wildly, her teeth nipping at
his shoulder. Her body was a hungry vessel, desperate to
receive him. "Please, Nat! For pity's sake . . ."

And then he was in her, his swollen shaft plunging hard,
gliding on the sweet emollient that her passion had released.

She cried out, her hips rising to meet his impassioned
thrusts. She was burning. Like the molten iron in the furnace,
melting, white-hot. The flames grew higher, consuming her,
swirling her into their midst, and ending with a great, fiery

explosion that shook her body and left her breathless. At the same moment Nat inhaled sharply, surged against her in a final thrust of triumphant possession. As he wrapped his arms around her, her violent quivering subsided into trembling spasms. She could feel the pounding of his heart against her naked breast.

In a moment her rapture had begun to give way to something else. All the years, all the arid years that she had denied her body, denied her very womanhood! A long-suppressed emotion bubbled in her heart, seeking release, until at last it burst forth. She began to cry, great wrenching sobs that shook her slim body.

Nat withdrew from her, sat up, gathered her in his arms. "Willough. My love. What is it?"

"I never knew . . . never knew a woman could feel that way. Oh God, I never knew!"

He held her close, letting her heart unburden itself. "Never?" he asked at last, his voice filled with tender concern.

She shook her head wordlessly. How could she tell him of the horror, the pain she had felt with Arthur?

"Dammit," he growled, "I should never have let you marry him."

She turned away, still filled with doubts. "No. Maybe Arthur was right. He called me frigid once."

He laughed softly. "Good God! After what just happened you surely can't believe that!"

"Maybe it was just . . . an accident. The emotion of the moment . . ."

"And you don't think it will happen again?"

"It never happened with Arthur. And I *tried* to be a good wife. A dutiful wife."

He kissed her gently. "You're all woman, Willough. No one ever made you aware of it, that's all. You were too afraid, perhaps. Too filled with what was 'right' and 'wrong' for a woman to feel."

"But, Nat . . ."

"How can this be wrong?" he asked. His hand caressed her breasts, her rib cage and flat stomach, then moved lower to the quivering juncture between her legs. He slipped his finger inside her, teasing her with steady, rhythmic strokes that left her gasping, her senses raised to a fever pitch. She could feel the hot bud of her passion swelling once again. Aching, yearning. Abruptly, he withdrew his hand. His eyes were twinkling. "Now tell me you're a frigid woman."

She laughed nervously, her voice shaking. "I feel like a glutton. Can it be possible to . . . ?" She couldn't go on.

"Now don't start being a prude again! Possible to what?"

"To . . . want you again so soon?"

He chuckled. "It's possible. And wonderful. And altogether what I was hoping you'd say. Because I'll never stop wanting to make love to you." He kissed her—a long, searing kiss that took her breath away, then pulled her under him. He possessed her once more, filling her with a joy that blossomed into wild ecstasy as his manhood claimed her again and again.

I'm a woman! she thought. And abandoned herself to the delirious pleasures of her body.

The next morning she didn't want to open her eyes. She could hear from the twittering of the birds that it was day. But to open her eyes would be to see the ordinariness of the room in Mrs. Walker's house. And there was nothing ordinary about the way her body felt—deliciously sated, fulfilled, warm, and contented. They had made love for hours, falling into an exhausted sleep as the first gray light of dawn had lit the eastern sky.

Of course, if she opened her eyes she'd see Nat. Her love. And that would be more wonderful still. She blinked once, yawned and stretched, opened her eyes.

Nat was standing at the window, staring out at the overcast day. He was dressed in his shabby frock coat. She didn't have to see his carpetbag waiting by the door; his bleak expression told her everything. "Nat," she said softly. He turned, his amber eyes filled with anguish. Her heart sank. "It's too late for us, isn't it," she said. It wasn't a question.

"I'm tired, Willough. I've been tired for a long time. After Gramps died there was nothing left. I was planning to go west. All summer long, I was just getting my strength back after the accident, earning some money so I could afford a grubstake. I just wanted to buy a piece of land away from the world. And now I can, with the money your father paid me."

"But *why*, Nat?"

"I want peace, Willough. There must be peace for me somewhere! There's still a war going on. Only now it's a war against everything I hold most dear—decent people, God's sweet earth—and the generals are men like your father. Maybe out west I'll find peace!"

"But you can't go! Part of the MacCurdy business is yours now."

"I don't want it. Men will still live and die . . . because of greed. Did you see the faces of Charlie and the other men yesterday? Suffering? Desperate?" He waved his hand toward the window. "And look out there. The ugliness, the destruction. Once upon a time, we knew how to keep a balance with nature. But not anymore. Maybe out west a man can live in harmony with the land. Without exploiting it. But here it's still war." He laughed bitterly. "Do you think it matters a damn to me if I'm on the side of the generals instead of the troops?"

"Oh, Nat. It doesn't have to be that way. If you're a general you can change things!"

His eyes were sad. "And what about us? How soon would you regret your unrefined lover?"

"Never!" she cried.

"Here in the North Woods, no. But what about in New York City? That life is too much a part of you. It would happen again. That inborn snobbery would win out. Your mother would see to it."

"I'll leave the city. I'll divorce Arthur!"

"Dammit, Willough, in some ways you *are* Arthur! Spoiled by civilization—like this land is spoiled."

"Oh, Nat, you're unfair. People change. I'm not the stupid girl who sent you away a year ago."

"I don't want to chance it. I'm too tired to go through it

all again. First the embarrassment, then the coldness. Then
the contempt, like a wall between us. The same as before."
His face twisted in agony. "God, Willough, I'm so sick of
war!"

"It wouldn't be like that." She was desperate. How could
she lose him?

"You don't understand," he said wearily. "Before I met
you, I managed to get along by cutting out my heart. You
brought me back to life. But you brought me something else
too. All the turmoil I was trying to escape. Do you realize
how often we fought? Quarreled over every damn thing? It
tore me to pieces. And the other night . . . God! It makes me
sick to think of it. I behaved in a way I didn't think was
possible. Degrading you like that."

"Nat, it doesn't matter . . ."

"Dammit, Willough, I nearly raped you! How can you be
good for me if you can bring out such ugly passions?" He
gulped, struggling against his emotions. "Gramps had the
right idea. To be alone."

"But I love you," she whispered, knowing even as she said
it that it was too late.

"And I love you. But that doesn't change anything."

She *had* to reach him. "What about Arthur? Have you
forgotten that he tried to kill you? That your grandfather's
death was his fault?"

He sighed. "I'm too tired even for revenge."

"I'm not! I'll make him pay."

He shook his head. "Don't waste your time, Willough.
He's not worth it." He limped toward the door, picked up his
carpetbag. "I've left a note for your father. There on the desk.
I've refused the partnership. He can get a new manager too.
If he's smart, he'll choose you. But he's probably too much
a fool for that. I've also written out a list of the agreements
we made yesterday with the men. You can fill him in on the
details." He picked up a battered cap and jammed it on his

head. His golden eyes were filled with tears. "You'll haunt me, Willough," he choked. "All the rest of my days. But I want peace. Maybe there's something out west, some unspoiled wilderness, that can give it to me."

Chapter
Thirteen

"We'll be getting into the Grand Central Station in half an hour, ma'am."

"Thank you, porter." Willough smiled, looked out the window of the parlor car. "It looks like a fine morning."

"Yes indeed, ma'am. Would you care for another cup of coffee from the dining car?"

"That would be nice." She rubbed at the back of her neck as the porter moved off. Sitting up all night on the train from Saratoga—even in the relative luxury of the parlor car— didn't exactly compare to traveling in Brian Bradford's car, but it hardly mattered. She wouldn't have been able to sleep anyway. Her mind had whirled with thoughts all night long.

She was surprisingly calm about Nat. He was wrong about her. After a year with Arthur, she wasn't the same person.

That idiotic child who'd been ashamed of Nat because he hadn't known which fork to use had vanished long ago. *Don't wish for something too much*, Grandma Carruth used to say, *or your wish is liable to come true*. Well, her foolish wish had come true. She'd had a fairy-tale wedding to a well-tailored gentleman with impeccable manners. And the morals of a guttersnipe.

After Arthur she'd have been *proud* to be Nat's wife. She sighed and brushed away a tear. But she never could have made Nat understand that. There'd been too much pain, too much hatred between them that he couldn't forget. And too much grief in his life, burdening his heart. She understood his need to be alone, though it brought her misery.

"I wish you peace, Nat," she whispered.

And Daddy too. All night long she'd played the scene over and over in her mind. Daddy in Saratoga, ashen-faced, drawn. And she—calm, controlled, seeing him clearly for the first time.

"I don't know how you did it, lass," he'd cackled. "Getting Nat to turn down the partnership! I didn't want to see it go to a stranger. Especially not after he put me over a barrel the way he did."

"I had nothing to do with it. It was his own decision."

"Well, all the same . . . I'm damned proud of you, lass. I had reports from Bill and Taggert. The way you handled the negotiations. And the fire. By thunder, I wish I'd been there! They're all saying the whole furnace house would have been lost but for you. You know, Willough, Drew's a disappointment to me. He came back from France to be my partner, then turned me down and went back to his fool painting after that little wife of his vanished." Brian cursed softly. "And after I'd advanced him all that money too."

"Maybe painting is what he wants to do. Have you ever seen his work?"

"I'm not interested in his work. And I'm not interested in him. You're the one. You've got a head on your shoulders. Come into the business with me. Right now. I'll give you a ten percent partnership right off the bat."

She almost laughed aloud. If he'd talked this way a month ago, she would have leaped at the chance. "I don't want it, Father," she said coolly. "Not any part of it."

"Are you daft? What do you mean, you don't want it?"

She sighed. "Tell me, Daddy. How soon would your daughter have been the currency for the *next* business deal?"

"What the hell are you talking about?"

"When you sent me to Nat ... what did you think he wanted?"

He thought about it, then frowned. "Why, that son of a bitch! I didn't think he was that kind of lowlife."

She felt a surge of fresh anger. "You helped Arthur black-ball him. Without a twinge of conscience! And didn't bother asking me about it. Under the circumstances, don't you think Nat was entitled to his revenge?"

"Willough. Lass. If I'd known ..."

"Would it have mattered? I begged you not to send me to him. That should have been enough."

"It was just that I was so worried. With the business and all ..."

"And I was your daughter. Oh God, Daddy, did you ever really *see* me?" Her bitterness was choking her. "I spent half my life trying to please you, and feeling guilty because I wasn't the son you wanted. Drew was smarter than I was. He ran as far away from you as he could."

"Damn Drew," he muttered.

"He's your son. You could have helped him. He's struggling now. He needs your encouragement more than ever. But all you ever cared about was your business. Your money." She took a deep breath, picked up her hat and gloves. She was suffocating in this house. "Good-bye, Daddy," she said softly.

His eyes were filled with terror. "You can't leave me, Willough! I'm a sick man! The doctor said ..."

She blinked back her tears. "I'm sorry for you, Father. I spent too many years caring about you more than I should have. You'll have to forgive me if I care less now than I should. Please have Martha pack my things and send them on to New York City. I'll not be returning to this house."

"Your coffee, ma'am." The porter bent above her.

"Thank you." Poor Daddy. She didn't hate him. No. The only hatred in her heart was for Arthur. For all the misery he'd brought her, for his unforgivable cruelty to Nat. But she'd deal with him, by God! And then? She wasn't sure what she'd do with her life after that. She only knew she felt a sense of freedom, thinking about the future.

Her confidence wavered on the carriage ride up Fifth Avenue. What would she do if Arthur was at home? She took a deep breath. She held all the cards . . . why should she be afraid of him?

Brigid met her at the door. She put a comforting hand on the maid's shoulder. "I was so sorry to be called away the day your brother died. Is your family managing?"

The soft brogue was filled with grief. "Thank you, ma'am, yes. Me other brothers are all workin'. It's just that . . . Kevin was special to me, I guess. And the T.B. is a terrible way to go."

"If you want a few days' holiday, I'll see that you get paid."

"No, ma'am. I reckon keeping busy is the best way."

She handed her gloves and hat to Brigid. "Is . . . is Mr. Arthur at home?"

Brigid's eyes opened wide. "No, *ma'am*! He came flyin' in here yesterday like a bat out o' hell, if you'll forgive my sayin'. Tore up your sitting room something fierce, then packed a bag and said he'd be at his club. Lillie and me, we cleaned up the room the best we could, but there's still a lot of papers we didn't want to put away."

"I'll take care of them, Brigid." Thank God she'd had the sense to put all the incriminating notes and papers in the bottom of her sewing box! It had always given her a perverse pleasure to know that while she sat with her needlepoint— Arthur smiling nearby in smug domesticity—she had his ruination at hand. Absentmindedly, she rubbed at her chin, still tender from his assault the other day. And the sooner the better, she thought. "I'll just go up to my room for a little while. It's been an exhausting trip."

Brigid bobbed politely. "Yes'm. Oh, Mrs. Gray. I hate to tell you this right now, you being so tired and all..."

"What is it?"

"Well, maybe you don't have to take care of it right away ...I can say I forgot to tell you...."

"Brigid!"

"It's only that your mother, Mrs. Bradford, sent a message round last night. She said she *had* to see you. The moment you came in. But she doesn't have to know that you..."

Willough smiled at the girl's thoughtfulness. "Thank you. But I suppose I ought to see her if it's important. Come up to my room with me. I'll just freshen up a bit. You can help me change. This suit smells of smoke."

"From the train, ma'am?"

"Yes." She thought of the flaming furnace at Mac-Curdyville, the life that she and Nat might have shared, had he stayed. "And from my past."

She was at her mother's within the half hour. Isobel Bradford reclined on her chaise in the parlor. She hasn't even bothered to dress! thought Willough. Indeed, the disorder of her mother's toilette was shocking. Her wrapper was tied together in a careless fashion, and the graying hair was straggly and unkempt. Her face was flushed, her hands twitched constantly. Nat had said once that she was addicted to her tonic, and Willough had scoffed at him. But if the tonic contained opium, then perhaps he'd been right. She'd been too young and stupid last year to realize *that*, either!

"You wanted to see me, Mother?"

"Yes." Her mother's eyes were dark and accusing. "Arthur was here yesterday. He told me that you had made up terrible lies and stories about him. And that you intended to go to the newspapers with your scurrilous charges!"

"Yes."

"He assured me there was nothing to them, but that you could ruin him in any event. Is that true, Willough?"

"He'll be fortunate if he doesn't go to jail."

"Oh!" Isobel patted her brow with a linen handkerchief. "That you could so brazenly admit it to me! You surely don't intend to go through with it. Think of the shame to the Carruth name!"

"The only shame I feel is in being foolish enough to marry him in the first place."

"But why are you doing this?"

She thought of Gramps, dying alone in his little cabin. Of Nat, crippled. Of her own happiness so cruelly destroyed. "To settle old scores," she said wearily.

Isobel's eyes filled with tears. "Willough, I implore you! Don't do it."

"Are you asking for yourself? Or for Arthur?"

"What do you mean?"

"Did Arthur come here yesterday and ask you to make this plea to me?"

"Why shouldn't he, the dear boy? He's too ashamed and hurt by his own wife's treachery to face you directly."

She laughed sharply. "What nonsense!" She thought: He *used* you, Mother. All those years that he came to call. And went away again with what he most craved. Influence. Respectability. And you thought he loved you, Mother. Poor snobbish Isobel Carruth Bradford. What would she think if she knew that the love of her life had once been a street arab? Artie Flanagan from Broome Street.

Isobel pressed her lips together, drew herself up in her most imperious pose. "You can't do it, Willough. I *won't* have a scandal!"

"He tried to kill me, Mother. And Nat. Up in Mac-Curdyville."

"There's nothing I can do to talk you out of it? You ungrateful daughter!"

"He tried to *kill* me! He's no good!"

"How sharper than a serpent's tooth it is to have a thankless child!"

The absurdity of it made Willough laugh. If Isobel wasn't quoting Grandma Carruth, she was quoting Shakespeare. She stood up abruptly. "If you have nothing more to say to me, Mother..."

Isobel's voice had become shrill. "You're not my daughter!"

Willough shrugged. "I never was." She turned toward the door.

Isobel sniffled and dabbed at her nose. "At least I still have Drew. He doesn't belong to his father now. Or that awful wife of his. He's *mine*!"

Isobel's voice had become shrill. "You're not my daugther!"

Willough frowned. What was it Daddy had said about Drew? She turned. "What do you mean, he doesn't belong to Daddy now?"

"He was going to go into the business with him."

"Yes. Daddy said he changed his mind." Something in Isobel's tone made her uneasy. She walked back to the chaise, leaned over her mother. "*Why* did he change his mind?"

Isobel's hands had begun to flutter helplessly. "Because he wanted to continue painting."

"But he didn't change his mind until Marcy went away. That's what Daddy said."

"Well, when he didn't have the burden of a wife to support, he was able to stay with his painting."

That didn't sound like Drew, thinking of Marcy as a burden. Willough sat down on the chair beside Isobel. She gripped her mother's hand. "What happened to Marcy?"

"I'm sure I don't know."

"I'm sure you do." Willough's voice was like steel.

Isobel fidgeted in her chaise, shook her hand free from Willough's grip. "Well, if you must know...Drew found her with another man."

Willough rocked back in her chair. "I don't believe you! What man?"

"It doesn't matter."

"What man? They'd just come home from a year in France. Who would Marcy know in the city?" Isobel's eyes had begun to dart nervously about the room. It was clear that she knew more. "*Tell me*, Mother!"

Isobel smiled, her mouth curled in a vindictive sneer. "It was Arthur." The words were clearly meant to hurt her.

"Good God, Mother. He was unfaithful to me five minutes after we were married. I don't give a damn about *him*." But Marcy? Willough frowned. That made no sense. There hadn't been many letters from Drew in Paris, but his love for Marcy was in every line. Unless big brother is a fool, Willough thought, his wife couldn't have deceived him. Particularly not with Arthur. Arthur wasn't that smooth a rake. He'd only duped her—Willough—that time in the boathouse because she'd been so innocent. A man can only seduce a woman, she thought, if she doesn't know what's about to happen. Or if she *wants* to be seduced. Neither of which would seem to apply to Marcy. "How did he manage to seduce her? I thought she was in love with Drew."

Isobel was beginning to shake. "You know these fortune-hunting women. They'll run after any man! Now fetch me my tonic. I'm feeling poorly."

Her mother was lying; she was sure of it. "There'll be no tonic, Mother. I'll smash the bottle right this instant unless you tell me everything!"

Isobel tried to rise from her chaise. "How dare you! Ring for my maid!"

"No! There'll be no maid! And no tonic! How did Arthur manage to seduce Marcy?"

Isobel began to cry. "I didn't want him to give up his painting," she whined. "He was going to. Just for that woman!"

"And so you sent Arthur to seduce her." Willough felt sick. "And how did Arthur manage it?"

Isobel held out a trembling hand. "For pity's sake, Willough, give me my tonic."

"How?"

"I . . . sent him a sleeping draught to use on her. I only did it for Drew. She was so common! She would have left him sooner or later."

Willough crossed to a table and picked up the bottle of tonic. She handed it to her mother. In a frenzy, Isobel gulped it down, closed her eyes, leaned back against her chaise.

"You horrible old woman." Willough's voice was filled with sadness, not anger.

Isobel's eyes blinked open. "You're mean, Willough. Mean and cruel!"

"Why do you hate me so, Mother?"

"Why shouldn't I? You stole Arthur from me."

A bitter laugh. "I give him back. But . . . no. It isn't Arthur. For as long as I can remember—your face changed, every time you looked from Drew to me."

"That's not so."

"If we didn't look so alike—Drew and me—I would have thought that"—she hesitated, then shrugged off the old restraints—"that we'd had different fathers."

Isobel gasped. "Willough! Please!"

"Oh, God, Mother! Don't you ever get tired of prudery? Of pretending such things don't exist? *I* do! Why can't we talk openly for a change? Who *was* my father? Some black-hearted gypsy who talked his way into your drawers and left you with bitter memories and a daughter you despise?"

"Your father was an animal."

Willough recoiled at the loathing in her mother's voice. "And Drew's father?" she asked softly.

Isobel sighed. "I suppose I owe you an explanation," she said at last. "The Carruths were a fine family. The finest in the city. But there'd been business reverses. Your Grandma Carruth wanted to arrange a good match for me. She was always telling me what was 'proper.' When Brian MacCurdy came along, I thought he was the handsomest man I'd ever seen. I found his earthiness exciting after the rich mamma's boys my mother had tried to marry me to. A big strapping man, with the roughness of Scotland. But with a hunger to improve himself. My mother hated him, of course."

"And so you married him."

"Well, he was rich. And I thought it was romantic and generous that he was willing to change his name to please me." Isobel stood up and began to pace the floor. "I was drunk on our wedding night. And of course Grandma Carruth had given me no warning of what to expect. I don't remember much, except that it was ... unpleasant." She wet her lips nervously. "It happened a few more times. I still found it unpleasant, but Brian was impatient, so mercifully it never lasted long. Then I found out I was carrying Drew. On my doctor's advice, I locked my door to your father." Her tense expression softened. "Then Drew was born. The sweetest child a mother could want. I gave him Carruth for his middle name, of course, though your father was angry about it. But oh! that child was a treasure. I devoted all my time to him."

"And Daddy?"

"I kept my door locked. I told him quite plainly I was no longer willing to submit to such filth. I think that's when he first began to take mistresses, but I didn't care. I had Drew. I had no room in my heart for a ruttish husband."

"Is it ruttish to want to make love to your wife?"

Isobel sniffed. "I'm sure I don't know what was in your father's heart, but nice girls don't enjoy that sort of thing!"

Willough thought: If it hadn't been for Nat, I could have been like her.

"And then ..." Isobel wrung her hands, "when Drew was around three, your father ... he was very drunk. He burst into my room, and started to tear at my clothes. Swearing and shouting in a drunken rage—'I want a *real* wife!'—As if I hadn't kept his home, and raised his son, and done all the things a wife is expected to do!"

Except go to bed with him, thought Willough.

"At one moment, hearing my screams, my maid rushed in. He threatened to beat her if she didn't get out." Isobel shuddered. "I still have nightmares about that night. My suffering. And the humiliation—knowing the servants were whispering behind my back."

"What suffering? Did he rape you?"

"Willough! Merciful heaven! How can you use such words?"

"Oh, Mother, I'm tired of propriety! Sick to death of dancing around things that should be said straight out! Grandma Carruth and all her nice homilies turned you—and me!—into priggish snobs! Damn what 'nice girls' would do or say! Did he rape you?"

Isobel nodded wordlessly, and sank back into her chaise. "But it was the last time he touched me," she whispered. "He went to MacCurdyville the next day, and when he came back a month later, I knew I was carrying you. I told him if he ever touched me again I'd kill myself. When you were born he named you Willough after his grandfather. Out of spite. Because Drew was *mine!*"

Willough was trembling. "It wasn't even me. All those years . . . I kept wondering what I'd done, wondering why you hated me. And hating you back. My God, I think I married Arthur to hurt you as much as anything else. And it had nothing to do with *me!*"

"Every time I looked at you, I remembered that night."

"And I thought I was named Willough because Daddy was disappointed that I wasn't a son! You and Daddy. What a pair. Was I ever really a person to either one of you?" Strangely, she felt no bitterness, only a sense of release.

"Your father was all to blame. When I got tired of his flaunting his women I insisted he move out. His revenge was to tighten the purse strings. If it hadn't been for Arthur, I don't think I could have endured the years of loneliness."

Willough laughed cynically. "It's a good thing you didn't *marry* Arthur. You might have been surprised. *Daddy* probably loved you, back then. Before your coldness drove him into the arms of Dame Fortune." She fought back her tears, remembering her last meeting with Daddy. "He doesn't have any other lover now. But Arthur? I don't think he's capable of love. Or ever was!"

"He loves *me!*" Isobel glared at her daughter with fevered eyes.

Willough felt a twinge of pity for this pathetic woman, bolstering her faded dreams with opium. "Then you can have him, Mother. I'm not as unforgiving toward my husband as you are to yours. Tell Arthur I won't do anything to ruin him. I just want a quiet divorce, as quickly as possible. I'll want custody of Cecily, and enough money to keep her well, but that's all." She hesitated, then leaned over and kissed her mother softly on the forehead. "How different things might have been if you and Daddy had tried to be a little kinder to each other." She smoothed on her gloves and headed for the door.

"Where are you going?"

"To salvage Drew's life, if I can." At the door, she turned. "Tell me. When Nat was here last year . . . the way you treated him. Was that on purpose? To humiliate him? No. Don't answer. I can see it on your face." Oh, why hadn't she listened to Nat?

"It was Arthur's idea!" said Isobel defensively.

"Yes. Of course. The favor you did for him. That he paid back by seducing Marcy." She sighed and went out into the vestibule.

Parkman hurried toward her. "Oh, Mrs. Gray. I'm sorry to disturb you. There's a policeman here. He says it's important. They sent him round from your house." He motioned to the uniformed officer, who waited politely near the door. "Do you want to talk to him here in the vestibule?"

Willough had an eerie presentiment. "No. Perhaps it's something that Mrs. Bradford shouldn't hear as yet."

"What shouldn't I hear?" Isobel stood at the parlor door, leaning against the doorjamb.

"It's a bit of bad news, ma'am," said the policeman, stepping forward.

"Then tell it and get it over with," snapped Isobel.

"It's only that . . ." He turned to Willough. The eyes were like a puppy dog's eyes, large and mournful. "It's Mr. Gray, ma'am. There's been an accident. A runaway brewery wagon . . ."

Willough turned cold. "Is he seriously hurt?"

The officer wrung his hat between his large hands. "I'm afraid he's gone, ma'am."

Behind them, Isobel began to gasp for breath, clutching at her bosom.

"Parkman!" cried Willough. "Get Mrs. Bradford to bed at once! Call Dr. Page. And make sure that Mrs. Bradford's maid doesn't leave her alone for a second until the doctor gets here. And she's to take no medication before the doctor arrives. She's just had her tonic. Be sure you tell the doctor that."

"Yes'm."

As Parkman helped the trembling Isobel from the room, Willough turned back to the policeman. "Is there anything I must do?"

"We'll need someone to come down to the morgue and identify the body."

"I'll come myself." It was the least she owed Arthur. "Must it be at once?"

"Well, no."

"It's just that I have an important errand to run first. Will it be all right if I can come in an hour or so?"

"Of course, ma'am." He cleared his throat. "You're a very brave lady, Mrs. Gray."

She smiled into the sad eyes. "It's my duty."

"Jesse, let's put the Seine painting over here." Drew squinted at the blank wall, noticed the way the light hit it at just the right angle.

"Sure enough, Drew." The tall man scratched at his muttonchop whiskers and glanced around the large studio. "But I want to put the drawings of your wife on that small wall. It makes a more intimate setting."

"If you think so." Drew turned away, stared at a speck of dust on the wall. He didn't know why he'd allowed Jesse to talk him into framing and hanging the pictures of Marcy. She haunted him enough in his dreams. But now, this last week, getting ready for his exhibit, he'd had to see that face a hundred times a day. That beautiful face.

Oh, Marcy, he thought in anguish. What did all this matter without her? Without her laughter?

"Come on now, Drew. Smile! You can't be *that* worried about the exhibit. Not after you had the brass to show with the Impressionists in Paris last spring!"

Drew turned about and managed a laugh. "Jesse, you're a mother hen."

"The homage Commerce pays to Art! I always knew when we studied together at the Cooper Institute that I'd go in to real estate with my father and you'd go on to greater glory as a painter."

"God bless your real estate!" Drew indicated the bright gallery. "You're more than a fair landlord. No rent! I couldn't ask for better than that. Nor a better friend."

Jesse looked embarrassed. "Humbug! The place was going begging anyhow! And I'm charging you for the gas. With no discount, mind you! And I expect a commission when you sell."

"*If* I sell." Drew sighed and put his hand on Jesse's shoulder. "You're not getting the best of this deal, old friend."

Jesse bridled. "Humbug! I didn't pay for the invitations for nothing! Tomorrow night, while you're receiving the acclaim of your admirers, I expect introductions to all the famous art critics, half the editors of the newspapers, *the* Mrs. Astor, and any visiting royalty whom my invitations have managed to snag!"

Drew laughed. "Agreed. And I'll even throw in introductions to any of my former lady friends who might come round."

Jesse nodded toward the drawings. "With a wife like that, you surely don't need them! When are you going to let me meet the little woman?"

Drew shrugged and turned away. "There'll be time enough. She's . . . in the country right now." And what am I going to do about her, he thought? Mother had been urging him to get a divorce. He was sorry he'd told her about that scene in the railroad car. But he'd had to tell *someone*, or go mad. He couldn't confront Arthur—not his own sister's husband.

But he wasn't ready to divorce Marcy yet. It seemed too final. And too painful. One thing at a time. After the exhibit opened tomorrow night there'd be time to think about Marcy.

"Joy unconfined!" Jesse leaned his head out the window, peering at the street below. With a grin, he pulled in his head and turned to Drew, his whiskers quivering. "There's the most *charming* creature who's just come in the door downstairs. If she's a friend of yours, you can start reimbursing me for the invitations immediately! Come in!" he said heartily to the gentle tap on the door.

"I'm looking for Mr. . . . Drew!" Willough smiled and held out her hands to her brother.

"Willough." He kissed her on the cheek, noticing how pale she looked.

"Hrrmph!"

"Oh. Jesse." Drew tried not to smile. "Willough, I'd like you to meet Jesse Brooke, an old and good friend, who's helping me put this exhibit together. Jesse, this is my sister Willough. *Mrs.* Gray."

Jesse's face fell. "Oh. Charmed, I'm sure, Mrs. Gray."

Drew chuckled. "Jesse was hoping . . ."

"Drew," Willough interrupted.

For the first time he noticed the dark shadows under her violet eyes. "What is it, little sister?"

"I'd like to talk to you."

"Here now," said Jesse. "Why don't the two of you just hop into the sitting room out back. I've got things to do here."

Drew led Willough into the small room behind the gallery, and indicated a worn chair next to the stove. He sat down opposite her. He frowned. He couldn't remember the last time he'd seen Willough looking so distracted.

She removed her pale kid gloves and smoothed them on her lap. "I . . . received your invitation. Of course I'll try to attend the opening tomorrow night. You must be very gratified and excited at the prospect."

He laughed mirthlessly. "Shall I be frank?"

"Yes." Her eyes were filled with sadness. "This is a time for frankness."

"It's all a bit hollow without Marcy. I didn't know how much I needed her until I lost her. That's as frank as I can be."

"Do you know where she is?"

"I assume she went back to Long Lake. To her uncle."

"Then go and get her, Drew."

He scowled. "Willough, it's none of your concern."

"Why not? You're my brother, and I love you. And you're miserable without her."

"For God's sake, Willough!" What could he tell her without breaking her heart? Destroying her marriage? "You don't understand," he said evasively.

"Then tell me."

He stood up and ran his fingers through his shock of black hair. All this time he'd kept it in, locked in his heart. "She's better off without me," he said at last. The words choked him. "When I first met her she told me she wanted to marry a rich man. I took it as a passing fancy of hers, a silly whim that had stuck in her brain. She can be so damn stubborn when she makes up her mind to something. But maybe it wasn't a whim." He looked around at the shabby room. "In which case, she's better off without me."

"And maybe your conscience is bothering you because *you* wanted to be able to pamper her, give her nice things."

That hurt. "God, yes!" he groaned.

There was no sympathy in Willough's eyes. "What a very selfish point of view, big brother!"

"What do you mean?"

"Did you ever ask her what *she* wanted? She knew you had nothing when she married you, didn't she?"

"Yes."

"But she married you."

"Yes." Could Willough be right? *No.* "Oh, hell!" he burst out. "What does it matter now? She made her choice the night..." He looked at Willough. She mustn't ever know. "Nothing. It doesn't concern you."

"The night you found her in bed with Arthur," said Willough softly.

"Oh, God, Willough, I didn't want you to know. I think I might have killed Arthur that night but for you."

She smiled gently. "Don't worry about my feelings, Drew. Arthur was never faithful. I just didn't think he'd sink that low."

"I thought you loved him. That's why I never did anything. And then"—his heart was breaking—"I'm not sure she wasn't . . . a willing partner," he choked.

"Don't be a fool, Drew!"

"I never could give her what she wanted."

"She probably never wanted anything but you."

He laughed bitterly. "She wanted money. And she wanted Arthur."

"You don't believe that."

He rubbed a hand across his eyes. "You didn't see her that night. I did. She was *enjoying* herself. The fancy trappings, the champagne dinner . . . She was holding him, kissing him, letting him . . ."

Willough stood up and put a hand on his arm. "Drew. She was drugged."

He staggered back a step. *"What?"*

"Arthur put something in her food or drink. She probably didn't even know what was happening."

His head was reeling. "Was he so unsure of his charms— that bastard!—that he had to drug her?"

"Oh, Drew! Don't be such a fool! He was so sure of her love for you. It was the only way."

"Well, he didn't succeed there, at least," he growled. I burst in on them before he'd had a chance to . . ." An iron band was twisted around his heart. "But why Marcy? Of all the women he could have had . . . why Marcy? I thought he was my friend. 'Uncle' Arthur! Damn him! And so stupidly brazen! Didn't it occur to him I'd find out?"

"He did what he intended to do," she said gently. "You were meant to find them together."

"What? *Meant* to? That's madness! What in God's name for?"

Willough blinked back her tears. "Oh, Drew, I'm so sorry. To break up your marriage."

"Why would Arthur want to break up my marriage? My life had nothing to do with his."

She hesitated. "It wasn't Arthur's idea," she murmured at last.

He didn't understand. "Then . . . who . . . ?" He didn't want to know. He didn't want to see the truth. "Oh, God, Willough. No," he groaned.

"She told me so herself. Not more than an hour ago."

"I don't believe it!" he said, even as he remembered how his mother had hurried him out the door that night. Just in time to walk in on Arthur and Marcy. He closed his eyes, fighting the pain. "Why would she do it?"

"She was desperate. You're all she's got."

"I always thought she loved me."

"She did. She does. Too much. Have pity on her, Drew. She's a pathetic old woman."

He pounded a fist against the wall. "And Arthur! I'll kill him!"

Willough shook her head. "No, Drew. He's not worth your anger. Leave him to God's judgment."

He sank back into a chair and buried his face in his hands. "Will she ever forgive me?"

"If you love her, find her and bring her back. *Fight* for your happiness, Drew! And don't be concerned about the exhibit. Your Mr. Brooke and I will take care of it. We'll see to the opening."

"I'm not concerned. With Marcy gone, all this"—he waved toward the open door and the gallery beyond—"appeared worthless." He looked at his sister. She seemed altered, somehow. Sad and calm and self-contained. Not at all the "little sister" he'd thought her. "And what about you, Willough? What about *your* happiness?"

She smiled through her tears. "I let my love get away. I guess I'll regret it forever."

And now she must go to Arthur.

She allowed herself to weep for him when she saw his face. The attendant at the morgue had pulled back the sheet for her identification. Arthur's face was pale, with just a small bruise at the graying temple to show where he'd been struck. Even with his eyes closed in death, there was a haughty air about him, the handsome mouth curved into the hint of a superior smile, the aristocratic mustache groomed just so.

Poor Artie Flanagan, she thought. Fighting his way up from Broome Street to a mansion on Fifth Avenue, only to be felled by a brewery wagon. It seemed such an ignominious death, such a squalid end to all his high aspirations.

She wept for him. And for her mother, who had loved him. They'd always been strangers, she and Arthur. And enemies, at the end. But she'd shared his life for a year; she'd shared his bed. She had borne his child. He was deserving of her tears. Perhaps he too had hoped for a better marriage.

She nodded to the attendant and turned away, drying her eyes and composing herself before she went out to her waiting carriage. For the first time she was grateful to Grandma Carruth. Her proper upbringing at least would see her through this long day.

She took out a small mirror from her handbag to look at her face; the lack of sleep last night had done more damage than her tears. She was pale, but it was a becoming pallor. Arthur would have approved: with her somber complexion, her haunted, dark-shadowed eyes, her constrained expression, she was the perfect picture of a grieving widow.

A widow. She looked more closely at herself, peering into her violet eyes. "Who are you?" she whispered. She had no one but herself now. Arthur was dead. Daddy's love had proven to be an empty shadow—fleshed out by her own needs. And Nat was gone, leaving her with nothing but bittersweet memories. She had no one but herself now.

She began to shake, fresh tears springing to her eyes. "Weeping Willough," Arthur had called her many a time. First in playful teasing, then in derision. But she'd been a child then. Stop your crying, you silly goose! she thought. No one but herself. She took a deep breath, feeling an odd sense of resolution. A door had been closed.

No one but herself. It would have to be enough.

When she reached the house on Fifth Avenue she found it in turmoil. Lillie greeted her at the door, tears streaming down her face.

"Oh, Mrs. Gray! Did they reach you at your mother's? Have you heard the terrible news?"

Beyond the foyer, in the drawing room, Willough could
see one of the parlormaids crying hysterically, and being
comforted by the cook; and the butler moved about the dining
room, morosely watering the potted palms. Only Brigid seemed
relatively calm.

Willough took the hatpins out of her hat, and handed hat
and gloves to the sobbing Lillie. "Brigid," she said, "do you
have your wits about you?"

The girl bobbed in front of her. "I think so, ma'am. 'Tis
a terrible thing, but there's nothing to be gained by all this
hullabaloo. It won't bring Mr. Gray back."

"No. Now listen carefully. You're to take my carriage. Go
around to Mr. Gray's attorney. Tell him what's happened.
Have him notify the proper parties and arrange for the funeral.
And I want a notice in tomorrow's *New York Times* obituary
column. Something that does justice to Arthur Bartlett Gray's
standing in this community. When you've done that, go to
Lord and Taylor. I'll need a mourning gown at once. Something that's already made up." She reached into her handbag
and pulled out a little square of cardboard. "Here. Here's my
card. Have them put the purchase on my account. Then take
the gown to my dressmaker and have it altered to my measurements. I'll want it by morning, if she can manage it. Tell
her I'll need at least two more black toilettes by month's end.
I'll leave the design to her discretion. Can you remember all
that?"

"Sure and I can, ma'am. You go on upstairs and take a
rest. You'll need your strength."

She sighed. "Thank you, Brigid. I *am* tired." She climbed
the red-carpeted staircase. The afternoon sun streamed through
the stained-glass windows on the landing and illuminated the
large antique canvases on the stair wall. Anonymous English
lords and ladies of another century. Arthur had always encouraged the assumption—by his modest silence to their
guests—that these were his ancestors. Poor Arthur.

She heard crying from the end of the corridor. Cecily. On
an impulse, she turned away from her room and went down
to the nursery. The nursemaid was there, frantically rocking

the cradle, to no avail. Each shake of the lace-draped cradle produced fresh wails from the baby.

The nursemaid looked up, her eyes filled with dismay. "Oh, Mrs. Gray, I'm so sorry," she said nervously. "It must be the colic. She's been like this all afternoon. I'll *try* to keep her quiet. I know with Mr. Gray . . . and all . . . that you'll want your quiet. Perhaps a bit of paregoric . . ."

"No, no, Hetty. It's quite all right. I'll stay with Cecily for a little while. Why don't you go down to the kitchen and see if you can calm Lillie and the others? I'll just sit here with Cecily."

"Yes'm."

Willough leaned over the cradle and scooped up Cecily in her arms; rocking the baby gently, she sat in a chair near the window. As she rocked and crooned, the wailing became a gurgling sob, and then soft hiccoughs. In a moment Cecily was sleeping. Willough smiled and held her child closer to her breast. What a pretty little thing, she thought, stroking the downy cheek and smoothing back the single brown curl. My little girl. Who never asked for anything but to be loved. What had she to do with her mother or her father—if they loved each other or lived with hatred?

Willough began to cry, bitter tears that traced burning paths down her cheeks. "Oh, Cecily," she whispered. "I'll try to do better for you than she did for me. I'll try. I'll try."

Chapter
Fourteen

D rew Bradford shifted the knapsack to his other shoulder and grimaced. He'd spent too many sedentary months in his studio; this climb seemed far more rigorous than it might have last summer. The path up Owl's Head Mountain was steep, and his load was heavy, with a warm blanket and several days' food.

"You know Marcy," Old Jack had said last night. "A body never can figure *what* she's thinking. And she might have lit out of the hermit's cabin by now. You'll need food if she's not up there. And enough to get you back here again."

Drew had rowed his boat to the far side of Long Lake this morning, following the current for a mile or so before reaching the creek that led to Clear Pond. He'd circled Clear Pond, felt the painful tug of old memories as he passed the lean-to on its shore. It was deserted now. The nights were getting too chill for the tourists and sportsmen to want to sleep in the open air. He'd rounded Clear Pond Island and seen the beach. Where he and Marcy had made love that glorious night. How long ago it seemed! Heading for the distant shore of Clear Pond, he'd finally seen what he had been looking for. It was just as Old Jack had described it—a rocky inlet, no more than a small indentation, and beyond it the beginning of the trail that led to Owl's Head Mountain. Coming closer, he'd seen a canoe, up-ended and pulled well out of the water. Marcy's canoe. That boded well.

In spite of the cool day, the climb was making him warm. He took off his frock coat and wadded it into a ball that he stuffed into his knapsack. A small stream bubbled alongside the trail; he knelt and drank deep of its sweet water. He sat and rested for a few minutes, peering through a break in the trees at Clear Pond far below. The September color was spectacular. The bright reds and golds of maple and birch and white oak, the blue-green of the evergreens, the clear sky.

He thought: I should come back here with my paints. Paris in autumn couldn't begin to compare to this glory! He laughed to himself. What a paradoxical fool he was! When he was painting—and Marcy gone—he was miserable. Yet here he was, about to get his wife back (God willing!), and all he could think about was painting!

Well, not all. It had been over two months, and his body ached with wanting Marcy, needing her. He yearned to hold her, kiss her, press her sweet form to his heart. He sighed and picked up his knapsack again, continuing on up the trail. He wasn't sure what she'd think when she saw him. The things he'd said to her in the railroad car—cruel, ugly words. And then to send her that money, as if she were a cheap...

Oh, God, Marcy, I'm sorry. Had she gone *willingly* to Arthur, it still couldn't excuse his cruelty.

Arthur, he thought. I suppose one ought to forgive the dead. Poor Willough. She must have already known when she'd come to the gallery. He'd only heard the news when he'd arrived at North Creek yesterday morning. He'd stopped off to refresh himself at the hotel before taking the stage to Long Lake. The day's news was just coming over the telegraph in the lobby, straight from the morning's *New York Times*: Wall Street was continuing to improve after the disastrous panic; ground had just been broken on the site in Philadelphia for the Main Building of the Centennial Exhi-

bition; Arthur Bartlett Gray, prominent New York lawyer and
gentleman, had been tragically killed in a street accident on
Wednesday afternoon.

Gentleman! Well, he could forgive the dead, in spite of
Arthur's heinous behavior. He wasn't as sure that he could
forgive the living. He hadn't wanted to see Isobel before he
left; he might have said things that he'd regret later. He'd
left for the Grand Central Station directly from Jesse's gallery
after sending a note to his mother, saying that he didn't want
to see her for a while. Not after what she'd done to Marcy.
And to him.

Willough was right, of course. Isobel loved him with an
unhealthy passion. He'd seen that before he'd gone to Paris,
when they'd quarreled over Marcy. But she had been so
contrite upon his return, so desperate to make amends that
he'd ignored his own better instincts. And then, of course,
her dependence upon drugs had probably clouded her judgment. He sighed. Perhaps he could find it in his heart to
forgive her eventually.

He looked up. The top of the mountain seemed to be in
sight. His shoulders ached. He shrugged out of the heavy
knapsack and put it on the trail. If Marcy was there, he'd
come back and get it. If she wasn't, he could pick it up on
his way back down the mountain. He chuckled, remembering.
Marcy'd probably take a fit, if she knew. With all her talk
about panthers and bears, and not leaving food around. But
he didn't really have to worry. There were still a few hours
of daylight left.

At the cabin Marcy slipped two cartridges into her double
rifle and leaned the weapon against the wall near the open
door. It was just common sense to be prepared. The nights
were getting cool. It wasn't cold enough yet for wolves, but
she'd heard noises outside, the last three nights. And there'd
been bear droppings just off the trail this morning.

She lifted the lid on the iron pot that hung over the cold
fireplace. There was still enough rabbit stew for her supper.
Maybe tomorrow she'd take her rifle and fishing rod down
to Clear Pond. If she couldn't catch a few trout, she might

be able to flush a grouse or two. She picked up the kerosene lamp and shook it. The liquid was nearly gone. Well, she wouldn't use it unless she had to; the fireplace would do just as well.

She looked around the snug cabin. The old hermit who'd lived and died here had built himself a cozy retreat. A stone fireplace, a box bed with a fragrant, balsam-filled mattress, a table and chair, with an old apple barrel for extra seating. There was even an oiled-paper window, with wooden shutters to close against the north wind in the winter.

Except for the kerosene, she had plenty of supplies. Flour for pancakes, coffee and sugar. Tea and a few tins of condensed milk. She could stay here until the last leaf fell. Maybe by then she'd be able to drive Drew from her thoughts. She sighed unhappily. Well, if she was going to heat up that stew for her supper, she ought to bring in some more wood and light the fire. She stepped out of the cabin and went around to the side, where the logs were piled in neat stacks. It had taken her two days to do that. She'd felled a small maple, dragged it to the cabin, chopped it into proper lengths. It would last her for a while unless there was a cold spell.

She stopped and looked about her, feeling the old thrill at being in her Wilderness. The cabin perched on top of Owl's Head. From here she could see for miles: the brilliant autumn foliage rolled down in waves of color to the sparkling lakes far below, glittering diamonds nestled among settings of rubies and golden topaz; beyond, the distant mountains were deep blue and purple.

My Wilderness, she thought. She felt again that enchantment that had moved her a thousand times. The mystery, the wondrous silence, broken only by the soughing of the wind through the trees below. There was peace here, in this remote solitude. She should never have left. This was where she belonged.

Except that she still loved Drew.

Tarnation, Marcy! she thought. It won't do you any good to mope about! She looked beyond the far mountains. There were clouds gathering in the distance, silvery wisps against the late afternoon sky. She wet a finger in her mouth and held it up to the air. It would rain before morning. She'd better bring in an extra load of wood.

She turned to the woodpile, then stopped. Drew had emerged from the trail and stepped into the clearing. Now he stood there watching her, that funny smile on his face. Her heart leaped in her breast, beating wildly in a tattoo of joy. And then shame, remembering the last time he had seen her—naked in a bed with another man. She felt the hot flush creep up from her bosom to stain her cheeks, to flood her with guilt.

He moved slowly toward her, his clear blue eyes on her face. She'd forgotten how tall he was, towering over her. He smiled again. "I still haven't painted that blush," he murmured, and swept her into his arms. He kissed her hungrily, his mouth warm and sweet on hers, his arms holding her tightly against his hard body as if he would never let her go. At last he raised his head. "Marcy," he said. His voice was husky in his throat. He looked toward the cabin. "Is there a bed in there?"

She nodded, her heart too filled with love and happiness to allow her to speak. He kissed her again, then picked her up, carrying her into the cabin and laying her gently across the bunk. He lay beside her, pulled the ribbon from her hair, and spread the burnished curls across the pillow. His eyes, devouring her, were filled with a tenderness that made her tremble. All the yearning, all the misery that had besieged her heart for months was gone, driven away by the sweet reality of her love beside her. "Oh, Drew," she whispered, and pulled his mouth down to hers.

And suddenly kissing was not enough. His impatient hands tugged at her shirt, fumbled with the buttons of her breeches. Laughing like children, they tore at each other's clothes. When at last they lay naked together she clasped his burning manhood and guided him to her, aching for the feel of his hard fullness within her. She gasped and cried out in ecstasy as he plunged, striking chords of feeling that she had denied for months. She wrapped her legs around him; he thrust into her again and again, his fierce passion taking her to heights she had never known. She was a great bird swooping and soaring above the mountaintops; a storm on the lake; a roaring waterfall. They exploded together in a dazzling sunburst of rapture that subsided into a throbbing quiet, like the cry of a loon dying away over a distant shore.

While he stroked the soft curls at her forehead, she lay snuggled in his arms, smiling in contentment. At last he roused himself. "It's getting chilly in here," he said, sitting up and reaching for his trousers. "I'll light the fire."

"There's no wood inside. I was just fetching some. Have you eaten?"

"Not since lunch. A cold sandwich on the trail."

"There's stew." They dressed in silence. There seemed to be no need for talk. Tarnation! she thought, I'm grinning like an idiot. But every time he looked at her, his eyes warm with love, she couldn't help but smile, the joy in her heart finding expression in her eyes and mouth. She cooked the stew, boiled some coffee, set the table. After he'd brought in the wood and lit the fire he perched on the apple barrel, watching, grinning at her. She found herself blushing—like an innocent girl, like a new bride—in the heart-stopping presence of her love. She hadn't thought she could love anyone as much as she loved him.

They ate in silence as the quiet contentment of twilight crept across the clearing and through the open door. At last Drew put down his fork and smiled at her for the hundredth time. "I love you," he said softly, covering her hand with his.

Her lips began to tremble with remembered pain. "I thought you didn't. Or at least I thought you'd stopped loving me, long ago. In Paris. Because I was such a burden."

"Oh my God. I thought *you* didn't love *me*! That you were miserable in Paris. Because of the money."

"Why should you think that?"

He smiled ruefully. "I couldn't forget that silly girl who wanted to marry a rich man."

"Oh, Drew. That *was* silly. But . . . I couldn't tell you, last year. I was so mixed up. And it hurt too much."

He pulled her hand to his lips, kissed her fingertips. "What, Marcy?"

"I told you once . . . or tried to. That my parents had died in an accident. There . . . there was an earth tremor. Our cabin . . ."

"Don't talk about it, if it hurts so," he murmured.

She fought back her tears. "But I *have* to. I want you to understand. Once and for all. I was *afraid*. A part of me kept thinking the mountains would kill me too. It didn't make any sense. But I was terribly afraid."

He nodded in understanding. "And you thought you'd be safe if you left."

"Yes. In a city. But . . . but Uncle Jack kept warning me how hard it was to live in the city without money. After awhile I got to be more frightened of *that* than staying here in the mountains."

He laughed softly. "Until you decided to marry a rich man."

"Don't make fun of me. I know it sounds silly now. But last year it seemed the most important thing in the world. To get away, and find a rich husband. And you just mixed things up. I was in love with you the minute I saw you."

His eyes twinkled. "Especially after I cornered you in the boathouse and kissed you?"

"No. Even before then. When you were drawing the picture of the deer on the path. Without any boots." She smiled. "Greenhorn," she said tenderly.

"But you thought I was poor. Until Collins told you differently."

"My heart and my head battled all summer long. But when I finally had you I knew that the nonsense of the rich husband had been just that. Stuff and nonsense. But I could never make you understand that."

He sighed in relief. "I thought you were miserable. And it was all my fault. Because we had nothing."

"Oh, Drew. I didn't need *things*! I was just unhappy in Paris because I thought I'd lost your love. I felt so helpless.

You didn't seem to want my help. To *need* me! And after a while I thought you were sorry you married me."

He stood up and pulled her into his arms. The cabin was now quite dim. His eyes were warm in the firelight. "If you'll come back to bed, I'll show you how much I need you. How much I love you."

There was still so much to be said. All the guilt she'd lived with since they'd parted. All the times—for so many reasons—she'd blamed herself. She pulled away from his arms, feeling the tears burning behind her eyelids. "How can you love me when I'm so wicked?" she whispered.

"What do you mean, wicked? My foolish dear Marcy."

"That night . . . you know. I'm so ashamed."

He pulled her over to the bed to sit beside him. "What do you remember about that night?"

"I . . . I remember having supper. And then . . . Arthur and I . . . I think we went to look at the rest of the car." She frowned and rubbed her eyes. "I remember taking a rain bath. I felt giddy. Like a kid. It seemed too silly. Oh, it's all such a blur." She couldn't meet his eyes.

"And then?" he prodded gently.

She covered her face with her hands. "I thought it was you. I don't know how I could have been such a fool, but I thought it was *you!*"

"I was the fool. A jealous fool! To think you could . . ."

"But I *let* him," she moaned.

He pulled her hands from her face, put his fingers firmly under her chin, turned her to face him. "You couldn't help yourself. He put something in your drink."

Her eyes widened in horror. *"What?"*

"It was a plot. To drive me away from you. And because I was a damned idiot, it succeeded."

She still found it incomprehensible. "Something in my drink?"

"Some kind of drug. Possibly laudanum. It didn't much matter if you were conscious or not. I only had to think you were unfaithful."

"But why would Arthur do such a thing? He's your sister's husband!"

"Was. He was killed the other day. Though I can't say I mourn his passing."

"Why would he do it?"

Drew sighed. "It was my mother's idea. She thought I'd be better off without you."

She frowned unhappily. "And maybe you would be, with your painting. I know how important it is to you."

He grabbed her by the shoulders, his eyes like blue flame. "Dammit, Marcy, don't talk that way! It means *nothing* without you! These last couple of months . . . I had to force myself to pick up my brushes. And in Paris I was so discouraged. It was *your* strength, your joy and love, that kept me from losing heart." He kissed her hard, then softened his kiss, his lips moving gently on hers, until she began to tremble with love and renewed longing.

She pulled away from him, her heart pounding, her breath coming in little gasps. "Tarnation, Drew Bradford," she whispered. "I *do* love you."

"Come back with me, Marcy. I want you with me. I need you with me."

She stood up and turned away. It was what she'd dreaded, knowing what her answer must be. "No. I belong here. This last week, up on this mountain, I've had a chance to think. I *belong* here. I feel the seasons in my bones. In my blood. In Paris the time seemed to drift away, the seasons blended together. Oh, I don't know how to say it. I guess I can use a word you and your artist friends would use. My days had no *form*. My life had no form. I'm *connected* to these mountains, Drew. Even my name. From Mount Marcy."

"There's no reason why we can't come back here sometimes."

"No. I belong here. Forever. I thought the mountains could hurt me, the way they hurt my parents. But the world out there is the real wilderness. Nature can be cruel, but she doesn't mean to be. Out there"—she gestured toward the open door, to the cities beyond the night sky—"the wickedness isn't blind chance. It's planned. Like your mother, and Arthur. Like Mr. Stewart in Paris. I never saw an animal attack that wasn't hungry or scared. Only people hurt one another for no reason."

"Maybe they're scared too," he said quietly. "I think my mother was." He shook his head. "That's not a good enough reason, Marcy. Unless you intend to spend the rest of your days in this cabin. Like a hermit."

"Of course not."

"Then you've got to be with people. What's the difference between living in Long Lake and living in the city? Especially if you and I are together? And we come back here sometimes?"

She twisted her hands nervously. "It's just . . . the temptation."

"What temptation?"

She'd had plenty of time to think about this too, to curse her own weakness. "Dang it, Drew! Maybe I *am* a fortune hunter!"

"What?"

"I *liked* that railroad car. I liked Arthur's attentions. I felt like a fancy lady. And I liked it when you brought me presents."

He pushed impatiently at his black curls, stood up and paced the small cabin. "For God's sake, Marcy! Why the hell shouldn't you like nice things? Especially after last year. The hard times. The miscarriage. You'd have to be a saint not to enjoy nice things after that!"

"Well, but if I stay here, I'll be away from temptation."

He crossed his arms against his chest and glared at her. "Have you done anything in the past two months besides dream up daft reasons why we shouldn't be together? What else? I can see from the look on your face that you have more doubts. Come on. What is it?"

"You don't need me," she said sulkily. "You have your painting. You don't really need me."

"I just told you I did!" he huffed. "What more can I say?"

"No. It's more than that. I'm not good for you. You nearly gave up your painting for me. You feel obligated to me."

"You're my wife and I love you!" he explained through clenched teeth. "I'm *supposed* to feel obligated!"

"Then what would happen if you couldn't support me? You'd give up your painting again. And I couldn't stand that."

"I swear to you I won't. I have high hopes for my exhibit. And even if it isn't a success, I can still get a job, while I continue painting. I can teach at the National Academy or the Cooper Institute. The important thing is that we'd be together."

She stuck out a belligerent chin. "And what kind of job could *I* get? I can't hunt or fish in the city. I can't be a guide!"

"You won't *have* to work! We'll manage."

"You see?" she said accusingly. "You don't need me. I'm no helpmate."

"Dammit, I'd forgotten what a stubborn devil you are! You're my helpmate just by being my wife and my love! If that isn't need, I don't know what the hell is!" He took a deep breath, cooling his anger. "I'm going back to the city. Are you coming?"

"No."

"You've made up your stubborn little mind, haven't you? No matter what I say! Well, I'm going down. I expect you in Long Lake."

She wavered. Maybe he was right. Maybe her arguments were foolish. *No!* She'd had plenty of time to think about it. It made sense for her to stay here. "I'm not coming."

He ignored that, and turned toward the door. "I'll be waiting."

Oh! He made her so hot under the collar! Who did he think he was, bossing her around like that? "You can't go down tonight," she grumbled. "It's already night. The trail will be dark. You'll have to stay here."

"I'll sleep on the floor," he said sarcastically. "We'll talk in the morning."

"There's nothing to talk about. I won't change my mind."

His eyes narrowed in fury. "Then you just might wind up with the sorest backside my right arm can give you!"

"Oh!" She glared at him and turned away.

"I left my knapsack and blanket down the trail. I'll go get them," he growled.

"Take the lantern."

"There's enough light. I'll be able to see. My things are just down the trail." He went out the door.

"Consarn him," she muttered. She slammed the kerosene lantern onto the table and pulled out a tin of matches. She struck one and touched it to the wick. No matter what he said, it was too dark out to see. She'd hear him crashing around in a minute, and then she'd go out with the lantern. Spank her, indeed! Dang him! She wouldn't be bullied into going back with him!

A terrible sound tore through the stillness. She gasped. She heard Drew's voice—half shout, half cry of pain. A long drawn-out howl that turned her blood to ice. *"Drew!"* she screamed. She snatched up the lantern and her double rifle and raced out the door. The sounds were coming from the trail—Drew's groans and cries, and an ominous growling noise. Hurtling down the path, lantern held aloft, she stopped in horror.

Drew knelt on the trail. Above him loomed a giant black bear, at least six hundred pounds, that reared up on its hind legs and slashed at him with razor-sharp claws. The contents of the knapsack lay scattered on the trail. Blood poured down the back of Drew's neck, staining his shirt; he raised his arms to ward off the bear's attacks. "Get back, Marcy..." he gasped.

"Lie down and play possum, Drew!" Roughly, Marcy set the lantern on the trail in front of her and raised the rifle to her shoulder. Drew flattened himself to the ground. The bear growled once, prodded the prostrate form, then turned his attention to Marcy. In that moment she aimed and fired. The great creature roared its pain as the bullet smashed through its shoulder, then advanced on her, swinging its huge paws in fury.

Drew struggled to his knees. "Marcy . . ."

"Dang you, Drew! *Stay down!*" She aimed again, feeling the cold sweat trickling down her back. She had only the second barrel to depend on; she'd left her cartridges back at the cabin. She murmured a prayer and squeezed the trigger. Straight for the heart. The bullet slammed into the bear. The beast staggered backward, grunted once, and crashed into the brush at the side of the trail. Marcy advanced cautiously; then, certain the animal was dead, she threw down her rifle and knelt to Drew. She gasped at the sight of him. His face and shoulders and arms were covered with scratches, deep gashes that traced bloody lines across his flesh. But the most serious injury was to the back of his head; the bear, in its rage at being surprised with the knapsack, had torn a great patch of his scalp away from the skull. Blood poured from the flap of skin, drenching Drew's shirt.

He laughed unsteadily. "I should have taken the lantern. The damn thing didn't like my disturbing his supper."

"Oh, hush," she said gently. She brought the lantern closer and examined his head. The skin, though badly torn, was still attached. But the bleeding was fearful. "We'll have to get back," she said. "You can't stay here." There had to be some way to retard the flow of blood. Gingerly, she lifted the skin flap and pressed it tightly against his head. "Can you hold this, Drew? Until I get a bandage from the cabin?"

"I'll try." He put his hand to his head. "Lord, that hurts!"

"I'll be right back," she said. "I'll leave the lantern here for you." She made her way back to the cabin, treading carefully up the trail until the light from the open cabin door showed her the way. She left her rifle; it would be impossible to carry. She picked up a roll of linen bandages and stuffed it in her pocket, filled her canteen from the water bucket and slung it across her shoulder. Drat! She would have liked some biscuits; Drew might need his strength before they got to Long Lake. She had a few toffees. She shoved them into a pocket.

She hurried back to him. Working quickly, she wrapped

the bandage about his head, pulling it as tightly as she dared to stem the bleeding.

He smiled up at her. "I guess I *am* a greenhorn. You always warned me not to leave food around. Let's go back to the cabin. I'll be all right after I rest for a little while."

"No. You're losing too much blood. Even with the bandage. We've got to get down to Long Lake, so your head can be stitched up properly. Can you walk?"

"I think so." He hauled himself to his feet, clinging to Marcy for support, then let go of her. "I can make it on my own."

She turned and picked up the lantern. "I'll walk in front of you. But if you feel your knees giving way, holler." They started down the trail. It was slow going. The path was steep. Twice Drew slipped, managing at the last minute to clutch at a sapling tree, and once he tripped on an exposed root and tumbled to the ground. Marcy noted with dismay that the blood had already begun to seep through the bandage. She helped him to his feet. "Can you go on?"

He shivered and smiled thinly. "Damn, it's cold!"

She frowned in dismay. "I should have brought your coat. I didn't think of it!"

"We'll manage." They continued on down. Drew was breathing heavily. Marcy turned to watch him, noticing the beads of sweat on his face, the pallor of his skin even by the dim light of the lantern. At last he stopped and sat down on the trail. "I'm getting awfully light-headed, Marcy." His voice was beginning to slur. "You go on without me. I don't think I can make it."

She set down the lantern. "Oh, bosh, Drew Bradford! There's no good my going without you!" She knelt to him and gave him a drink of water, then unwrapped the toffee. "Here. Suck on this. It'll keep up your strength." She helped him to his feet. "Put your arm around my shoulder and lean on me." The trail was wider here. They proceeded side by side. She held the lantern in one hand, lighting the path; her other arm, firmly wrapped about his waist, was soon wet from the blood that continued to pour from his wound.

By the time they reached the bottom of the trail, Drew was staggering. He blinked his eyes, desperately trying to stay conscious. Marcy let him rest while she pulled her canoe out of the brush and righted it. Drew's boat was here as well, but the canoe would be faster. She pushed it partially into the water, then turned back to Drew. Grunting with the strain of his weight, she managed to help him into the canoe. She waded into the water, hooked the lantern onto the bow of the canoe, then scrambled into the stern, launching the canoe at the same time. She paddled quickly around Clear Pond, straining through the darkness to find the entrance to the creek that led to Long Lake. The sky was black, thick clouds scudding across its dark expanse. Despite her years in the wilderness, her eyes that had grown used to seeing in the dark, it was difficult to make out shapes. She cursed softly as she saw the lean-to on the shore of Clear Pond; she'd gone too far, missed the creek. She turned the canoe about and headed back. She looked down. Drew lay in the bottom of the boat, his eyes closed. "Drew!" she said. *"Drew!"*

He grunted and opened his eyes, managing to smile weakly at her. "Marcy . . ." he whispered.

She peered through the darkness. The lantern illuminated just a small patch of shore ahead, but she managed to make out the creek, and headed down its narrow way. She maneuvered the twists and turns, running aground once on a shallow stretch. She jumped out of the canoe into the water, and tugged and pushed until she'd worked the small craft back into the center of the creek; then she regained her seat and took up the paddle again.

The wind had begun to blow. The storm she'd seen far off was moving in. Gusts of wind whistled through the trees and shook their light craft. Dang it! she thought. It wasn't too bad here in the creek, which flowed into Long Lake. But once they hit Long Lake itself, there might be danger with a storm. The settlement was only a mile or two away from the creek entrance—on the opposite side of the lake. But the current of the lake ran in the other direction. She'd be battling the flow as well as the storm. Worse than that was the knowledge that if she couldn't win out over the current, their small boat would be swept down the length of the lake—at least eight miles. And there wasn't a cabin or guide in all that uninhabited way to which she could turn for help. And unless she could make it back soon, Drew would bleed to death.

She came out onto Long Lake as the mists rolled in, damp clouds that swirled around her, gusting fitfully. The kerosene lantern had been sputtering for the last ten minutes, its fuel nearly used up; now, with a small hiss, it died. Only her instinct, the feel of the strong current under the canoe, guided her. She fought against the movement of the water, seeing the whitecaps on either side of her fragile boat each time the wind parted the mists for a second. She could only guess she was headed in the right direction.

At her feet in the boat, Drew began to shiver and moan feverishly, his voice barely distinguishable above the whistling of the wind. Oh, God, she thought, let him not die!

She fought against the current, her muscles straining, her arms quivering with the agony of each tortured stroke, until wind and waves and night were one enemy, against which she battled to the edge of exhaustion. She had no idea how long she struggled. The storm blew down, sheets of rain that drenched her; savage winds that whipped her hair about her face. She moved in a delirium of storm and wind and pain. As the storm abated, she was aware that the sky was lightening; it must be nearly dawn. She had been on the lake all night long.

The lake was dim, though the sky brightened in the east. She saw no sign of life. Oh, God! she thought. Could the current have carried them down the length of the lake, despite her efforts all night long? If they'd gone past Round Island it might be hours more before she could get help for Drew.

She leaned over him. He was so pale, so still, his damp hair matted to his forehead. She lifted his head for a moment, and was heartened to see that his eyelids fluttered. But her hands were covered with his blood. How long could he last?

She lifted her eyes to pray to the heavens, and sobbed aloud for joy. She saw lights, closer than she would have hoped. She strained her eyes, seeing shapes more clearly as dawn advanced. Sabattis's Boardinghouse. Just up on the hill. God bless Mrs. Sabattis! If she hadn't been up early to cook, Marcy would never have seen a light. She headed the canoe in the direction of the shore, grateful that the pull of the current had slackened; in another few minutes the canoe was on the beach. She scrambled out of the boat and raced up the hill, bursting in on the Sabattis family at breakfast. She knew she must look a sight, her clothes drenched from the storm, her arms covered with Drew's blood.

"Quick!" she said. "On the beach! Drew's been attacked by a bear! Oh, help me, please!"

Tom Sabattis and his father jumped up from the table. Trembling violently, she reached out a quivering arm to them and crumpled to the floor.

Chapter Fifteen

"Tarnation! What a smell!" Marcy came into Uncle Jack's room, closing the door behind her. She crossed to the window and opened it to the crisp autumn afternoon.

In the wide bed Drew stirred and plumped at the pillows

behind his back. "The doctor spilled some carbolic acid while he was changing my bandages."

She moved to him and brushed back the black curl that drooped over the strip of linen at his forehead. "How does it look, did he say?"

Drew patted the back of his head gingerly. "He thinks once my hair grows in, the scars won't even show."

She rubbed a tender hand across his cheek. "Scratches are almost gone."

He grinned up at her, one eyebrow raised in mockery. "Pity. I was hoping to be able to tell everyone my wife did that."

Her eyes narrowed in pretended anger. "I can oblige you, you varmint!"

"I don't know when! I've spent more than a week alone in this bed." He indicated a small trundle bed in the corner. "Even Uncle Jack in his cot is beginning to look good to me!"

She giggled. "Oh, bosh! You know you were in no condition. And neither was I. That was a fearsome cold and fever I came down with. Even if I wasn't as sick as you. Though every time Uncle Jack put another mustard plaster on my chest, I almost would have traded places!"

"Poor Marcy. And all to save my life."

She felt herself blushing. "Don't, Drew."

He smirked. "I just want to hear you tell me again how I don't *need* you!"

"Stop funning me. That was different, and you know it!"

"Well then," his mouth twitched in a smile, "you can stand guard outside my studio with your trusty double rifle. I can think of a few wolves and other creatures I'd just as soon keep from the door!"

She smoothed the edge of his quilt, unwilling to look at him. "I don't want to argue with you now. You're not in a fit condition. But I hate to leave here. I meant what I said, up on the mountain."

His eyes were suddenly serious. "I know. I've had a lot of time to think, lying here. Even if you agreed to come back to the city, I don't think you could be happy there."

She put her arms around him and kissed him. "Oh, Drew," she said unhappily, "what are we going to do?"

"I'll set up my studio in Long Lake or North Creek. There's no reason why I can't paint here."

"Oh, no, Drew! I won't let you do that for me. You *must* be in the city. To study. To teach. And to be near the dealers and the galleries. I'll go with you. Wherever you want to be."

"I want to be where you'll be happy. We'll stay here."

She shook her head stubbornly. "No!"

He glared at her. "Dammit, Marcy, do you *want* us to be separated?"

"You know I don't."

"Then we'll stay here. And not another word about it!"

She *couldn't* let him make such a sacrifice for her. "No, Drew, I..."

"By God," he muttered, reaching out to grab her by the shoulders, "Uncle Jack has the right idea! I've had enough of your stubbornness!"

Her eyes widened in fear. "What are you doing?"

He pulled her down to the bed, slinging her roughly across his lap. "What I should have done last week on top of the mountain. Or a year ago. Or every time that chin of yours jutted out to defy me!"

She wriggled furiously, her face buried in the quilt. His arms were strong, holding her down, immobilizing her. She gasped as she felt his hand tossing back her skirt and petticoat, leaving her thin drawers as her only protection. "Drew!" she wailed, steeling herself for the first sharp slap.

He laughed suddenly. "Of course, now that I have you in this position, there's a heap of other things I can do besides spank you!" He began to tickle her, his fingers working their way up from her buttocks and hips to the top of her drawers and the sensitive line around her waist.

"You lop-eared devil!" Giggling, she twisted and turned, managing at last to swivel herself around so she could grasp one of the pillows behind his head. Still lying facedown on the bed, she tugged loose the pillow and swung it at him.

He grunted as the downy softness of the pillow connected with his shoulder. "This means war, Mrs. Bradford," he said, and released his hold on her waist to reach for another pillow behind him.

She scrambled away from him on the bed, warding off his blow as she saw the pillow come crashing down. Getting up on all fours, she attacked again, this time managing to smack him across the chest. There was a ripping sound. The air was filled with feathers. "Oh, drat!"

He crowed in triumph. "Ha! You've an ill-equipped army, ma'am!" He gave her two blows on the rump with his pillow, sending her sprawling on her face.

She struggled up, puffing at a feather that had lodged on her nose. "I'll fight to the death, sir!" She hit him again with her pillow (careful to avoid his injured head), laughing as the down came flying out in a rush of feathers.

The bed looked as though it were caught in the middle of a snowstorm. Drew waved his arm furiously to clear the air. "Do you intend to choke me to death?"

She straddled him on the bed, glaring at him with determination. "I intend to win this war, by fair means or foul! See how *you* like being tickled!" She attacked him without mercy, while he grabbed at her tormenting hands and tried to wrestle her away from him.

There was a knock at the door. Marcy froze. Tarnation! she thought. Here she was, perched on the bed, her skirts still up around her knees, and feathers all over the place!

Drew smiled innocently. "Come in."

"Drew Bradford, you devil," she hissed, scrambling from the bed just as a young woman came into the room. She was dressed in black bombazine trimmed with black crape, a black hat with a small sheer black veil, black gloves. Even without her mourning garb, Marcy would have recognized her—the tall, slender form and strong features so like Drew's, the same dark hair and blue eyes, though the eyes held a hint of violet, unlike Drew's paler blue. Marcy smiled shyly and held out her hand. "You'll be Willough."

Willough moved toward her, hands outstretched, and kissed

her on the cheek. "Marcy." She turned to the bed. "How are
you, big brother? When I didn't hear from you I figured you
were either happy with Marcy—and too busy to write to
me—or too miserable to want to." She smiled and indicated
the disordered room. "The former, I should guess!"

Drew welcomed his sister's kiss. "Thanks to you, Willough."

"They told me in North Creek about your accident. Are
you well cared for, Drew?"

"Drew was mighty lucky," said Marcy. "There was a doctor
staying at the boardinghouse."

Drew nodded. "Dr. Waugh is up here to look into estab-
lishing a sanatorium for consumptives. He seems to feel that
the air of the mountains is beneficial. *He* certainly was beneficial to me!"

Willough pulled off her gloves and sat on the chair that
Marcy had drawn up to the bed. "I would have come sooner,
Drew," she said, "whether I'd heard from you or not. But I
had Arthur's funeral arrangements to make . . ."

Marcy bit her lip. Arthur Gray. The horrible scene in the
railroad car. But he *had* been Willough's husband. "We were
sorry to hear . . ." she began.

Willough laughed sharply. "Nonsense. We were none of
us sorry."

Marcy thought: I like this woman. Drew *said* we could be
good friends.

"I'm almost surprised to see you in mourning, Willough,"
said Drew. "Under the circumstances. But I suppose it's only
proper."

Willough shook her head. "For Arthur's death, I'd almost
be prepared to wear holiday colors! But perhaps I'm mourning
. . . someone else. Besides . . ." she pointed to her gown, sparingly trimmed with the crape, instead of with the yards of
crape required for full mourning, "I've slighted my mourning
already. I shouldn't be wearing this for another six months.
Mother's scandalized, of course!"

At the mention of his mother, Drew's face darkened.

No, thought Marcy, I can't let it stay this way. "How is

Mrs. Bradford? I've been meaning to write to her and tell her about Drew. I'm sure she'll be concerned."

"It's probably just as well you haven't," said Willough. "I've seen her a few times this week. She's distraught enough over Arthur's death. The poor thing. She's probably the only one who *did* care for him. And now ... Daddy's sick, you know."

"No, I didn't. Does he finally need you as a partner, little sister?"

Willough stood up and walked to the window, gazing out over the lake below. "As a matter of fact, yes. But I turned him down."

Drew laughed. "We both seem to have lost our blind spots. Now what?"

Willough turned and leaned against the sill, a quizzical smile on her face. "You haven't asked me, big brother."

Drew reached out and pulled Marcy close to him, holding her hand in a tight grip. "I've been afraid to," he said hoarsely.

"Well, to begin," said Willough briskly, "your friend Jesse is a treasure. He handled the opening of the exhibit magnificently. I stayed away. Not because I didn't want to be there, but because the inappropriateness of a grieving widow's presence would have reflected badly on you. I think Jesse's in love, by the way."

"With you?"

"No. It seems there was a Barbara ... a friend of yours, I believe ..."

Drew grinned up at Marcy. "Yes. A charming thing."

"You polecat," she muttered. "Wait'll I bring Zeb Cary around!"

He laughed, then turned back to Willough, his eyes suddenly dark with uncertainty. "What about the show, Willough?"

She fumbled in her purse. "Would you like your reviews first?" She pulled out several newspaper clippings. "The art critic of *The New York Times* considered you a celebrity, having shown with the Impressionists in Paris. He seemed to feel that though their works have elicited much criticism, it cannot be denied that you 'bring a freshness to your paintings that has not been seen on these shores in many a day.' The man from *Harper's* waxes positively lyrical. Your works 'radiate assurance,' he says. 'The majesty of the wilderness is rendered in colors never seen before.' 'Truly remarkable,' et cetera, et cetera."

"What about my Paris paintings?"

Willough indicated the stack of clippings. "The general opinion seems to be that your *métier* is to be found here in the Adirondack Wilderness, not on the confining streets of a city." She smiled in pleasure, looking from one to the other of them. "Though several of the critics commented on the remarkable series of drawings of the artist's wife, so imbued with love and tenderness that the viewer is moved to tears. You're very fortunate, Marcy. Most women must rely on a spoken avowal of love."

Marcy trembled, seeing the look in Drew's blue eyes. "I always knew I was lucky."

The blue eyes twinkled. "Damn! It means I can never stray. My drawings will give me away!"

Marcy pinched him on the ear. "Drewry Bradford! If you ever stray, your wife will find another black bear!"

Willough cleared her throat. "Don't you want to hear the rest?"

"Is there more?"

"Well, only a contract from Currier and Ives. They want to reproduce several of your paintings for lithographs. And commission a series on the major mountains and lakes of the Adirondacks."

"My God." Drew was still clutching Marcy's hand. She could feel him trembling. "A commission? And they're willing to pay?"

"Quite handsomely, according to Jesse. But you'll have to work out the arrangements."

Marcy smiled at Drew. "A commission to paint in the Wilderness."

He grinned back. "I reckon we'll have to *live* in the

Wilderness, then. If that doesn't break your heart, Mrs. Bradford." He turned to Willough. "I don't believe all this."

"You're quite successful now, big brother. There's talk of making you an associate of the National Academy of Design. And one more thing. If you live here, I suppose you'll have to have a house."

"We'll manage until the commission comes through."

Willough laughed and stood up, coming over to the bed. "Perhaps you can manage on this for the time being. Jesse sold a few of your paintings." She handed Drew a bank draft.

He leaned back in the bed, his eyes wide with shock. "Five thousand dollars?" he whispered. "We can live comfortably for a year on *three*!" He gulped and stared at Marcy, fighting back a sudden rush of emotion. "What'll we do with it, Marce? How about a house on Round Island?"

She wiped away her happy tears. "I'd like that, Drew."

"No, come to think of it. The first thing you're going to do is take some of that money and buy yourself the fanciest dress you can find."

"But Drew . . . "

He frowned. "And I don't want to hear a lot of nonsense about it being wicked to like nice things! *Do you understand*, Mrs. Bradford?"

She nodded obediently. She wasn't certain she still wouldn't earn that spanking if she didn't learn to curb her stubbornness. "Maybe Willough would help me shop in North Creek."

"No. You'll come down to New York City and stay with me for a few days after Drew has recovered. We can go on the most delightful shopping trips while he cools his heels!" Willough turned to Drew and smile apologetically. "I'm a very rich widow, you know. Arthur knew how to make money, if nothing else." She picked up her gloves and smoothed them over her slender fingers. "I'll leave you two alone now. I'm sure you must have a great deal to talk about. I'm staying at Sabattis's Boardinghouse down the road. I'll be there till day after tomorrow." She leaned over and kissed Drew on the forehead, then hugged Marcy warmly. She moved to the door, then turned, her eyes sparkling with tears. "I envy you both," she whispered. Then she was gone.

Marcy fell into Drew's arms, laughing for joy. All his hopes, all his dreams! Somehow the sufferings in Paris seemed worthwhile, meaningful. If only to bring more sweetness to this moment. He kissed her hard, grinned at her, sat her down beside him on the bed. He talked of his plans, the house they'd build, the future, with children and warmth and laughter. He talked of his need for her, for her strength and encouragement. She thought her heart would burst, all the love bubbling up within her.

At last he stopped, and gazed at her, his eyes grown suddenly heavy-lidded with passion. "Is there a lock on that door?" he said, his voice husky in his throat.

She gasped. "Drew, you can't! You're still weak!"

"Dammit, I'm not *that* weak!"

"But Drew . . ."

"Listen to me, you stubborn imp! Throw the bolt on that door!"

She stood up. "Yes, sir." She moved to the door, threw the bolt, turned to face him. "Now what?"

He brushed away a few loose feathers and grinned, his eyes twinkling. "Now, Mrs. Bradford, I want to see how fast you can get out of those clothes and into this bed!"

Willough climbed the steps to the Sabattis's veranda. She felt tired, and filled with the old longing. She *did* envy them so, Drew and Marcy. So much in love. So happy together. Drew had always loved to laugh. Marcy obviously brought him joy. She fought back her tears, forcing Nat's memory out of her head.

A red-haired young man with spectacles arose from a rocking chair on the veranda and stepped toward her. "Mrs. Gray? I'm Dr. Waugh. I understand you've been looking for me."

"Only to thank you, doctor. I'm sure you saved my brother's life."

"I only finished what that noble little wife of his began. Dragging him down the mountain like that, then fighting her way across the lake in a storm." He shook his head. "Remarkable."

"And my brother will be fine?"

"Oh, yes. The greatest risk was always that he'd lost so much blood he wouldn't be able to fight off the shock or the infection. Fortunately, he's a very vigorous man, in the prime of health. And the infection was mild."

She smiled. "It was fortunate for us that you were here. Drewry tells me that you are considering a tuberculosis sanatorium here in the mountains."

"Yes. I'm inspired by Dr. Trudeau, a very brave physician who himself is stricken with the disease. He has had several healthful summertime visits to Saranac Lake. He seems to think that the fresh air is salubrious. And I've heard others speak of the cleansing powers of the evergreens, particularly the balsam fir. It is widely held that the air is purer where there are many conifers, and that the scent of the trees themselves, when drawn into diseased lungs, is highly beneficial."

Willough thought of Brigid's brother Kevin, dying so tragically of consumption. "It would be wonderful if your sanatorium could provide relief to sufferers."

The doctor nodded. "The disease kills one of every seven Americans now. And mostly the poor."

"You would provide room for the poor, doctor?"

"I would hope to. Alas, I have not the resources. I have a small practice in Brooklyn Heights. It's scarcely adequate. But perhaps if I can take up a subscription among my patients and neighbors..."

Willough thought quickly. "A subscription? Nonsense! You'd raise scarcely enough money to build one wall of your clinic! That's not how I'd do it at all!"

He took off his spectacles and polished them. "How *would* you do it, Mrs. Gray?"

"It's a matter of common sense. The people who fall ill are workers, laborers. They're a burden to their employers as well as themselves when they're ill. It seems to me that the rich people who own the factories and the mills would pay handsomely to support a hospital such as yours. They would get a better day's work out of healthy workers."

He shrugged. "If I knew many rich people . . ."

His resignation was maddening! "*I* do!" she snapped. "It's a simple matter—a few intimate receptions and luncheons, a few words to the right people . . ." She frowned. "How did you plan to provide the materials?"

He flushed. "Frankly, I hadn't even begun to think of that."

Wouldn't Arthur cringe if he could know what she was contemplating! "I know some contractors. Friends of my late husband. I'm not sure, but I suspect I might be able to persuade them to donate materials and services for your hospital. In honor of my husband's memory." And out of fear of his *wife's* memory, she thought sardonically.

"That would be quite generous of them."

She was warming to the task. It would be an exciting challenge. "I don't suppose you've decided on a site as yet."

"No. That's one of the reasons I'm here. To look around in the region."

"Well," she said, smoothing her gloves primly, "there's not a thing we can do until you make up your mind."

He smiled and replaced his spectacles, allowing his gaze to examine her thoroughly. His eyes were pale gray and clear.

She stiffened under that searching appraisal. "You have a most insolent stare, doctor!"

"I'd like to see you out of your corsets."

She gasped. "I beg your pardon, doctor!"

He grinned good-naturedly. "Only in the interests of scientific research, you understand. I'd like to see if you're as stiff-backed without them!"

It was a gentle rebuke, but it hit home. It was the least she owed Nat's memory, to bury Willough the snob once and for all. She exhaled, her face softening, and smiled sheepishly at the doctor.

He nodded in satisfaction. "I suspected you could smile." He crooked his arm in her direction. "Will you take supper with me?"

She slipped her arm through his. "I'd be pleased to, Dr. Waugh."

He led her into Mrs. Sabattis's kitchen. "I'd very much like to discuss the possibility of a partnership, Mrs. Gray."

Brian Bradford leaned back in his chair in the house in Saratoga. Beyond the windows, the evening shadows were lengthening. He sighed heavily. The day was dying. The trees were shedding their leaves with the dying season. He'd never felt so alone in all his life. He had a sudden yearning to be back in Scotland, amid the purple heather and the sweet mists.

He'd managed to lose it all. His wife. His son. And now his daughter. All he had now was his business. Safe and solvent because of Nat and Willough. But useless to fill the empty places in his heart.

He sighed again. Drew had never been his son. He'd never given the boy a chance. He realized with a pang that he'd never even seen one of Drew's paintings. And now the word from the city was that Drew had had a stunning success. No thanks to his father, who'd been willing—my God, *eager!*—to destroy his son, the artist.

And Willough. So capable and strong. He'd never been able to see beyond her sex. Not until it was too late. There'd be no one now to inherit the business when he was gone. Not even Arthur. That was a blow, Arthur's death. He wondered how Isobel was taking the news. If she hadn't become so completely addicted by now that she was oblivious to the world around her.

Isobel. He regretted her the most. How had they managed to get to this pass? That terrible drunken night when he'd abused her. He hadn't meant it. He'd wanted her so badly, hungered for her. Was he at fault, because his appetites were too coarse for her delicate nature? Was she at fault, colder than she should have been, filled with all the fears that that damned mother of hers had put into her head? And the time had gone by, and the apologies had died on his lips. And then his needs had driven him into the arms of other women. And after that she could never have forgiven him, even if he'd prostrated himself before her and kissed her feet.

He leaned back and pressed the dull ache just below his heart. Supper hadn't sat well; perhaps a small brandy would settle his stomach. "Martha!" he bellowed. He closed his eyes, feeling the weight of his loneliness pressing against his lids. He heard the rustle of Martha's petticoats. That was odd. It sounded like silk. Martha must be getting fancy these days.

And perfume. But that wasn't Martha's perfume! He struggled to sit up, opening his eyes.

Isobel smiled gently. "Martha's busy in the kitchen. With the dishes. Do you want something?"

"What are you doing here, Belle?"

"You haven't called me that for twenty years. Willough told me you weren't well. I thought I'd come to see for myself." She looked around the large parlor with its balcony and stone fireplace. "This is a handsome house, Brian. I'm sorry I haven't come before now." She sat in a chair opposite him, a small crease wrinkling her brow. "You don't look well. Not at all, Brian. I want you to come back to the house in Gramercy Park. To be near the proper doctors."

"I have to be near the business."

"Of course you don't! You can run it just as well from New York City if you have the proper manager. You did it in the old days."

"In the old days I had my health."

"Then sell the business. The ironworks. And the sawmill too. If you can't run them yourself, why do you need the burden?"

He thought about it. "Yes. The market is coming up again. I can get a good price."

"And then you can invest. You've made sound investments in the past."

"Arthur always advised me. I'm sorry, Belle," he said, as a flash of pain crossed her face. "I forgot."

She pulled a lace handkerchief from her pocket and dabbed at her eyes. He saw that her hand was shaking.

"Have you had your tonic?"

She stared at him, hollow-eyed, and ran her tongue across her dry lips. "I'm . . . trying to break the habit. Dr. Page says it isn't good for me."

"I'll help you all I can," he said quietly.

She looked at her folded hands, clasped tightly to keep them from quivering. "Would you like me to read to you for a little while? I'm not tired."

"If you wish."

She stood up and pulled down a book from the shelf. "Would you like Mr. Dickens?"

"Yes. Please."

She seated herself near the kerosene lantern. The light shone softly on her face, easing away the years and bathing her still vibrant beauty in a warm glow.

He felt overwhelmed by grief, by the waste of years. "I've lost my children, Belle," he said hoarsely. "I've driven them both away."

She looked up at him, her face etched with sadness. "So have I."

"We're both a couple of old fools."

She nodded and looked down at the book. She began to read. Her voice was clear and beautifully modulated, with the vital ring to it that had captured his fancy twenty-seven years before.

He smiled at the bent head, held with such pride and dignity. He was a damned lucky man to have her as his wife. "By God," he said, "you still have more class than any woman I've ever known, Belle."

Willough walked along the shore of Long Lake, breathing deeply of the sweet night air. The moon was full, bathing the night and the lake in a silvery glow. In the distance she could hear the mournful hoot of an owl. This is what Nat meant, she thought. This peace and serenity. This beauty and solitude that civilization was trying to destroy.

She'd noticed the wasted tracts all along her journey from North Creek. The burned-out patches of forest; the streams choked off by jammed logs, leaving only dry beds; the flooding where ponds had been diverted to provide banking grounds for the lumbermen. It isn't right, she thought. It's time to build, not destroy. To give back to the land what had been plundered. She thought about her supper with Dr. Waugh. Here was something she could do that had real benefit. They'd buy a large, unspoiled tract, keep it in its natural state. Build their small hospital. Use Nature in the way she was intended to be used, in harmony with man.

And this was a good place. Perhaps she'd build a house here. Near Drew and Marcy. It would be a good place to raise Cecily, at least part of the year. Somehow, in this setting, she could keep civilization from doing what it had to her and to Isobel. And Arthur. There was a timelessness in these woods—the thought that the same mountains and lakes had been here for generations before and would endure long after they were gone. Somehow it made the petty concerns of the city almost meaningless. Isobel with her sense of propriety. Brian with his need for money. And poor Arthur, with his pathetic desire to hide his humble beginnings beneath a cloak of respectability.

She sighed, feeling a contentment she hadn't known was possible. She turned back toward the boardinghouse. There were only a few lights shining in the windows. It must be quite late. She'd excused herself when Dr. Waugh had gone to bed, and slipped out into the night, needing the time to think, to sort out her future.

It would be a good future. She thought of Isobel and Brian. Two sad people trapped in an unhappy life together. *She* would never have stayed married to Arthur all those years, no matter what. It was a pity that her parents hadn't had the courage to divorce; they probably would have been better off. Well, maybe when she built her home here she'd invite them to come and visit. Perhaps the air would be good for Daddy's health. And she might get Mother to break her drug habit.

She mounted the steps to the boardinghouse and slipped quietly in at the door. She felt tired, but strangely elated. Her life was useful. With a goal, a purpose. Nat had given that to her too: By reaching out to help others, she was finding fulfillment for herself.

She opened the door to her room and walked in, closing it gently so as not to disturb the other boarders. Mrs. Sabattis had left the kerosene lamp turned low. She adjusted the wick; the flame sprang up, bathing the room in a golden glow. She turned toward the bed.

Nat was standing by the window.

"I got halfway to Ohio," he said softly, "before I realized I couldn't live without you."

She leaned back against the door, too stunned to say a word.

"I heard about Arthur," he said. "When I went looking for you in the city. I'm sorry."

"Nat." Her voice was trembling.

"I've almost nothing left. I'll have to start again. I can't afford much. And I'll not take charity from you. Or Brian."

"I'm through with Daddy. I turned down his partnership. He'd probably welcome you with open arms."

"I'm not sure I'd take it. If I did, I'd have to run it my way, pouring back the money into the land, to preserve the Wilderness."

"And what about the peace you were looking for?"

He laughed softly. "I saw families going west. Hundreds of them. I started thinking. There's not going to *be* any wilderness left, any unspoiled places unless we take a stand. It suddenly seemed damned cowardly of me to run away, seeking something that I'd lost years ago. I can't bring back my innocent youth. I can't bring back my family. But I can take a stand. Here. And fight for what I believe in. Maybe if I could get the laws changed..."

"Why don't you run for the state legislature?"

"I'm not sure I can afford it. Not right away."

She hesitated, hoping he'd take her words in the right spirit.

"I know a very wealthy Fifth Avenue widow who'd love to support your run."

"I couldn't possibly take her money." He smiled gently, and the dimple appeared in his cheek. "Of course, if she were my wife, I'd feel differently about it."

Her lip began to quiver. "Even if she's quarrelsome?"

"I reckon I don't mind that as much as I thought. Besides, the quarrels always seemed to be about sex. And if memory serves me, I think we resolved that problem. And very satisfactorily, too, I might add!"

"And what if she's a snob?"

He grinned. "A *damnable* snob, as I recall I told her the first time we met."

"What if she's a *damnable* snob?"

"She wasn't entirely to blame. I think I was a bit defensive. I reckon she can help me smooth the rough edges. It won't hurt me, especially if I go off to the state legislature."

"But, Nat . . ."

"And I won't let her get *too* uppish."

She stared at him. It was too wondrous to be believed. Her love had come back to her!

He smiled and looked at the bed. "Dammit, woman," he said softly, "how long are you going to stand there?"

She felt the chills start up her spine, remembering their last glorious night of love. She pulled the pins from her hat and put them aside with her gloves. With the hat still perched precariously atop her head, she crossed the room to him. Reaching his side, she laughed for joy, pulled the hat from her head, and skimmed it clear across the room, watching in delight as it skidded under a chair. She turned back to him. His amber eyes glowed with love.

"Happy birthday," she whispered, and melted into his arms.

_____ *Postscript* _____

On May 15, 1885, the governor of New York signed into law a bill which said, in part, that the nearly seven hundred thousand state-owned acres in the Adirondack Mountains would be kept forever wild as forest lands. What trees there were on those acres could not be removed, nor could the land designated as Forest Preserve ever be sold or exchanged by the state. The law became known as the "Forever Wild" law.